John Daulton
www.DaultonBooks.com

DANCE OF
DESTINIES

Book Five: The Galactic Mage Series

John Daulton

This is a work of fiction. All characters and events portrayed in this book are fictitious. Any resemblance to real people or events is purely coincidental.

DANCE OF DESTINIES
Book 5: The Galactic Mage Series

The phrase "The Galactic Mage" is the trademark of John Daulton.

Cover art by Cris Ortega

Interior layout by Fernando Soria

DEDICATION

To Max and Janice. How much I admire you both
cannot be expressed in words.

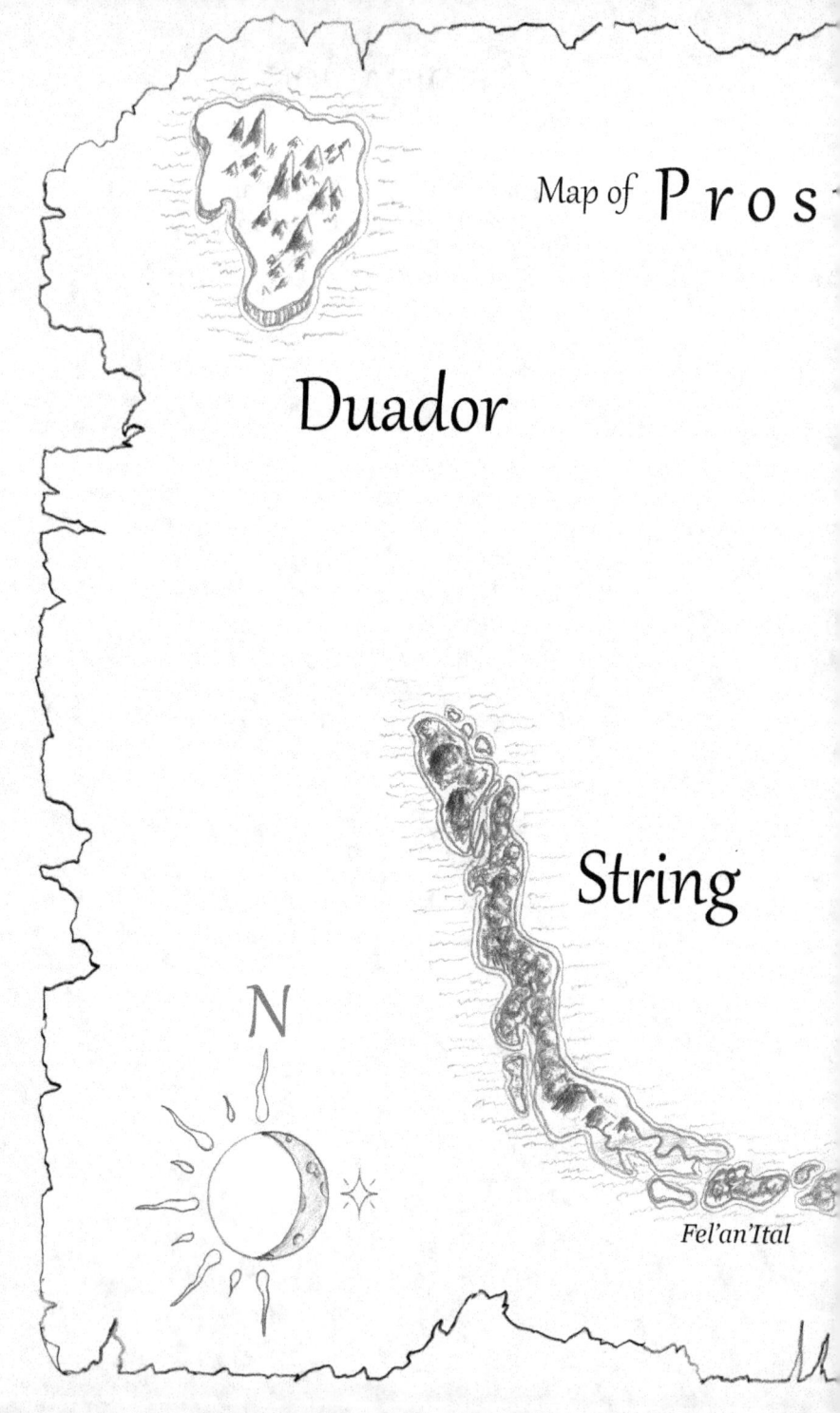

Map of P r o s

Duador

String

N

Fel'an'Ital

rion

Orc Spur

Sansafrax

North Mark

Mt. Pernolde

Kora Mon Dae

Daggerspine Mts.

Sarbol City

Alumall

Calico
Castle

Leekant

Dae

Great Forest

Gulf of Dae

Sansun R.

Gardavar

Crown City

Pompost

Valenrider

Hast

Big Branch R.

West Mark

Sandsea Range

Desertborn R.

Three Tents

Queen's Mark

Sandsea Desert

Corvon

Solydae

ington

Gallspire Mts.

Gallenwood

Angrost

Tok Rottan

Feshtie R.

Twee

Pengrost

Kafisk

South Mark

Lalt Point

Murdoc
Bay

Kurr

Kolat

Chapter 1

Altin could not tell how long he'd been in the ochre gel. When he woke up, the lights were out on his spacesuit. Nothing worked. He couldn't move his arms or legs. Only his head swiveled, enabling him to look around through the glass of his helmet. Orli was there beside him, trapped in the same ochre blob as he was, but he couldn't see her face. She was turned away just enough. She was alive, he knew. He'd seen a wisp of her hair on several occasions, the tips of a few blonde strands that swept into view as she moved her head around. He'd done the same, glanced about within the confines of the helmet, taking in what had become of them.

What had become of them? Altin could hardly say. They were inside the alien ship. That much was sure. He and Orli were held in a blob of ochre jelly, or at least that is how it appeared to him, as if they'd been frozen together in some strange kind of gooey ice. The blob sat upon an enormous grate, one that spread out in all directions, its length and breadth lost in darkness, a distance Altin had no way of measuring. What he could see all looked to be made from the same green-brown material that the ship's hull was made from, a substance Orli had described as "some kind of protein." Long beams of the stuff crossed each other in a

1

perfect grid, the beams roughly a pace wide, and the square gaps between at least six paces on a side. It was hard to say more about it because the jelly through which he looked made a hazy effect. Details were hard to make out.

Looking up, he could see another grate, or at least he could see a section of one, high above. Here and there along its underside were dull, hazy lights, some green, some orange, some blue, all pale as if seen through a mist. They traced the lines of the beams that formed the grate, spreading out in all directions above him, and just as did the grate he and Orli were on, it stretched away until it vanished into hazy darkness. From where he was, it looked to be an island in the steamy black above him, a great grille with foggy edges all around, simply floating up there.

There were other lights upon it as well. On top of it, not attached to the underside. These came from objects. Enormous things, bulky and dark mainly, but marked here and there by glowing patterns and shadowy protrusions that sometimes moved. Larger motion sometimes passed above them, streaks whipping by, smears of color like one sees in thin layers of oil floating on water. These objects would flash by, blurs like windblown clouds, lighting up the dark things on the platform above him, if only momentarily. Then they would be gone. Altin did not know what the colored things were, but he reckoned the bulky objects they illuminated in their passing were alien machines.

He'd gone through a few spates of panic early on, stuck there as he was. When it occurred to him that Orli was there with him, that had been the worst. He'd reached out for mana to save her, and himself, but found none. He could see it. It was all around him, the same pink mistiness that it always was, or at least, that it had been since the day Blue Fire had given him the green stone, the pulsing green marble that was the Father's Gift. That mana was there, but he couldn't reach it. He was on the inside of a manaless bubble. An empty pocket, perfectly round, all around him. It was very large, though he had no way of measuring it in distances meaningful to a physical world.

That had panicked him. Seeing her there, and seeing the mana all around, but unattainable. He'd spent some time shouting, nearing hysteria for a time perhaps, helpless as he was—as they were. First he shouted at her, that she might hear him, shouting so loud and so hard the skin of his face prickled and stung, sweat wrung from him by the force of his urgency. After he shouted in anger for a time, then, finally, came the frustration, which wore him out.

When that had passed, it occurred to him that, with all the lights extinguished on his suit, he was probably going to use up all the air. He knew that much about how it worked. Which made him wonder about Orli's air. He spent more time watching for that flick of blonde hair.

Sometime after he'd fallen asleep. Woken up. Panicked some more. Grew angry again. Tried for mana several more times. Slept. Woke. And slept. He felt as if he were recovering from being drugged. He didn't know if he'd slept for hours or days. It occurred to him then that he should probably be dead of thirst if it had been too long. He might be close to it now. Which meant Orli might be too.

That was the first time he noticed the brown tubes thrust into the ochre jelly blob that held her, jammed through it and through her spacesuit. None of them were much thicker than his thumb. They ran like roots across the grate and disappeared into the darkness. One was pushed into the center of her suit's heavy back panel. The other two went in at the top of it, one just behind each shoulder. He assumed he had the same.

Whatever these aliens were, they at least didn't want them dead. Not yet, anyway.

He saw no sign of Roberto, which he counted a good thing. To count it otherwise was not something he was willing to consider. And he supposed Roberto might just be on the grate behind him out of view. He could not know.

What he did know was that now, some indeterminable number of hours or days or ... years ago, after being captured, he was awake. He wondered why. And then the ochre jelly began to melt away.

At first he thought it was some trick of light. The air beyond the jelly did seem to move in a way, but soon after, it turned clear. The thickness of it diminished. Shadowy ripples of viscous fluid flowing marked where the jelly ran like melting fat, though it ran sideways, not straight down, as if gravity came from the left. It slicked away in strands to his left, stretching like mucus being blown off in a strong wind, long stringy lines of it flapping in the air. Bulbous ends of these tacky ropes would flap onto the crossbeams, stick there, then bow in the middle, bent by the wind again until they would break off and ooze down through the grate. Upon seeing the force of what blew it so, Altin wondered if perhaps they were still outside on the surface of the stormy red planet, the planet he'd once thought of as Red Fire, now a world he hoped would become a healthy, living Hostile being named Yellow Fire.

As he watched the ochre jelly melting and blowing away in front of him, the edge of the ochre jelly blob thinned and got nearer and nearer to exposing Orli inside. Soon it melted enough that part of her suit was out, like she'd been carved from it and the excess had blown away. Then the rest of her was free, the last of the goo blowing off her like a thin sheet carried off in a hurricane. She staggered forward, slightly right, one step that nearly took her off the edge of a beam, then, buffeted by the wind, she staggered a step back the other way, where she collapsed onto her hands and knees less than a half hand shy of falling through the grate at the other edge of the beam.

Altin cried out as he watched it. Horrified. His hands

4

wouldn't move, though he tried to reach for her.

The ochre jelly was melting around him, the edges nearing as it thinned.

Soon he was partially free. He could hear the wind against his helmet. And other sounds. The thuds and pulses and hissing of massive machinery. Something roared in a dull, distant way. He prepared to brace himself against the impact of the wind. The remaining ochre jelly melted and blew away.

He leaned into the wind. Staggered like Orli had, overcompensating right, the effects of whatever had been put in him making balance difficult, and something pulling at him from behind. The wind caught him and shoved him left. He fell to his knees to prevent himself from stumbling over the edge. Just as Orli had.

She turned, still on hands and knees, and saw him. Their eyes locked. Hers moved with the gasp of her relief. She was crying immediately. She hadn't had the luxury of seeing him there behind her all that time.

"I'm fine," he shouted, not sure if she could hear him over the noise all around, not to mention through his helmet glass.

They crawled to one another and clutched each other tightly. He didn't dare take his helmet off, though he wanted to so desperately it burned in his chest.

"Are you okay," she shouted, like him, neither opening her helmet's visor nor removing it entirely.

"I am," he shouted back. "I'm fine. Confused, a little frightened, but fine."

She smiled. So beautifully. The tear streaks on her cheeks reflecting the lights on the grate above them in a dim, pearlescent line. "I was so afraid," she said. "I thought you were dead. I knew you weren't. I kept telling myself you weren't. But I was so afraid."

"I had the advantage of seeing you there," he admitted.

"But I too panicked more than once."

"Where is Roberto?"

"I don't know."

They both turned about, still on hands and knees, balanced there precariously on the pace-wide beam, peering into the darkness. Everything was hazy. Droplets of liquid that looked like water formed on their helmet glass. Streaks of steam fogged it and cleared in places.

"Can you cast a seeing spell?" Orli called through the wind. She pointed downward through the gap in the giant grating, her thick-fingered glove directing Altin's gaze to a platform below them like the one they were on and the one he'd seen above them. It was just visible through the steamy, windblown darkness. It had to be at least a five-hundred-span drop.

"We're in some kind of bubble," he said. "The mana, it curves all around. I can't cast anything."

"Shit." She looked up at the grate high above. It too was five hundred spans away. "Shit," she repeated. "We have to find him. We have to get out of here."

It was true, but truth means little enough sometimes. He looked into her helmet, waiting for her to look back. In a few moments, she did. She was breathing more easily.

"God, Altin, what have we done?"

He was afraid she was about to say, "I told you so." She hadn't wanted to go out into the storm and look at the alien spaceships with them. He and Roberto were the ones who had wanted to leave the safety of his tower, now known as "the boot," standing safely at a distance from the alien vessels. But they'd talked her into it. The aliens hadn't made any hostile moves on them, and, well, adventure was practically Roberto's middle name. So they goaded and teased and ignored her warnings. And now here they were, at least the two of them. And Roberto MIA.

"I don't know," he admitted. He noticed sweat beading on

Orli's upper lip. He could feel it running down his own temples too, down his ribs inside his suit. "It's awfully hot in here," he said.

"Yeah, it's really bad," she remarked, watching as a puff of steam blew past. "We've got to get moving."

"What about those? Do we dare try to remove them?" He pointed to the three tubes in her suit. He traced the lines of them snaking off into the dimness across the crisscrossed beams.

She took note of them, seemingly for the first time, and tried to turn in her helmet to see where they attached. She looked back and acknowledged the ones in his own suit, which he hadn't seen but knew were there for the dragging weight of them.

She turned him carefully around and studied them for a time.

"Well, this one probably explains why we are still breathing," she said. He could feel that she touched something at the back of his spacesuit, presumably the lower of the three. "But these two, I'm not sure. Given that we aren't dead yet, I'm thinking these are feeding tubes of some kind. Or maybe some kind of anesthesia or tranquilizing gas. Maybe both."

"That was my thought as well. So do we remove them, or does that kill us instantly?"

She let him turn back around. "Your guess is as good as ...." She let that thought die as her mouth fell open. She tilted back, upright on her knees, and gaped. "Oh no."

"Oh no, what?" he said as he turned to see what she was staring at.

Looming above him was the strangest and most enormous creature he had ever seen.

Chapter 2

Roberto walked along the edge of the huge ramp. It curved out of an opening in the giant spaceship like an arced, extended tongue. There were no buttons or levers at the end of it where it touched the ground, nothing to indicate a means of operation or communication as he had hoped there might be. There weren't even any letters or other symbols on it, nothing to suggest an enchantment or some kind of magic was in place, some useful spell like the sort of thing Altin's people might put in place of a com station or even just as a doorbell.

Altin and Orli had gone up to the belly of the ship. They looked really small from where Roberto was. It was pretty mind-blowing how big this damn thing was. Thirty-one miles long was a whole lot of ship. This damn ramp was three-quarters of a mile to the top.

"I wish I could take my glove off," Altin was saying to Orli over the com. "This stuff has a really strange look to it. It's not wood, but it kind of looks like it. Or maybe bone."

He was talking about the weird stuff the ship was made out of. The two of them were all the way over by the ship itself, messing with the hull, but Roberto dropped to a knee when Altin said that and verified that the ramp was indeed made out of the same kind of stuff. It looked rough, a texture like the outside of an avocado.

Whatever it was, what was more important was what was up there. The aliens hadn't sent out a welcoming committee, but they also hadn't sent out troopers to kill or capture them. Given the latter, Roberto figured they were on pretty safe ground at this point. He had to believe that not everything in the universe was going to be violent. And any culture capable of developing technology on the scale of this massive ship must have learned how to work together. And besides, Roberto was a glass-half-full kind of guy.

He started up the ramp again. He considered saying something to Altin and Orli, but he knew as soon as he did, Orli would start in on him about him being a dumb-ass or something. Which he was well used to, coming from her, but there was no sense bringing it on needlessly. Besides, he just wanted to have a peek.

"It's some kind of protein," Orli was saying to Altin as Roberto climbed. She said something else, but Roberto couldn't focus on it given that something was coming over the arc of the tonguelike ramp and rolling his way.

"Hey," he managed to get out. "Something's coming." He took a couple of steps backward down the ramp, glanced at the surface of the planet, and decided six feet was close enough. He jumped off.

"What is it?" Orli asked.

"I don't know," he admitted as he landed. He moved farther away from the ramp. His heart was pounding. "But whatever it is, it's really big." He sure hoped that whole "learning to get along with each other" thing came true, and he was really rooting for a half-full glass.

The object continued to roll down the ramp, still at least a quarter mile away. It was a round-bodied thing, a vehicle of some kind, with an egg-shaped central portion and two enormous hoops on either side as wheels. There was something in the egg shape, but he couldn't make out what. He assumed it was one of the aliens, finally coming out to say hello.

He tore his gaze away long enough to raise his arm. He tapped up the video controls for his helmet's visor. He set it to record. It was pretty thrilling to think he might be the first guy in history to video these things. If they didn't eat his face off or blow him up with some kind of titanic anal probe, he'd be famous for all of time.

The vehicle had a light, which it held on a flexible sort of boom, or maybe tentacle. The light grew brighter and brighter as it approached, so bright it lit up the dust in the air.

Roberto zoomed in the camera as close as the helmet's optics would allow. There was definitely something inside of the vehicle. "Whoa," he muttered under his breath, then, louder, "What the hell is that?"

"I can't see it from down here," Orli said.

Roberto glanced over to where they were and saw the two of them shuffling back, leaning back and trying to see the top of the ramp, which he knew they couldn't from that angle.

"What's it look like from over there?" she asked.

"I don't know," he said. It was pretty hard to explain. "Like two huge hoops rolling side by side around a giant glass egg." Man, that sounded lame, and it was going to be recorded for all of history. "There's some puffy balloon thing in the middle of it with a bunch of spaghetti arms. I'm getting it on video, though." That wasn't any better. The guys on the news feeds from Earth always sounded way cooler than that.

"Maybe this is the creature coming to greet us finally," Altin was saying. Roberto wanted to agree, but he wasn't so sure. The light was getting really bright, and the vehicle was right above the two of them now. Nothing about it seemed too warm and welcoming. The tentacle reached out toward the edge of the ramp. It clearly knew they were down there. It stretched over the edge and started down toward them. The glare was so bright Roberto could hardly see them in it.

A second tentacle shot out from the top of the vehicle right after, whip quick, and it arced over the edge of the ramp, bloated at one end, and ejected something globular.

"Oh shit!" he managed to get out.

The tip of the tentacle recoiled as if it had just spat something down at Roberto's friends, and then they were encased in some kind of wiggly goo. A third tentacle came down right after, this one holding a large tubular device, with a sharp end like a probe. It jammed the probe into the jelly, and something sparked.

"Hey, Orli. Altin. You guys all right?" he asked.

No answer.

"Hey, Orli. Seriously, don't screw around. Answer me." He waited a half second. "Altin? You guys getting me?"

Still nothing.

Roberto ran toward them, into the wind. The sand blowing rasped against his helmet glass.

The beam of light from the tentacle changed colors. He looked up. A new tentacle was holding a different device. It looked to be made from the same avocado material as the ship and the ramp. The wiggly iceberg of jelly in which Altin and Orli were trapped began to rise.

"Shit. Orli!" he called. He ran faster. "God damn it, Orli, say something. Altin, come in. Jesus. This is Roberto. Altin Meade, can you hear me? Orli? God damn it."

He drew his blaster and thought about blowing the light to hell. But the blob and his two friends were now over a hundred feet in the air. The drop would kill them.

"Orli?" he called again, but there was nothing coming back. Not even a crackle or a hiss. He saw that all the lights on their suit packs were out. That wasn't good.

He ran back to the base of the ramp. This time he was with the wind, and it gave him speed, though he fell three times. The third time he actually leaped as he felt himself losing his balance and let the wind carry him that much farther before he bounced to a stop. He got to the base of the ramp and sprinted up it as best he could in the damn suit.

"Hang on, you guys, I'm coming," he called. His blaster was still in his hand.

The spaghetti-armed monstrosity in the giant vehicle had them up on the ramp now. He could see them both hovering above it, still suspended by the dimmer light at the end of the tentacle boom.

A quarter mile had never seemed so far away. Up and up he ran.

He was close enough to take a shot. He stopped, dropped to a knee, and aimed carefully for a section of the tentacle from which the suspension light came, about a half yard from the tip. He fired. The tip bent downward, as if hinged, cut halfway through by the searing shot. The yellowish jelly holding his friends plopped to the deck. Roberto was up and running. "Take that, you spaghetti fuck," he called as he ran.

They were only a hundred or so yards away. He pushed himself for speed.

Another tentacle came out through the top of the egg shape. It took up the device that the wounded tentacle had let go. Once again it lifted the jelly blob up. The vehicle turned and began to roll away, back up the ramp and toward the opening in the ship.

"Oh no you don't. Eat this, bitch!" He dropped to his knee again and fired another shot. This time the laser beam struck some kind of barrier and angled off into the sky. "Like I didn't expect that!" He switched to conventional rounds as he ran closer. They wouldn't be any good from this far away. The vehicle was moving away too quickly. He had to shoot anyway.

He aimed and fired. He couldn't tell if he hit anything or not. Nothing happened. He fired again, then three more after.

The vehicle stopped.

"Hah! Now you see how it is. Give me my friends back." He ran farther up the ramp.

A tentacle reached out toward him. It held an oblong black device. He wasn't sure what it was, but he didn't like it, so he stopped and shot at it too. Three shots, *crack, crack, crack.*

Something happened in the air in front of him: it rippled, like barely visible smoke rings being blown at him. The force blew him backward eighty feet, and were it not for the slope of the ramp, the landing might have killed him. As it was, he struck hard and his breath was knocked from him. He slid another sixty feet before coming to a stop. He'd damn near slid off the edge of the ramp. The seventy-foot drop would have finished him.

He got up, realized his gun was gone, and immediately fumbled for the sharp pair of pliers in his suit's tool kit. "This shit isn't over yet!" That's when he realized all the lights were off on his suit too. All of them.

He paused, thinking. He looked up and saw the vehicle was already getting up and over the hump in the ramp, heading into the black hole that would take it inside.

He refocused, looking at the blank glass inside his helmet. Nothing. No video, no temperature readings, no oxygen monitors.

"God damn it!"

He wouldn't be any good to them dead.

Chapter 3

The creature snaked a tendril up into the steam-filled wind, a tentacle perhaps, for there were round structures along it like suction cups, though from the distance, and the steamy darkness, it was hard for Orli to be sure. The tendril flapped and fluttered as it rose, much as the mucus had when the ochre jelly was melting away, but it climbed steadily higher. Its ascent was guided by a number of the small discs, which flattened out like giant oval dinner plates, spreading out from the center of the tendril and angling here and there, some upward, some vertical to the direction of the wind, like the rudder and ailerons of an old-fashioned airplane.

She saw it rising in the distance behind Altin where he knelt in front of her, watched it climb right up to the large grate high above them. She followed its flight, saw it wind itself around one of the cross members of the grate, and then, right after, it seemed to haul the most colossal creature out of the darkness from down below.

"Oh no," she said as she watched it emerge from the shadows.

"Oh no, what?" Altin asked, turning and following the direction of her gaze.

Up rose a billow of gray material, looking rather like a colossal parachute made from a film of mucus. It bloated with the prevailing wind, and it followed the tendril upward for a time, growing larger and larger as it drew near. Soon it was high above them. From within it, descending out of the space inside the gray, filmy dome, came a long body, at least three times longer than the billow was deep. She thought immediately that the creature looked like a soft, lumpy-stemmed mushroom made of snot—with lots of tentacles.

It was enormous. The billow, inflated and massive as it spread wide above her, had to be at least a hundred and fifty yards across, and nearly as deep inside. And the body that came out of it was a mucous gray tube that couldn't be any less than three hundred yards long. It had two bulbs, a small one up inside of the billow and another at the center, and at the end of its very long, cylindrical body it narrowed, like the tapering of an insect's thorax, though soft and seemingly malleable. An odd puckering of flesh at this terminal end reminded her of someone about to spit.

The large central bulb seemed to recommend itself as the creature's head and face, or at least something approximately so, despite being located where it was. It swelled at the middle of the long, tubular body, not much below the line of the billow's edge, and appeared as if the creature had swallowed something enormous and oblong in the way of a python that has just had a meal of something extremely large. Around the equator of this bulbous area blinked three large, silvery eyes, massive half spheres that bulged out of black eye sockets, each of which were formed by concentric rings of black flesh like stacked rings embedded in the soft flesh.

It was also from this bulbous central part of the creature's body that the tentacles came. One of them, the first tendril she had seen, emerged near the top of the protuberance and now stretched taught like a guy-wire up to the grate above, holding the creature in place despite the wind. Several other tentacles waggled freely, loose and streaming like smoke plumes in the currents blowing by. Five sprouted from the bulb above the eyes, spaced evenly around, and five more emerged from beneath those blinking orbs, also equally spaced all around, ten tentacles in all.

The creature snaked a tentacle down at the two of them, Altin and Orli standing there. Once again it flattened a few of its discs out to guide the tentacle toward them. It came waggling down, its tip flexing, not quite sharp, and it tapped once against the back of Altin's head.

"Oh God," Orli said as Altin muttered something profane and entirely Prosperion.

The tendril tapped twice more on Altin's helmet, then right after, and quick as a dart, it dove down through the grate beneath him. It threaded its way back up and wrapped itself around the beam several times, while yet another tentacle came down and slithered around him, wrapping him up in a stack of coils.

"I can't imagine this is going to end well," Altin said, though he sounded more curious than afraid.

Orli could hardly believe he was so calm. She jumped up and tried to pull the tip of the tendril away, intending to unwind it. She couldn't budge it. It might as well have been three-inch rebar. She reached for her blaster. It was gone.

"I think it's trying to do something," Altin said, still remarkably restrained. "I can feel pressure all over my suit. It's like a thousand fingers all over me, squeezing and prodding me everywhere."

He was jerked up and away before she could reply. She screamed his name. The tendril curled up into the blowing mist. Another tendril came down, this one having been first sent up to the platform above, wound through it, and sent back down. It locked together with the tip of the one that had Altin wrapped up. Both went taut between the two grates, with Altin like a joint in the middle of them.

There followed a loud, sucking sound, and in that moment the creature sucked its puffy parachute-like billow in. The massive dome of shimmering flesh vanished almost too quickly to be seen, settling into the smaller bulbous area that she'd noted near the top of the creature's body, situated up inside the billow earlier. That bulb became pregnant with the billow's mass and now matched the central one for size, the whole thing together looking like two scoops of snot-flavored ice cream on a mucous cone—a five-hundred-yard-long one with tentacles and eyes.

From the larger, central bulb a light came on, emitted from one of the creature's eyes. It shone down on Altin, the beam bright and tight, as focused as any spotlight could be. It beamed into Altin's face, and she could only guess how blindingly bright it must seem to him, being that he was at least two hundred yards closer to it than she was.

The beam changed colors, from white to blue, then green. The tentacles around Altin flexed. Gaps opened up here and there between the coils. Still the light shone. Orli shouted up to him, but she knew he couldn't hear her over the infernal wind and all the other noise, the roiling rumble from down below and all the thumping and hissing coming from everywhere.

Altin was upside down now. Another tentacle had been brought to bear and was prodding at him again. It was too dim to make out his features in the darkness, with the distance and with the misty wind, but she was sure he must be terrified.

Then he was coming down again. The tendril that had been wound through the grate above elongated, stretching and thinning some as it lowered him down. Orli realized as it did so that there were colors flashing all up and down the creature's body now. All the colors of the rainbow, dappled with gray, making patterns on its skin. The lights flashed on the puffs of steam that blew by, painting them to ghosts of rainbows. Orli realized the steam was rising up through the grates.

The added illumination from the enormous creature revealed more of the area around her. She could see that the grate they were on was indiscernibly long. She was sure she could see for a half mile in either direction at least, and yet there was no sign of a terminal wall in any direction. Just blowing mist. And strange alien machines.

Huge formations of the rough, green-brown protein rose up from the grate, the material shaping the alien constructs. They were blocky and towering, dotted with enormous glowing bulbs. The nearest had long flutelike chimneys, or so they seemed to her, which rose straight up and disappeared through the grate above. Levers thrust out thrice as long as she was tall. Holes were sunk into it as well, perfectly round and, by her best guess, about the perfect diameter to stick a tentacle inside.

There were other machines beyond it. The largest were giant melon-shaped things that sat upon the grating, braced in place by what looked like woven nests. The melon-things she thought might be reservoirs of some kind, tanks perhaps, but whatever they were nesting in was translucent, a dull seaweed brown, and having the look of coiled hose. Light pulsed dimly from inside of the strands, suggesting they were hollow and contiguous, and perhaps filled with something liquid moving inside.

These structures, reservoir and brace, were also attached to long chimneys, which again ran straight up and vanished through the grate above. More bulbous lights glowed here and there along their length.

There were other machines, many others. All of them massive and impossible to define. In some ways, they seemed very familiar, obviously equipment with functions like any other machine. But the sheer scale of them made function impossible to guess.

Altin was taken to one of them.

The creature traveled across the grate by hauling itself against the wind. One tentacle was locked to the grate Altin and Orli were on, the same grate with the machine it was heading toward. Two more tentacles were stretched up to the grate above now. The titanic being pulled itself against the gusting wind with these taut lines, its limbs like ropes, and with yet another tentacle, it laid Altin down upon the flat surface of a machine that was some quarter mile from where Orli was.

Orli couldn't see him anymore. She could only see the enormous creature at work. She gathered up the three tubes that were plugged into her suit and ran as quickly as she dared along the grate, making right-angle turns to zigzag her way to him over the crisscross network of beams.

A puff of steam came up from below, thick like fog, and as it blew over her, she thought she might be in danger of heatstroke if such occurred too often. Her spacesuit wasn't cooling at all that she could tell, and sweat ran from her in rivers. Worse, the steam made it hard to see, forming droplets on the helmet glass and making traversing the grate dangerous at best.

The light above grew brighter as she approached. She paused long enough to look up.

Another of the massive alien creatures blew into view, coming from the opposite side of the machine that Altin was on. It simply appeared out of the darkness like a phantom on the wind. It caught itself with tentacles wrapped around the grate above, stopping its flight abruptly, then sent more tentacles down toward the grate in places around the machine. Soon it had guy-wired itself in place beside the machine as the first alien had done. The two creatures began flickering and flashing back and forth, prismatic colors sliding up and down their lengths. It added a little extra light to help Orli run.

And Orli was a runner, her conditioning supreme, but the damn spacesuit and the damn tubes attached to it and the damn crisscrossed beams of the grate made movement agonizingly difficult. And then there was the wind.

As she neared the machine, she quickly realized that it was so huge that she couldn't possibly see what was happening on top of it. She'd have been better off staying where she was. At least back there she'd had some kind of angle. All she could see up close were the three tubes that had been plugged into Altin's suit hanging down the side of the machine like lengths of coarsely made rubber hose. "Altin," she cried out, knowing it was pointless. It was.

Something was being lowered from the darkness high above the upper deck of the machine. A light came on, glaringly bright. It came from the surface that Altin lay upon, shining upward and illuminating whatever it was that was coming down.

The object was a three-pronged device with long and thick tubes like fingers protruding from a blocky central mass. Attached to the blocky section of the device were lengths of the same hose-like material Orli had seen the melon tanks nesting in. These hoses, or pipes, or whatever they were, ran upward through the grate and attached to some other very large device mounted on the underside of the grate above. She could see it well because of how bright the light was shining up from the machine Altin had been set upon. These tubes, sinuous as they were, appeared to be the lone source of support for the large, three-pronged device, suggesting they must be tremendously strong.

The fingerlike prongs themselves, and the central mass from which they came, were made from the same green-brown material that seemingly everything else on the ship was. But the tips of them were different. On each was a black half dome that shone as if made of glass or some kind of semisolid liquid. None of them were quite the same size, nor were the prongs themselves identical in thickness or in length. Whatever they were, the shortest, thickest of them was being lowered right down at what had to be where Altin lay.

First she thought he might be crushed. Then she wondered what they might be doing ... or emitting. She hoped he wasn't being irradiated to death.

She considered climbing up one of the tubes jammed into his suit, but thought better of it. What if she pulled it out and it really was his only source of air?

She needed to do something.

Think, Orli, God damn it, she told herself. Think. Take a breath and do something.

She turned her gaze downward. Looked through the grate at what was below. The ship was huge. She and Altin couldn't go up easily, but they could go down. What was down there?

The light from the machine was blasting upward, but there was still enough bouncing back from above, plus the prismatic color coming from the two massive aliens, to reveal quite a bit below, though often the light bounced off streaks of blowing steam, which turned white and still reminded her of spirits streaking past. Some were very large, and their passing obscured everything in blinks of ghoulish mist on a field of darkness.

The platform below her was identical to the one she was on. The machines were different. But there were many of them.

The ballooning billow of an alien streaked into view from her left, barely twenty yards beneath her. It came so quickly it startled her. None of its body lights were on. Or at least, not very brightly, not like the two doing whatever was happening to Altin glowed. This one had little flickers of color that shimmered here and there on an endless field of mucous gray as it blew past. It took nearly half a minute for it to glide by.

She watched after it, hoping in the dim luminescence that she might spot the silhouette of one of those chimneys coming up nearby, something she and Altin could shimmy down.

Of course there were none.

There were no wires, no ropes, no pipes, tubes, or that weird, glowing nest material anywhere in sight. The only distinguishing anything at all was a triangular bit of prismatic light probably a half mile away, ironically pretty and optimistic in color, but nothing hopeful in the end. If it had wires or pipes she could climb, she damn sure couldn't see them from here. Which meant there was nothing. Just a five-hundred-yard drop at least. With what had to be a fifty- or sixty-mile-per-hour crosswind in between. Not good.

She turned back to look up at the, well, the examining table Altin was on. What else could it be?

She saw that a longer, narrower cylindrical prong of the three was rotating into place above Altin, or where he had to be—for what else would that machine be pointing itself at? The first one, short and fat by comparison, rotated away as the mass twisted. It ended up sticking out like the pinky of some posh Prosperion noble drinking tea. The new cylinder locked into place with an audible thud. It was so loud Orli could feel it through her spacesuit boots. This prong also had a black dome at the end, slightly smaller than the last.

The newcomer alien drew itself up and looked into something on the far side of the protein mass above. Whatever it was cast a blue light that reflected in two of its giant eyes.

It watched for a time, then lowered itself again. And

then, to Orli's absolute surprise, an image of Altin appeared upon its body, as if projected from the back side of a bulbous white sheet. The image was huge, Altin's face clearly visible beneath the helmet glass, eyes wide but his expression calm. She could tell he was trying to control his breathing. That was good. He was still keeping his head.

The rest of him, the image of him, showed itself down the length of the alien's long body. Altin's head appeared broad and distorted across the bulbous part, and the rest of him, somewhat elongated, stretched down a forty-yard segment of the narrow, lower part of the alien. It was as if the creature itself were a video monitor, or at least, nearly so. The image was a little hazy, but not much, and she hardly knew if that was the effect of the image itself, the steam in the air, or the fog coming and going on her own helmet glass.

Patterns of light and color flashed over the image. Dark patches too. The first creature responded with colors of its own. Altin's face appeared on its bulb too, then grew and got so large it vanished, replaced with only the metal ring around the seal at the base of Altin's helmet.

The second alien reflected that image back. More colors and dark patches mottled the helmet seal depicted on their bodies. The alien that had been looking into the device pulled itself back up toward the big mass out of which the prongs and all the translucent hoses ran. It stared into the dim glow coming from up there again. Three of its tentacles were moving about on the top of the machine where Altin was. Orli had no way to know what they were doing to him.

Then the alien's whole body turned blue, bright blue like the sky on a clear Prosperion day. It flashed three times, and right after, the first alien did the same.

Altin's spacesuit helmet came bouncing over the edge of the machine a moment later. Orli barely had time to realize it—she hardly noticed something so small moving in such a place of massiveness. She saw it as it fell, realizing what it

24

meant. She ran for it, jumped the corner of two gaps in the grate, trying to catch it. It bounced on the beam directly across from her, rolled down its length, and spun there. She jumped the corner of that gap and dove for it just as a gust of wind blew it over the edge. She watched it fall until she lost it in the darkness.

Chapter 4

Roberto appeared in Calico Castle, near an old suit of armor on a pedestal. It was placed in the corner of a massive dining hall, in which he'd eaten numerous times before. The high vaulted ceilings above him were lost in darkness, as was the long table at the center of the room, most of it, anyway. The double doors across the way were open, and light came in from the hallway beyond, illuminating the high, arcing backs of three chairs at the end of the table and making pitchfork silhouettes of the candelabras near that end, none of which were lit.

He let go the breath he had held back on Yellow Fire's new red world, a long and potentially final one drawn as he had pulled his helmet off. It was nice to know that it hadn't been his last. He glanced to the shattered remnants of what was once a pale sapphire and shook his head. Altin called them "fast-cast amulets," enchanted gemstones that held a single teleportation spell. Roberto called them lifesavers. He only hoped his would be enough to get Altin and Orli help. He didn't think they were going to be in a position to use the ones they wore right away, not while being stuck in some kind of alien goo.

He ran out of the dining hall, helmet still in hand, and

headed out into the courtyard. He cast his gaze about, but there was no one there. He called for Tytamon as loudly as he could. The doughty old kitchen matron, Kettle, came waddling out of the castle, wiping flour from her hands on equally flour-dusted skirts.

"What's with all that racket, now?" she asked, looking ready to scold him for it regardless of the contents of his reply.

"Where's Tytamon? I need a ride to ... I need ... crap, I don't even know where I need a ride to."

Who could he get to help that could do anything about Altin and Orli's predicament? He could go to Little Earth, a forty-acre base that the War Queen had provided for the Earth fleet's use when it first arrived on planet Prosperion. But then what? It's not like the fleet had any way of getting to Yellow Fire—not without a wizard. Not without many wizards now, given Altin's circumstance.

"Calm down, lad," Kettle said. The frenzied look in his eyes had turned her irritation into something more useful to them both. "Think a bit, now. Where is it ya need ta go? Tell me now, an' we'll see ta gettin' ya there quick as ya like."

"*Citadel*," he said. "I need to get to *Citadel*. Those aliens that landed on Yellow Fire have captured Altin and Orli. They took them into the ship."

"Oh, sweet Mercy, not again," Kettle cried. "Do ya all got nothin' else ta do than go about the stars tweakin' the nose of ever' new creature ya run across? Weren't it enough what nearly done fer us last year?"

Roberto let out a long, slow breath. He could see Kettle working herself up into a fright, which wouldn't serve anyone. It was his turn to strive for calm.

"You're right," he said. "But it's too late to do anything about that part now. We've got to get help."

"Are they all right? Are they hurt?"

"Well ...." He paused and had to think about that. He

didn't think they were hurt. But he hardly knew. "No," he told her. "They were unharmed last time I saw them." It wasn't exactly a lie. "But I didn't get to talk to them before they went into the ship, so I think it would be best if we had *Citadel* there. You know, in case the ... uh ... the meeting doesn't go well."

"I dinna just bounce off the potato wagon and inta the pot, young man," she said, "and this here ain't potato-me boilin' fer mash."

His face crowded in around itself as he stared at her, his mouth half-open. "What do potatoes have to do with anything?"

"It means don't treat me like a child, boy. Now if they're in trouble, I need ta know."

He straightened, looked her directly in the eye. "Kettle, they were alive the last time I saw them. I don't know what's happening to them now. But I do know the aliens had a chance to kill me—easily, I think, if they'd wanted to—and they didn't. So, while I admit I don't really know anything, that part I *do* know, and it's all completely true. I think they are okay. Maybe. But I don't like it, and I need Tytamon." He watched her face for her reaction. She seemed satisfied.

"He was outside this mornin', workin' with them girls a' yer crew on that fancy black floor you've got him and poor Altin makin' out there."

He knew where Altin's teleportation pad was being built—a project Roberto himself had inspired—but he let her lead him across the courtyard and out through the gates. The armored guards looked back and forth between them as Roberto and Kettle ran through, sensing something amiss, but unable to detect anything to which they might put their halberds.

In his spacesuit, and with Kettle as agitated as she was, it was a bit of work for Roberto to keep up with her. Her stout frame and round, florid cheeks gave a false impression about her when it came to speed.

Soon they rounded the corner of the castle and were heading into the meadow to the east. There was a bulging section of the castle wall now, arcing out into the grass and made of lighter stone than the rest. It was a new construction, an extension Altin had added to accommodate the frequent absence of his tower, the boot, these days. Beyond its curve, another hundred paces out into the meadow, lay several large black stacks of tiles, nearly a yard square, piled five feet high. All around them were heaps of stone, barrels of pitch, wheelbarrows full of wisteria and blackroot, and mounds of various types of clay, some dry and cracked, others wet and glistening in the sun. Weaving around all of this were several members of Roberto's crew, most having eschewed the glittering purple corsets of their *Glistening Lady* uniforms in favor of tank tops more suitable to heavy work under a springtime sun. Sami, Fatima, and Betty-Lynn were all pushing wooden wheelbarrows full of clay over to a frame staked to the ground, their muscular bodies leaning into them as the creaking wheels bounced over rocks and in and out of animal burrows. Roberto's fourth brawny bodyguard, Chelsea, pushed a gravity sled from the other side of the site toward the frame, hers stacked with at least a half ton of stone, while his lean but lovely navigator, Tracy Applegate, singularly still in uniform, worked with an axe chopping down strips of wisteria to length. And there amidst them all, attired as always in his gray robes, was the ancient wizard, Tytamon, Calico Castle's original tenant and a man approaching his eight hundredth birthday.

The great wizard heard them coming and looked up from his work. He set down a block of the black material he was making, a substance called engasta syrup, which he made from the ingredients all around. When formed into tiles and assembled together into a platform, the material could be transformed by transmutation magic into a box large enough to accommodate very large things. Objects and people could be teleported about in these boxes without troublesome accidents, and, in the particular case of the work in progress, spaceships could be sent across distances that were, prior to the advent of this magical device, impossible. A spaceship teleported in that way would not have its fusion core extinguished—as was the case when teleporting ships directly, "out of the box"—and it would not require a total restart of all the systems aboard. In the boxes operated by the Transportation Guild Service, Roberto's own ship, the *Glistening Lady*, had gone back and forth between Prosperion and Earth a few times in what was little more than a blink in time. But without such a convenience provided by the TGS, a teleport by his friend Altin, unboxed teleportation, required a five-hour span of drifting helplessness while the ship was essentially rebooted from its very core. That time could be as much as several days for the fleet's largest ships.

And so it was that Altin, and now Tytamon, were building their own private version of the massive teleportation platforms that the TGS was building in choice locations across the galaxy. The existence of this private platform was not public record just yet, but given how politicized the whole galactic transportation topic had become over the last year, it had seemed prudent to pursue in reality what had started out as just a casual idea. The whole point of having one at Calico Castle was help in situations like the one in which Roberto, Altin, and Orli now found themselves. A situation that Tytamon picked up on right away.

"Might I assume by the nature of your attire that my apprentice and his new bride are in some difficulty again?" Tytamon began as they approached. He said it with a nod toward Roberto's spacesuit and the helmet in his hand.

"Yeah, you can assume that. They've been taken aboard a spaceship at the alien dig site on Yellow Fire."

"Hmmm," hummed the weathered old sorcerer. His thin lips pursed beneath the snowy whiteness of his mustache, though they were barely visible. "That does sound like them. How urgent is the danger? None of you seemed terribly concerned about the aliens when you took the tower back out there."

Roberto couldn't help rolling his eyes. He'd just done this with Kettle. "How urgent does it need to be? They're on a damn alien ship, stuck in some kind of alien snot ball, and now I can't get either one of them up on the com."

"Hmmm," hummed to ancient sorcerer again. He pulled gently on his long white beard as he thought about it.

Roberto tried to be patient. He knew the man was a genius. He knew the man was the only wizard on the whole planet able to cast spells in all eight magic schools, at least that's what Altin called them: schools. Tytamon was an Eight. The only one in Prosperion history, apparently. So, it seemed reasonable to let the man think. But, well, what was there to think about? They needed to do something.

"Sir," Roberto began, as politely as possible. "We need to get moving. Unless you think you can, you know, zip in there and zap some lightning, maybe a fireball or two, and then, well, get them out of there ... it's time to get to *Citadel* and get this rescue party moving."

"Given how things went the last two times Prosperions encountered a new race of beings, I should think we might take a bit more care this time, don't you?"

"Not when my best friend is frozen in some kind of jelly, and one of those giant spaghetti assholes tried to shoot me with ... with a sonic blast or something."

"They tried to shoot you?"

"Yes."

"Well, that does change things a bit. You hadn't mentioned that they shot at you, unprovoked." His bushy white brows drooped over his eyes for a time, then he set his gray eyes back on Roberto. "It was unprovoked, wasn't it? What were you doing when it shot at you?"

Roberto's eyes glanced away for the barest moment. He didn't even want them to. They just did. He frowned, emitted a low sort of growl. "Shooting at it," he admitted.

"You shot first?"

"It had my friends. What was I supposed to do?"

"But you said they weren't harmed."

"I said I don't know if they are harmed."

"Right. There are worlds of difference between them." He looked to Kettle then. "I suspect we won't be back in time for dinner," he said.

"Weren't ta be the first time," she replied. "I'll have somethin' waitin' fer ya, all the same. Just in case."

He smiled, his expression softening, affectionate. "Hardly the first time, indeed." They exchanged a pair of sighs that spoke more than ten thousand words might have, and then she turned and tottered off back toward the gates.

When she was gone, Tytamon sighed again, this one different than the last. Resignation, certainly, but determination too. It was the sound one makes when about to embark on a long and wearisome journey, a journey all too familiar despite the destination unknown. It was the trek of tedious responsibility, down another rough road in a long line of them. It was the sound of time weighing heavily upon a man. "Let's be off, then," he said when he'd blown it out. "But we'll begin with the Queen."

"Whoever," Roberto said. "Let's just get some wizards on the way. Preferably a whole crapton of them. And maybe a few platoons of mechs just to be safe."

"We shall see," said Tytamon. The great sorcerer closed his eyes and began chanting straightaway.

Chapter 5

Pernie appeared beside a rushing river, flanked on either side by the elf Seawind and the old woman Djoveeve. She knew that the river was the Sansun, because she'd known that they were going to come to Crown City, the capital of Kurr and the city where the War Queen lived. Pernie had met the War Queen before, and even fought in a battle with her. She was very excited to see the Queen again. The last time, Her Majesty had tried to order her around, but Pernie was about to become the *Sava'an'Lansom*, so she was sure that would change things quite a lot. Besides, Pernie knew a lot more about the War Queen now.

Before she'd been dragged off to the Isle of Hunters in the elven lands of String, Pernie has spent just enough time in school to have learned lots of facts about the magnificent Queen Karroll. It was said that her armor made her all but invincible. It had been enchanted by great diviners two hundred years ago, and one of its main magicks was that it defended her with the force of her own courage. Pernie did not understand how that could work, but it sounded very impressive. Besides, the War Queen fought with a broadsword that was longer than Master Altin was tall, and it was nearly as wide as Pernie was. She read that the War Queen was the greatest warrior on all of Prosperion, and that even the Royal Assassin, Shadesbreath, couldn't beat her in a fight.

Pernie didn't know if that was true, but after spending just over a year in training with the elves, learning how to be their Sava'an'Lansom, she rather hoped it was. The Sava'an'Lansom, or "assassin of the vale" when translated from elven to the common tongue of Kurr, was supposed to be the guardian of the High Seat, which apparently was what the elves called their ruler, although Djoveeve had explained to Pernie that they didn't really have a ruler in the way humans did. But Pernie didn't care about that kind of thing. All she knew was that after a year of being knocked around by elves, of being struck by their spear butts and kicked by their swift, accurate feet, she had a place in her heart that was rooting for some representative of humanity to fight better than the elves—Pernie being human and all. With all the stories she'd heard about the elves as she was growing up, especially the way people paled when they spoke of the dreaded Shadesbreath in low whispers, as if he might be lurking there in the room, it gave her hope for her own abilities to think that the most deadly fighter in the world was a human and not an elf. She could hardly wait to see the War Queen again, this time with much less fighting going on all around.

And see her they would. Seawind had told her that she must go to the human school. In some weird form of elf logic, it turned out that the best way for her to become the bodyguard of the elven High Seat was to learn from humanity. Elves didn't make very much sense sometimes, but Pernie was fine with it. She was going to learn from the humans on Earth, not the boring ones here on Kurr. She was going to learn everything Orli Pewter knew, and then, when Orli Pewter died—maybe by accident, as one could never be too sure about such things—Pernie would be ready for Master Altin to fall in love with her.

36

Pernie could hardly wait.

Seawind led them out from behind the clump of bushes they had appeared behind. He pulled the long green cloak he wore about himself and drew up the hood even though it was a pretty spring day. She watched as he changed the pale green hue of his skin to the tanned tones of Pernie's own flesh, though he did not change the seaweed-green color of his hair.

"Come, little Sava," he said, "let us go get you to Earth."

Pernie followed along behind him as they entered the city. Growing up at Calico Castle, she'd always thought that the walls of that gray stone fortress were high and mighty indeed. But now she saw that they were not. Calico Castle was hardly a cobbler's hovel compared to Crown City. She had to tilt her head so far back to see the top of the walls that she was nearly looking straight into the noontime sun.

The guards at the gate made no particular notice of them as they passed through, and Pernie thought their scarlet capes very beautiful. She wished she had a scarlet cape instead of the boring elf-made clothes—dumb brown pants, dumb short boots, and a plain green tunic with no sleeves. That last was kind of pretty in a shiny sort of way, but it was plain. She felt like she should be wearing something better now that she was here and about to see the War Queen. Pernie wasn't normally the sort to care about such things, but she really did want to impress Her Majesty this time.

The trek through the city was a long one, and it took them the better part of two hours to arrive at the spectacle that was Unification Avenue, rebuilt after the war in even greater glory than it had before. Pernie gasped as she gazed down it toward the Palace. The boulevard was enormous, a hundred spans wide and five hundred long. The trees along its sidewalks were still not as the old stories said, as the healers with their growth magic hadn't had time to coax the newly planted replacements back to half-measure altitudes.

But the statues were all back, tall and regal, old kings, famous warriors, and all the gods, major and minor, depicted in glorious poses down a wide median that divided the avenue. The least of them stood twenty spans high, and some, the five-armed god Anvilwrath with all his weapons in hand, had to be no less than ninety spans.

Pernie and her two companions walked down this central avenue, and she gawked and gasped. She had been in Crown City once before, but she'd flown in right after the orcs captured Calico Castle and only got to see one corner of a military compound. This was much better than that. They passed the statue of the Huntress, the divine guardian of the goddess Mercy, and just as in the stories, she had her great bow across her back and a spear forty-five spans long raised and aimed as if to pierce the sun above. Pernie thought the minor goddess looked a little bit like her, if only a little, but there was certainly a touch of similarity around the eyes and nose and perhaps a little more in the way her hair hung long around her shoulders and down her back. But someday it would all look like her. Pernie was going to grow up tall and strong like that, she knew. And she already knew how to use a spear.

At the end of the avenue was one last series of statues, three in a row, side by side, all of which were enchanted into motion, replaying short ten-second scenes. The centralmost was enormous, nearly as large as that of Anvilwrath and the great gods. The scene it presented depicted the mighty War Queen doing battle with an orc that was twice her height and at least three times as wide across the shoulders and chest. He was a monster. And he bore a battle-axe with two huge blades, each as wide as a wagon bed. The War Queen's face was twisted in defiance as she swung her sword. The orc roared as he swung the axe, so loud it made Pernie step back. His mouth gaped like a cavern as he did so, and it was so large Pernie thought she might have been able to stand upon his tongue and not be as tall as his teeth, two of which curled out from his mouth like tusks, thrusting up from a jaw that was broad and square. The marble Queen raised her sword and blocked a blow of that mighty axe, and the crash of the two weapons made thunder and sent sparks out in a rain of fire. She roared back at the orc, and the sound was terrible and glorious. Then the statue was still for a time. Pernie got goose bumps running up her arms.

On either side of that statue were slightly smaller ones, the one on the right depicting mounted men and warriors on foot, battling with orcs that crushed in all around them. It came to life right after the Queen's statue battle settled down. The men leaned from their saddles and slashed at their enemies, who jabbed with long spears back at them. They all shouted and cursed and growled, and the clank and clatter of their armor and swords mixed with the thuds of wooden spears pounding on shields of steel. Their battle went on for ten seconds too, and then it settled back to the white silence of the enchanted stone. Then the last statue's enchantment began.

The statue on the left depicted yet another battle scene, this one showing humans from Earth in their splendid battle gear, machines that they wore like suits of armor, and from them sprayed death on light beams and tiny arrowheads that Pernie knew were called bullets. Pernie loved bullets. Roberto had let her shoot bullets from his gun one time. And the laser too. She liked the laser, but the bullets made an excellent sound and the whole gun recoiled in her hand. The weapons of the Earth warriors cut through the limbs and face of a hideous monster with many legs and eyes like spiders' eyes. It had sets of mandibles all lined up in a row, which opened and closed, clacking loudly as they gnashed, a distorted and mutant face attached to a crab-like body with great mashing spheres where its crab claws should be, huge, round hammers big enough to crush mammoths into patty meat. But the Earth machines blasted into it, alien and powerful, and the demon limbs broke, blasted apart until it collapsed like an old swamp house on rotted pilings. Pernie watched and sighed and wished she could have an armored machine like that too. Maybe she would one day, now that she was going to Earth.

"I notice they didn't bother to carve our friend in that," Djoveeve observed as they walked past the statue of the Queen.

Pernie looked at it again, but couldn't fathom what the old woman meant. She saw Seawind look up at it too. He acknowledged whatever the old assassin had intended him to see, doing so with a single nod, but he said nothing and no emotion crossed his face. They seldom did.

The three of them came then to the enormous Palace gates. Pernie's pulse raced. The walls were so high she couldn't even guess how tall they were. At least twice as high as those that ran around the city. And these were mirror smooth. They looked like marble, but Pernie knew from the stories that they were so full of enchantment magic it had taken tens of thousands of magicians hundreds of years to make them as they were.

It was frightening to think, as she stood there, that the orcs and the demons had almost gotten through. How could anything get through all of that?

The guard at the gatehouse came out. His plate armor was gilded with gold and polished to a mirror shine. His cloak was red like the others were. Once again Pernie wished she had more impressive clothes.

"Business?" the guard demanded.

Seawind pulled back his hood.

"Mercy's ghost," the red-cloaked man said, stepping away. His face paled, and Pernie thought it was fun to see how scared he was. She'd used to think elves were scary too, but she didn't anymore.

The man went back into the gatehouse. A few minutes passed, and after, the gates swung open enough to admit them.

A herald approached down a main avenue that ran around a fountain and took up more space than all of Calico Castle did. He was riding on a golden disc that glided above the ground.

He came to a stop above the shimmering paving stones and simply hovered there, the flying disc barely three finger widths off the ground. "Please," he said. "If you will accompany me. Her Majesty is being notified of your arrival now."

"Thank you," Djoveeve answered, sparing the elf having to remember his human courtesies. She made to reach for Pernie's shoulder to nudge her toward the disc, but Pernie was already standing on it, right next to the herald and grinning ear to ear.

Djoveeve and Seawind followed suit, the elf's face as inscrutable as ever and Djoveeve's brightening a little in the glow of Pernie's exuberance.

As they sped through the outer reaches of the Palace compound, Pernie gaped and pointed this way and that, crying out, "Oh, look at that" and "Djoveeve, do you see?" all the while. She must have asked, "Can't we just go touch it for a minute?" forty times by the time they got to the Palace proper and the stairs.

Pernie was nearly delirious at seeing them. She'd never seen such a great stack of steps before. "Look at it," she gasped. "It's as high as a mountain!"

"And it might as well be one," Djoveeve grumbled. "And I'll have to climb them in these old bones." She didn't look pleased about that.

"Your jaguar form will make it easier," Pernie told her matter-of-factly. "Or the crane fly."

"I don't think that would be a good idea," Djoveeve said.

"And you will not do any magic while we are here either, do you hear? Not one jot, or you'll have all the guards on us in an instant. I don't want to spend my last few decades rotting in a jail cell."

"I would come get you out," Pernie said. "I'm not afraid."

"All the same, young miss," said the herald, "you'll do right to remember what the Sava'an'Lansom has said. There is no magic cast here without permission from Her Majesty, the Lord Chamberlain, or, in special circumstances, the Captain of the Guard."

Pernie was more interested in how well the man spoke the elven words when he pronounced Djoveeve's formal title as the current assassin of the vale. It came right off his tongue, easily. She'd been working very hard for over a year to learn the elven language and make it sound pretty the way the elves did. He did it as easily as if he'd said it a thousand times before.

They climbed the stairs on foot, which didn't bother Pernie at all, angling slowly upward toward the enormity of the massive central spire, which loomed above as if it were trying to spike the sun before the Huntress with her spear could. The rest of the Palace was a golden panoply of towers and turrets and sprawling battlements. It was too bright to look at for very long, so Pernie mainly watched where she was going, and watched Djoveeve.

"They use floating discs for the flat spaces, and yet we walk up the steps," Djoveeve complained when they were nearly three-quarters of the way to the top. "It's hard to imagine how our people achieved anything, isn't it, little Sava?"

Pernie had never seen the woman tired before. But then, Pernie had also never seen the woman travel much without using one of her animal forms. It was the first time Pernie really saw her as being old, old in a withering way, not just old in a gray and wrinkled way.

At last they reached the palatial doors, cast in bronze and inlaid with gold that sparkled in the sun, and Djoveeve took a moment before them to catch her breath. She caught Pernie looking at her, and glared in mock anger. "Come back here when you are three hundred and three years old, then see how well you do." She winked, and Pernie smiled. She had a lot to be happy about. She was about to stand before the mighty War Queen as someone important now.

Chapter 6

Pernie grew very impatient waiting outside of the throne room, even though the wait hadn't been three minutes yet. She could see all the people inside, and it was quite crowded today. A great milling about of regally clad courtiers and applicants hummed and buzzed in dialects from all over Kurr. Pernie had seen pictures in books and in the illusions cast by storytellers and traveling bards, depicting many of the styles of clothing people wore when they came to see the Queen, and many of those were evident for real within. Some of the faces she recognized as well, as if characters from those books and stories had suddenly turned real. There were even a few she already knew, great figures of wealth and power whom she'd seen visiting with Master Tytamon and Master Altin back at Calico Castle.

The noise that came from inside that room was such a constant din that she could only grasp bits and pieces of conversations. She tried, but she couldn't follow any of them. She leaned and twisted trying to see the Queen, but she wasn't tall enough. It didn't help that Seawind and Djoveeve had pushed her behind them as if she were a child. Which, she supposed, technically she was, but she didn't appreciate being treated like one. She was the Sava'an'Lansom, after all. Or at least, she almost was. Then they wouldn't treat her like that anymore. No one would.

There came two loud cracks of the herald's staff upon the floor, each sounding like a strike on a colossal drum. The herald's voice boomed out over the crowd after. It was a spectacular sound, thunderous and loud. "Seawind of the White Meadow, Speaker of the High Seat and emissary of String." He paused a moment, then went on. "And Djoveeve Ledgerwotch, Sava'an'Lansom, Protector of the High Seat."

Pernie wrinkled her nose at that. She hadn't known Djoveeve had a last name before. She didn't think the Sava'an'Lansom needed one. Pernie had a last name, but it wasn't real. Her last name was Grayborn, but they called all the orphans that if they didn't know who their parents were. Pernie was not going to tell anyone her last name when she was Sava'an'Lansom. One day, her last name would be Meade. Then she would tell everyone.

She waited for the herald to call her name, even if it was going to be Pernie Grayborn for now, but he didn't. He simply finished off after Djoveeve's title with "and ward." Seawind and Djoveeve were moving through the doors, the old woman turning back to make sure Pernie was coming along.

"But he didn't announce me," Pernie protested. "Her Majesty won't know who I am."

Djoveeve smiled over her shoulder at her. "Oh, she'll know, little Sava. I promise."

Pernie followed, but she wasn't too happy about being relegated to "and ward." She glared at the herald as she walked by, but he did not look down at her. Pernie didn't think his gold-trimmed livery was as nice as it used to be. She knew she could take that big staff from him and beat him with it too. Plus he had an ugly nose.

The crowd froze as they passed along, gasps and murmurs preceding them but falling to silence as they drew near.

Pernie looked from side to side and saw them all gaping at Seawind. Nobody even looked at her. Nobody looked at Djoveeve either, or at least not much. Important people don't see old women and children. That rankled too.

Someday they would see her.

Pernie peered between Seawind and Djoveeve, looking through the space between their hips. She could see the Queen now.

The War Queen sat in her throne upon a dais, several steps separating her from the people all around. She was bright and majestic, just as Pernie had known she would be: all dressed in shiny plate armor of solid gold to match the regal chair, her armor and her seat sparkling, picking up the light from stained glass windows high above. Best of all was the giant broadsword slung across the back of the throne. It truly was enormous, and Pernie thought it might be twice as long as she was tall. She hadn't gotten a very good look at it that day the orcs attacked them outside Calico Castle. But now she could see it just fine. She really wanted one.

At length they came to stand right before the monarch, and Seawind and the Queen exchanged formal greetings, which included a lot of calling each other *friend*. "Hello, friend Seawind" and "Hello, friend Karroll" and then *friend* this and *friend* that. Pernie tilted and tipped, trying to get a better look. But it seemed that the Queen and Seawind were going to talk forever about boring things.

She sidled to Djoveeve's left and looked around. She saw, to her surprise, that Master Tytamon was standing there. She was still mad at him for grabbing her by the neck and casting a counter magic spell on her just because she tried to kill Orli Pewter again. She understood why he did it, but she was not going to talk to him today so that he would know that she was mad. More surprising, and more fun, was the discovery that standing next to Tytamon was her friend

Roberto from planet Earth. He was nice and funny. He was wearing a thick, stuffy sort of suit with lots of lights and lumps like the one Master Altin had been wearing that day he came back from the big red Hostile world all covered in blood. It had almost killed him, the planet, not the suit, but Pernie saved his life. If it had killed Orli Pewter, that would have been all right.

Finally they got around to paying attention to Pernie. Seawind and Djoveeve parted just enough to allow her to squeeze through. The old woman reached back and guided her forward unnecessarily. When Seawind said, "The future Sava'an'Lansom, your own Pernie Grayborn," even Tytamon looked surprised.

Pernie, of course, ignored him, and instead smiled at the Queen. "Hello, Your Majesty. You are very golden, and your sword is the best one ev–"

Djoveeve hushed her, hissing, "Curtsy, child. And be silent. You are before the Queen."

Pernie glowered at her, but she did remember that she had forgotten to curtsy. Kettle had taught her how to curtsy on many occasions–"Just in case," she'd say–so Pernie executed one perfectly.

The Queen smiled and looked down at her as if she were someone's mildly amusing new kitten. Pernie saw it right away. It was the same look most grown-ups gave children they had only passing interest in. The War Queen looked back to Seawind and nodded, then to Tytamon. "Well, she is as impertinent as all the rest raised at Calico Castle, Master Tytamon. Why am I not the least surprised?"

"I do what I can, Your Majesty," said the ancient wizard. "But the old castle does seem to draw the most independent sorts."

"Indeed," the Queen agreed.

Pernie didn't like when people talked about her as if she weren't in the room. She frowned at Tytamon, but Roberto was bent forward and looking at her with a warm expression on his face. He saw her. He winked at her, and he had the look of mischief on his face, though it passed very quickly. Pernie thought he looked kind of scared. She wondered what could make a man like that look that way. She wondered if that was why he was wearing the bulky Earth suit he had on. It seemed like only bad things happened to people when they were wearing one of those.

"So what is it that you require of me this time, friend Seawind?" asked the Queen. "I've given you my subject to be trained as bodyguard to your High Seat. Has Miss Grayborn proven inadequate? I can give you any other subject as you and the treaty require. Simply say the word, and they will serve."

"She is quite adequate, friend Karroll," Seawind said. Pernie thought she saw the War Queen flinch at that, as if she'd been bitten by an ant somewhere deep in her armored pants. But it passed quickly. "The time of Tidalwrath is near. The prophecy requires that we send this child to the new world for a time."

The Queen looked startled by that. It was only a flash of it, but Pernie saw it. She'd felt exactly the way Her Majesty had just looked many times, especially whenever Kettle caught her sneaking cakes, or when Nipper caught her trying to get one of the big crossbows out of the Calico Castle armory again. There'd been so many times where Pernie had worn such an expression over the brief course of her ten and a half years that recognizing it on someone else's face was like looking in a mirror.

It was gone as quickly as it appeared, however, and the royal countenance was once again as placid as the surface of a mountain pond. "And *which* new world would that be, friend Seawind?"

"Earth," he announced.

The placid pond became more so.

"Why, of course," she said, her tone light and, to Pernie's ear, relieved. "And your timing is excellent. We were just this morning talking about that very thing." She pointed with her golden scepter into the crowd. "You, there, what's your name again? Come hither."

A man in his middle years came forward. He was tall, well dressed. His hair was black with wisps of white at the temples, brushed back over his head and shiny just like his boots. Pernie thought he was very handsome, although not as handsome as Master Altin.

The man bowed and answered as asked. "Ivan Gangue, Your Majesty. Third seat on the Transportation Guild Service council."

"Yes, that's right. Ivan Gangue." She looked back to Seawind. "Councilman Gangue here came this morning with a petition for a thousand ... what do you call them again?" She looked impatient as she waited for Gangue to answer her.

"*Visas*, Your Majesty. The Northern Trade Alliance refers to them as visas."

"Yes, of course, visas. The TGS feels that the NTA has been too stingy for too long, and my people have finally got that skittish planet full of blanks to get over their fear of magicians long enough to allow a few Prosperions access to their world. Frankly, it's about time, as the whole thing is entirely insulting. So, friend Seawind, as I said: your timing could not be better." She paused and looked to Pernie for a moment, then back at the elf. "Might I inquire as to why she must go?"

"Yes, friend Karroll, you may inquire." Seawind put on a smile, but everyone in attendance could tell he did so as a formality.

Her Majesty regarded him for a time, expectant, and when nothing followed, she prompted first with a raising of her eyebrows, then a few moments after with a circular on-with-it-then movement of her scepter. Neither of those worked, however, so she had to say it aloud. "And the reason would be ...?"

"Because it suits the prophecy."

"Oh, dear Mercy, friend Seawind, of course it does. It always suits the prophecy. If not this one, then some other. But what I'm after is the reason for *why* it suits the prophecy." She propped up a smile much as he had done.

"I cannot say, friend Karroll."

"*Cannot* as in you are unable for reasons of ignorance, or *cannot* as in you are compelled by some power to keep secrets from me?"

"We all have our secrets, friend Karroll."

She actually laughed. Pernie thought it was likely a real laugh too, because the Queen looked up at the ceiling for a time and her golden breastplate actually moved up and down upon the royal bosom for a while, making the lights reflecting in it shift around. When she looked back, her gaze was steady, the humor in it fading like a spark that's fallen to the ground.

"Councilman Gangue, do you anticipate complications with the NTA officials on this little deviation from your list?"

"They asked specifically that half the thousand be blanks, Your Majesty. And the other half, who may be wizards, must be enchanters willing to take full-time positions casting Greater Common Tongues enchantments throughout NTA facilities for the period of one year. They also require that no teleporters be sent to the planet yet, enchanting school or not."

"Yes, yes, I am well aware of their fear about our people blinking into their banks and their bedrooms for their gold and for the love of watching blanks fornicate."

"Yes, My Queen."

She looked back to Pernie. She frowned. "You're the little

one who teleported into the tower the afternoon we took back Calico Castle, aren't you?"

Finally the Queen was paying attention to her. "Yes," Pernie said. "I am. Master Altin said it was my animal magic coming out, and I—"

"Is that going to be a problem, Councilman Gangue?"

He looked uncomfortable. Pernie glowered at her.

"Councilman, you see that I have an emissary of the elves standing here asking me this favor, do you not?"

"Yes, Your Majesty."

"So I'll tell you what. I will agree to another year having our people treated like sneak thieves and Peeping Toms in the name of appeasing the fearful nature of the Earth people if you can convince the NTA immigration folks of the value of helping me deal with my ... obligations to elven prophecy. If you cannot arrange it, I will find a way to have the entire council replaced, repercussions or no, and your successor can get this done." She finished with a smile that required far more architecture to hold it up than the previous few.

He still looked uncomfortable, but he agreed. "I will arrange a place for the girl among the thousand, Your Majesty. We will include her in the student exchange. I'm sure the NTA will agree to one teleporter once I explain the circumstances. They may require particular conditions, but I shall appeal to Director Bahri personally if I must."

"Good. You do that." She looked to Seawind then. "Satisfied?"

The elf nodded, an inclination of his head that was more subtle bow than affirmative.

"Very well, it is settled." To Ivan Gangue the monarch said, "Off with you, then. You've won your suit." To the elf, "Will there be anything else, friend Seawind?"

"No, friend Karroll. You have the appreciation of my people."

"A great reward, I am sure."

Seawind began backing out of the room. Djoveeve did likewise, placing a hand on Pernie's chest and propelling Pernie back as well.

Pernie didn't want to leave, but she could tell she was supposed to. "Goodbye," she said to the Queen, but Her Majesty had already turned back to Tytamon and Roberto standing there.

"So, Master Tytamon, this is what I *can* do for you and Captain Levi about our missing friends ..." the Queen began.

Djoveeve was saying something to Pernie, making it hard to hear the Queen. The crowd was murmuring all around. Pernie really wanted the Queen to at least say goodbye to her, but Djoveeve dragged her along. The last thing Pernie heard as she was pushed out of the throne room was Roberto's voice, raised above the crowd. "Are you serious? How the hell am I supposed to give a crap about gold and Goblin Tea at a time like this?"

He said it very loud, and Pernie didn't think you were supposed to talk to the Queen that way. Which made her smile as she went out.

Chapter 7

The trouble with capturing wizards—beyond the fact that they were wizards—was that they tended to be well connected. Even those of lowly ranks and single schools of magic were popular amongst their friends. If they were wealthy, they were connected, and if they were poor and of ranks low enough as to keep them that way, they were still likely to be earning wages by their paltry skills. Snatching a wizard who would not leave a noticeable absence was akin to stealing expensive art. A clever thief had to understand that it would be missed, and there had to be a discreet buyer somewhere waiting to take it forever away. Art, however, did not call for help telepathically.

Black Sander would hardly count his three captives as art. Two were orphans, a local boy of nine years who had just begun manifesting a talent for healing and another boy of fourteen, a D-class enchanter from Solydae. The younger of those two was a lucky find, and Black Sander had spotted him by chance only yesterday. Black Sander had been returning from a visit to the marchioness and had barely gotten into Murdoc Bay when he came upon the lad.

Some reckless teamster had run down a dog on the street, and the boy had found the animal where it had dragged itself off to die in the shadows of an alley. Black Sander heard the boy crying and peered around the rubbish heap to find the filthy lad holding the dog in his lap. As often happens with young sorcerers of that age, the emotions in him triggered his magic, and just like that, the dog was healed. Black Sander counted it a stroke of luck, a blessing from the god of thieves, Sobrei the Swift, and he snatched up the boy and brought him to the tannery.

Black Sander bought the older boy from a crooked orphanage director in Dae, a fellow who was a regular provider of such things for the black market and slave trade. Black Sander promised the man double bounties on any other fledgling magicians he found for the period of ninety days. He just needed them to be without telepathic gifts, or at very least, before they were sent off to be trained in magic and learned how to use their telepathy. A tall order, but quite possible for a man in the position of orphanage director.

The third wizard captive was hardly a wizard at all. Black Sander was almost embarrassed to send her. She was old, and looked far older than her years. Bathilda Hornblower, a sanza-sap addict—when she could afford magical highs—and an opium user when she couldn't, which was all the more pathetic. She was the only one of the three he was shipping to Earth that he was confident nobody would miss. She lay at the back of the large wooden crate, slumped in the corner like a corpse. Her breathing was a leaky bellows rasp. She was a sad sight, but she was an A-ranked seer, which the marchioness' diviner had verified. El Segador had explained quite clearly that, at least for now, his employer was interested in anyone with a mythothalamus. Jefe, said employer, was fixated on the organ of magic, which was unique to humans from Prosperion, and it was based on that fixation that Black Sander had suggested they might include a few animals as well. Study was study, after all.

Animal magic was not as refined as human magic, but it worked on the same principles for the most part. And it was the purpose of Jefe's scientists on Earth to discern the nature of how that organ worked. It had been agreed that animal samples would be welcome as well.

And so it was that the three humans were being pushed toward the back to make room for smaller animals in cages that Black Sander's doughy henchman, Belor, and the burly sailor Twane were carrying in.

"That's got it all," Twane was saying as Black Sander watched. The brawny man set a wire cage with two yellow birds in it on top of a box containing a Zergot's marmoset. The latter had a nasty bite and a gift for invisibility, and the former were capable of regenerating themselves after injuries. There were others as well, nothing dangerous, none capable of doing much damage if they got away, and all in all, Black Sander was sure that for the first shipment of magic users going off to Earth, Jefe and El Segador would be pleased.

"If that's all of it, then let's get it nailed shut. I want a canvas wrap on it too, just like we would if we were really shipping hides. Seal that box up tight. We don't want any accidents."

It was true, too. With the two orphans in there next to the unconscious whore, weeping and whining, eyes wide and lips trembling with fear, there was a real danger of the teleport going wrong without a properly sealed box. Teleportation magic worked best if the teleporters were sending an object rather than individuals. A body inclined not to be teleported could resist a teleport in the same way one resists wetting the bed while sleeping or resists breathing while submerged. Some reflexes happen on their own, and the terrified were impossible to teleport. Anger wasn't much better. But, in a box, well, a person could tremble and wet themselves all they wanted. The box would not resist at all.

So Black Sander's men set about the work of closing it up tight, making sure it would make it to its destination without incident. Black Sander turned to the group behind him while the others worked. These were his teleportation crew. Three teleporters, a seer, and a conduit.

The conduit was hardly in better shape than the prostitute in the box. He wore the traditional red of a conduit, an old set of robes, faded and filthy. He could afford to buy all the sanza-sap he wanted, and he clearly did. His tongue was permanently gray for it, as if he were dead.

"All right," Black Sander said. "Let's not make a carnival out of this. It's one box and one teleport. Kalafrand, have you given Conduit Wanderfrond the location?"

Kalafrand turned a blank look up at Black Sander, his wide face and wide eyes the physical expression of the open spaces in his mind. He'd heard the question but hadn't processed it. Z-class wizardry resided within that thick skull, if only as a seer. He was brilliant with sight magic, it was true, but so dull witted in every other way, he could apply no creativity to his gift on his own. It was akin to tragedy.

"The basement," Black Sander said patiently. "In San Francisco. The compound on planet Earth. You remember the room where the man Annison, Thadius Thoroughgood's old cast-master, lies with his brain all pulled apart and soaking in buckets?"

"Oh, yes," Kalafrand said, the lamps all lighting up in the vacant house of his head. "I remember."

Black Sander suppressed a sigh. "So have you given that location to the conduit?"

"Oh. No. I haven't."

"Then let's get it going, shall we?"

"Right," said the Z-class seer.

The red-clad conduit got up lazily from the chair he'd been sitting in and moved it out from the wall. Black Sander took other chairs and arranged them roughly in a circle.

"You," he said, pointing to the T-class teleporter they had "on loan" from the marchioness' contact in the TGS. "Help me. You've done this before. Let's go. You're the lead teleporter anyway. It's your head that will pop if it doesn't go right."

The man left his place leaning against the wall and sulked his way to the nearest chair, which he set in the rough circle pattern Black Sander had under way around the conduit's seat. The conduit was already seated, his elbows on his knees as he ran his fingers through the remnant wisps of hair on his blotchy bald head.

"You're sure you are up to this?" Black Sander asked for the second time since bringing the conduit in.

"I'm fine. Stop asking me or I'm going home. I don't care how much gold you have."

"It's a long way," Black Sander said. "And a lot of mass in there. You said yourself we've only just got enough teleporters in this concert to pull it off, and barely enough mana draw. I can't afford to have this shipment get lost."

The conduit got up and teetered a little, but straightened right away. "I said I'm fine. Ask me one more time, and I leave. That's no idle threat. Do you know who you are talking to?"

Black Sander closed his eyes and let the wave of impatience pass. Conduits were notoriously conceited, a rare breed of people, whose usefulness for bringing multiple magicians together was invaluable. They had no natural magic of their own. They were simply oddities of nature. But they were useful oddities. They were also renowned as drunks and liars, yet there wasn't much to be done about attitude. Especially for a clandestine enterprise such as this.

"It's ready," Belor called across the room to him. "You can send it now."

Black Sander looked to the crate where his assistant

stood, dwarfed by the mighty figure of Twane. One was the epitome of a life indoors, the other a man whose thirty-odd years had almost all been spent at sea.

Black Sander turned back and took one of the seats around the conduit. He, like the Z-class seer, would participate in the concert cast as a mana channeler. He had no gift in the school of teleportation, but his illusionist's rank was W, and with that, and the fact that he was a Two, he could add a magnificent amount of mana to the conduit's mana pool. With the sulky T-ranked teleporter and two other teleporters, an M class and a J, they calculated that it would be enough. He hoped inexperience wouldn't be a handicap as he glanced over at the two lower-ranked teleporters the marchioness had sent him. Neither of them could be more than seventeen.

"Just remember what they taught you in school," Black Sander said, for his own benefit as much as that of the two younger teleporters there. The truth was, even Black Sander hadn't done this since he was in school either. His time at the two-year school for young wizards—mandatory for any young wizard on the continent of Kurr—had been a long time ago.

"Let's just get going," said the conduit. He was sitting up straight now, and his eyes were open and alert, if as red as his robes. "You, T class, what's your name?"

"Paeter," said the trembling man.

"You're doing this, so you start the spell and feed it to me. Master Sander and the dullard Z, send me yours after. Just channel the mana. Don't start thinking about spells. You hear me?" The conduit was looking directly at Kalafrand. Black Sander didn't blame him. Kalafrand nodded that he understood.

Black Sander hoped he hadn't just signed on to something that was going to get his mythothalamus burned out, but, well, the gorgon was already at the ball. Nothing left to do but put your head down and dance.

The teleporter calmed himself, closed his eyes, and started chanting. The conduit's eyes flared a little wider than before and took on an elsewhere look.

Black Sander hesitated long enough to see if Kalafrand set himself to work channeling mana rather than casting a spell. The seer's eyes were closed and his lips pressed loosely together in a dull smile. Good.

Black Sander closed his eyes and opened his mind up to the mana too. He could see the pink and purple whorls of it churning all around. There was some movement sliding toward a vacancy that pulsed like a candle nearby, a flickering nothingness. He figured that slide was Kalafrand. Z-class mana draw was truly something to behold, even from an idiot and an idiot that was only a One. He gathered up mana on his own, swept it up, and pushed it toward the flicker that he knew was the conduit's beacon. He pushed the mana to it and watched it be pulled in like water down a drain. He pushed more and more until he was channeling constantly, as much as he could. It was more mana than he'd ever channeled before. But he kept on, channeling at max.

The river of mana he channeled grew faster and faster, sucked into the conduit's mind with more and more force. The river thinned, stretched out. Thinned more. He tried to channel faster so it wouldn't thin out and break. He couldn't channel more. He was a W-ranked illusionist, very powerful, rare power even. He even had a D class in sight, the second school adding more strength, but he was at his max. That was all he could give.

The line of it stretched out farther and farther. The conduit's flickering, lightless flame pulsing more and more. Then the flame burst in the silent, thunderous way of massive spells being cast. The mana thread broke too. He couldn't be sure if it broke before, after, or during the concussive release of the spell.

There followed in the next instant a very loud pop, a singular sound like someone had dropped a huge slab of marble flat upon the floor. He felt the brim of his hat flex as air sucked toward the sound.

He opened his eyes and looked to where the crate housing the animals, orphans, and whore had been. It was gone. That was a relief. He turned back to the conduit. "Well, Conduit Wanderfrond, have we done it?"

Wanderfrond shrugged. "I'm not sure. It didn't feel quite right."

"Kalafrand, quick. Have a look. Is it down there, in the basement?"

Kalafrand set his powerful sight magic to work, looking across the galaxy to distant planet Earth. He mumbled the seer's song for a time as he looked around. Black Sander clenched his jaw and waited impatiently. Even the disinterested conduit appeared interested in the result.

Kalafrand's eyes opened and looked to Black Sander. "I seen it," he said.

"Well?"

"Best I show you, sir. I'm not as good with words."

Black Sander nodded and lowered the telepathic block he normally kept in place. "Go on, then."

The seer sent him what he had seen, delivering the images right to Black Sander's mind. A few boards lying on a sunlit lawn. Half a canvas thrown over a bush by a window. Another board half-stuffed through a wall near a bright red smear of blood.

The image twitched, and then he was looking into a basement. There was a heap of boards on the floor and half a body sticking out of the west wall: the fourteen-year-old boy. A few of the boards moved, and the younger boy crawled out of the heap looking bewildered. He pushed part of the pile off the old prostitute. Black Sander could see her breathing regularly as she slept. She'd missed the entire thing.

Chapter 8

Altin held his breath as the giant creature wrapped a tentacle around his helmet. The sinuous tendril snaked around the seal at his neck, and with a *pop, pop, pop, pop*ping of the clasp, the helmet was off. He was sure he was about to die, and he wasn't looking forward to the searing in his lungs he was certain would come upon his first breath, which he delayed as long as he could. He reached out for the mana for perhaps the fiftieth time in the last ninety seconds, but it just wasn't there. It was out there, all around them, but he was trapped in this damned bubble of a ship. He felt as if he'd been embedded in a crystal ball, like being stuck at the center of great *Citadel*, with no way to get out. And Orli was down there all alone. Once he was dead, she would have no one. He hoped that somehow Roberto had gotten away. Roberto was Orli's only chance now. He'd come through before. Altin had to believe he would again.

He held his breath until primal biology kicked in and forced him to gasp. He steeled himself for the agony, the fire of some toxic atmosphere.

There was none. Oh, it burned, that much he got as he thought he would. It just wasn't how he'd thought. The air felt as if it were on fire. Like, actually so. Immediately his lungs felt the heat of all the steam, and there passed a span of time where he wondered if he could possibly bear that kind of heat.

But, with each successive breath, he realized that he could. Uncomfortable, yes. Wet, even more so. He suspected if they kept him here very long, he would either drown by slow accumulation of fluid in his lungs or simply die of pneumonia in time.

But he could breathe.

He stared up at the alien staring down at him. He could see himself reflected clearly in one of the creature's eyes. He would have kicked in the silvery ocular bulge were it not still twenty spans away—and if his legs weren't bound together by a damned coiled tentacle. He thrashed around in its grip, or tried to, anyway, then relented. He swore aloud.

The cylindrical object that had been lowered down over him, seemingly a device being used to examine him somehow, descended even closer than it had been. The half dome of black glass at the tip got so close he was sure it was going to crush him, press right through his chest and smash him into the brightly lit table upon which he was being held.

But it stopped, only a hand's width above him. Whirring noises came on dim vibrations from somewhere inside. The light at his back was so bright that it reflected blindingly from the dome. He squinted and turned his head.

The tip of a tentacle flattened itself out and wriggled close to his head. It slid under his cheek like a spatula, all the way under, then wrapped around the back of his head, where it gripped him, rotating by force until he was facing the black-domed prong again.

The machine whirred and vibrated for a while.

Altin could see the second alien better than the first. It was reflected in the dome of black glass. He saw images of parts of his spacesuit on the creature in the reflection. He couldn't decide if the images were in the glass or actually being created by the creature's skin.

Or perhaps fear was turning his brains inside out.

Colorful patterns crossed over the creature's body, over the image of himself, like the sort of thing in a children's kaleidoscope. Some were very intricate. Altin thought that, were he not being looked over like some specimen in Doctor Singh's laboratory back on the fleet ship *Aspect*, he might have been able to spend more time appreciating how beautiful they were.

"Listen," he said, his lungs sore with the brutal humidity. "I'm not sure what you have in mind, but I think that unless you wish to give the wrong impression to my people and the people of planet Earth, and not to mention our Hostile friends, you ought to go about getting to know us a bit more slowly."

Neither of the creatures made any indication that they had heard a word he said.

"Really," he went on. He had no other choice but to try. "I don't know what passes for courtesy on your world, but where we come from, one does not simply snatch someone up and begin poking and prodding about their bodies. Not only is that considered poor diplomatic policy, it's downright rude. And, as I understand the nature of diseases and that sort of thing, it might be dangerous if your medical skills are not up to it. Not only for me, but for you. Who knows what innocuous bit of ...." He paused, tried to remember what Orli called all the invisible bits of contamination that got into making a disease, but he couldn't recall just then. "Well, whatever it is, you might have already caught it. So if you don't want it all the worse, perhaps you could set me down, and we can have another go at this in a less offensive way. I promise not to hold this against you, as I am sure you can't possibly know how things are done on my world. If there's anything I've learned in my brief excursions in space, it is that there are ample opportunities to get off on the wrong foot—or tentacle—and purely by mistake."

He knew he was rambling, and he hoped he didn't sound hysterical. He didn't feel hysterical, but he didn't suppose it was too far off.

The giant aliens did not reply.

"Orli!" he shouted. "Orli! Can you hear me?"

He got no reply from her either.

"Orli, are you all right? Have they taken you for inspection too?" He looked about as best he could, which incited the tentacle tip to clutch his head more tightly and hold him still.

Orli did not answer. He hoped she wasn't doing something reckless. She wasn't much different than Roberto when it came to these sorts of things, and she was as likely to start shooting as her friend was if other options did not present themselves right away.

"I would also like to warn you," he said to the alien, "that if you hurt my wife in any fashion, your best option right after will be to kill me straight off. For if you let me live, and if I manage to get out of this mana hole you've built around us here, I can assure you, I'll put you and your gods-be-damned ship straight into that mountain you've parked beside. And what sort of diplomacy will that be, eh?"

Neither of the aliens appeared to be much concerned with his threat. And so, for some ridiculous length of time, he lay there waiting to either die or be released.

He thought for one brief moment that he heard Orli cry out, the sound startling him, piercing like a rapier through the heart, but then it passed. He strained to hear it again for quite some time, but nothing came. He told himself it was the wind.

That wasn't so much of a stretch. There was a lot of wind. It was nearly as windy in this infernal ship as it was outside on the surface of Yellow Fire.

He wondered how Yellow Fire might be doing just then. He wondered why these aliens were here. Why were they digging for Blue Fire's poor, unlucky mate, digging for Yellow Fire's newly rekindled heart? After perhaps millions of years lying dormant, his planet-sized wife bereaved and mourning for all that time, the moment he is brought back to some semblance of health, along come more aliens going after him. The poor Hostile chap hardly had time to hug—or whatever constituted a hug—rapturous Blue Fire, and now it was all on thin ice again.

Not that anything like ice could survive in a steam bath like this ship.

He wasn't sure if he'd dozed off or been hallucinating, but all of a sudden he was flipped on his face. Something rough happened to the back of his spacesuit, and he saw the three tubes slide away, apparently under their own weight. All three open ends went right off over the edge of the table, two of them leaving trails of liquid, one trail clear and watery, the other not far from the hue and texture of the ochre jelly he'd been in. Something made a snapping sound right after, and then something jarred him at the back. The alien snatched him off the table, and for a time he was being waved about in the air as if he were being held by a pampered noblewoman trying to dry her freshly painted fingernails. The motion was not frantic or violent, but it did seem at least careless to treat him so. At least at first. It turned out that the creature was moving, shifting and unwinding the tentacles that locked it to the grate upon which the machine sat and heading off for somewhere else. The next thing Altin knew, he was flying. He and the alien.

It happened so fast Altin hardly had time to realize what was happening. First, the creature, which had apparently swallowed the ballooning billow into a smaller bulb near the top of its body while it worked, reared back and, well, spat the thing back out. It blew out like a giant bubble, much in the way children on the islands of Angrost and Pengrost blew them with chewed-up wads of *hgat* leaf. But this one was so large, and it blew to full size so quickly, that the violence of the inflation filled the air with a thunderous noise, loud even over the roar of the wind. In the instant that followed, the creature was snatched off the grate, and Altin snatched with it. It occurred to Altin in the moments right after that he might have been hurt by such sudden velocity, but somehow the tentacle that held him did a fair job of mitigating most of the shock, at least the physical variety.

And so he was sailing through the darkness. He thought he heard Orli's voice again, right after they took off, but he was waggling around too much to know where to look.

Flashes of light went by him as he soared along. They flew over—and under—grate upon grate upon grate. He got the sense that each grate was on the order of several measures long, at least as measured in the direction they flew, separated by spans of dark emptiness. They were traveling down the length of the ship, so he could not tell how wide the grates were. He thought perhaps they might stretch all the way across, as he saw no vertical supports anywhere. But he could not be sure. Orli's people had things that defied gravity. And these creatures obviously had some ability with mana, if the manaless bubble around the ship—or that *was* the ship—was any evidence.

He saw other aliens as he and his captor flew along. Some were working at various tasks, anchored to the grates with tentacles like tent wires reaching up, out, and across at various angles. Others flew past, going back in the direction from which Altin had just come. Those rode upon air currents blowing the opposite way, riding wind on a level below the grates over which Altin and his alien ... escort flew. He surely hoped it was an escort and not an executioner.

He wondered at what oddities the creatures were, and

once again thought this might not be as bad as it seemed. He thought that perhaps it was promising that the creatures worked together, suggesting a cooperative nature and, at least between themselves, some degree of civility. He surely had reason to cling to that idea. Though he might just as easily be on his way to the slaughterhouse right now. It did seem, however, that he was hardly big enough to be much of a meal for creatures of this size. There was also some hope in that. Unless he was but a bit of caviar. A single egg of the novafly perhaps. He cringed as they flew on.

The alien carrying him angled left, toward a bright oval light that glowed with the orange hue of starfish. As they neared the light, he could see it was anchored to the far edge of another grate. The alien flew right over it. It reached up with two tentacles and grabbed onto the grate above them. Another two tentacles grabbed the grate near the light. It pulled itself—and Altin—down toward the light.

The wind changed, buffeting him all around. It whisked and whirled, but much less violently.

The alien pulled them into the change of wind pattern, sending out new tentacles to grasp farther down the grate. Another tentacle reached off into the darkness beyond the light, grabbing something unseen above, out of sight and at least a quarter measure away. He wondered what it was.

The creature pulled them onto another grate, and then spidered along it for a time, across the direction of the wind and right along the edge of the grate. Looking out over the edge, he saw a vast expanse of nothingness off to his left, a wide gap between this grate and the next. When the creature reached up into the darkness again, they were climbing up a wall. It was the hull of the ship, or at least it seemed to be, for it was solid, made of that same green-brown protein as everything else, and it had a gentle curve to it.

The alien snaked its tentacles up the surface, buoyed some by occasional updrafts that couldn't have been a third of the strength of the wind that had carried them through the ship. But it was enough to help with the climb in intermittent puffs. In short order, they were at what Altin realized must be a hatch, for there were controls near it, and it housed a very large window that looked up into the storm clouds of Yellow Fire's roiling sky.

The creature sent a tentacle toward a giant boxy shape that looked as if it had grown out of the wall. There were holes in it arranged in geometric patterns, several of which had lights nearby. The creature thrust the tip of a tentacle inside several of these holes in a rapid sequence. Altin had the feeling he was about to be taken outside.

So he *was* going to die. He sighed. He thought they might be going to kill him by mistake. Maybe they didn't understand what his helmet had been for. What a terrible way to go.

"I can't breathe out there, you know?" he said.

The creature, as usual, made no response.

They waited there for several minutes. Altin realized the clouds were getting closer. And closer. Soon they were in them, and Altin could see nothing but red-and-gray mist. It reminded him of his first explorations of the gas giant Naotatica back in his home solar system, now so very far away.

Something scraped against the hull beneath him, a dull sound blown up to his ears on an updraft.

He looked down and saw that something was coming up the wall. It was another alien, though this one entirely different than the others he had seen. It was much smaller. No more than fifty or so paces long—large by comparison to his tiny human body, but minuscule compared to his original captors. The newcomer appeared to be made of the same sort of mucous material as the bigger ones, but it had no billow and no bulbs. It was longish, with three eyes—left, right, and center—and its not-quite-cylindrical body tapered to a tail that ended with a hook. It had three long tentacles emerging from beneath its eyes, like a mustache with only three long hairs. It was with these that it climbed the wall, gripping it with its little suction cups. On the hook at its hind end—and, by comparison in size to the hook itself, barely appearing more than a tiny droplet of milk—was Altin's spacesuit helmet.

"I hope you're not going to throw me out," Altin said upon seeing it. "Because I'm not leaving without Orli."

Chapter 9

The lady they gave Pernie to be her fake mother leaned down and buttoned the top button on her uniform collar. The woman's breath smelled like mint. It always smelled like mint. Or sort of like mint. Mint in that fake way people on Earth made fake natural stuff. She handed Pernie a navy-blue sweater to pull on over the light blue shirt. It was itchy and way too hot.

The woman, Sophia Hayworth, stood and watched as Pernie wrestled with the stupid sweater. Once it was on, the woman reached behind Pernie's head and pulled her long ponytail out from under it, letting the golden waves fall free, still nearly halfway down her back. Pernie wouldn't let them cut it.

"Well, don't you look smart," Sophia Hayworth said in that chipper voice she always used when talking to Pernie. She smiled down at her, obviously pleased, like someone who has just finished putting together an arrangement of flowers that came out nicely.

Pernie turned and looked at herself in the wall monitor that doubled as mirror. She looked dumb. The shirt was dumb and the sweater was dumber. The plaid skirt was dumb too, hanging down to her knees, of which there were about two finger widths visible before they were consumed by dumb blue socks that itched just like the dumb sweater did. The shoes were the dumbest. They were shiny like polished leather, but made out of something fake. The soles were hard and made out of some dumb Earth material that was too slick to grip the ground very well.

"I can't run in these," she said for the fifth time since having been fitted in them.

"You won't need to run in them, sweetheart," Sophia Hayworth said. Every time she talked, her voice was just like a children's song. It made Pernie want to punch her in the throat, even if she was trying to be nice. Pernie's fake mom lifted up a pair of blue-and-white shoes made out of something else that was fake. "These are your running shoes. You'll wear them when you have gym."

"I don't want to have gym," Pernie said reflexively. "I hate gym." She didn't know what gym was, but some things had to be said on principle.

"Well, I'm sure you feel that way right now," said her fake mother. "But you will see."

There was a bunch more of that sort of thing that followed, and eventually Pernie was taken out of the blocky gray house in which she now lived—Sophia Hayworth told her it was "paid for," which Pernie was made to understand was an important thing. They walked three blocks down one street and two blocks up another. They sat together, Pernie and her fake mother, until a vehicle came along on quiet black wheels and parked in front of them. On the side of it were the words Carson-Millerton Junior Military Academy, painted in black upon the gray-and-blue side of the vehicle. Her fake mom had been teaching her to talk and read for the last three days, in anticipation of school starting. She was picking it up fast. It had helped that she'd learned a little while helping Orli Pewter learn to speak the language of Prosperion, but Pernie was a quick learner too. She was going to learn all their words, and all their science too, but she wasn't going to tell them that.

"Here's your bus," Sophia Hayworth said. "It will take you right to school. You see in the front that it is bus number thirty-five. Remember that number. That's the bus you'll need to get on to come home. I will meet you here this afternoon."

"What if I don't want to come *home*?" She said the last word derisively.

"Then you can sleep in the streets where the other stray animals live, eat garbage, and hope nobody runs over you with their car."

If that was supposed to scare her, it didn't. Pernie could teleport right through one of those dumb cars. If she could blink away from an elven spear, she could blink away from something like that. Although she had promised Djoveeve and Seawind that she would not cast any magic while she was here. "Not one word. Not even telepathy," Djoveeve had told her. "It's part of the agreement made by Her Majesty herself. So your promise is the promise of a future Sava'an'Lansom made to the Queen of Kurr." Pernie had agreed to it even though she was mad at Her Majesty for not saying goodbye to her when she left the throne room that day. But she understood that queens could be very busy sometimes, so she supposed it was all right if they were rude occasionally. Pernie was rude sometimes, too, so she didn't think it was fair to stay mad at the War Queen.

"Fine," she said in her best Earth words. She wore a translation pin buttoned to her collar. One of the enchanters she'd come to Earth with a few days ago had enchanted it with the Greater Common Tongues spell. He'd done it for everyone in the box with her, the teleportation chamber the TGS had sent them in.

Sophia Hayworth's husband, a man named Don, had given her a little device that was hardly bigger than the tip of her thumb. It had a curving bit of fake wire—they called it plastic—that wrapped around her ear. The device had a fat, white button that pulled out on a length of metal thread. If Pernie put the button in her ear, the device translated words for her as well. But it was slow, and it was weird listening to people say something in one language and then have it spoken right on top of that language in another. She thought it was a pretty poor substitute for the translation spell, so she left it in a drawer in the room Sophia Hayworth had given her to use.

The door to the vehicle opened, and an older man who looked in some ways like a much older version of Roberto smiled down at her. "Well, howdy," he said, seeming very happy. "Welcome to Earth. You know you are my very first Prosperion passenger."

Pernie shrugged. She looked to Sophia Hayworth, who placed a hand gently on her back and nudged her toward the steps that would take her up into the bus. They sure didn't use any horses on this world.

"Go on," Sophia Hayworth said. "Don't be afraid."

Pernie spun on her. "I'm not afraid," she said. She wasn't either. To prove it, she climbed right up the stairs.

The driver was still smiling, like it was his birthday or something. She turned and looked down a long, narrow aisle that divided rows of seats on either side. There were at least thirty other children staring back at her. Some were very little, like maybe only five or six years old. Others were older than Pernie by four or five years, maybe even as old as seventeen or eighteen. Every one of them looked at her like she was painted pink and green.

She looked down one row and back up the next. A little girl Pernie's age stared at her with eyes so wide Pernie thought they might roll right out of her head. The girl saw Pernie looking at her, and her eyebrows ran and hid beneath bangs that were slightly arced and cut perfectly straight across her forehead. Pernie realized that the girl, and the rest of them, were all dressed exactly the same as Pernie was.

"Arrr!" Pernie growled at the girl. She feinted, like she might lunge into the seat at her. The girl screamed and slid against the side of the bus, hitting it with a thud and no room to run.

"Hey now, you be nice," said the bus driver. "You want to make a good impression here on your first day. That's no way to make friends."

Pernie turned a bored look on him. "I don't need friends," she said. "I'm only here to learn."

There was an empty seat three rows down on the left. She went to it and sat down near the window as the door swung shut. She was sure she saw Sophia Hayworth sigh.

Chapter 10

Pernie sat at a little square table that was attached to its own seat. They called it a "desk," but it didn't look like one. Someone had made the whole thing all one piece, and she couldn't move the chair closer at all. The desktop lit up and glowed, and she could move images around with her fingers. All the other students in her class had desks just like it, though they were all much better at using them than Pernie was.

It wasn't much different than the tablet Orli Pewter had let Pernie play with back at Calico Castle, and it wasn't much different than the interior wall of her room at Sophia Hayworth's house. She knew how to make things move. What she didn't know was how to stop from opening up the wrong things.

The teacher talked very fast, and Pernie didn't even know what half the things she was telling them to do meant. The translation spell worked perfectly fine for most things, but there were some concepts that Pernie simply had no contexts for. Things that were completely alien. Things like "drag and drop" and "copy and paste" meant nothing to Pernie. And when the teacher would give out what were obviously simple requests, Pernie would get lost. She couldn't find anything to paste anywhere, and there were no symbols that looked like glue bottles or even a dead horse. It was all so confounding, and she knew it was because she didn't know all the little things.

She'd looked to the girl on her left, but that one was pointedly looking anywhere but at Pernie. She'd looked to the girl on her right, and it was much the same, though Pernie caught her staring out of the corner of her eye every time Pernie turned to look at her. The boy behind her looked just as scared as the girl on the bus had looked, and the girl on the bus was the girl sitting in front of Pernie. There wasn't even anyone she could ask. And she damn sure wasn't going to raise her hand and ask out loud. They all wanted her to be stupid, Pernie could tell. And she would rather die than give them that satisfaction. She'd just have to figure it out herself.

Fortunately, the teacher was a nice lady and didn't say anything about how terrible Pernie was at everything. When it came time to show answers on the big, whole-class monitor that crossed the front of the room, the teacher had mercifully disabled the feed from Pernie's desk.

It was pretty embarrassing anyway. Pernie knew that the big black rectangle on the wall display—third from the bottom and second from the right—was hers, because it was the only big black rectangle on the whole board. The rest of the surface was lit up with colorful rectangles, each with answers written in bright white Earth letters that glowed. The other students knew it too, but nobody said anything. Pernie thought that was smart of them because she didn't want to have to break anyone's leg. She knew that would be a bad way to start out in Earth school.

"Be careful and be patient," Djoveeve had said. "It's frightening to go somewhere completely new. Do you remember how you felt when you came to String last year? Well, it will be just the same on Earth. Perhaps even more so. The ways of an alien world will be disorienting. So remember your breathing techniques. Stay calm. Keep your magic in your mouth and your fists in your pockets, little Sava. Promise me."

That had been the first of the five hundred billion times Djoveeve had made Pernie promise not to do magic or hurt anyone.

After a while, the class broke for what the teacher called "recess." All the kids got up and started moving toward the door. Pernie stayed where she was and tried to figure out the desktop screen. There had to be a way to make it go back to what the teacher kept calling the home screen. But which stupid icon was it?

She pressed one twice in a row. It opened up a new screen that started playing a video. She knew how to close it, so she did. She double-tapped another, and it opened up four new boxes, which everyone called windows. She tried to close that, but the one she touched started a whirring sound that Pernie could feel vibrating through the desk.

A thin layer of the desktop make a clicking sound, and it swung up, a section all along the far edge of the desk and about two hand widths high. Now there was some kind of contraption being depicted like an illusion spell in the air, sort of hazy, but floating there above the desk. Pernie recognized that it was showing some kind of space machine design.

"Stupid old–" she started, but cut herself off.

A boy coming up the row on her right, headed out to "recess," stopped and placed a hand on either side of the image floating in the air. "Like this," he said, moving his hands together until both palms pressed flat. "Holographic stuff all closes like this. Hands together, then push it back into the desk." He pushed one hand down, flat against the middle of the desk. The little section of the surface closed itself with a few seconds of whirring and another click.

"See?"

She looked up at him, frowning. But he only smiled back. "I'm Jeremy," he said. He reached out a hand for her to shake. "My granddad is the custodian here. Everyone calls him Gabby. That's why I can afford to come."

Pernie frowned again, different this time. He could afford to come because everyone called his grandfather Gabby? Pernie was sure she was never going to understand this world.

"Don't worry," he said cheerfully. "They all looked at me like that last year."

"Like what?" she said.

"Like they look at you. But it's okay. I'm not afraid of Prosperions. I've already read everything on them. I am going to go there someday."

"Humph," Pernie said. But she decided he was probably nice. "So what does this thing do?" She pointed to the green ball with the little white line. "It keeps opening other stuff, and I can't make it go away."

"Oh, that's your global-net access icon ..." he began. They spent their recess getting Pernie settled in on her desk.

Chapter 11

"I assure you, my friend," the man called Jefe repeated, "we have no concerns about the accident. We are all in new territory with this." He smiled reassuringly beneath a mustache that was thick and long, the shiny black ends pulled out and waxed, shaped into upward-curving hooks. Black Sander watched Jefe's eyes for signs that the words hid the reality, but there was nothing glimmering in those brown orbs but glee. The man was happy with what he'd gotten, despite the damage to some of the contents in the crate.

"I appreciate your patience with us," Black Sander said. He looked behind him at the wreckage of the wooden crate and the body of the boy. Pieces of the older orphan lay in a gory heap on the basement floor. Part of him hung out of the cinder-block wall, strips of red meat looking like something wolves have been chewing on. Black Sander knew the rest of the body was somewhere in the earth outside the basement, pulped most likely and fertilizing the lawn. "We have to be careful which teleporters we employ, and the War Queen has her eye on everything. My employer assures us that there is another we can bring in for future casts, and we'll make smaller loads from here on out."

"Yes, yes, I understand completely." Jefe stepped to Black Sander and put a hand on his shoulder. He had to reach up to do it, as he was a good deal shorter than the Prosperion. "I have read about your TGS operation. It seems your transportation guild has all its teleporters working on platforms. It is good that you have found any of them for our work here."

"The TGS has always been a stingy and controlling entity. As a subset of the Teleporters Guild, it's got astonishing authority even over its own parent guild. It always has, being the primary means of modern travel across Prosperion, but with the mechanisms for traveling across the stars being put in place, I am sure the TGS will become nothing but unbearable in time. My sources tell me they even make the Queen uncomfortable."

"Yes, I can imagine it is true. They are in a position of great importance in the galaxy now. And it's a kind of importance that your War Queen will have a hard time controlling one day. The NTA cabrones here on Earth are at their mercy as well. Your TGS will be a great force in the galaxy very soon." His eyes glinted as he said it, and Black Sander had to grin. Here was a man who understood power.

"They will. Of that there is no doubt. We've taken steps to get our people on the inside."

"This is good," agreed Jefe. The blue-eyed El Segador standing beside him nodded as well. "But now is a good time to set plans in motion for the alternatives."

Black Sander grinned again. "You would have us move more quickly than my employer would. You are the dragon to her dire rat."

Both Earth men laughed at that. They said something together in the language they called Spanish, and then Jefe said, "I like that. I like the things you say, Prosperion." He looked back to the wreckage, then to the young orphan and the old prostitute, the latter now on her feet, though looking wobbly. She leaned against a wire birdcage that had been brought down to replace the one that had been destroyed by the errant teleport. Only one of the little birds had survived.

"Jefe," said El Segador, "let's take those two upstairs and get them set up. Doctor Gaspar is anxious to get started with the new specimens, and we need to get their magic neutralized."

"Yes," agreed Jefe. "Besides, I think our friend Annison will like to have some company."

Black Sander could hardly believe that Annison was still alive. He'd been held captive on this world for months and months now, with his skull opened up and his brain cut into parts, all of them wired together by Jefe's team of scientists and kept functioning somehow. It was all in pursuit of learning about how Prosperion magic worked.

Black Sander accompanied them, following along as they mounted a short staircase and moved through the bowels of Jefe's mansion. The basement, one of three, sat beneath three stories of construction meant to emulate an older style of architecture, obviously from some period in Earth's history, for there were no buildings like it elsewhere that Black Sander had been to. He hadn't been on Earth often, or long, having only first arrived a little over a month ago, but he'd seen enough of it in person and on the information system they called the global net to know that this place was different.

The style of the main building as well as the outbuildings and the furnishings all around matched perfectly with the style depicted in the large, colorful paintings and murals that were everywhere. They matched too with many smaller images, little square depictions in shades of gray that featured men in hats with brims so wide they made Black Sander's wide-brimmed hat seem a skullcap by comparison. These were all dark, rugged-looking men, often with wide mustaches like Jefe's, though not curled like the one he wore, and almost all of them carried weapons that looked like a cross between the laser rifles of modern-day Earth and something more in keeping with the stock of a Prosperion crossbow. Black Sander knew these images were images out of time, for the men in them often stood beside horses, which was certainly something he saw nothing of during his time upon the strange, technological world.

He wondered, now that he had come across this planet powered by plastic and electricity, if one day his world might seem the same. He wondered if the paintings and portraits of his people and their horses might someday fade to black and gray. He wondered what that future Prosperion might look like.

They arrived in the room where Black Sander and his two hosts had first met. Inside, just as he had been on Black Sander's first foray onto the compound, lay Annison, strapped to what looked to Black Sander like an elaborate, technological version of a barber's chair. Though he wouldn't have thought it possible, he thought Annison had actually lost more weight. The thin blue sheet that covered his body revealed nothing more than the lines of a skeleton. The face that he'd once known to be fleshy and alive was now so gaunt, the cheekbones so prominent, the man was indistinguishable from one who'd been dead for months.

Annison no longer moved. His eyes were open, but they were rolled up so far that his pupils were out of sight. He looked as if he'd gotten glass replacements and the ocularist forgot to paint the irises and black dots. As before, his brain was cut up and its parts separated out and placed into trays, each sitting in a bath of some fluid that was obviously meant to keep the tissue alive. Thin wires, like silver thread, connected the pieces to one another and to what remained of his brain still inside the open cavity of his skull. This too was liquid filled.

All of it was attached to monitoring equipment set up

around and behind him. The machines that had been damaged or destroyed during the initial skirmish that ensued when Black Sander had arrived had all been repaired or replaced. Some tables had been moved or removed as well, and now there were four more barber's chairs set up with their own monitoring stations around them.

"I see you are open and ready for business," he remarked upon seeing the empty chairs.

"We are," said Jefe. "And we are putting in another lab just like this one in the room next door. I will fill this whole floor of my house up with them when we are done. I will know how magic works," he said.

"What is it you want it for?" Black Sander asked. "If I may ask. If that is too bold, then forgive me and leave me to my ignorance. I am certainly not at liberty to speak of my employer's aims, so in this there can be no fair exchange."

"I am not ashamed to admit it," Jefe said. "I take my country back."

"How so?"

"Long ago this land belonged to my people. Men came from across the ocean and took it from us. Over the course of centuries, they drove us farther and farther west and south. They humiliated us. They used us like slaves and stole our resources. They used us."

He paused and said something in Spanish to El Segador, who pushed the two captive Prosperion casters toward the chairs. The slender woman called Doctor Gaspar came in right after with two other men. They set to work binding the magic users down—not that any force was required, as both were too shocked (or rummy) to resist.

"But they thought we were stupid," Jefe went on. "That was their mistake. They thought we were barbarians. They used us for their politics. In time they let my grandfathers grow strong because they thought my grandfathers were weak. They let us build an army right on the border they imposed upon us. And then the weather changed. They tried to stop it and made it worse. So the climate changed and the seas climbed and the hunger came. The diseases came, and the world filled up with war. They tried to contain it. They had all the best technology. The biggest guns. But they were weak with pride. They were divided and disorganized. We were used to being hungry. And we worked like surgeons." He pointed to the doctor, who was now looking at the orphan boy. He smiled. "We came in and took our land back. Most of it, anyway."

"How did you do it if they had bigger guns and better technology?" Black Sander was genuinely intrigued.

"Our people were already on the inside, thanks to the Great Cartels. They were the visionaries who beat the arrogant people at their own game. When the corrupt government of the United States made deals with one cartel against the next, that cartel sank its fangs deeper into their country. So it went for nearly a century before the world collapsed. By the time the famines were everywhere, the government of the United States was stretched too far and wide. Their greed and corruption broke their economy, and the whole world nearly died for a time. Three hundred years, there was nothing but war and destruction. Pockets of civilization fortified and struggled to just survive. Disease flourished. Science declined.

"But we never lost sight of what we wanted for ourselves, our honor. We only had to walk in and reclaim what was ours. Some of it was easy. The western, coastal part of the old United States was soft. They had allowed their government to disarm them, so they rolled over like dogs. This city, San Francisco, was the crown jewel of them all. This compound was the first my forefathers built in the land we took back from them. It is a place of great history.

"Other parts of the old United States were more difficult. Not all the citizens in the middle parts of the country were unarmed. They rallied together, formed militias, and we fought for centuries. That was when the cartels came together under Rafael Francisco Arellano-Muñoz, who is an ancestor of the president and my ancestor too. Together they created what you see now, the new Mexico, three hundred years after the world came out of the dark ages again. We are strong and proud. But there is one part of our country still left to take."

"Which part is that?"

"Texas," Jefe said. "The Republic of Texas is the last. Their pride made them separate from the remaining parts of the United States. That was what allowed the NTA to crack the safes of the planet again. The same families who had controlled the world for a thousand years started again there. But we will take Texas. When we reclaim it, then we will be whole. Then we will look to the stars."

Black Sander nodded, an appreciative thing. "I wish you all success with your campaign. I should think you and my employer have more in common than I thought."

"I will want to meet your employer one day," he said. "But for now, they can keep their secrets. You come from a world where people read minds. I do not want my mind filled with secrets that can be stolen. That could jeopardize our new friendship. I am satisfied with mystery. For now."

Black Sander inclined his head. "Thank you. Things will go more smoothly that way." His expression was a little flatter than it might have been due to the way Jefe had pronounced that last bit. But not much. Such was the way with men like that. They couldn't help themselves. The marchioness would have said it too. If not with her lips, with her eyes.

He wanted to ask how, precisely, Jefe planned on using magic to retake the lost territory called Texas, but he suspected he'd probably milked enough information for now. So he changed the subject entirely.

"I'll get you another wizard to study and a few more animals to replace what was lost by the end of the week," he said. "I'm sure my employer will appreciate some portion of the agreed-upon payment as a show that the incident has not marred our relationship."

Jefe said something to El Segador in Spanish again, and then smiled easily. The crow's feet at the corners of his eyes lengthened considerably. "No, amigo. You will be paid in full. I know that you will do as you have promised."

"Good," Black Sander said, carefully concealing his relief. He did not want to have to listen to the marchioness' complaints, and the whole thing was already awkward enough. "I will have a few of my men sent down to help clean up the mess. As soon as the basement is clear, we will send smaller crates back down the moment our additional teleporter arrives."

"Do not worry about sending people. My men will clean the mess. You have your man with the far seeing just watch down there. When we are done, we will turn out the lights, all but the one near the stairs, just as we did last time. There is no reason to put your men at risk moving across all that space."

"Well, it's not normally a risk," Black Sander said. "Though I admit, there is perhaps a bit more risk than is strictly necessary, as we are not the TGS."

"One day, we will be," Jefe said. "You will see."

Chapter 12

Orli tried to mark the descent of Altin's helmet after it fell through the grate, but it was gone. A few bounces on the next two grates, and then it was lost in the mist. The way it moved when it fell through each grate suggested the winds changed directions in each subsequent layer, which meant by the time it reached the bottom, it could have been blown anywhere. She'd never find it now. But that was all right. They had their fast-cast amulets. She'd get to him and break the gems. That would get them home. It wouldn't be the first time she'd resorted to it.

She climbed to her feet, careful to brace against the wind, and stared back up toward the bright light and the three-pronged machine with the bulbs of black glass. She knew what they were and what the aliens were doing. They were examining him. Like some specimen. It infuriated her. They were just as bad as ... well, as bad as her own people had been to him when they first encountered the Prosperion sorcerer.

It occurred to her that the whole universe might be filled up with inquisitive, thoughtless assholes. She hoped she was wrong, but it sure was shaping up that way. Again.

She had to get Altin off that table. She had to get up there someway. Which meant she needed some way to climb. She'd already ruled out the lengths of tubing leading into Altin's suit, though they hung down the side of the machine like the inviting vines of some old-fashioned lover's fairy tale. She could be the hero and rescue him from the tower. But she wouldn't chance it. Pulling them out could be the end of him—assuming the loss of his helmet hadn't already been.

She turned and traced the length of the three lines running out of the back of her own spacesuit instead. Perhaps where they led, there would be more like them. Maybe she could figure out what they did, figure out a way to take them out, and turn her suit's power back on. Assuming the power packs weren't simply drained. There was no telling how long they'd been in that yellow jelly stuff.

Orli tried to remember how much she'd seen since being in it, how much she'd witnessed since that light had reached down over the edge of the ramp when Roberto called. But she couldn't recall anything after that. She didn't remember coming into the ship. She didn't remember being put up on the grate. There were no memories of these hoses being attached or any aliens doing anything to them at all.

She must have lost some time. But how much?

She followed the three hoses to another massive bit of alien equipment not too far away. This machine—and that's what it was, she was sure, a machine—stood at least forty yards tall. The tubes from her suit, at most three inches in diameter, jutted from the side of it, some sixty yards up. She looked behind her and saw that Altin's hoses were also attached to this machine, for she could follow them around to the other side.

She walked all the way around it, hoping there might be another set. If it could serve two captive humans, perhaps it could serve more.

No such luck.

She decided to go to the next machine down the line. Maybe it would have something she could use. It didn't. It was just a big green box. A few lights high above. A smaller version of the oblong tanks on the other side of Altin's examination machine bulged out from one side, different but not unlike the ones sitting in the nests of coiled hoses.

Maybe she could use that nest stuff. It looked like it was woven together pretty tightly, but it was worth a try. She started across the grate for the nearest of those tanks, hoping that the translucent seaweed-colored tubes wouldn't be too heavy to move. The fact that she was able to drag around as much as the three tubes attached to her suit gave her some measure of hope, though the farther she went, the more she had to lean against their weight. Perhaps the other stuff was an even lighter material. She doubted it, but it wasn't like she had much else she could do.

She was downwind of Altin by perhaps forty yards, and she thought she heard him call her name. She stopped and looked back at him. She still couldn't see him yet, not even from the angle this distance afforded her. She saw the aliens flashing images of him and flashing patterns back and forth. She wondered how long it was going to take them to figure out that she was just wandering around. She wondered if they were that unafraid of her, of all humans. They certainly had charged right on down onto a Hostile world and started digging with no hesitation at all, so they clearly had no fear of either Hostile or human as evidenced by that. But still, you'd think they wouldn't want her to get away, being as they'd gone to the trouble to capture her. Unless they were that confident in their ability to catch her again. She looked down through the grate and shook her head. Or else they just knew she was too tiny to do much or go anywhere.

Three steps closer to the tank and she realized why they

weren't too concerned with her escape. She couldn't drag the hoses anymore. It was simply too much to pull. She turned back and yanked on one of the tubes. She could barely drag it half a foot.

She yanked harder. So what if it broke or came loose from the machine. If they wanted their specimens alive, they'd better be ready for accidents. Especially if they left them free to roam around. She hauled back on the tube with all her might.

Nothing.

"Damn it!"

She looked back down through the grate. Then realized she was an idiot.

She felt around her waist, and sure enough, there was her Higgs prism, still attached to her belt. Right where she'd put it. "Idiot," she breathed aloud. "Get it together, for crying out loud." She sounded like Roberto.

She pulled the small device free of its pocket on her belt. She was about to set it to zero, but paused. The damn wind was going to make this difficult. She looked up again to where Altin was. One of the aliens had pulled him out of the light and was waving him around in the air. She barely had time to shape the question in her mind, when the alien shot out its parachute billow from an opening in the top of its long, narrow body. The wind filled it instantly with a pop that was so loud Orli heard it from that distance, through the wind and through the helmet glass. The next thing she knew, Altin was flying right over her head. The tentacle holding him drooped so low she could almost touch him as he went past.

"Altin!" she screamed, but it was too late. He was gone, the glimmering of the alien fading into the darkness, growing dim.

"Fuck that," she said. She set the controls to zero and jumped into the wind. She flew out after him for some thirty yards, then, *BAM*, hit the end of her tether like a steel wall.

She bounced and waggled in the wind, bobbing up and down in the wind like a damn kite. One gust drove her down to the grate, where she hit hard and bounced back up again. A little bit harder and she'd have broken her leg. A little bit left and she'd have gone down through the opening in the grate. She fumbled with the control on her Higgs prism, and, waiting until she drifted directly over a beam, she set herself down again. She stood there trembling. She looked up into the darkness where Altin had been.

He was gone.

The tears began to burn in her eyes, frustration quivering her lips. Then a tentacle grabbed her and wound her up tight.

She tried to fight it off. She thrashed and wriggled in its grips. "Let me go, asshole," she shouted. But the alien had her in its clutches.

It had had to let out some length in the tentacles it was using to anchor itself between the grates, and she absently noticed that it retracted the tentacles to drag her back into place. It clearly had no issue with the weight of the tiny Earth creature or the three tubes in her suit.

She was placed on top of the machine where Altin had been. She could see a huge patch of smooth material like glass. She assumed that was where the light came from.

The creature reached up another tentacle, which fluttered near her helmet glass. She felt the pop of a latch as much as she heard it.

"Oh shit," she said, as the second one popped. Then the third. Then the last. The air hissed out of it. So it had still been pressurized. That was interesting. She heard the helmet bounce across the tabletop and then heard it no more.

The creature mashed her down on the flat glass, rolled her onto her back. Lying that way was beyond uncomfortable because her back bent over the bottom edge of the suit's bulky dorsal unit. The light behind her glared.

The contraption with the cylindrical prongs began lowering toward her. It rotated with a whirring and clicking sound, and a larger bulb was brought to bear on her. She knew it was examining her somehow. She hoped it wasn't gamma radiation or something worse to barbecue her guts. She didn't feel anything. It moved closer. More whirring. Then the first prong, with the smaller black glass dome, rotated back. It lowered all the way down to within an inch of her face.

"Fuck you," she snarled. She spat on the glass. The black semisphere remained there for a while. She saw the creature's color shift to various patterns, most of them the color of peach flesh, with the faintest hint of red. She could hear the bulk of the machine whirring above her.

She rolled her head around trying to get a better look at it. She wondered if another alien had come along. They moved so silently. None had. But the one that was here pushed another tentacle into the space beneath the lens—she was confident that's what the black glass was—and held her head in place.

"I hope I give you some terrible disease, asshole," she said.

The alien colored some. She could see it in the tentacle around her. Redder, a slight shift toward the color of a fine Prosperion wine. It gripped her a little tighter.

Had it understood her threat?

"That's right, you heard me. I'm going to infect you with some little pathogen your people have never heard of. Some virus I got from Earth or Prosperion. Maybe something from the Hostiles. You're going to rot in horrible agony."

No response came that time.

Of course it was stupid to think it had understood.

The lens whirred and moved down her body some, stopping just below her waist. It made more whirring sounds, and it pulled away almost a foot. Another lens rotated into place, this one rather brownish glass, and it moved within inches of her pelvis. Clicks and whirring sounded again. She hoped they weren't irradiating her ovaries. She still planned on making babies with Altin, God damn it. If the universe would stop screwing with them.

She thrashed and tried to break loose. The tentacle grew redder still. She wanted to believe that meant she was hurting it, but she knew she was not.

The machine made more sounds and moved back up, once again right over her head. It clicked and rumbled for a time. Then the first lens, the smaller of the black ones, rotated back into place. It drew so close it just touched her skin, right between the eyes. It moved down her face, mashing the tip of her nose as it passed. It went sideways, first left, then right. It pulled back a few feet, and the tentacle flipped her over and slapped her back down, face-first. This time far less gently than it had at first.

She could hear the machine whirring and clicking again. It touched her hair, twice, which sent shivers down her spine both times.

There followed a longer period of whirring sounds, growing dimmer with distance. She turned her head to look. She could see the alien full on. It wasn't red anymore. It was fading from a pale blue back to the mucous gray.

Something felt like it was crawling all over her suit. Like a thousand fingers prodding and squeezing her. There was a lot of thumping and clicking. Something tore loose back there. The pressure around her body lessened for a moment, followed by an upward, sequential squeezing. The dorsal unit of her spacesuit thumped onto the table, all the jet packs, main computers, and, worse, her oxygen. Another tentacle snaked down, grabbed it, hauled it up near the alien's eye. It looked at it, turned it over a few times. Then it hurled it out over the side of the machine. It flew out, caught briefly in the wind, then plunged out of view.

The coils were twitching and groping all around her again. All the little finger-sensations crawling all over her. She was rolled onto her side. Some of the tentacles at her chest and abdomen rose away. She could see the little discs along the bottom of the tentacle working dexterously, opening up her suit, spreading the front access wide. Another tentacle snaked inside of it and wrapped around her waist. Its flesh was astonishingly hot. And wet. The discs were hard like plastic, with burrs that poked her skin. The first tentacle, the one that had coiled around her, spread the spacesuit apart so wide it ripped at the crotch, while the new tentacle pulled her out of it like a banana out of a split down the center of its peel. The tentacle that had been holding her head actually shoved her head under the helmet ring to get her out.

The tentacle holding her spacesuit whipped back, jerked forward, and threw the suit over the edge of the machine with the motion of a fly fisherman. The wind caught it, puffing it up as if it were a small, blocky version of one of the alien billows. It rose up into the airstream, spinning lazily higher for a moment as the wind blew it away, way out over the grate, where it began fluttering down. The alien manhandling her lifted her high enough as it flopped her over that she actually got to see her spacesuit fall down through a gap in the grate. Lost. Just like the backpack and helmet were. Like Altin's helmet was. Like Altin was.

She looked down as she was being rolled over and noticed the amethyst fast-cast amulet dangling from her neck. It bounced against her sternum and swung out again. She caught it and pressed it against her steam-soaked flesh. She couldn't decide if she should let it go—so they didn't realize she valued it—or keep holding on. She could rip it off and hide it in her bra. But if they took that from her, it would definitely be gone. She thought about using it now. She should go back to Prosperion. Get help. What could she possibly do for Altin here, at this point, this circumstance, all alone on a massive alien ship in her goddamn underwear?

What would he want her to do?

She knew immediately what that would be. He'd want her out of here. Right now.

But she wasn't going to leave him.

But ... she had to. She had to get help. Tytamon and her dad. These damn aliens were three hundred yards long. That was just one of them.

God. What to do? What to do?

The alien slammed her down on the examining table again. Her arms and legs were free this time. She kicked at it. She bit the tentacle. She might as well have tried biting through the insulation on a plasma coil.

She didn't want to leave him.

He'd trusted her alone before. Down below this very spot. Down in the bowels of this planet when it was still Red Fire. He'd believed in her being on her own. He'd had no choice. He'd promised her.

But she'd promised ... they'd promised to die together before they'd ever separate again. She couldn't just go.

But they were already separated.

She could find him, though. Maybe. God, no, she couldn't. How in the hell could she find him on this ship? Not now. Not without the Higgs prism. She couldn't even get off this goddamn grate.

The alien was moving three more tentacles her way.

Shit.

She fingered the amulet in her hand.

She had to do it. It was the only way.

Two tentacles began snaking around her legs, one at each ankle, winding up nearly all the way to her knees. A third was moving straight for her hand.

She yanked the fast-cast amulet off her neck, snapping it

at the clasp. "I'm coming back, Altin. I swear I am. I love you." She slammed the amethyst on the tabletop. It shattered like glass.

Nothing happened.

She was still lying there. She lifted the broken amulet up and stared at it. "No!"

The third tentacle wrapped around her free hand, all the way to the elbow. The one that had been holding her around the waist withdrew and bound up her other arm. Another one came down and reached out over her, out over the edge of the machine and down toward the grate. It anchored itself there.

She saw another branch off and slither up above, out to the side. The alien was tethered in place by five of them now. Two above, two below, and one out to the side. Orli could only watch, increasingly terrified. Nothing was working anymore. There was nothing she could do.

The creature hoisted its bulk up until the lowest portion of its long body was above the edge of the examining machine. It angled itself at her, directing the length of its body at her as if it were a rifle. She could see a small iris-like valve at the very end of it, like a sphincter. It began to pucker, and the flesh around it appeared to bloat. The color there changed to a dusky green.

"Wow," she snarled. "What are you going to do, shit on me?"

She braced for something terrible, cringing and only barely willing to look. Whatever was about to come out of that thing was probably going to hurt.

She waited for quite some time. So long that she grew tired of cringing. What the hell was it waiting for?

She waited some more. At least a full minute. Maybe two. Maybe ten. She wanted to punch that thing right in its puckering anus. Or whatever that orifice was. And then something snapped beside her. Something big and loud, a tremendous crackle in the air. Something right beside her head. That's when the orifice spat.

Chapter 13

"That's correct, Miss Grayborn," Mrs. Beckman said while staring at the board where Pernie's drawing of an electrical circuit glowed. "And do you know why that is?"

"Because it's got extra lectrons," Pernie replied. "And negative wants to run to positive."

"Correct again. You've got a gift for physics, Miss Grayborn. You'll want to pronounce the *E* on the front of the word *electrons*, but I have to tell you, your English is coming along splendidly as well."

It ought to be, Pernie thought. That was practically all Sophia Hayworth ever did with her. They did English all afternoon when Pernie got out of school. She'd be waiting for Pernie there at the bus stop. They'd walk home, and then Pernie would keep learning again. She actually learned more from Sophia Hayworth than she did from school. At least some things. Jeremy was teaching her about robotics. He had a robotic arm that he was building just like a human one, and it actually worked. Or mostly it did. He said that the school wouldn't let him have the parts he needed because they cost more than his grandfather Gabby could afford. But he didn't mind. He told her he had an uncle named

Crook, who was going to get him a synthetic frame kit. He told her he was going to build his own android and grow human skin for it. He told her that a well-made android could sell for three hundred thousand credits, which was enough to buy a townhouse by the park.

Pernie didn't know too much about townhouses or parks, but she'd learned enough about his android to think she might want one someday. He said they did all your cleaning and chores for you, and would even protect your house from burglars if they came in. The good ones looked just like people, but he said that was the hard part. "Most of them don't move right. Sitting still, you can hardly tell the difference," he said. "But once they start talking, they just never look the way a person does."

"Why not?" she'd asked.

"I think it's the wiring or something," he said. "Even the NTA guys can't do it, and they got the big bio-printers that just run androids right off. Theirs look perfect lying there, but there's something about them too. I've seen them on the net. There's a show called *Synthlink* that I love to watch. They show all the new ones. Someday I'm going to have an invention on there."

Pernie didn't know too much about all of that, but she did know she'd rather be in the science lab messing with Jeremy's robot arm than in here parroting lessons back to Mrs. Beckman. The class spent way too much time on stuff she didn't care about. She didn't care about Earth history, that was sure. Although some of the net videos from World War III were pretty fun. Especially the part where the United States almost fell apart, but then they killed everyone in some other country across an ocean, and then another country that was their ally did the same to a fourth country, and then everyone got scared that everyone in the whole world was going to die. She found out she was in the country called the United States, which was the country that won the war along with its allies. Although some of it did fall apart, but she couldn't remember which ones—which states—left. Even though they won, they didn't want to be part of the United States anymore. And someone else took some parts away, another country. Or they took some back. Axico was the name. Or something like that. Or Axis. Or maybe both. But that was the part of history that was boring, so she had trouble remembering it all. But she did like the big guns and explosives and especially the antigravity fighter planes. They were sleek and fast, with blue fire blowing out of them, and a fun shimmer underneath to keep them from falling out of the sky. The people who got to fly in them were powerful warriors who could kill as many people as they wanted to.

Jeremy told her that if they wanted to, those pilots could drop one bomb big enough to kill a whole city. He said twenty of them could blow up the whole world and kill everyone.

Pernie thought death was very interesting, but she wasn't sure why someone would want to kill everyone. Then what? That seemed kind of dumb.

Mrs. Beckman was asking another student about electrons, and Pernie found that she knew the answer too. The circuitry seemed simple to her, and even though her reading wasn't so great, and her history was terrible, she could hardly understand how anyone couldn't make perfect sense of that. It flows like water. What's not to understand?

The student was struggling with the idea of open and closed circuits, arguing with the teacher that it didn't make sense that a closed circuit was how you let the electricity through, when an open one made more sense. "How can anything get through if it's closed?" he asked. Pernie thought he must be dumb, too.

She looked up at the clock. Only five minutes until lunch. Lunch was boring. Nobody did anything but stare into their tablets or net visors, or maybe, a few of them anyway, would talk.

The bell that was really a buzzer went off. Pernie closed her desk computer down. She was pretty familiar with it all now, but she was still the last one done. Jeremy was standing there beside her when she was finished.

"Want to work on my robot after we eat?"

"Okay," she said.

They walked together down the hall toward the cafeteria. Pernie looked around as they walked, but nobody looked back at her. Nobody looked at anything. Everyone looked at their tablet screens or into the lenses of the small plastic visors that they wore. That was the first thing everyone did when she and her classmates left the classroom. The bell rang, and out came five tablets and thirteen visor sets. The kids with the tablets all walked along, staring down into their devices, smiling and laughing at them sometimes. Tapping this or that, as if they were doing work. But they weren't, Pernie knew. They were just talking. Writing notes back and forth like people on Prosperion did with their homing lizards sometimes. Although these kids never stopped. Some were playing games, though mostly the boys.

The kids with the visors made Pernie want to laugh. At first she'd thought they all looked very strange, but now, after almost two full weeks, she thought they were funny. They rolled their eyes up to look into the narrow little visors of plastic that jutted out from above their eyebrows. Sometimes she could hardly see the color of their eyes. They reminded her of the stories Kettle used to tell her of zombies brought back to life by necromancers in the olden days. Pernie had always thought the stories of zombies were made up, but she laughed and thought they must have all moved to planet Earth.

The upside of having an entire hallway filled with people who weren't paying attention to anything was that she and

Jeremy could hustle right on through them all and get very close to the front of the lunch line.

"There she is," said the lunch lady with the wide, fat cheeks and the smiling eyes. "How's my tough little Prosperion darling doing today?"

"I'm not your darling," Pernie corrected her yet again. She corrected her every day. She was fairly sure this round-faced woman was trying to be nice, but Pernie didn't have time for it. If she stopped and tried to talk to the lady, the people in the back of the line got mad. They made snide remarks, and then Pernie wanted to break their legs. She couldn't, though, because Djoveeve and Seawind had made her promise a hundred million times.

"Now why you gotta say that every time?" the lunch lady asked. "You all need to learn to be nice to folks when you come down here."

"I am nice," Pernie told her as she held up her tray. The lunch lady flopped a heap of white stuff on her plate that the menu on the wall said was supposed to be potatoes. Pernie didn't know if potatoes on Earth were supposed to be the same thing as the word translated to for potatoes on Prosperion, but she sure knew that mashy stuff didn't taste like anything that Kettle had ever made. The meat was worse, and the vegetables had no flavor at all. Pernie thought that someone during the war must have dropped a bomb that killed flavor from everything.

"Well, you go on, then, darling," said the lunch lady. "You keep on being nice, and I'll keep on doing likewise. Have a nice day now."

Pernie stopped and frowned at her, and considered telling her again to stop calling her darling. Jeremy was just pulling back his tray. "Go on," he said, seeing the look on her face. He'd only been her friend for twelve days, but he could already spot the little storms that got to brewing sometimes. "She's just trying to be nice," he repeated for the lunch lady, who was already talking to the next kid in the line. That kid pushed up against Jeremy with his tray.

"Get going, dipshit," the kid said. "You're clogging up the line."

Jeremy didn't look back, and tried to urge Pernie on.

Pernie turned her little brewing monsoon on the boy who'd pushed her friend. He saw her look at him and glared right back. She slapped the tray out of his hand so fast neither he nor Jeremy saw more than a blur of her hand. It clattered noisily to the floor.

The boy was beyond startled, and he recoiled spastically, flinching away from her and making a very embarrassing panic face for all to see. In the moment after, he glanced to the tray on the floor then back up at Pernie. She leaned her little face forward, her gaze predatory, inviting him to say or do something else pushy or mean. His eyes widened for a moment, then he bent and picked up his tray. He turned and lifted it up for the round-faced lunch lady without so much as another glance in the direction of Pernie or her friend.

When Pernie and Jeremy were finally seated, at the far end of a long row of tables and benches, Jeremy stared across the table at her, openly amazed and perhaps a little terrified. "He's a seventh grader," he proclaimed. "Are you crazy?"

"I don't care," Pernie said, grimacing as she took a bite of the mashy white stuff they called potatoes. "Size doesn't mean anything. Neither does age. Not even weight or weaponry. Nothing does." She'd killed the king of the sargosaganti; she knew for fact that this was true.

He frowned at that. He, unlike her, enjoyed the food here, and he ate heartily. "Why do you say that?"

"It just doesn't," she said. "And you shouldn't be afraid."

"But I am," he announced, perfectly at his ease. "But that's okay. I don't come here to fight. I come here to learn."

That's what Pernie had said her first day on the bus.

Nobody else had said that before.

"Well, you still shouldn't let them push you. They'll just do it again."

"We'll see how much they push when I make my android."

That lit up Pernie's eyes. "Really?"

"Oh yes," he said. "I'll make mine a full combat droid. I'll program him so he can even wear the big battle suits. The Tesla-Matsura Six, even. Mine will be the first mech-pilot android. Mine will be so close to human that it will be able to control everything in it too. All the heads-up stuff and twitch controls. Then they'll see."

"Why don't you just make a big robot like the arm in the robotics lab?"

"Because machines don't have instincts. You have to have a human brain. That's why I have to make an android. You have to get the human part. The skin, the nerves, the brain. It has to be human enough to hook into the mech, but machine enough to think a million times faster than we can."

Pernie thought that made robots sound like elves. "Elves don't have instinct either," she said. "Maybe they are robots inside."

"Elves?"

"Yes, they are a different kind of people on Prosperion. I know some. They are teaching me how to fight. But I'm not supposed to talk about that, so I can't say anymore or they won't teach me how to ...." She blanched and snapped her teeth together in an awkward grin. "Well, I'm not supposed to talk about that either."

Jeremy looked like he really wanted to know super bad, but he didn't make her say. That's why she liked him. He didn't make her talk about things she didn't want to. Sophia Hayworth did. Sophia Hayworth was always asking, "What's wrong, sweetheart?" and "What's on your mind?" But that was okay. Pernie kind of liked Sophia Hayworth most of the time. She was teaching her a lot, and she never got mad. Pernie had even stopped thinking of her as "fake mother" most of the time. She was just Sophia usually.

Don Hayworth was nice too. Don said he would teach her how to play baseball this weekend. She didn't know what that was, but Don said it was an old game that everyone loved to play. Playing would be fun. She'd been very focused on learning everything. The more comfortable she got with the computers and the devices the Earth people made, the more she learned—and the more she learned, the more she began to think that it might be harder than she thought to learn everything right away. She also thought Orli Pewter might know more things than Pernie had originally anticipated. And Pernie was very far behind. But one game of baseball would be okay.

And some time working on Jeremy's robot.

When they were done eating, and Jeremy was done eating most of Pernie's food, they headed to the science room to spend some time on just that very thing. Jeremy had to take the thumb apart, because it wasn't working properly.

She sat watching him struggle with it for a time, and finally asked, "What are you trying to do?"

"I have to get this tensioner off. It's like a ligament, holds the joints together. But it's super tight. And if I nick it, it will tear right through."

Pernie watched some more. Jeremy's hands and face were trembling with the effort of trying to get the pieces apart. "It's not supposed to be this hard," he said.

"Are you sure you're doing it right?" Pernie couldn't know for sure if he was or wasn't. She wasn't trying to be mean. She just wondered. She had been watching him for a while, though, and she was pretty sure she knew what he was trying to do. The tool was very simple, and she thought it might just be that he was kind of weak.

"Yes, I'm sure. I don't know why it won't work."

"Can I try?"

He looked up at her. She was absolutely serious. She could tell he was afraid she would break it.

"If I break it, I'll buy you a new one," she said. "I have money, you know. Master Tytamon sent me a lot of money. Or he had a lot of money made for me here." She shrugged. She hadn't figured that stuff out yet because it didn't seem to matter and it was really boring.

Jeremy paused, and pulled his chin toward his throat. "You had money made?"

"Yes," she said. "They did something with a heap of Tytamon's gold back on Prosperion. He gave it to the man from the TGS office, who said he would turn it into money here on Earth."

"Oh," Jeremy said. He looked back at his project.

"So will you let me try it?"

His mouth shifted back and forth across his face.

"I won't break it," she said.

She was sure he was going to tell her no, and she was preparing her best pouty face, when he reluctantly agreed. "You're sure you can get me another one if it does? At least the tendon and ligament? They cost a lot, you know. Eighty credits each."

She smiled happily. "Of course I can. I have enough to buy that thing you said was where you park."

"That what?"

"You said you wanted to buy something near where you park. In town, by your house."

One eye closed as he scrunched up the left side of his face, trying to figure out what she was talking about. Then it dawned on him. "A townhouse by the park."

"Yes, that was it. I can buy you one of those if you'd like."

It was his turn to frown.

"Come on," she said, reaching for the tool. "I promise I

won't break it."

He was just staring at her, like he was trying to decide something. She reached for the tool in his hands, a small metal rod with a hook. He didn't snatch it from her when she gently pulled it from his grasp.

She moved around the workbench to where he was, shouldered him gently aside, and quickly found where the joint was he'd been working on. She pushed the hook underneath the expanse of dark gray material that looked like polished string. She tugged on it gently, and found it to be on very tight. She pulled a little harder. Still nothing. She continued to pull harder until, just like that, it popped off.

She turned triumphantly to him, presenting him with the tool. "I told you I could—"

He was crying.

Chapter 14

The Earl of Vorvington sat at his opulent desk in his opulent offices on the top floor of the opulent Castles, Inc. building. Castles, Inc. was a construction and transmutation business the portly nobleman was forced to operate to augment the paltry earnings his earldom provided.

Still, his station gave him advantage in business, and he was privileged in his contracts, operating almost entirely for the Queen, who awarded to him almost every job his company bid on. In the aftermath of the war, he was making a fortune repairing damage to the city, in particular to the Palace walls, as he was one of the few people with access to any wizards at all these days. What the TGS hadn't taken, Her Majesty nearly had, and with Her Majesty tied up in her own affairs more so now than at any other point in his memory, she'd given him all the more leeway to get things done. Which was good. Leeway provided a man of opportunity with, well, opportunities. And a man like Vorvington prided himself on his vision when it came to such matters.

Speaking of which, he was just stuffing a set of very special plans pertaining to a section of the Palace wall into an ivory tube when a knock came upon his door, announcing the arrival of a diviner from the temple of Anvilwrath. She was a young acolyte, very pretty, whose name was Klovis, as he recalled. He'd been expecting her. He opened the door and gazed at her, a smile creasing his fleshy face.

Her face was stern but comely, high cheekbones and a narrow nose above lips that likely did not smile much. But most noticeable about her was the scar, a long, straight line cutting from just below her throat down between her breasts and vanishing into her rust-colored robes. It was narrow and well healed, the slight rise of it only a shade paler than the rest of her flesh, but she made no effort to hide it, much less have it properly removed by a cosmetic healer. Rather, she seemed to wear it with pride, and his eyes were even directed to it by the copper spearhead medallion she wore suspended from a copper chain around her neck. His tongue crept out from between his lips, wetting them, as he thought about where that scar went.

"The Grand Maul says that it is done," the young priestess said. "Your people have dug it out. He thanks you and assures you that you and he and … that everyone is on the same line of the prophecy." She handed him a sealed envelope. "Here is what you asked us for in return."

"Right," grinned the earl, ignoring the envelope in his hand in favor of studying the scar. The neckline of her robe had shifted when she handed it to him, revealing another finger length of the wound. He'd heard that scar ran all the way to her nether parts, carved into her by the claw of a demon. He licked his lips again. "You're very pretty, you know."

"I'm sure that I am grateful that you say so, My Lord." She spun and left.

He watched her go, the pendulous movement of her robes tracing the athletic body underneath. His fingers twitched, his hand shaping itself as he imagined what her buttocks might feel like to the touch. He imagined clutching it, and his breath quickened. There were other advantages of station as well, pressures that could be applied, favors called.

But the marchioness would be furious if she caught him. And she watched.

He looked down at the envelope. It was the Grand Maul's seal. That wrinkled old demon made Vorvington twitch. Half a millennium at least, that cripple of a man had been asserting his influence in this city. Long before Her Majesty was here. He was as patient as he was old, and he had the light touch of a thief. Of a weasel perhaps. But powerful. A Five: two Ws and a T at the top, which was a lot of magic in a body so frail.

Vorvington opened the missive. It read:

The office of your dead nephew. You will find it there. The key. Follow it.

He actually laughed. Damned diviners were all the same. All those years in a wheeled chair rolling around in the darkness under the temple of Anvilwrath had made the Grand Maul even more abstruse than all the rest. But they were all the same, diviners, mystics, blathering nonsense most of the time. Often their "visions" were only explained in retrospect. He could go find anything in Thadius' old office, an acorn or an old pot of ink, and if things shaped up well for the old priest and his prophecies, then of course *that* had been the key. If things went poorly, well, then it would be Vorvington to blame. He'd found the wrong thing. Or he'd misread it. Or he'd followed it to the wrong place.

What in nine hells did it mean to follow a key, anyway?

Nonetheless, the marchioness would be expecting him to do it, so he did. He closed up his desk and tucked the note inside his ivory case, rolling it up and stuffing it into the plans.

He wheezed a little by the time he made his way down the stairs to Thadius' old office. In truth, he hadn't been in the room in well over a year. Not since Thadius had died. He'd been fond of his nephew—at least, as fond as a man like Vorvington could be of a man with Thadius' temperament. Thadius had provided him a vicarious life of seduction and depravity, stories shared over fine bottles of wine, stories of things that Vorvington was no longer allowed to do.

He sighed as he looked upon the dusty desks. There were two: one had been Thadius' and the other had belonged to the transmuter Aderbury, whom Her Majesty was so fond of. The man was a fabulous transmuter, perhaps the most artistic of them on all Prosperion, but the poor bastard was flying *Citadel* now. Vorvington liked Aderbury well enough—he'd certainly made the earl a fortune with his exquisite talents melding stone—but, all of that was done now. Vorvington was making do with what transmuters he could find in Aderbury's absence, and he'd brought on a great deal more numbers of blanks. They were dreadfully slow, but they worked cheap. That was the beauty of a blank: you could pay them a pittance, and they'd take it for fear they might not have enough to eat. They did all the work, and produced nearly everything, and yet they were ever willing to leave all the wealth to the nobility, satisfied to live on what they were handed back from the sale of what they themselves had made. It was a beautiful system, and Vorvington was eternally happy to have been born on the right side of it.

He rummaged through Thadius' old desk. He had no idea what he was looking for. A key. What kind of key? A key-key, or something else? Some kind of epiphany? Some object or document that would suddenly flash an idea into his mind?

Maybe he was looking for a map. Maps had keys. Perhaps he was supposed to follow it.

He went through every drawer. There were heaps of parchments, documents, plans, and maps. None of them prompted any sort of epiphany. None of them did anything at all. He could name every project for each of them from memory.

Maybe it was something else. A book open to some prophetic page. Maybe a quill had been laid aside, and now, by the hand of fate, lay pointing at something vital somewhere in the room, or perhaps at a suggestive portion of some painting on the wall. It was just the sort of idiocy that a diviner might rely on—especially a five-hundred-year-old crippled one, rolling around in Anvilwrath's tomb picking through the rubble of a war he did not predict, at least not in any way that counted meaningful, meaningful in the way of preventing it or even leaving time for preparation.

He looked and looked, but there was nothing. There were no pens, no knives, no ivory toothpicks. There were no revelatory lines in the dust, no fringes of carpets or angles in the arms of a damned chair ... nothing that pointed conspicuously to anything in any pictures on the wall. There was nothing. Not even an actual key.

He sighed and turned to leave. He was wasting his time. Let the marchioness send her own private diviners to come do something with the Grand Maul's message. He'd been looking for a half hour and it was nearly dinnertime. He hadn't eaten since tea, and that was nearly three hours ago.

He looked one last time around the room. There was nothing. Not even anything on Aderbury's desk. Although he hadn't looked through it. The note said Thadius' old office, not Aderbury's.

Still, he supposed he should, just so that he didn't get berated by the marchioness. The young priestess Klovis had stirred his loins, so he might as well try to stay on speaking terms this evening with the marchioness.

He opened the top right drawer, and lying there was a key ring with a handful of keys. Vorvington cursed. "Sons of harpies, all of them." He took the ring and looked through all the keys. None of them were spectacular. They were simply regular old keys. One key to the building, another to the basement, one to the room on the third floor where they kept the more important designs and patent documents. There was a house key and three more smaller ones that likely unlocked chests or drawers. There was literally nothing among them remotely remarkable.

He looked around the office for a box or a trunk that he might unlock with one of the smaller keys. There were none. There were no small boxes in the other desk drawers. There was nothing.

He shook his head, his breathing heavy now for the effort of bending down and rummaging through everything. Then it occurred to him that it might be obvious after all. The damn house key. That was *the* key, and he already knew where it led. It led to Aderbury's home.

He had to go to the records office on the second floor, but as it was his business, it was only moments before the clerk found the address. Vorvington's driver had him at the premises in twenty minutes more.

No one answered his knock, and the key on the ring fit exactly as Vorvington figured it would. He went inside. There was no one home. He looked around, saw nothing out of the ordinary. He ran his finger over the table in the front room. It was lightly coated with a film of dust. So was the counter top in the kitchen and surfaces every where he looked. Nobody had been there in weeks.

He looked around some more, rummaging through the kitchen and the pantry. He went through closets. He went through bedrooms. He had no idea what he was looking for.

He found Aderbury's study as he made his way down the hall. He opened the door and went in. There was a desk, a few shelves full of books, and a cabinet upon which sat a homing lizard cage. The lizards were all dead. Starved to death by the look of them, that or thirst. They were all shriveled up like dried apricots. He wondered if that was why he was there, if they were the sign he was supposed to find. Some sort of ironic clue.

It didn't seem likely.

He went to the desk first. Aderbury's desk at Castles, Inc. was where he'd found the key. He was prepared to check for locked drawers, but there in the center of the desk, set there prominently as if left out for him to see, was a set of plans for the strangest series of fortresses he had ever seen. Nine of them, vaguely like those hastily built in wilderness areas, depicted as having been built upon formations that looked like rock. Eight of them formed a loosely shaped circle and were joined to the ninth at the center, connected by ramparts that arced ridiculously, high humped and steep at both ends. There were other pages to the plans as well, interior plans and top views and other details pertaining to customized transmute spells required for the making of them. None of it was particularly unusual other than the design.

He looked them over and couldn't fathom why anyone would build such a thing. Which meant they had to be what he was looking for. He scooped them up, rolled them, and stuffed them into his ivory case as well. Perhaps the evening would work out after all.

He stopped for a bouquet of enchanted parasiniums mixed with red rosebuds and a cloud of baby's breath before returning to the TGS station near the Palace, a small, private one operated only for the nobility. He hoped the songs the parasinium blossoms sang would work nicely with the designs he'd found and a jot of wine or nine to put My Lady in the mood.

Chapter 15

Roberto stared out over southeastern Houston toward the water. San Jacinto Bay glittered brightly in the sun, the rusting supports of an old bridge rising from it like giant needles pushed through blue fabric. Pleasure boats stitched white threads across the water, and Roberto sighed as he thought about what might lie beneath them as they sailed leisurely along. There'd been an island there once, Alexander Island, slowly eroding over time and finally drowned when the climate changed a half millennium or so ago. If he hadn't had his hands so full—if the Queen's inexplicable demands that he work the Goblin Tea business "in the name of long-term security" didn't swamp his days, and if the fact that his best friend in the world wasn't MIA on some damn alien ship didn't swamp his every waking thought—then he might have relished the idea of being out there on one of those boats too. Maybe throw on some diving gear and go see if he could find some prewar artifacts. He blew out another long breath. The view from his sixty-fifth-floor office suite was spectacular, but today, like the rest of the last thirteen days, the scenery couldn't cut through his mood.

He turned back into the room and shook his head. "It's

bullshit," he said. "I can't believe we are here doing this crap right now. Those bastards up on Yellow Fire, assuming they even are still on Yellow Fire, could be doing anything to Orli and Altin right now. It's been *two* freaking weeks! I'm telling you, I'm having a really hard time getting my head around why Her Majesty insists this Goblin Tea empire is a priority. I've already got a hundred and sixteen stores open. I literally am selling every coffee bean I've contracted for. And she wants me to get more and do more? 'Deal with anyone you have to,' she said. I can't even deal with my contractors, much less those shady bastards out of Murdoc Bay. And there's plenty more of those kind here too. Between taxes, permitting, and bribes, I can't get my infrastructure to grow fast enough to keep up with supply or demand." He jerked his hand in the direction of the computer terminals at which Deeqa and Allen Greenfeld, the man he'd made CFO to help hold the business together, worked. "We're making more money than you guys can even count on two computers, and it's still not enough. How greedy can she possibly be?"

"You made the deal with the devil, Captain. Best learn to like the scent of brimstone," Deeqa said. Her smooth cheeks rounded with the ensuing smile. "But it's not so bad when you mix in the sweet smell of our coffee. And it pays handsomely." That last bit was why she'd signed on, after all.

Deeqa Daar was Roberto's copilot on the *Glistening Lady*, but she had rapidly become a crucial business partner too. He'd stolen her from a miserable job on a rusty old freight ship, and he considered that one of the best negotiations he'd ever made. Not only could she fly the hell out of a spaceship, she had a great mind for business and an even greater one for ... navigating the decidedly cloudy spaces between right and wrong. She was as comfortable in a bar fight as a boardroom, and when it came to tax codes,

Roberto figured she was at least a thousand times smarter than he was. Between her and Allen, the business was making money hand over fist. And he was fine with that.

"Besides," Deeqa went on, "Her Majesty said she'd talk to Director Bahri and get some people out there as soon as possible. You worry too much. Orli and Sir Altin will be fine."

"Yeah, that's what she said, but 'as soon as possible' in Queen time doesn't mean the same thing as it does to regular people. And I don't like waiting." Roberto turned back to the window and stared out again. "I swear, if anything happens to Orli ... well, I'm just saying. Her Majesty better not screw around."

"Or what? Are you going to fly the *Lady* in there, guns blazing, and ... what?" She shook her head, and the light from her computer screen glinted up and down the stack of gold rings that bound up a stem and bushy tuft of her hair, a Qurac, she called it, after a sacred tree of her homeland.

"I'll go myself if I have to. I don't care how big that ship is or how hard that damn alien hull material is. I'll blow that thing wide open and get them out personally. I'm only giving her a few more days. That's it. For all I know, that's going to be way too late. She just isn't doing anything."

"We all care about Orli and Sir Altin," Deeqa said. "But nobody in their right mind is going to fly the *Lady* in there solo with you against spaceships the size of damn cities." She paused, then amended, "Okay, Chelsea and Betty-Lynn would. Probably Fatima. But nobody else will."

Roberto's shoulders drooped. He turned back. "I know," he said. "It just pisses me off. I hate feeling helpless. And I can't give a crap about building a damn chain of Prosperion coffeehouses while my best friend is—well, I don't even want to think about it."

"Then don't. Look, you have a contract to fulfill. Her Majesty said she would get some mages over there at Yellow

Fire. You've got Altin's old boss working on it too. Isn't that man supposed to be some kind of superhero, raised from the dead and invincible?"

Roberto nodded, his mood lightening some at the mention of Tytamon. "That's true. And he is the guy who taught Altin everything he knows. He's got an extra one of those magic schools on Altin too. Altin's only got seven of them. Tytamon is an Eight. Apparently that's super hard-core."

"Exactly," said Deeqa. She smiled and gestured to the door to his private office. "So why don't you go in there, call Brent down in reception, and have him send the next guy up. Do your job, and trust others to do theirs. We'll get our friends back."

He scowled, but she was right. He just had to get the Queen her money. That's all she cared about anymore. It was weird. And yes, it was his money too. He used to care about it. And maybe he would once Orli and Altin were safe. But now, well, having them missing sucked anything like fun out of the enterprise right now. He should be doing something for them. Earning money now felt like earning ransom ... that he had to pay to his own damn ally!

He went into his office and flopped down into the high-backed chair behind the big desk. The whole rig was replica seventeenth-century Spain, baroque and as close to authentic as he could get. At least it was real wood and not synthetic, but he was waiting for a new set to be made back on Prosperion. When that came, he could cut this stuff up for firewood. He reached out and tapped the com controls. "Brent, send in the guy from San Francisco, please."

A moment later the door slid open, and in walked a man wearing a business suit that could not have cost him less than twenty thousand credits. Roberto watched the fabric shimmer, then shift from a gunmetal gray to a muted brown that was the perfect complement to the colors of the office carpet and other furnishings. It was the kind of thing politicians wore. He was clean cut, of medium build, blond hair trimmed short, bright blue eyes, and a nose that was a bit too round to be pleasant looking upon his face. He carried a large tablet computer in an alligator case.

"Good afternoon, Mr. Levi," he said as he reached out his hand to Roberto. "Or do you prefer Captain even while you are here in Houston?"

"Captain is fine," Roberto said. He thought he detected a hint of an accent in the man's voice. He stood and shook the man's hand across the desk. He found his grip to be strong and sure. "Please, take a seat, Mister ...." He let that tail off, clearly an inquiry, as he directed him to one of two replica armchairs, also made to match the desk.

"My friends call me El Segador."

Roberto cocked an eyebrow at that but let it pass. "Can I get you something, Mr. Segador? Water, whiskey, or Goblin Tea? I've got a thirty-six-year-old scotch that is so good it will make you want to play bagpipes, and, of course, my Prosperion specialty was brewed barely a half hour ago."

"That scotch sounds excellent. I could use the jolt after three hours on the tube," El Segador said as he sat down.

"It's a long way from the Bay Area to Houston on that thing." Roberto poured the drinks as he watched his visitor settle in.

"Yes, it is. And NTA customs agents are not as pleasant coming this way as they are going back to Mexico."

Roberto delivered the scotch and then took his place behind the desk. "Yes, well, there are unsavory elements in Mexico these days."

The man called El Segador nodded, admitting this was true. "A sad and seemingly permanent state of events. Our poor country has been in turmoil since its very first days. So many empires have cut their way back and forth across that blood-soaked land it almost forgot what it originally was. But she is a great country, before and now, and one of the few real beneficiaries of the third world war."

Roberto nodded. "I always thought, as I read the history, that that was a bit ironic, calling the war that, given who rose out of it and all."

El Segador nodded, smiling as he sipped on his scotch. There followed a brief period of silence as he whirled the brown liquor in the glass and sniffed it as if it were a rose. "That is damn fine scotch. I thought you might have been exaggerating."

Roberto agreed and played a few notes on imaginary bagpipes. El Segador smiled again, tipping his glass slightly in toast toward the song in the air before taking another sip. Roberto set his glass down right after, small talk and courtesies done. "So what can I do for you, Mr. Segador? You didn't come all this way to sip scotch and chat about ancient history. What have you got for me?"

"I'm here to offer you distribution opportunities in Mexico," he said. "I represent a small conglomerate interested in a partnership."

"I'm only just off the ground here in the NTA territories," Roberto said. "Mexico is a whole new set of headaches." He knew perfectly well he wanted into Mexico, as bad as every other country and corporate exo-nation on the planet. But he wasn't going to tell this guy that.

"Of course it is. But, as you can imagine, it is a set of headaches we are well used to, so to speak. Which is why we are suggesting a partnership. We will buy as much of your Prosperion coffee as you want to sell. Sell it to us through our licensed companies in the NTA nations, or directly to my people in Mexico, straight from your cargo bays. Either way, as you please, and either way, we'll operate under your franchise name and preserve your global brand. We will submit to your franchise rules and inspectors, too. Contracts will specify that, and your brand will be represented pristinely throughout Mexico and its territories exactly as you intend. We, of course, will gladly make cultural suggestions if you should be interested in tailoring the business to local tastes, but that is entirely at your discretion. We simply wish to leap at the opportunity to be the first rather than a follower in the Goblin Tea industry." He flipped open the tablet he carried and turned it on. He spun it around and pushed it across the desk toward Roberto. "That is the complete proposal. There's even a personal message from President Domingo Rios-Muñoz himself. He would have come today, but, as you can imagine, he's very busy. He would like to meet you someday soon."

Roberto prevented his eyebrow from rising at that last bit. The Mexican president wanted in on the action too? But then, why should that surprise him? Roberto was partnered with the Queen of one world and working under the extremely unusual permissions of Director Bahri and the NTA. Of course the Mexican president sent a private message. Hell, he probably really did want to meet with him someday.

Roberto skimmed it over. Everything seemed to be as El Segador had said. He tapped in the code to the main office network and, with a flick of his finger, copied the proposal into his own system.

"All right, Mr. Segador, I've got a copy. I'll have my people look it over and get back to you. You'll understand that I have obligations to the Queen, and there are some rules in my contract with the NTA that I haven't gotten around to reading yet. I don't have to tell you how slick those guys are when it comes to finding ways to force exclusivity."

"No, you don't. They are slick, without doubt. They didn't take control of half a planet's wealth by accident."

"They damn sure didn't," Roberto agreed.

"And if there are rules that bind you," El Segador added, "there are other opportunities besides Goblin Tea that might not have been taken off the table by the NTA lawyers."

"Such as?"

"Well, it's not my intent to pry, but I can't help wondering what your cargo holds are filled with on your return trips to Prosperion? It would be a shame to think you go back empty." Again came that easy smile, and with it a hungry narrowing of the eyes.

Roberto laughed. "No way, man. Do you have any idea how sticky all this is? My deal with the Queen to do this is a lot weirder than you can possibly imagine, and it gets weirder every day. There was a short little window to get this going before all the cockblocks got set up. And even now, the TGS is furious that I have my own set of friends who teleport my ship back and forth sometimes." He grimaced inwardly as he thought of Altin's plight, but he kept up his poker face. "So is the NTA. They watch my ship like a hawk the moment I'm anywhere in range. But the TGS is going to end up being the worst of the two in my opinion. It's only a matter of time before they control everything shipping. If they had enough teleporters, they'd cut out freighter ships and trucking entirely and just teleport direct. Who is to say they won't in time? That's how big they think they are going to get. You watch."

El Segador laughed. "Yes. That's how we see it too. But for now, the situation is as it is. I understand that magicians are in short supply after the war, so you don't need to make any decisions immediately. Just keep the suggestion in mind."

Roberto wondered who the man had been talking to, but he kept that thought to himself. He'd probably already said more than he should have—Orli and Altin missing was messing with his head. He smiled instead. "I will. Thanks." He polished off his scotch. "Is there anything else I can do for you?"

"No," said the man, taking the dismissive cue without the least blemish to the congenial expression upon his face. "I look forward to hearing from you." He tossed back the last of the scotch as well. "And thank you for that," he said as he placed the empty glass on the desk. "That alone was worth the trip."

Roberto smiled, almost laughed, and shook the man's hand. "Thanks for coming. I'll be in touch."

The man left as efficiently as he came in, and Roberto joined his two companions once more in the outer offices of the suite.

"There's something about him," Deeqa said as soon as he was gone.

"Were you listening?" he asked, nodding toward her computer on the table nearby. He already knew.

"Of course."

"So why do you say that?"

"Who has he been talking to?"

"About what?"

"About the mages."

"What do you mean?"

"How does he know that mages are in short supply after the war?"

"It stands to reason. Everyone knows the casualties on both sides were staggering. They show images of Crown City under siege all the time on the net."

"Maybe," she said. "I don't know. It's just ... something. And what does *El Segador* mean? That is Spanish, isn't it?"

"Yeah. It means someone who harvests stuff, like someone who picks crops or gathers fields. Literally it translates to: 'the harvester.'"

Deeqa thought about that for a time, her jaw working. Then she shook her head. "Do you know what a harvester is, Captain?"

He shrugged, quirking an eyebrow.

"Someone who reaps. And if there is but one of them, as in *the* harvester, then there is, well, but one who reaps."

Roberto nodded, in a "no-shit" sort of way, but there was something in her expression that made him rotate his hand in front of him impatiently, urging her to get on with her point.

"He is not just *a* reaper. He is *The* Reaper."

That put a frown on Roberto's face.

Chapter 16

The little alien—little by comparison to the one that held Altin in its grasp—suction-cupped its way up the hull to the window. Altin hadn't realized how big the window was until he saw the strange creature crawl across it with its hooked back end and its three twitching mustache tentacles at the front.

The larger alien reached a tentacle out and took the spacesuit helmet from the hook on the smaller alien's rump, at which point the little one scurried away back down the wall.

The tentacle snaked up and set the helmet back on Altin's head. The sinuous limb wrapped around him, head and shoulders, and he could see through the helmet glass the discs on the tentacle writhing and working. *Click, click, click, click* went the locks on the helmet. The tentacle coiled farther down. Things were thudding against his back. The lights came on inside of his suit. He heard a brief click of static. "Orli!" he called out.

Air blew inside of his helmet. It was cool. Or cooler. Anything was cooler than the steam pit of this vessel.

Finally the clunking at the back of his suit stopped. The lights went off. He called Orli's name again.

The tentacle pushed him toward the window, the giant hatch.

"You really are going to throw me out?" he said. "By the gods, why?"

He was going to fall what had to be at least several miles if he was as high in the blowing clouds as he thought this window was relative to the planet's surface. Was that what they were hoping for? Or did they just want him out there until the air they'd just recharged in his suit ran out, the whole ordeal simply something as mundane as an experiment with his equipment?

But then it occurred to him that, whatever they were up to, if they put him out there, he'd get the mana back—or at least he hoped he would. But then what? He couldn't get Orli out. Hell, he couldn't even get himself back in. The ship was a mana-free zone. What if they left? He knew he wasn't going to fall to his death, but they didn't. And it wouldn't matter. They could take Orli away.

The alien reached two tentacles to the controls near the hatch. It poked the tips into holes. Lights flashed along the rows of color. Loud thumping sounds came from above.

He looked up and saw what at first looked like a house being lowered from above. Like everything else in this place, it was made from the green-brown protein. It was suspended from thick ropes made of, of course, more protein. It swung down over him. The alien lifted him up and put him inside. The object was a five-sided box. The open end, at the edges, was slightly convex. Altin absently wondered if they were going to teleport him somewhere.

The box moved toward the hatch. Altin realized the box was slightly higher and wider than the hatch. The alien put him in it and held him there until the leading edge of the compartment was barely three hand widths from the hull. Then the tentacle let him go. It uncoiled itself quickly and slithered down out of the gap. The box clamped tight against the hull. Altin stared out the window. He was so high up he couldn't see the ground. Just red, dusty clouds blowing all around.

They really were going to jettison him.

The edges of the box glowed faintly, a dull brown light that illuminated the seam for a time. He could feel more than he could hear a crackling sound. Then the hatch itself began to vibrate. White plumes of air and steam flickered out and were snatched away by the raging wind. Then all was roaring and loud. The fury of the red planet's ever-present storms. It buffeted Altin violently as the hatch opened, swinging down and away.

The moment it did, Altin felt the gravity change. He braced himself to be crushed, as he had been the first time he lowered the Polar Piton's shield on this world. But he wasn't. He was reaching for his Higgs prism, hoping he knew how to work it well enough, when he realized he was fine. The gravity had just changed. A little. That was all.

He didn't understand what the aliens wanted him to do. He damn sure wasn't going to leave Orli behind. The back wall of the box began to creep closer to him.

They were going to push him out.

It came very close, within a half step of him. He turned to watch it. Backing toward the edge. He reached for the mana. It was still all in a bubble around him, though he was very close to the edge of the confinement. Maybe if he jumped out.

He was going to be pushed out in a second anyway.

Then the wall vanished. So did the floor. All of it, all around him, was just gone. The whole ship. He panicked, clutched for the wall he'd been standing near, his knees bending, bracing for extra balance he did not actually need.

He was still standing on something solid.

Something touched the front of his suit. He reached forward, felt it. Solid. Moving. The back wall was still coming at him, invisible now.

Out of reflex, he looked for the mana again.

There it was. The pink mist. Everywhere around him, returned to him at last.

"By the gods!" he muttered. In that instant, he cast a seeing spell back onto the tabletop where they'd examined him, half-expecting it to be gone, invisible like the rest of the ship. It wasn't. Orli was lying there. An alien had stripped her suit away and now held her down, stretched like a prisoner on an invisible rack in only her underclothes. It held itself above her, the bottom portion of its body poised and puckering, about to launch something vile from its nether parts. Or worse.

That was all he needed. It was hardly even a thought. It was the seed of a thought, the barest flicker of an idea, and he teleported himself there. Right to her.

He appeared beside her. He spared only an instant to catch his balance in the ferocious wind, glaring up at his enemy. His brow furrowed, and he reached back into the mana. He gathered up vast clouds of it in his mind, drawing it in as he drew in the breath that would fuel it, a fireball that would engulf the creature entirely.

The blob of ochre jelly flew through the fireball even as it formed by Altin's spell. The blob struck Altin at the same moment the fireball struck a crackling barrier. The flames wrapped around an energy field for a moment, then blew back on the wind at him. Altin cried out, but no one could hear him but himself. He was encased in an ochre blob again.

He waited for the flames to pass, staring helplessly down at where Orli lay. He screamed at her, watching the fire blowing away. It was gone in an instant.

Orli lay steaming and motionless. He'd killed her, his own wrathful fireball the thing that did it. He should have just teleported them home. So stupid. He'd had the chance.

She was looking up at him. She smiled. Her mouth moved. She said something to him. He gasped, almost a sob. She was alive. He could breathe again, with something to be grateful for in all that wet, blowing steam.

"I'm sorry," he called out to her. Shaping the words carefully that she might read his lips. "I'm sorry. I tried. I'll think of something. I love you."

He reached for the mana again. It wasn't there. He was in the gods-be-damned manaless bubble again. "By the eyes of the gorgon, you will suffer for this," Altin swore up at the alien. "You shall see. We are not playthings!"

He vented out a few more strings of threats and frustrated epithets. All he could do was watch helplessly. He stared back at Orli lying there. She stared at him. She was so beautiful. She had the face of a goddess, perfect, a likeness like those that had been carved into every statue of every feminine deity across Prosperion. And she loved him. Foolish, reckless, bumbling him. She let him marry her. And this was her reward. Pinned to a table by aliens, half-naked and as vulnerable as she could possibly be. Steaming no less, nearly burned to a crisp by the man who'd sworn to keep her safe. Rage and frustration filled him so full he was sure he must go insane. He thought it impossible to feel so wholly consumed by helplessness.

He was wrong.

Another alien roped and towed its way toward them, its tentacles reaching up and down, hauling itself against the wind. He thought it might be the same alien that had taken him away, but he had no way to be sure. He was only sure he wanted to kill it in some horrible way.

The recently arrived alien snaked a few tentacles high and low, guy-wiring itself between the grates again. It positioned itself as it had been when the aliens were examining Altin before.

It wrapped a tentacle around the blob of jelly he was in

and moved him, setting him aside like some captured pawn on the edge of a chessboard. It left him there, then reached up into the darkness. Lights glowed, and a bulky upper portion of the pronged machine lowered toward Orli.

Altin could see her depicted in an oval of light at the center of the protein mass, a clear, rounded shape like an eye. He could see her image in it, larger even than he could see her in real life only fifteen paces away.

The machine rotated its conical arms and the black bulbs of glass. The alien on the other side of the tabletop flickered more colors and patterns across its flesh. Altin saw Orli lying there, an image of her visible on the alien itself.

The alien nearest him flickered something back. It turned the machine with the eye-monitor toward the other alien. More colors flashed. That alien snaked tentacles up and did something on the other side of the machine. More colors. Altin could see Orli's belly now. It was depicted bright and clear upon the alien's bulbous central part, an extreme close-up. He could see her navel and the soft blonde hairs, tiny upon her bare flesh, made more visible by humidity and sweat.

The farther alien spun the machine back toward the first. There was something pink and whitish on the eye-shaped screen. Altin didn't know what it was precisely, but it was much like the sorts of images he'd seen on Doctor Singh's examination machines in the sick bay of the *Aspect*. They were looking inside of her.

The machine moved up and pointed over Orli's skull. Again Orli could be seen in the eye-like monitor, her beautiful goddess face. Light patterns flashed across the bodies of both aliens. Orli's face was distorted on the alien's body opposite. More patterns flashed between them.

The image in the eye-monitor changed. Altin recognized it immediately. He'd seen that image, or one like it, many times. It was a human brain.

The image repeated itself on the alien opposite him. Then it swelled, seemed to go inside the brain. There were long, arcing things, and two oblong objects depicted there. More patterns flashed between them.

The alien near Altin ran its tentacles around the machine, touching things, inserting the tips into holes. The image of what had to be Orli's brain moved to match the image on the alien's body bulb. The alien near Altin began to shift color some, turning pinkish and then a faded shade of burgundy.

The other alien flashed another brain image, briefly this time, different, though clearly human, but it passed too fast for him to pay attention to it.

The alien above him turned from burgundy to pale blue, then gray again.

There followed a brief exchange of patterns, then the alien holding Orli down released her arms. First one tentacle uncoiled, then the other. One tentacle released her left leg, and Altin dared hope they might let her go. Then the tentacle binding her right leg jerked her off the table and flung her away like a bit of trash.

Altin watched her sail off into the darkness. Then she was gone, leaving him to scream her name.

Chapter 17

Black Sander related the last part of the story to the marchioness, who sat upon a couch that was embroidered with quotes from her long-departed father, the Margrave of South Mark, last to fall in the great war that had finally brought all of Kurr under one rule a pair of centuries back. She'd been particularly attentive as Black Sander related the part about Jefe's desire to take back the place called Texas. Now that Black Sander's report was done, she sat quietly, a faraway look in her eyes as she absently stroked the barrel of a Colt M-9XR laser rifle, one of several weapons Black Sander had delivered to her. "Absolute state of the art," El Segador had said of it.

Black Sander stood quietly, watching her, waiting. He had nothing more to say. He'd been paid. He needed to get back to Murdoc Bay and see about sourcing more stray wizards. It was not the sort of crop that was going to be in ready supply.

As if reading his mind, the marchioness finally spoke. "They've sent five hundred sorcerers to Earth," she said. "Enchanters, all of them." She set the weapon down beside her. It lay upon a quote that read: *With its eyes open, the littlest basilisk makes statues of dragons.* "I hope your friends are not foolish enough to go after them."

"I cannot say, My Lady. Jefe and his man El Segador are aggressive. And well connected."

"Well, they'll all have some sort of devices in them," she said. She rose and went to a long table that sat beneath a mirror of the same length on the wall. She pulled a shiny object from a plastic crate sitting there, a half-span steel bar with a black-handled grip at one end. She pressed the button at its base, and it began to hum. She turned back to him. "What did you call this again?"

"It's an ion baton, My Lady. Don't touch it on anything. It's like a stick of lightning magic without the flash."

She grinned and pushed the button again. The humming went away.

"What did you mean by 'devices in them,' My Lady?"

"I meant exactly what I said." She fingered a handheld laser pistol, one of several, stroking it like it was a beloved pet. "Something the Earth people insisted be stuffed inside their bodies somewhere, wizard and blank alike. A very small machine that allows them to be tracked at all times."

Black Sander nodded. That was good to know. "I will mention it," he said. "Although I suspect men like Jefe and El Segador will already be aware of such things. It is likely a common practice on their world. Like the runes we tattoo onto criminals here on Prosperion for the diviners to find."

"Indeed." She went to the last crate on the table, where the rifles were. "Speaking of which, my diviners have twice caught Crown City diviners divining me. I do hope that none of your local boys have thought to profit from both sides."

"They haven't, My Lady."

"Well, don't you think it odd that that gold-plated imbecile in Crown should be poking around at me just now? What with all her ... other activities?"

"She's never trusted you, My Lady. It hardly seems a

surprise. Who knows what might have slipped from Lord Vorvington's tongue. He is a heavy drinker, after all."

She spun on him then, her eyes turned to slits. "You will fail me far sooner than Vorvington ever will, commoner." She spat that last as if it were the worst of epithets.

Black Sander realized he'd stepped on an enchanted stone with that one, so he apologized immediately. He began moving toward the door. His business here was done anyway. For now.

"May I go, My Lady?"

She turned back to the box of rifles. "Is this all there is?"

"No, My Lady. There are five more cases of each at Gevender's. For now. And we have accounts under various names on Earth with NTA credits totaling three and a half million."

"Is that a great amount?"

He nodded toward a parchment lying on the end table near the couch, where the marchioness had been sitting moments before. "I've included the conversions for NTA credits to gold crowns and silver marks on that list. The NTA is very efficient about posting that sort of thing on the global net."

She returned to the couch and took up the document. Her lips curled in. The lines radiating around the grim stretch of her mouth looked like little shadow flames. "I want a thousand of each," she said. "Everything in those boxes. Can he deliver that?"

"I don't know, My Lady. But I imagine that he could given a little time."

"See to it. And see to your men. If one of them is leaking information, I want his heart on a plate."

"Yes, My Lady. Will that be all?"

"No. There is one other thing."

He tilted his head, expectant, his hands curling the wide brim of the hat he held as he waited.

"On the subject of leaked information: I need you to leak something for me. And I need it leaked so that it gets to the director of the NTA."

Black Sander did not allow his expression to reveal the volume of his curiosity. "Yes, My Lady?"

"Can you do it?"

"Of course."

"Then let them know about Sir Altin Meade."

"My Lady?"

"He's been captured by aliens, you fool. Don't you read the *Crown City Sentinel*?"

"Of course I do. So do the people at the NTA. I'm certain they are already aware."

"But are they aware that Her Majesty intends to leave him there?"

"She what? But I thought Meade was her favorite. The Galactic Mage. He's a pet."

"It seems he *was*. I've got news that a plea was made to her to send *Citadel* to rescue Sir Altin and the new Lady Meade. The appeal came from the Earth woman's friend, the captain of that spaceship we've seen flying toward the plantations. Our plotting monarch gave him platitudes and vague promises, but would not commit. Even Tytamon the Ancient could see it, for he was there and misses little. The royal fool yawned and promised, and sent them away. And then, three days ago, Vorvington saw a *Citadel* teleporter delivering something to the Lord Chamberlain to give to the Queen. It was a collection of seedlings."

"I don't understand, My Lady."

"Idiot! There are no plants on the red world. Sir Altin is not on a planet where anything grows."

"Perhaps *Citadel* is fighting Sir Altin's captors on a different alien world. Perhaps the aliens have taken him away."

"They haven't." She went to the far side of the room, to

another table, upon which sat a small black box made of enchanted tarwood. She took off the lid, and a mirror appeared, the box expanding in an instant and becoming quite large, with the mirror sticking up out of it even larger. The mirror was beautiful, its frame made of carved bones that twisted around one another. A sizable emerald was mounted at the top of the frame, and in the gaps of the contours were carved tiny replicas of the fleet ships upon which the first humans from Earth had arrived.

The marchioness closed her eyes, and for a moment she was silent, her expression consistent with one engaged in telepathy. She opened them shortly after and pulled the smashed remnants of a small fleet communications device, one of their collar pins, out of a fold in her skirts. She touched the emerald with one hand and pushed the rumpled com button into a slot near the bottom of the mirror with the other.

Black Sander moved closer. He was well aware that the mirror was enchanted. He'd been the one to get it for her. He understood that it had been enchanted by Sir Altin Meade himself, a gift for Orli Pewter back before she'd become his wife, locking sight magic that was bound to her into the mirror. He had made it so that he could find her and speak to her through it, though much of the speaking part was wound into associations with Earth ships and technology, the magic woven together by those inexplicable cross-school strands that only a wizard who was a Seven or Eight could do. It was a monstrously complicated spell, exquisitely complex, and it had been woven so tightly around Sir Altin's lover, around them both, that it was almost useless to anyone else at all. But the marchioness' Z-ranked seer, the idiot savant Kalafrand, had managed to burrow into the enchantments well enough that the marchioness could spy on Orli now, if only visually. Kalafrand had somehow muddled the mirror's listening ability when he'd wormed his way into what Altin Meade had cast. But seeing was enough, and as long as Orli was near her new husband, the marchioness could also spy on him, the Queen's Galactic Mage.

"Look for yourself," she said once she'd finished the process Kalafrand had given her for activating the enchantment. "There is the wife of Sir Altin Meade."

In the mirror was the image of the Earth woman. She was encased in something dark and yellow. She wore one of the suits the Earth men wore when they went outside their ships or tramping about on alien worlds, places where there was no air or no air that was any good. There were no lights blinking on the suit like Black Sander knew there usually were. She did not move. She did not blink.

"Is she dead?"

"I have no idea," replied the marchioness. "But wait. It gets more interesting."

There came a knock on the door.

"Enter," said the marchioness. In came Kalafrand. The marchioness did not turn to greet him. "Show him what we found the other day," she said, stepping away from the mirror and gesturing for the lumbering seer to draw near.

Kalafrand said nothing and set his hands on either side of the pale gray frame. He closed his eyes and chanted for a time. The image of Orli grew smaller as the perspective in the mirror moved away some, drawing back to a vantage two spans distant.

"Stop," the marchioness commanded. She pointed with the negligible tipping of her head. "Look who's there with her. Like little bugs in amber."

Next to her in a very dark place was the Galactic Mage. He too was encased in the yellow material, and he too wore a spacesuit that had no lights glowing on it. Both of them had three dark lengths of some kind of tubing pushed into the amber-like material they were in, all of which drooped like limp rope from them and then disappeared into darkness at the edge of the mirror's vision.

Black Sander stared at the two figures for quite some time, and the marchioness let him. "Their eyes are open," he said after a while. "Yet they do not blink. I think they are dead."

The marchioness grinned. "That, my friend, is what I want you to get out."

"But why?"

She turned back to Kalafrand. "Go on, pull out all the way and show him the hole."

Kalafrand pulled back the view in the mirror so rapidly that in seconds they were staring down on a vast spread of land, a red land ravaged by churning winds. Plumes of red dirt blew into the air and smeared the clouds like filthy paint, the whole of the place a great, violent tempest. Still, visible through all that were four dull shapes that dominated the landscape, long greenish-brown objects, nearly identical. They lay in a formation around a large expanse of the red land, at the center of which was a massive hole. The thickest plumes of red sand blew up out of that cavernous opening.

Black Sander studied it for a time. "What am I looking at?" he asked.

"An excavation," she announced. "Those four monstrosities are the ships of the aliens who took Altin Meade and the Earth girl. They've been at this dig for two straight weeks."

"What are they digging for?"

"Vorvington says they're after the heart of a rekindled Hostile world."

"I don't understand."

"Of course you don't. And you don't need to. The point is, look at them. What do you see?"

Black Sander stared into the mirror for another long stretch of time. It was hard to know what to make out of it all. He started piecing together details. It was difficult to tell how big the mountains behind the ships were, but if they were anything like Prosperion mountains, then those spaceships had to be very large. Measures and measures large. Which meant, by comparison, the hole was large too.

"It's all very massive," he said. He knew that wasn't what she was looking for.

"No, you fool. Look. What don't you see?"

What was he supposed to say to that? "I don't know, My Lady. I confess you have the advantage of knowing what your purpose is."

"There are no Prosperions, you dullard. Where is the rescue? Where are the siege craft? Where are the allies from Earth in their machines?"

Black Sander looked back and saw that it was true.

"Perhaps the rescue is still in the planning stage."

"Even if I thought that was true, how well do you think the people of Crown City will take it, learning that their beloved Galactic Mage and his Earth bride are so low a royal priority that now, two weeks after his abduction, she has done nothing?"

"Not well, My Lady."

"And the people of Leekant?"

"Even worse."

"And imagine this: what if the people of Prosperion, and the people of Earth, discovered that aliens have come through that opening and are now digging down to a new heart that has been placed in that world? A new heart meant to bring it back to life! The world that killed over a million people between our two planets. How do you think the people will take *that* news, as they still weep each night over their dead? How popular do you suppose that will make the War Queen when the people learn that she allowed it to happen?"

"Not popular," he said. "But as I understand it from my

sources, the heart of that world was easily destroyed last time with the use of fleet explosives. Lady Meade did it herself. Surely the NTA will have required measures be taken before they would allow the resurrection of the Hostile. They lost more lives than we did. I am no expert in the war-making ability of planet Earth, but I know enough now to understand that the simple push of a button would be enough to detonate incendiary devices placed there. It seems implausible to me that anything less would have been acceptable to them—assuming they were consulted, which I can't believe they would not have been. Reason suggests the threat from that Hostile source could not be counted credible. It is surely already locked into the guillotine."

"Since when does the general populace need a credible threat to fear? A plausible story is all they require, and even an implausible one will suffice if the message is delivered with style."

Black Sander nodded. That much was true. And if the outrage of the War Queen having abandoned the Galactic Mage to aliens wasn't enough to incite the people to anger, surely the threat of danger brought on by a reckless ruler could be set into the public's collective mind. Many weren't too happy with her anyway, not after the war, regardless of the outcome. The sweaty glow of victory dulls in the dust of digging graves.

"But what if she does launch a rescue?" he asked. "It may truly be that she is setting plans in motion as we speak. Those alien vessels are very large. Like laying siege to a city, I should think."

"You and I both know Crown City can have battalions in place in less than half a day. Even if she were arranging for reinforcements from Earth—war vehicles and those delicious walking armor machines of theirs—well, they'd still be there by now. The TGS has been working for over a year. She's got more than ample resources to execute a rescue."

Black Sander frowned as he stared into the mirror. "So why aren't they there fighting, then? Is she afraid of the aliens? Are those ships a threat that we, Earth and Prosperion combined, cannot thwart?"

"For the last two, I have no answer. I do not know. But for the first, I can. She is not there fighting because she is fighting elsewhere."

"She's what?"

"She's gotten us into another war already. One that has already begun."

He turned from the mirror to regard her. "It has? With whom?"

"She's kept that secret well, so far. But soon, very soon, I will know. She's not the only one with a stable of diviners, you know. I'll dig it out of her. Then things will change."

Chapter 18

Pernie was impatient for the school day to end. It was the start of her third week, and finally Sophia was going to let her walk home from the bus stop alone. The woman had been babying her since she got to Earth, and Pernie was more than ready for some alone time. She would have had some a week ago if she could have figured out how to get out of the house without setting off the alarms, but that place had more wards on it that any nobleman's castle ever did. All she'd done was unlock one window and slide it open, intent on having a look around in the dark—since there sure wasn't any way Sophia was going to let her go out and explore the city during the day, apparently—and off went the sirens. The alarms were so loud she would have thought orcs were pouring down from the mountains to invade the whole city. Lights had come on in the yard, dogs around the neighborhood barked, and that was it. Pernie got caught.

"You can't just go out in a city like Reno at night," Sophia Hayworth said. "There are people who go about at night who aren't the sort a little girl ought to meet—and, yes, that includes little girls who have been taught by Prosperion elves how to defend themselves, do you hear?"

Pernie heard her, all right. But mostly she heard the alarms. It was like being in prison. But fortunately, she did have Don on her side. Don Hayworth was not fixated on danger and safety all the time like Sophia Hayworth was. In fact, the very next morning, while Pernie was putting on her scratchy clothes getting ready for school, she heard Don and Sophia arguing over what Pernie had done.

"She's not like other kids," Don said. "And she's definitely not like Angela. You can't just stuff her in her room and expect her to be content devouring books."

"But she is!" Sophia Hayworth said. "She's already through the third grade material. That's a whole grade level every week. She'll be ahead of them all in two months if she can stay on course."

"I didn't say she isn't smart. I said she isn't Angela. She's an outdoor girl. You've got to let her run sometimes. Let her look around. You read Angela's last email from Calico Castle. That's not an ordinary kid in there."

"I did read it, and that only makes it more important we keep her where we can see her."

"You need to trust her, honey. She needs to be free to make some mistakes."

"Angela didn't need to make mistakes."

"Yes, she did."

Pernie didn't know what that meant exactly, but he said it in a weird way, and the kitchen got pretty quiet downstairs for a while. Pernie was putting her hair up in the requisite ponytail—because apparently she was supposed to look just like all the other dumb little horses in the herd—when she heard Sophia say, "Fine. So what do you want me to do? Just open up all the doors at night? Should I get her a gun, so if she wanders all the way downtown, she can defend herself?"

"Honey," came Don's reply, part empathy, part exasperation. "How about you just let her walk home from the bus by herself? How about just that to start? None of the other kids her age have parents walking them back and forth. I think she can handle that."

More silence followed. Pernie decided she definitely liked Don Hayworth the best. They'd played baseball last weekend, and Pernie hit every ball he threw at her. She could see how he was going to throw it before he even let it go. It was like watching sugar shrimp, and she paid attention to his fingers on the ball. And he was much slower than an elf when it came to the rest of him. His body gave away what he was doing well before any motion was complete. So Pernie "dinged" every one of them, as Don had said. He said she could make a hundred million credits a year as a professional baseball player one day, playing for one of the NTA corporate teams.

Pernie thought that sounded pretty weird. Why would anyone pay people to play a game? Besides, money was boring. Everyone on this planet talked about money all the time. Talking about money had made Jeremy cry, although Pernie still didn't quite know why. Nobody talked about money when she was growing up, and the people at Calico Castle had more of it than almost anyone.

But today was the day she was going to walk home from the bus stop by herself, so none of that other stuff mattered at all. She just had to get through lunch, and a few more hours of class. Then she was finally going to explore her neighborhood, maybe even go up into the mountains rising up so temptingly all around. She wondered what kind of creatures lived up there. She hoped there was something she could tame like she had tamed Knot.

She missed Knot a lot. Djoveeve had told her she wasn't supposed to use any magic, not even telepathy, but twice now, late at night, she'd sent a bare little flicker to her bug back on String, just to make sure he was okay. He was. He was doing his bug thing, under the low clouds of the wispy ferns, running around in the powdery yellow dust, sucking dry the eyeballs of any creature that grew weary and slept, laid low by the dust's effect. Pernie was glad he was happy, and she'd let the sounds of the jungle calm her, heard through the vibrations he sensed in all those tiny feet of his. She could listen to the jungle, to the rustle of the other bugs, and forget about the frustrations of her long, book-learning days.

She didn't think there would be any creatures quite like him in the woods, because Sophia Hayworth said there weren't any animals—or people—on Earth that had any magic at all. But Don had been quick to point out that, technically, nobody actually knew that for certain. He told Pernie that there might be creatures on Earth with magic; people just didn't know how to tell. He told her that long ago the native inhabitants of Reno and surrounding areas used to believe that animals had magic. He said that it still might be so.

Sophia Hayworth had rolled her eyes and said, "Don, you're going to confuse the poor girl. She just got here. Can we stick to the facts for now?"

He'd shrugged across the dinner table at Pernie after that one, and it was then that she'd begun to see him as something of an ally.

"Miss Grayborn?" asked Mrs. Beckman, apparently for the second time. "I don't see you working. Are you having trouble, or do you have the answer already in your head?"

What answer? She must have drifted off. Pernie looked up at the big board monitor at the front of the class. Mrs. Beckman had written a math problem up there. A missing-number problem. Pernie still couldn't figure out the purpose of making math problems with letters in them, being that letters were supposed to be for spelling, but the answers were always obvious anyway. "Seventeen," she said. "The X is seventeen." She sounded bored, because she was bored. The other kids all looked up from their desktops at her. She shrugged.

Math was the worst. She thought it was boring. Not because she thought doing it was boring, she actually kind of liked that part, but because they moved through it so slow. Sophia Hayworth had already gotten her through the math program for the whole year. She said Pernie was as good as her own daughter, Angela, at math. "Now if you would just put more effort into reading, writing, and history," she would say. Pernie didn't care about history, and she didn't have anything to write about. She didn't mind reading, though. She just only liked reading stuff that wasn't boring.

Mrs. Beckman grinned a big smile at her. "That's correct. Very good, Miss Grayborn." She did that a lot.

There followed two more problems, but Pernie was looking out the window at the mountainside. She wished she were there. She wished she were flying over it in one of the NTA fighter planes, dropping bombs on the orcs that came to invade the town. She wished she could go that fast. Faster than Knot. Faster than Taot. Faster than "the speed of sound" Jeremy had told her. That's how fast Pernie wanted to go.

Fortunately, Mrs. Beckman didn't call on her for the other math problems, the ones she called *algebra*, and soon enough the drone of the bell marked that it was time for lunch.

As regular as the bell itself, Jeremy was standing beside her while the rest of the class cleared out. She had already shut her desk down, so she got up and led the way out of class. They joined the herd of tablet tappers and visor zombies moving toward the cafeteria. She glanced down at the screen on the tablet of one boy as she swerved around him to get by. He was playing something where two men were depicted, fighting with swords. One of them, wearing red armor with pauldrons that were way too thick and wide to be useful, lunged at the other figure, who was wearing blue pants and black boots but no armor at all, not even a shirt. That was probably better than the bulky, impossible armor of the first.

The red warrior's lunge was a fake. He followed with a second one that was so slow Pernie wondered why the blue warrior didn't take his throat out and maybe make a pot of tea in the interim. The blue warrior made a low, sweeping kick instead, which was dumb given the opening he had, and then the red warrior cut off his head.

A boy behind Jeremy shouted, "Hah. Ritchie, you suck. I own you."

"No, you don't. You got lucky. I missed my combo."

Pernie listened to them for a moment and realized the boy behind Jeremy was the one who'd been playing the red-clad fellow with the unlikely armor.

"Is that some kind of fight simulator?" Pernie asked the boy near her. "Like the flight simulators I read about over at the fort?" She'd been reading about pilot training over the last few nights, and found out that there was a huge NTA fortress nearby called Fort Reno. People learned how to fly fighter planes there, and even how to fly spaceships like Roberto did.

The kid beside her stopped, saw who it was, and recoiled. He stepped away from her as if she were about to stab him with a real sword.

The other boy stepped up in his place and smiled winningly. "Kind of," he said. He was taller than Pernie by almost two full hands—or eight inches in Earth measurements. He had thick, wavy hair, dark and combed back over his head, dark enough that it really set off his very light blue eyes. "It's a game: *Blades of Death XIV: Return of the Lich.*"

"What do you win?" Pernie asked, stopping to take the tablet he turned toward her so she could see.

"Nothing," he said, still grinning. "Except telling people that they suck." He made a face at his friend, who was still standing a step away. Jeremy stopped and waited beside her, shifting uncomfortably.

"You're that alien girl, aren't you?" the tall boy asked. "From Prosperion."

Pernie nodded, but she was looking at the game. "How do you make it work?"

He showed her, quickly going through the controls. "Combinations are here," he said, showing her how to find the list on the game's menu screen.

She perused the list and clicked to the second page, then the third. "Are there more, or just these three pages?"

He laughed. "That's sixty-four combos," he said. "Most people only use ten or twelve."

She found an entry called "practice" and opened it. There were several warriors depicted to choose from. She picked the one that looked most like her, even though it was a much older woman with bosoms that were larger than her head. She had blonde hair at least, and she fought with a quarterstaff that wasn't so much different than a spear.

She went through the motions, getting the feel of the controls. There weren't that many buttons along the edges of the tablet, and only so many more around the edges of the screen. The image of the warrior woman leaped and spun about. The quarterstaff made very loud noises that didn't sound anything like reality, but there were nice streaks of color that followed in the wake of spins, cuts, and thrusts.

"Okay, so how do we play?" she said, cutting off something the boy was saying in midstream.

"You want to play ... against me?" His brow crinkled to convey the absurdity of the idea, but his smile suggested he was happy to oblige.

"Why not?" Pernie asked.

He laughed, mostly an air sound through his nose. He leaned over and looked at her screen. "Well, don't use Starfaze. She's weak, and that quarterstaff sucks until you unlock her fourth power—and even that sucks compared to Raven or Princess Drax, if you want to play a female."

"I like her," Pernie said.

"It's your funeral," he said. "Ritchie, give me yours."

Ritchie handed his tablet to his friend.

"Prepare to go down ... uh ... What's your name, anyway?"

"Her name is Pernie," Jeremy blurted. He said it very suddenly, and it sounded odd. He stood beside her now, but then didn't say any more.

The tall boy looked at him, gave a dismissive sniff, and returned his attention to Pernie. "Okay," he said. "Accept my request."

A square appeared over the top of the blonde woman with the huge bosoms and the quarterstaff. Pernie supposed her name must be Starfaze.

The image shifted. She was looking at eight small squares across the screen, each depicting a scene, like the set of a traveling minstrel's play. "Where you want to fight?" he said. "Arena is easiest. Ghetto has lots of stuff to climb. Desert is good for your quarterstaff because you can flick stones, Mars is fun because—"

Pernie clicked the first one on the list. It looked like some kind of purple street. A moment later she saw her figure, Starfaze, standing there. The man in the oversize armor stood opposite her.

"You ready?" the blue-eyed boy asked.

Pernie directed Starfaze up to him and struck him down. It only required three successive "combos" to do it. The last blow, called "Coup de Grace," had Starfaze pounding her opponent into the purple street with the butt of the quarterstaff.

Pernie frowned as she watched it, fake red blood spraying

everywhere as the body was mashed and pulverized into a pile of intestines and gore. Pernie's frown deepened as Starfaze put her hands on her hips, her head back, and laughed. The words "You Win" appeared on the screen.

The tall boy was staring at his screen as well, and he looked up with surprise upon his face. One side of his mouth began to turn up into a smile. "Damn," he said.

She handed him the tablet back and made a face.

"What's the matter?" the boy called Ritchie asked as she walked away. "Too much violence?"

Pernie turned back long enough to say, "That's not what guts look like." Then she and Jeremy went in to eat.

Chapter 19

As the bus came to a stop, Pernie looked out the window at the empty bench on the sidewalk. There was no Sophia Hayworth there today. Pernie smiled. She looked out past the bench to the tall buildings beyond the neighborhood. Some of them rose almost as high as the Palace did, though none of them were so broad and powerful. These were more like the uneven teeth of a very crooked bit of jaw. Horse teeth mostly, all squared off at the top, though there were a few sharp fangs to be seen. Many of them were still broken from the Hostile attacks during the war.

"I see they let you out on your own this time," the bus driver said. "You be careful out there, you hear? This here is a nice neighborhood, but don't you go off toward downtown."

Pernie got off the bus without saying anything and turned in the direction of Sophia Hayworth's house. She walked that way until the bus was gone around the block.

The nearest mountains were several measures away—several miles away. The toothy buildings were pretty close. If Sophia Hayworth was right and there really were no magic animals, she supposed the real adventure must be over there in "downtown." The bus driver was the second person who had worried about what was over there.

Pernie set off immediately.

The neighborhood itself quickly bored her. The houses looked the same, concrete structures poured by the big machines Jeremy called "printers." There was a street she traveled down on the bus ride to school that had several of them at work. The printers looked like four giant table legs to her, taller than a four-story house, and atop them were long metal beams. Attached to the beams, running across the space between the table legs, was a row of vats and hoses. The vats sat atop another beam that ran back and forth, and projecting from the bottom of the vats were pointed openings from which the concrete spewed. Jeremy said other things could spew out of them too. He told her they could make the whole house right there, plumbing, electrical, and all. He said in the old days before printers, people had to do it all. Pernie had seen enough things being built at home to think that Prosperion must be in the "old days."

So Pernie had watched over the course of her first two weeks of bus rides as two of the printers printed twelve houses in as many days. They all looked exactly alike, but Jeremy said people would paint them and dress them up so they took on "personality." Pernie wasn't too sure about that.

One thing she was sure about was that the whole neighborhood was made of lots of those same kind of houses. She noted that sometimes the design changed a little bit. Some blocks were made up of three-story houses, some made up with fours. Other blocks, like Sophia Hayworth's, were all one- or two-story homes.

Pernie used the towering buildings, viewed down streets and over the occasional patch of trees, to guide her on her way toward downtown. She passed by a park on the way. A man and two boys were there, sitting on curving plastic seats that hung from a frame. They were burning something and inhaling it through little tubes of glass. The man waved at her to come over, but Pernie ignored him. She didn't want to inhale anything through a tube of glass.

Downtown took longer to find than she thought it would, but eventually she was close enough to walk down its streets. The buildings were even taller than she'd thought they'd be. There were cars moving about everywhere. There were a lot more of them than there were in Sophia Hayworth's neighborhood.

Pernie wondered if she could get across to the other side. That seemed like it might be fun, but she thought they might likely stop. All the drivers were computers. The people in the driver's seats were really passengers. Jeremy told her that computers drove everything but fighter planes and that they even drove those sometimes too. That's when she found out that the bus driver on her bus didn't really do anything. He was just there to keep the kids out of trouble, apparently, and in case the computer malfunctioned. Jeremy said they never did, though. But he said humans made better pilots because they had better instincts, which was why he still had a lot of work to do on his android. Pernie did understand, though. It was the same reason the elves wanted a human to be Sava'an'Lansom.

Pernie decided to see if the computer drivers were as quick as an elf could be because, even if elves didn't have any instincts either, so far they were all much faster than she. At least all the ones she'd gotten to try to fight with, anyway. Which was really only one. Seawind. She wondered how fast the Queen's Royal Assassin must be. She thought he would be fun to fight with. Except that he would probably cut her up into little pieces right away. Just like Starfaze had pulverized the man in the oversize armor in the video game.

She looked left, then right, then left again. She assessed the speed of the vehicles coming from both ways. Three lanes each. Most of the vehicles had wheels, though there were a few of the fancier ones that flew by "antigravity." She was still trying to figure out how that worked. She didn't know enough science yet.

She figured she'd be better off not getting caught under anything with wheels, but she couldn't help wondering what would happen if one of the gravity cars went over her. She imagined it would feel hot, because the air grew sort of hazy under them, like it did in the courtyard at Calico Castle on hot summer days. Maybe it would burn her. It was probably best if she didn't find out. Maybe she'd ask Jeremy first, and then if he didn't know, she could try next time.

For now, she contented herself with just running between them all. She figured she could dodge them easily enough, for they weren't going very fast. Certainly not the speed of sound. Maybe as fast as a running horse was all.

She checked both sides once more and made her move.

A big truck in the nearest lane hissed to a stop. Pernie dove forward and rolled into the third lane. She knew there was a space between two cars that gave her time for that. She was on her feet and ready to dive for the median when she realized all the cars had stopped.

All of them.

The traffic in all lanes was at a complete standstill, up and down the street as far as she could see in both directions. The cars that had stopped in the nearest intersection formed Ts with those that had been coming the other way. Some of them were so close to each other that barely a hairbreadth separated front bumpers from driver's or passenger side doors, paused just short of collision.

Pernie turned and examined what she'd done. She stepped across the median and looked down the lanes both ways, all the way down and out of sight. It was all stopped. It was as if she'd stopped the whole city. She thought that was interesting. And fun.

She smiled at the man in the tall truck in the first lane. He had rolled down his window and was yelling at her. She turned back and saw that a lady had gotten out of the car across the median Pernie had just come over.

"Sweetheart, are you okay?" the lady asked.

"Yes," Pernie said. "They all stopped in time. Look." She pointed down the avenue, where the cars were still stopped everywhere. "That is very fast reflex. Even without instinct."

The lady made a face at that, but it quickly went away. "Are you sure you're all right? Where's your mother?"

"My mother is dead," Pernie said. "She has been for a long time."

"Oh!" said the lady, sounding startled. "I'm sorry. But, how about your father? Or your guardian? Who's supposed to be looking out for you?"

"My father died a long time ago too. Master Tytamon looked out for me the most, even though really it was Kettle who did. Master Altin was supposed to, too, but then the elves took me away when I tried to shoot Orli Pewter in the heart. Now Sophia Hayworth is watching me, but I don't need her to. I look out for myself most of the time. I don't need a guardian. Someday I will be the guardian of the High Seat, so they really need me."

The lady looked at Pernie for a time, her hands on her knees, her expression bewilderment. "Well, you shouldn't be out here all alone. You could have been hurt. And you've caused a traffic jam. Come on now, let me take you home." She reached out a hand for Pernie's. "Where do you live?"

"I can find my way," Pernie said. She turned and started across the street. She remembered what Sophia Hayworth had said, however, so she turned back because she was supposed to "try to be more polite." "Thank you for stopping to make sure I was okay." She smiled and then headed off across the street again.

When the lady finally got back into her car, and Pernie

was safely on the sidewalk, the traffic started up again. Pernie watched all the cars go. She saw the people in them staring at her. Some of them very angry, others laughing or smiling. Pernie smiled and waved at them.

She didn't think downtown was such a scary place. There were nice ladies who made sure you were okay, and there were cars that would stop the whole city just to make sure you were safe. She couldn't imagine what Sophia Hayworth was so worried about all the time.

Pernie made her way along the boulevard again. She spotted down one street, far to the left, a row of buildings that were still broken from the war. She wanted to go see them. She hoped maybe she would find a dead Hostile.

Master Altin and Orli Pewter had seen Hostiles. So had Roberto and even Master Tytamon. Pernie was practically the only person at Calico Castle who hadn't seen one yet. So off she went, her steps lively as a sprite.

The sidewalk got more and more broken the farther she went along. Weeds grew out of the cracks everywhere, and it seemed that nobody came along and picked the garbage up. Some of the garbage included broken cars, even a few of the fancy ones that didn't need wheels, or at least that hadn't needed them at one point in history.

Pernie went to each of them in turn, climbing inside and crawling over the seats. There were big holes in the front panels, and lots of wires hanging out. She could tell someone had torn out the vehicle controls. They weren't so unlike the control panel in the bus for her not to know it wasn't supposed to be like that.

In the backseats she found mostly garbage. There were lots of little tubes of glass that reminded her of the ones the man and the two boys in the park had been smoking through. She wondered if it was the same kind of smoke that Master Tytamon and old Nipper used, although they never smoked from little glass tubes. But she was rapidly coming to realize there were going to be many things that were different from Prosperion. Djoveeve had told her, "To blend with the enemy, you must bend with the enemy," but Pernie didn't think she was going to bend so far as that.

By the time she'd finished exploring her third trashed gravity car, the light was growing thin. The mountains threw a cool haze over the city, and the buildings began to shrink into it.

She hadn't even gotten to the broken ones yet.

She crawled out the broken back window of the gravity car she'd been exploring and dropped onto the sidewalk. She took off at a jog. If she hurried, maybe she could find one dead Hostile before heading home. She was sure if she ran the whole way, she could still make it back to Sophia Hayworth's house before it was too dark.

She realized a few blocks later that she needed to cut over another street to get to the biggest and most ravaged of the buildings. She spotted an alley that ran all the way through, so she turned down it.

There was a man relieving himself on a wall by a dumpster that was painted green. There were dumpsters just like it behind the cafeteria at school, but Pernie was pretty sure nobody got to pee behind them. She stopped and told him so. "That's a dirty thing to do, you know."

He turned to look at her, and she saw that the whites of his eyes were nearly as red as blood. What wasn't red was so hazy it was almost orange. He had red rims around them too, like old Djoveeve's were pink, but his face wasn't three hundred years old. She thought he might jump at her. He looked like a demon standing there, but she realized straight off that those red eyes were vacant and dull.

He smelled terrible.

She decided to ignore him and continued on. She could hear voices coming from the other end of the alley anyway. They sounded excited, young men shouting and whooping.

She could hear breaking glass. She thought they must have found a Hostile in the rubble. She ran to see.

There were seven of them, all boys. They were older than she was, but not by a lot. Maybe the older two were past eighteen. The youngest couldn't have been much more than twelve.

They were throwing bottles at someone who was running away down the alley across the street. They were laughing and swearing like the man in the stopped truck had been.

She didn't think the retreating man was a Hostile, but she stopped and watched.

The man was soon out of range of the last bottle the boys could find, and the one boy who'd been chasing the man left off chasing him and started back. He was the one who saw Pernie first. He made a face, although Pernie couldn't quite make it out in the darkness that was settling in, and he pointed. His friends turned to see what he was pointing at. They saw Pernie all at once.

"What the hell are you doing down here?" the twelve-year-old said. She could tell he was trying to sound tough.

The other boys laughed at him and started teasing him with "Ooooh" and "Ohhh."

"You're so damn scary, aren't you, Artol," said one of the older boys.

"Yeah, Jesus, Artol. Where was that shit back at the liquor store?"

The oldest of the boys approached her. He came with his head tilted sideways and sort of stooping some, one hand out as if Pernie were a stray animal that got loose from some neighbor's yard.

"Hey there, little girl," he said. "What are you doing out after sundown? Didn't your mommy tell you there would be bad people out?"

"Is that who he was?" Pernie asked, pointing down the alley across the way. The dark silhouette of the running man was just then turning down into the other street.

The young man turned to his companions and gave them a what-the-fuck? look, at which they all burst into laughter again.

"Oh, yeah," said the young man, sounding earnest. "He was bad. Super bad. But don't worry, we chased him away so he can't hurt a pretty girl like you."

He looked back to his friends, made a question of his lips and the way he kinked his head.

Two of the boys just a bit younger than he was seemed to understand the expression and cringed, though it was barely visible. They shook their heads and backed a step away.

"Aw, come on," said the older boy. "Don't be pussies."

"I don't know, man. What are you thinking?"

"I don't know. I'm just saying. Nothing. Whatever."

"Maybe she's got money," said one of the boys who'd backed away. "She's got the look of a spoiled piece of crap. Just loot her ass."

The nearest boy stepped forward. "Come here," he said. "You got your mommy's net card on you?"

A black-haired boy with an unruly puff of hair stepped forward to stand beside the nearest one. "She won't have no net card, fool. Look at that shit she wearin'. Fuckin' scanner baby, man."

"Then we'll take her prints and irises with us to a casino. Get some chips." The eldest of them lunged at her, intent on snatching her off the ground.

Ducking under and stepping away from him was easier for Pernie than dodging game attacks with Starfaze had been.

The other boys went into hysterics as their elder friend stumbled two steps into the alley as Pernie dodged his lunge. He turned back and looked at her. "What the ...?"

Pernie would have answered, but the twelve-year-old

shouted, "Five-oh. Five-oh," and took off sprinting down the alley in the direction the "bad man" they'd been throwing bottles at had gone. Two more of the boys were right after him.

Pernie looked down the street where the boy had pointed. Blue-and-red lights were flashing so brightly they lit up the walls of the buildings up and down the street. A car approached.

"Shit," said a couple of the other boys, and they took off as well. The oldest made to run down the alley from which Pernie had come, but she tripped him as he launched into motion, her foot darting between his ankles in the time it took for him to think. He staggered several steps, trying to catch his balance, and then crashed headlong into the side of the dumpster where the red-eyed man had been peeing only a few moments before. Pernie didn't know where that man had gone.

The car with the flashing lights pulled up in front of the alley and turned a bright spotlight down that way. Pernie, barely a pace away from the car, had to blink into its blinding brightness and ultimately turn away.

"You there, by the dumpster, don't move," came a very loud voice over a tinny-sounding projection mounted to the car. It looked like a very short trumpet to Pernie's Prosperion eye.

The young man had disentangled himself from the soggy refuse near the dumpster and was starting to run away again.

Two hissing sounds issued from the car, *fffft, fffft*, and Pernie saw the young man stagger again, pitch forward, and fall face-first to the ground. He slid for a few Earth feet and then lay motionless.

Two men emerged from the car then. Pernie saw their boots sticking out from under the blinding glare of the spotlight, which hid the rest of them.

"Are you Pernie Grayborn?" one of them asked.

Pernie blinked into the glare. "Yes," she said. "Who are you?"

"Reno PD," came the reply. "We got a missing persons report from a Sophia Hayworth that matched a report from a commuter earlier today. Miss Hayworth is worried sick about you and, if I'm honest, pretty pissed."

"So?" Defiance cemented itself in place upon her face.

"She wants you home, young lady. And she wants you home now."

"So?" Pernie repeated. "She's not the Queen, you know? She's not even my mother." Pernie hated it when people told her what to do. Especially strange men hiding behind bright lights.

"Well, she's your legal guardian, so that's good enough. Now come along. We're going to take you home."

Pernie thought about running, but she looked back at the man lying face-first in the alley and thought it might not work out any better for her than it had for him. Not with whatever that was that had gone hissing by her. She shrugged. "Fine," she said. "But I don't need a guardian."

Chapter 20

Roberto was trembling as he stood before the Queen, and it damn sure wasn't out of fear. At least not fear for himself. The only reason he hadn't launched himself into a complete fit of profanity was because the last remark out of his mouth had prompted the Royal Assassin to appear. The elf, whose place near the golden throne was well known but seldom visibly occupied, shimmered, and then there he was, a lean figure of black-armored death, decked in leather that did not creak when he moved, and which bristled with the hilts of daggers and knives of varying size, all protruding from this joint and that seam. His appearance garnered gasps from the assemblage of courtiers and petitioners and even a smattering of applause from a group of schoolchildren who'd been brought in on a field trip. Their visit to the throne room was cut short right after, however, for the Queen sent all visitors and courtiers away with a "Get out, get out, all of you!" All but Roberto and Deeqa Daar, that is.

When at length the Queen addressed Roberto again, her tone was as tight as a piano wire—which on Prosperion most people thought of as a garrote.

"Captain Levi, it is only by my appreciation for that abundant confidence of yours, which earned you your teetering privilege here, that I do not have you carted off and flogged. But you test me too far if you continue in such fashion." She tipped the royal scepter backward toward the Royal Assassin standing near her elbow. "You see how you've made my serpent come slinking from his hole?"

"Your Majesty, I mean no disrespect, but it isn't fu—it isn't right." He somehow managed to self-censor most of the profanity. He really was trying not to completely lose his cool. "It's been sixteen days. I've got nothing. The TGS people won't send me back to the red planet. They won't even tell me why."

"They are not yours to command, Captain. And I must tell you, I believe the fortune I am so rapidly making you has quite gotten to your head."

"Fuck the money!" he snapped. So much for self-censorship. "My friends are dying up there, and nobody is doing a goddamn thing. Bahri can't get there because your people—the ones who are clearly not mine to command—won't send any fleet ships to Yellow Fire either. They won't. Bahri tried. General Pewter sent the request. I thought this whole TGS thing was supposed to be a joint venture—you know, where both sides give a shit equally."

The Queen's scrutiny narrowed, and Deeqa, standing next to Roberto, put her hand on his arm. Roberto looked up at his copilot, his eyes ablaze with frustration and rage. She looked deeply into them, her own eyes, dark and patient to his dark and furious, speaking a warning that he trusted her enough to heed.

"Your Majesty," said Deeqa then. "If I may speak."

The Queen waved her scepter in the air in front of her. "If you think you can do so with some restraint. I admit I have need of you both ...." She paused and seemed to let go some of the energy that Roberto's semi-tantrums were winding up in her, before going on. "I really do." She looked at Roberto. "Good Captain, I do. We are friends. I need you to have some faith." To Deeqa she said, "Go on, my dear. Speak."

"The trouble is that the aliens must be almost at the depth of Yellow Fire's heart by now. The original estimates were that it would take them three weeks. It's been over two weeks now. We have no idea what will happen when they reach that depth, but it is my opinion that they are after the heart stone. Maybe even the Liquefying Stone around it. All of it. Given how rapidly they can dig, I believe"—she looked at Roberto—"we believe that once they are down to the main cavern, they'll clear it all out and be gone in a matter of days. If they go back through that wormhole—which is what we believe it to be—well, then Sir Altin and Orli will simply be gone. Forever."

"Not forever. My diviners will find them if that happens," the Queen replied, waving that last bit off. "You forget, dear girl, that we Prosperions have gifts your people do not. We are quite adept at finding things."

Deeqa inclined her head, accepting that. "This is true, Your Majesty. And a great gift it is. However, what can your people do if that rift in the space above the planet opens into another dimension? Or perhaps just into another place in space and time? Do you have magic for that?"

The Queen harrumphed and looked irritated. She glanced over her shoulder at the Royal Assassin, who did nothing but watch Roberto.

"My point is not to cause trouble, Your Majesty," Deeqa continued. "I merely wish to ... augment Captain Levi's point. Failure to act immediately could mean the absolute last we ever see of Orli and your Galactic Mage."

She harrumphed again. "Send for Guildmasters Alphonde and Meste," she called out to the herald standing near the doors.

"Yes, My Queen," he said, and shuffled past one of the two Palace guardsmen in their gold-trimmed armor and crimson capes.

"I really just need news, Your Majesty," Roberto said. "I know you need the money ... for whatever secret reasons you won't tell me." He made no attempt to hide how irritated that secrecy made him given how much work and stress that need was putting on him just now. "But I can't concentrate on your heaps of money if I'm spending my energy worried about Orli and Altin all the time."

"Well, I hired you because I thought you were the sort who can keep his head," she said, her own displeasure equally unveiled. "However, I will see what we can learn together, so that you can put your mind to rest."

"My mind resting is only part of the point, Your Majesty. I want to know when *Citadel* is going to show up. And when I can expect the TGS to comply with the request of a two-star general."

"The two-star general is the father of one of the missing," the Queen pointed out. "And I advise you again, young man, to pull in your claws. We are not enemies here, and there are things you do not understand."

"Yes, Your Majesty. I am abundantly aware of that. I'm trying to be a good little soldier here, but I feel like you are making me fight blind."

"If I tell you to fight blind, Captain, you will do it. Now be silent." She turned impatiently toward the door.

As if by her command, the door swung open and in came the herald followed by three figures: a one-eyed old man, a black-robed woman of roughly thirty years, and an even younger redheaded woman in gray robes, who Roberto recognized as the teleporter Envette. The black-robed figure led the rest forward, and as she approached, Roberto could see that her face was gaunt and she had puffy circles beneath her eyes. Her hair hung lank and oily around her face and over her shoulders. Her robes were muddy, and altogether she had the appearance of one who has not bathed in many days. The other two looked no better.

"Guildmaster Meste," said the Queen, greeting the powerful young diviner as if the woman did not look like she'd just been summoned from a gladiator pit. "It's so nice to see you again." The War Queen's smile was tighter than her tone was, and Roberto saw something cautionary in the aspect of her eyes.

Cypher Meste curtsied, and returned the Queen's smile. "Thank you, My Queen." She took a place beside Roberto quietly. The Queen greeted the one-eyed Seers guildmaster, Master Alphonde, and the powerful young teleporter with equally confounding cordiality, though the two of them remained standing behind Roberto, Deeqa, and Guildmaster Meste.

Roberto glanced back when they did not come stand beside them and noticed that Envette's gray robes, besides being heavy at the hem and elsewhere splattered with mud, also had smears near the knees that looked more like blood than mud.

"Thank you for coming," the Queen said. "I know your present work keeps you busy these days. But Captain Levi here is being thwarted in his efforts to produce the funds so necessary to your work these days for worry over the fate of Sir Altin and Lady Meade. Has *Citadel* been working on that problem as I asked?"

Cypher Meste drew in a breath and spent a few seconds longer than Roberto thought she should have needed before finally speaking. "Yes, Your Majesty. We are working on it still."

Roberto waited a moment for more to follow, and when none came, he turned to look at her. She really did look terrible. Like she'd been sleeping under a bush in a rainstorm for at least a week. But she didn't have anything else to add, apparently.

He looked back to the Queen, but she didn't seem like she

intended to press. So he did.

"So ...?" he said. "What's going on? Where are they? Altin and Orli, are they out? Do you know where they are on the alien ship? It's a big ship. Is anyone going in there to get them? A hostage negotiator? Some diplomats? A body recovery team? What?"

The diviner kept her eyes on the Queen.

The Queen traced a half circle in the air with the end of her scepter, the end of which came finally to rest, pointing at Guildmaster Meste. The cessation of the scepter's motion coincided with the lifting of the royal eyebrows.

"We are not prepared to send anyone in just yet," the guildmaster diviner said.

Roberto looked from her to the Queen. That was obviously one of those truths that were still lies. He looked to Deeqa next, who, with the barest motion, shrugged.

"So whose blood is that?" he asked. He turned and pointed to Envette's robes. "Did something happen that you guys don't want to tell me about?" He turned back to the Queen. "Look, I'm not totally calling BS here, but ... come on. I'm not an idiot. There's a whole crapton you aren't telling me. How about some truth, here, eh?"

"Some situations are delicate, Captain," said the Queen. "But I give you this assurance: your friends—our friends— are still alive. Are they not, Guildmaster?"

"They are," said the young diviner. At least that truth didn't sound so much like it was hanging by the neck.

"You've seen them?" Roberto asked.

"I have."

"Like for real? Or in ... you know, the spooky mind stuff?" He wriggled his fingers in the air around his head.

She looked at him for the first time, genuine empathy in her eyes. "The spooky stuff. It's what I do. But Guildmaster Alphonde there has seen them too, with scrying spells and far sight. That is as good as with the naked eye." She tipped her head backward to indicate the guildmaster standing behind her.

Roberto turned back to face the one-eyed old man.

He nodded that it was true. "I've seen them," he said.

Roberto turned back. That was good news at least. "And how about the hole the aliens are digging? How close are they to Yellow Fire? Have they dug him up yet? How long until they set off the explosives we wired down there with all of that? Is he even still alive?"

"He is alive," Cypher Meste replied.

"Your answers are getting short again," Roberto said.

"You asked for truth," said the Queen.

Roberto stifled his next outburst, snuffing it to a low rumble in his chest. Once contained, he went on. "I just want to know how deep the hole is. I can't get any data on it. Are they through? I need to know how much time we have, in case what Deeqa told you about the wormhole is right."

Cypher Meste looked the question to the Queen, who nodded, saying, "Tell him."

"Not yet."

"How soon?"

"Four days. Five at most."

"So when are you guys going to make your move? Are you going to rush in and save Yellow Fire at the last minute? Are you waiting on something?"

Nobody said anything. Roberto watched them. His eyes narrowed as he started shaking his head. "Then what? You can't wait till they go in. It's all wired to blow. If they mess with the heart chamber, they might set off the ...." His voiced tailed off, and his mouth dropped open. "Oh my God." He looked, eyes wide, to Deeqa, then back. "You *are* waiting. That's it, isn't it? General Pewter or someone on Earth is waiting to push the button and blow it all up once the aliens get down there, aren't they? That's been the plan all along!

Nobody wanted Yellow Fire back to life anyway. That's what all this awkward short-sentences stuff is, isn't it?"

"Military strategy is not the role of a merchant ship captain, Captain," said the Queen. "Speculate as you will, but I've answered your questions, and I've done so despite your hotheadedness. I should think you will be grateful now, and have faith that I am doing everything that can be done in the face of an unusual and unanticipated alien threat."

"*Merchant* ship captain?" Roberto stared up at her, incredulous. "Is that all I am?"

"What was it that you thought you were doing, Captain? Do I need to get you a dictionary? Now move along. I have other matters to attend, and I'm sure you would prefer it—as would your friends Sir Altin and Lady Meade—if we returned these three wizards to *Citadel* so that they might continue their work."

Roberto started to say something, but Deeqa put a cool hand on his arm again. He was calm enough to bite the comment back. "Yes, Your Majesty." He had to say it through clenched teeth.

"Have faith, Captain. Do your part. You don't see all the pieces on the board just yet. We need money, good man. We need lots of it. For reasons I am not going to explain. Just do what you have agreed to do. Do your work, and I'll do mine. If everyone stays on course, it will all come out fine in the long run. Won't it, Guildmaster Meste?" She looked to the V-class diviner, who nodded but did not look Roberto in the eyes.

Chapter 21

Orli started when the loud pop sounded near her ear. She winced, and one eye closed reflexively. She had time to look up at the alien with its ass end pointed at her and realize the pop hadn't come from it. She turned and saw Altin standing there. His eyes were closed. He drew in a breath. A splatty liquid sound erupted with a whoosh from the alien just as a furnace seemed to open up right above her.

Altin had cast a fireball, launched at the alien's bulbous body like a meteor. She squinted in the glare of it, unable to help but watch. It all happened so fast she didn't even have time to hope it incinerated her captor. She merely witnessed.

The fireball appeared to strike the alien full on, but in the half second after, Orli realized the flames were wrapped around some form of shield. Then the fiery tongues of yellow and orange blew back at her on the wind. She turned her head away, reflexively trying to cover her face with her arms but unable to for being stretched taut by the alien's tentacles. The fire washed over her. It was almost like lying in Taot's breath the day the dragon blew its fire over Calico Castle's walls. Friendly fire, in the most literal of senses. Again.

This fire, unlike that day she fought against the orcs, was brief. The wind in the ship blew the flames over her quickly. She could feel her skin dry out, the sweat and the steam slicking her body evaporating instantly. But it was enough to spare her hideous burns.

She turned back to see if Altin was on fire. She dreaded seeing it. He was standing up. He would have been in the heart of the flames, unlike her, lying beneath the worst of it.

But he was not aflame. No, he was in a blob of the goddamn yellow jelly again. Just like when they'd first found themselves aboard the ship.

"Altin!" she called to him. She could see him calling back, through his helmet glass and through the goo. He looked heartbroken. And relieved. She smiled, wanting to comfort him. "Oh, Altin. I love you. We'll figure it out."

She saw him say something. She thought he was probably saying the same, trying to reassure her that they would get through this somehow. She saw him say, "I love you." That was clear. She smiled again. Then he was swearing. She could tell not so much by the recognition of word shapes upon his lips as by the rage in his eyes. It agonized her. He would be blaming himself, wanting to save her. The helplessness would burn him worse than a fireball.

Another alien arrived. It drew itself up over the machine. It reached a tentacle down and moved Altin in his blob aside. It snaked more tentacles up, and once again the machine was lowering down.

The two aliens spent time going through the same processes that the lone alien had, running the machine back and forth over her. Orli was sure they were irradiating her to sterility this time. Machines that big could hardly be delicate enough for human bodies. It just didn't seem possible.

The aliens flashed their light patterns back and forth, and she decided they had to be communicating in that way, probably talking about her like she were some rat in their lab. They were probably discussing who was going to cut her open or push the pin into her brain. Maybe they were congratulating themselves in anticipation of the accolades they would receive when they got back to their own world: "Why, look here at this new species that we've found. This one is a female. Just look at how she reproduces here. And look, a fine primitive brain." The other aliens would all flash their lights and pat the new heroes of scientific discovery on the bulbs with lots of bulb-patting tentacles. Praise for their new great prize, Orli Pewter of planet Earth. She sighed, then realized she was wrong. At least in that. She would die Orli Meade of Prosperion.

The tentacle holding her right arm let it go, followed by the one holding her left. Then her left leg was free. She started to sit up, wondering if this was it, the moment they were going to drive the probe into her prizewinning rat brain.

It wasn't.

With a great yank that felt as if it were going to jerk her leg right out of the joint, the aliens threw their prize away. Just like that, Orli was flying through the air.

She flew out over the edge of the machine and out over the grate—it reminded her of a waffle iron. It reminded her of looking down on the redoubts in *Citadel*.

The momentum of the toss carried her fifty yards or more, but soon she was falling down. She tried to expand herself, to catch the wind she'd been thrown into and glide, but she couldn't. It wasn't blowing hard enough to hold her up.

So she fell. The grate hurtled up at her. She was going to hit one of those thick protein beams, and that would be it.

She had to dive through one of the openings in the grate.

She angled herself and tried to use the wind that way. The grate grew closer.

She had to pick her target.

She could clear that one, she thought, spying one. Maybe. No, she'd hit it. The one before instead.

She ducked, dove down, sliced through the air like a hurtling spear.

She made it under the farthest beam framing the square gap, but her heels clipped the lowest edge of it. Pain shot up her legs as she spun from the impact, her head flung up when her feet rebounded off the rough surface. The impact threw her into a sprawling backspin, and right after, she dropped into a blast of wind going in the opposite direction as the current above the grate. It struck her in the chest and straightened her, blowing her back the other way for twenty feet. But she was still falling.

Toward the next grate.

It was barely four hundred yards away.

Three hundred.

Jesus!

She tried to flatten out and slow the fall again. Nope. Not enough to mean anything.

One hundred yards.

Fuck me!

She angled down again, getting a small measure of control over her flight. She calculated which gap she would have to dive through.

That one. No, that one.

The beams seemed to be so much wider than the gaps now.

She shot through the square patch of emptiness cleanly this time. No impact on her heels.

The wind coming the other direction hit her like a bus.

With her head down as it was, the blast rolled her over, bending her at the waist and spinning her wildly. Now she was dropping like a rock. She had to turn, twisting in the air, trying to get her bearings. She was only a hundred feet from the grate.

Shit.

She dove straight down and gauged she was going to get pushed by the wind right into a crossbeam, so she angled at the last second. She nicked her toes on the way through.

A blast of steam hit her as she passed through this time as well, blinding her. Her toes burned like they were in boiling water after grinding down the beam at speed. But she wasn't thrown off her trajectory, at least not until the switch in air current hit her again, blowing her back the other way. It flipped her over once more, but this time she adjusted more quickly and was soon angling down, plunging toward the next grate with the wind whistling in her ears.

There was a massive piece of machinery in the way.

She spread-eagled as best she could, made a sail of her slender body. A laser beam might have caught as much wind, at least so it seemed.

She tipped herself, yawing her body, trying to catch some help from the wind to blow her over the machine, give her a shot at a gap in the grate beyond it. She wasn't going to make it. The machine was too big. She was going to hit that thing at 110 miles per hour.

A blur of gray shot past her, just below her. An alien streaking by. Its billow nicked her as it went past, spinning her wildly out of control. She spun and caught a blast of air churned by its passing, which rolled her as she commenced falling again. She hit one of its trailing tentacles—or it hit her, it was impossible to know. She bounced again. The sinuous limb gave beneath her weight, but even so, the blast of pain that followed told her she must have broken a rib. She hit another tentacle right after. God, that hurt. She was spinning wildly now. A third tentacle, barely the tip, whipped up in the wind and smacked her across the back. The welt would be enormous if she lived.

She couldn't right the spinning, and she could barely

glimpse the grates whipping across her field of view. She couldn't even tell which grate she was looking at when she saw flashes of crossbeams spinning in her vision. Was that the one above or below?

The sound changed right next to her head. The wind faded some, echoed differently off something close. She saw a streak of the green-and-brown protein whistle past. The lull in the wind lasted a breadth of a second, then, *wham*, she was hit by a new blast of hot, steamy air.

She used it to stop the spinning. She flattened out again. The next grate was coming fast. She could see an end to it. An edge of the grate, like the rim of some great black chasm beyond it. She glanced out over the darkness. Way off in the distance, maybe a mile or two away, there were lights. Other grates in the distance, other levels. From here she could make them out fairly clearly. They were decks. Platforms one above the next. She could see below, like staring into a black abyss, that there were more going down into the darkness. Many more. Miles and miles of them.

The one immediately below her was coming up fast. She couldn't tell if she was going to clear the edge or not.

She wasn't. The wind was blowing her back over it, not out over the abyss.

She dove, got her angle right. She made it through another gap, three sections shy of the edge.

"God damn," she muttered as she passed through.

She turned and started angling back the other way, anticipating the change of wind. It came, just as she expected. It blasted her back the other way. At least that much was predictable!

She got her body under control right away, and fanned herself out enough to let the wind carry her out over the abyss. She looked up and saw that she must have just missed the edge of the grate above that last one. Maybe there was a God. Maybe just blind-ass luck.

She managed to get herself a good forty feet beyond the edge of the next platform, trying to get herself as far out over the abyss and away from the grate edges as possible. She wanted some space to work with so the next level's wind wouldn't blow her back over them again. She wasn't sure she could keep diving through the eye of the needle, so to speak.

She shot right by the platform, plenty of room to spare. She gritted her teeth. Some small measure of victory.

She rotated as she fell, staying flat and steering with the wind against her palms. She was ready for the next change of the wind.

It hit her just as she expected it to. She made an arrow out of herself, tried to knife through it as best she could, trying to avoid dealing with the grate.

No luck. It blew her back over the edge of the next level. She ended up having to dive through a gap again. But she made it, and only one gap from the edge. The next air current change would get her much farther out over the open space. She was sure she could prevent having to dare those damn gaps again after that.

The wind change hit her, and she was totally ready for it. She managed to angle almost two hundred feet away from the grate she was falling toward. Now she had it down.

She managed to be almost four hundred yards over the abyss by the next sequence of alternating winds.

She stayed that way over the next two after that.

How long was this going to last? How long could she possibly fall?

She looked into the depths as she fell, able to focus on something other than what was immediately in danger of flattening her. The wind was roaring in her ears. Tears mixed with the condensation of steam, all of it running up her body in hot streaks that blew off in her wake like the dust from a comet's tail.

The steam was getting thicker as she fell, and hotter, which hardly seemed possible. She could see the lights of the layered grates come to an end. Seven layers left.

What now?

Another alien shot past her. Again a glancing blow, cushioned some by the inflated nature of the soft flesh. She spun out of control again. Darkness, little rows of light from the grates. A tentacle hit her and spun her the other way, a powerful slap that sent her spinning farther out over the abyss.

An updraft hit her like a battering ram, and for a moment she felt as if she were rocketing upward again.

She wasn't. She was just falling slower now. Not much slower, she quickly realized, still plummeting at what had to be eighty miles an hour or more.

She got her spin under control and flattened herself into the updraft. The steam coming up in it, the heat, was unbelievable. She wondered if she was blistering. By God, it was hot.

Now what?

A waggle in the wind made her shift her arms. The buffet stopped, but her new body position caused her to knife sideways.

She shot out of the updraft and was suddenly hurtling downward at full speed again.

Shit.

She angled back, trying to find the updraft. But where was it? She wasn't a goddamn bird.

Then she saw something fluttering.

She squinted into the darkness. Did she see something fluttering? Maybe she was going mad right before she hit the bottom deck. There was going to be a bottom deck. She could see the platform lights coming to an end on either side of the abyss, rows of lights on the grates, which together looked like ladders climbing to the top of the ship from its dark, unseen bottom regions. The last rung was twenty seconds away. She supposed madness was the best way to enter into death. No fear that way. She could die thinking she was a bird, fluttering amongst the rest.

The flutter came again. More of a shadow against the darkness. Light bouncing off a puff of steam shaped it in relief. It was man shaped.

A headless man. Tumbling in the wind. Perhaps madness was upon her in full.

It zigged and zagged wildly. It puffed and shot up above her. Or she shot past it.

Something in the updraft. The air column was right there!

She leaned, yawed her body again. She swerved to her right.

Bam, there was the updraft again. It rippled the skin of her face with the violence of slowing her. She felt like she was shooting skyward again. Though she knew she was not.

The man shape fluttered to her left. It was cartwheeling past her now. Spinning back out of the column of air.

It was her spacesuit.

Shit!

She rotated and flattened, took as much braking effect as she could get out of the updraft. Now she was a bird. A bird of prey. She watched that fluttering object fall. She waited until it passed the grate it was falling by. She watched it. Watched for which way the wind blew.

The spacesuit spun in the new layer of air. It swooped up, came back toward the updraft. It nicked the edge of the updraft and ballooned, it whirled and spun up, then, leaflike, it fell away again, turning slowly and bouncing along the column of air like some bewildered tumbleweed.

She angled her body and shot down at it. She knew she was going to eat up what little space she had left to fall.

She shot toward it. It came up faster than she thought. It

was turning. She was going to miss it. It turned back. She dove right into it. Hit it hard. The plastic edge of a belt compartment cut her open above the eye.

She didn't care. She fought to untangle herself from it. The roar coming from beneath her was incredible now. It was a roiling noise that was louder than the wind. The steam was unfathomably hot.

She fumbled for the back of the suit. A new blast of air turned her over, spun her around. She didn't care. She felt a strand of cable in her hand. She slid her hand to it. Grabbed the small device dangling there. She clutched it, drew it to her. She couldn't see what was on the little screen. She didn't have to. She knew which way to turn the dial.

She turned it quick, all the way. The steam was so thick now she couldn't see at all.

A blast of wind hit her. Blew her sideways. She was still falling. But she knew it was momentum now.

The roiling noise was like thunder, the steam scalding.

She hoped she could find the updraft again.

Something struck her hard. She bounced off it. Saw the shadowy form of an alien gliding past. She bounced along the curve of its billow, slowing some. Probably another broken rib. She rolled and tried to push off with her legs, but it was moving far too fast.

She pinballed around inside its trailing tentacles for a time. The upward whip of the last tentacle tip that struck her sent her spinning off vertically. She gripped the object in her hand like it was the very core of life.

It was.

She was alive. Drifting on the wind. Her Higgs prism in hand.

Chapter 22

The crowd of applicants, suppliants, and courtiers outside the throne room doors filled the grand hallway like a gilded fair. The costumes they wore—or at least they were costumes in Roberto's eyes on this day—were gaudy and opulent. Their perfumes filled the air as loudly and anonymously as did the drone of their voices, all together in a lively mumble, punctuated here and there by the shrill noise of some woman's laughter or the lecherous low undertones of men at lusty wit. To Roberto it all seemed one big party being thrown despite the teetering fate of his best friend and her new husband, Sir Altin Meade.

"You and I both know this is all bullshit," he said as he pushed his way through the crowd. "Almost all of that was lies."

Deeqa matched his pace easily with her long strides, but she said nothing. The courtiers paused as the two of them passed, most long beyond any awe at seeing people from another planet, but more than a few stricken by Deeqa's dark, statuesque beauty. She was not a regular feature of the Palace, and so she at least was new.

"So why is the Queen lying to us? What is she covering?" he pressed. It was almost a private rant. "And what the hell were those three *Citadel* mages into? Did you see them? They looked like shit. Envette had blood all over her knees, like she'd been crawling in it."

"You don't know if it was hers or someone else's," Deeqa pointed out.

"I don't, but I have a vivid imagination," he said, shouldering past two men wearing matching coats of blue velvet. One of them turned with an eyebrow raised and his mouth opened, prepared to say something. But he saw who it was, the burly Earth warrior whom everyone in Crown recognized on sight for his role in saving the city during the war. That eyebrow lowered some, and when the fellow saw the feral look that flashed upon Deeqa's face, his mouth shut as well, just before he turned around. He'd obviously seen something in her eyes, in the angles of her whole body, that promised she'd not learned to fight in rooms with climate control enchantments, taught by kindly instructors who spoke of honor as they explained point systems, trophies, and tournament rules.

"Fear is the child of imagination and ignorance," she said as they cleared the worst of the crowd.

"I know. But that redhead is an X-ranked teleporter. I've worked with her. She's a combat teleporter, the kind they send into dangerous stuff. What if they sent her in to get Orli and Altin out? What if that blood was her kneeling next to one of them? You know? Checking on them."

"The child grows strong, and the parents are proud of what you say."

Roberto frowned. It took him a moment to get it, and when he did, he forced himself to let the unprofitable what-ifs go. "Fine," he said. "But it's still bullshit. The Queen isn't going to do anything. That much is obvious. She says to trust her, but when it comes to the lives of my friends, I don't trust shit. We have to do something. We can't just leave them to … to whatever. And don't tell me I have a contract and job to do. You said that the last time we were here, over two weeks ago, and look what we've gotten—what Orli and Altin have gotten—for my efforts of *not* doing anything. If I thought I was getting the whole truth, I might be okay going back and hawking coffee for another few days. But right now, I feel like I'm drowning in lies."

"Captain! Wait," came a labored voice from behind them. "Captain, please, a moment."

They stopped and turned back. The fat figure of the Earl of Vorvington was just pushing through the last of the crowd plugging up the hall. His cheeks were florid, and he was huffing as he approached. He wiped sweaty hands on his red-and-gold doublet, and then reached out to shake Roberto's hand in the Earth-people style.

"Captain, I could not help overhearing some of what you were saying just now, as you passed through the assemblage there. I apologize for eavesdropping, but ... well, it is a habit one acquires after a century or two at court."

Roberto cocked an eyebrow to Deeqa, who shrugged and looked down at Vorvington, waiting for whatever came next. "Yeah, I get it," Roberto said. "No worries. What can we do for you?"

"I am under the impression you are as concerned and frustrated by the lack of information regarding our incredible Galactic Mage as I am. And his sweet wife, of course, whom I understand is your old crewmate."

Roberto knew perfectly well that Vorvington knew perfectly well that he and Orli were close. He might not know Vorvington at all personally, but he did know the man had been present for most of the goings-on here at the Palace since this whole Prosperion adventure began. Goddamn nobles. They were worse than the politicians back on Earth. If that was possible. "I am," was all he gave as reply.

"Well," said Vorvington, "I should think that makes us

something on the order of confederates." He moved in close. "Or at least prospectively so." He reached fat-fingered hands around and placed one each in the small of Roberto's and Deeqa's backs, for which he received a you-are-about-to-lose-that look from the latter. He smiled and gave them each a gentle shove toward the end of the hall anyway. He glanced back over his shoulder once, and said, "Come, let me not slow you down. We can talk as we move along."

Vorvington chattered on the whole way down the long hallway, guiding them swiftly and efficiently out while deftly avoiding saying anything of importance. The man had an ability to redirect conversations that was astonishing, and by the time they were at the front gates of the Palace, Roberto was actually distracted, and amused, by how good he was at it.

They reclaimed their weapons, and soon after, Vorvington had them in a carriage, heading toward the city's northern gate.

"Have you ever had wooly rhino ribs braised in orange-rind and sorsopal-root glaze? I know a place—out of the way and quiet—that will leave a mark on your very soul when you are done. The proprietor, a discreet man, swears the sorsopal root's real magic is not the illusionary swarms of bees, but a touch of something more in keeping with a love elixir of some kind. I assure you, you'll enjoy nothing so much on all of Prosperion, excepting perhaps prospon, of course, but how rare are the gifts of the novafly?"

"I think your nephew Thadius did enough damage with love elixirs for my lifetime, Mr. Vorvington," Roberto said. "How about you get to the point? We're out of the Palace now, so let's just cut the shit and get to it."

Vorvington's wide face stacked atop the retracting rings of his jowls and fleshy neck as he recoiled from the remark, unused to such treatment from any but the Queen and the marchioness. "To begin, young man, it is not 'Mister' but

Lord Vorvington, and secondly, keep your voice down. We cannot trust everyone on the street to be as discreet as the man at the Rhino's Horn."

"You're the one who brought us here. You're the one calling me 'young man,' and you're the one who brought up the love elixir. So if you want to keep me mellow and in the mood for title games, then stop jerking me off and tell me what we are doing here."

"Yes, I suppose that elixir comment was a bit insensitive. And while I admit to no wrongdoings on the part of my nephew—he was framed by his man Annison, I'll have you know—I do apologize. As for the rest, well, then let us get ourselves out of town."

He leaned back in his seat, and stared out the window then, in absolute silence and without looking the least perturbed. They might have been taking a leisurely sightseeing trip around Crown City.

At length they were out, and soon the carriage was making its way along the smoothly paved river road, heading west in the direction of Leekant.

Roberto and Deeqa exchanged glances but remained silent until finally Vorvington spoke. "There's something Her Majesty is not telling us," he said. "You and me both. And I make it my business to know what is happening."

"Yeah. We covered that already back there in the hall."

"Well, Captain, you are privy to things she does not discuss with me. And, if I'm being perfectly candid, you are also privy to information about what's happening on Earth. I can only assume, after all your years in the fleet, you have many friends and acquaintances here and there throughout the NTA."

Roberto offered a mild sort of smile, patient, and he lifted his eyebrows, encouraging the earl to go on.

"I'm offering you a trade, Captain. An information exchange. If Her Majesty won't tell me what is going on, then I must piece it together myself. I am in hopes that, between what you know and what I hear, I—we—can discover what is occurring on that red planet up there, and just why our mutual friends Sir Altin and Lady Meade continue to be in absence."

"If I knew anything, I'd tell you. I don't need to be hauled out into the middle of the prairies to some rhino cafe to tell you that. If you got something I can use, can't you just out with it? What is it you want to tell me ... Lord Vorvington?"

"*Citadel* hasn't been anywhere near that planet."

Roberto's encouraging brow dropped like a deadfall. "What are you saying?"

"I'm saying that I saw those three *Citadel* sorcerers come out of the throne room. Two guildmasters and an X-class teleporter. They were covered in filth."

"Yeah, go on."

"And what did they tell you?"

"They said Altin and Orli are alive. That the hole isn't deep enough for the aliens to get to Yellow Fire yet. That's it."

"That's all?"

"Yes, that's all."

"You're sure. They told you nothing else?"

"Lord Vorvington, if I wanted to dick around with you, I'd just whip it out, okay?"

"By the gods!" he said, again stacking up all his neck fat. But he recovered quickly. "My point, Captain, is that if indeed that is all the news you heard, do you not think it a bit overkill to summon two guildmasters and an X? She could have told you all of that herself."

"She was trying to, but I wasn't buying it."

"She could have summoned Master Aderbury."

"If *Citadel* is in battle, I don't think pulling the captain off it makes sense."

"I assure you, two guildmasters and an X have less time

to spare than one transmuter captain. Conduit Huzzledorf is more than capable of doing what needs to be done in the course of ... how long were the three of them in there with you? Three minutes? Five?"

Roberto sent a sideways glance to Deeqa. She won most of the poker games on the *Glistening Lady* for a reason.

"So what are you saying?"

"I'm saying, if *Citadel* wizards are being brought out of ... whatever has them all looking like that, just so that they can assure you that everything is fine, well, one has to wonder what isn't fine."

"That's pretty much the way I see it. But, I have to be honest, Lord Vorvington, we're still wading through the land of shit I already know."

"A land with which I am also familiar."

Roberto looked back to Deeqa again. He felt like they were going in circles. Deeqa actually beat him to the question.

"Lord Vorvington, what, specifically, do you want from us? An answer in under ten words is best."

"I want to know where *Citadel* is."

Roberto rolled his eyes and slumped back into his seat. He knocked on the ceiling of the carriage and called out, "Hey, driver, take us back."

"Captain, please," Vorvington said. "As I said, bringing those three proves something. There's a fight somewhere, perhaps a war. I don't know where it is, but I have reasons to suspect it is not on the red world. And if it is on that world, if we've got people doing battle with those aliens on Yellow Fire, we need to know. We need to know either way. The truth is that Her Majesty's political hold is tenuous. The people are still reeling from the last war. If she is trying to single-handedly take on an alien enemy, anywhere, without adequate support—and I assure you that none of the nobles have been asked to send troops—then we should be in a position to force her to include us in that decision, or at very least in formulating the strategy—not only for the sake of Sir Altin and Lady Meade, but for the troops on *Citadel*, and possibly for all of Prosperion. We have to find *Citadel*, Captain. Our work starts there. Her Majesty is a brave and honorable woman, but she can be secretive, and she can be brave to the point of recklessness. We want her success, even if we have to force it on her."

"Right," said Roberto in a tone that suggested otherwise.

"I am in earnest."

"I'm sure you are. But I don't know where *Citadel* is. That's why I'm here, remember? You do understand it flies around on magic, right? It's your ship, not ours. It doesn't show up on radar or any other scans, including my satellite probe—unless it wants to. And last I heard, they aren't logging their flight plans with the NTA."

"Yes, but you could still tell us if it really has gone to Yellow Fire."

"Did you even hear what I just said? The only insight I have into what's going on up there is a standard probe, in orbit no less. I can't control it without being there. Hell, I can't even see the damn thing on my own from here because it hasn't got its own entanglement array. I can only communicate with it when it's in range of the surface relay that we hooked up to the entanglement trigger—the one the NTA required that we wire into the explosives nest—and since that is their system, not mine, I can only do that through the NTA on Earth or through the general at Little Earth. In short, I got a limited view with limited access."

Vorvington made a show of leaning back into his seat, a display of patience. "Surely you've already done all of that, of course. Lady Meade's father and all that rot."

"No shit. That's what I'm trying to tell you. I don't know jack. *Citadel* isn't there, at least not above the dig site or in orbit somewhere obvious. I can't even get a good reading into the hole for all the goddamn sand blowing everywhere, and I know right where to look. Even if *Citadel* was there, it could just go all invisible or whatever and I'd never know. It could be parked right in front of my probe and I'd never know it. Bottom line: I haven't seen anything."

"Be that as it may, what if I could give you information that you could use in your machines to calculate where she's sent it? So we can determine if it really has gone there."

"Where else would it be?"

"That is what we would like to know as well. Like I said, I have information that I cannot make full use of without your help."

"What kind of information?"

"Lady Meade, before she became so, did some work for some associates of mine who were in turn working with a pair of students from the university in Crown. The youngsters were able to work out some maps and some magic that Lady Meade was then able to use to calculate the location of the red planet you now call Yellow Fire."

"Yeah, we heard. It was a star map and an illusion spell. Tribbey Redquill and Caulfin something."

"Caulfin Sunderhusk. Yes, those are the two. That is the idea."

"So what, you want me to check out a map and a 3-D image spell?"

"I do."

"And you actually have a map and a spell?"

"Very nearly, yes."

"Why me? Why us? They just did a big student exchange at the university, a thousand of them last I heard. Why not get one of them?"

"There are numerous reasons, the most important one being a matter of scrutiny. The reality is, Captain, that you are the only person from Earth who has as much liberty as you do. Not simply in your access and activities, but in your, well, in your freedom from prying eyes."

"Yeah, we know. Mainly thanks to Altin casting all that protective magic stuff on my ship after those douchebags were trying to sneak aboard and spy on me."

"Yes, well, he's done a fine job of it. And, since we are being open about these things, Her Majesty enacted some prohibitions about casting divination spells at you and your ship as well. A direct invasion of royal privacy. You've got more working for you than you know."

Roberto glanced to Deeqa, who let him see that she was, as he was, surprised and yet not surprised.

"Fine, so I look at your maps. Run a few cross-references on some star charts. Second-year-at-the-academy stuff. Then what?"

"Then you discreetly hand the information off to me."

"And what if *Citadel* is not at Yellow Fire? What if it's at Earth? Or somewhere else?"

"That's what we are hoping to learn."

"You know what, Lord Vorvington, whatever you really want is still nowhere near the tip of your tongue. So I'm just going to say no right now unless you tell me what you think she's doing. Seriously. Where do you think *Citadel* is? And like Deeqa said, ten words or less."

Vorvington's eyes darted to the tall Somali, then back to Roberto. He made a point of slumping, defeated. "There are those who fear she has gone to the world you call Blue Fire and begun the work of harvesting Liquefying Stone."

"She what?" Roberto turned to Deeqa, who did not look even marginally surprised.

"I am afraid that is my concern, and that of others as well. My diviner discovered it. A clear indication that Her Majesty is after more Liquefying Stone." He straightened himself, pushed his hands flat over his velvet breeches, and pressed out the wrinkles along his fat thighs. "If the alien excavation on the red world is as we believe it might be, then there is a source of Liquefying Stone being threatened by a very large and very unknown agency. So, we feel, I feel, that Her Majesty may be hedging her bets and going after the only other abundant source available ... before it is too late."

"That could kill Blue Fire," Roberto said. "Or piss her off real bad. The Queen knows that. She wouldn't do it, no way." He glanced to Deeqa and back to the earl again. "Would she?"

"They do call her the *War* Queen." It was not a question. "And the diviners saw clearly that she's gone after a source of more of the yellow stone. It is certain."

"Well, shit."

"Indeed."

He stared out the window for a time, thinking. "Fine," Roberto said. "I'll read your star maps to confirm it. But you need to do something for me."

"Of course. I had no intention of being the only beneficiary of our luncheon on the river." He looked out the window at the alders and cottonwoods going by. The river was a wide blue stripe running easy and smooth, the channel deep this far from the source and heavy with the late spring rains. There was still no restaurant in sight.

"I need harbor stones. And I need a lot of them. I can't sit there with my thumb up my ass trying to clear NTA customs and then dealing with the damn TGS bureaucracy. It took us a day and a half sitting on our hands just to get back here today. Nobody will even talk to us about going to Yellow Fire. Orli and Altin will be in specimen jars in some damn alien laboratory before we ever get back there at this rate."

The gilded earl held up his hands, palms up and out at his sides. "I can't get you through the TGS system any faster than you can. They are Her Majesty's people, not mine. And if I'm being honest, only barely that."

"I thought you guys were on the same side."

His cheeks colored a little, and he looked out at the river again. "Yes," he said, as if speaking to the terns flying over the water, "but they are an entity apart. Frankly, I doubt she controls them as well as she thinks she does. I have no pull there. Not anymore."

Roberto harrumphed and shook his head. But that was rather the point. "That's the problem I have. Which is why I need harbor stones. You guys made them for the fleet ships before. So I know it can be done. I need a bunch of them. I need at least ten each way, here and back to Yellow Fire. Maybe another ten each to go back and forth between Earth and Prosperion. Hell, make it an even sixty and get me ten apiece back and forth from Yellow Fire to Earth."

"You won't get them going between the red world and Earth, but the others could be done. However, your problem is still the TGS. And the enchanters. What you are asking for will require a small concert. You'll need a conduit—hard enough to find—and you'll need a whole stack of teleporters and enchantment mages. The TGS has gobbled up every teleporter beyond what is absolutely necessary for commerce and intra-continental travel, and all the best enchanters that weren't already on *Citadel* have just been sent to Earth as part of the student exchange. I really do want to help you, but what you are asking for is simply not feasible."

"Well, then you didn't come to the bargaining table with much, did you?"

"Why not get your friend Tytamon to make your stones? There is no other wizard on Prosperion who could do it on his own—other than Sir Altin, of course, and he's not on the planet, which is rather the problem you and I both share so exactly."

Roberto was fairly sure Lord Vorvington couldn't give a crap about Altin, but he didn't call him on it.

"Well, if you can't do that for me, what can you do?"

"I can help you find, and hopefully free, your friends. I

realize that does not give you any more than I am getting out of this, but, well, I think it still has value. Don't you?"

Roberto shook his head again. He knew that he'd been played. But Vorvington was right. And he was offering more than the Queen.

"Fine," he said. "So where's the wizard with the maps and the 3-D spell?"

"Why don't we meet outside of Murdoc Bay, an hour after sunset tonight. That will give me time to get the last bit of divining done. There's a good stretch of flat land above the cliffs at the top of the Decline. Perhaps you could land a measure west of the road. We'll meet you there."

Roberto exchanged glances with Deeqa again. She shrugged. It was his decision to make.

"We'll be there."

They sat in silence all the way back to Crown, forgoing the rhino ribs in favor of ending the façade.

Chapter 23

Sophia Hayworth didn't shriek. She didn't wail or cry. She didn't even put her hands on her hips like Kettle would have. In fact, Sophia Hayworth in anger was the exact opposite of Kettle in every way. Where Kettle would have been all red faced and shouting—and a couple of whip-strike smacks on Pernie's backside with that big, nasty wooden spoon she had—Sophia Hayworth was the very picture of calm. In fact, not only did her voice not go up in pitch or volume like Kettle's would, it actually came down.

She sat across from Pernie and stared at her seriously, but she did it in this patient sort of way that irritated Pernie to no end. Don Hayworth was still talking to the man from "Reno PD" at the front door. They were talking about baseball, though, so Sophia Hayworth was free to come look at Pernie now in her annoying, patient way.

"I only asked one thing from you," Sophia Hayworth said. "I asked that you come straight home. Can you explain why you were unable to do so?"

"I already told you. I wanted to find a dead Hostile." Pernie let go a patient breath of her own. How many times was she going to have to answer that question?

"You went downtown. You knew that it was dangerous.

Even the bus driver told you it was dangerous."

"But it wasn't," Pernie said. She fiddled with her fingers on the tabletop.

"Yes, Pernie, it was. Those hoodlums you encountered were dangerous. The young man the police arrested is a known criminal."

"He didn't seem dangerous to me," Pernie said. "And he and his friends even chased a bad man away."

Sophia closed her eyes and seemed like she had to concentrate very hard for a moment. Pernie thought she might be going to get mad, but she didn't. When she spoke again, she was still talking in that calm way. "He was dangerous, and you put yourself at great risk, young lady. Not only yourself, but the rest of us: me, Don, and even your guardians back at home, Mr. Tytamon and Ms. Kettle. We are all trying to do our part, building history and trust between worlds, and if you run off and do something reckless like that again ... if you were to be hurt, a lot of hearts would be broken, and a lot of work on the part of many people doing other things you cannot conceive just yet—it would all be put in jeopardy."

The surface of the plastic table was textured to look like wood. Pernie scratched her fingernail into the little ruts of the faux wood grain. To the touch it felt hard enough to be wood, but it seemed silly to make plastic wood when wood wood was just as good. Jeremy had showed her how there were many things that could be made from plastic, too, many to count. He said there were even plastic bones in case something bad happened to your regular ones.

"Are you listening to me?"

Pernie looked up. Sophia Hayworth was obviously waiting for an answer, because her eyebrows were both high up on her forehead. "No," Pernie said.

Sophia's mouth dropped open, and between the raised brows and the dangling chin, her face looked very long.

Pernie wondered if they could make plastic jawbones, which she knew were kind of bendy and had teeth in them, or only just straight bones like leg bones and arm bones. She'd seen her own leg bone once, back on the Isle of Hunters. It broke right out of the skin. It hurt a lot, but it was also very interesting.

Sophia eventually closed her mouth and started talking again. Pernie only heard the last part about "what are we going to do with you?" because Don Hayworth came in. The Reno PD man was gone.

Don looked down at Pernie and grinned at her, a proud thing, the same look he'd given her when she was hitting all the baseballs he threw at her. "The lieutenant says you damn near knocked that guy out. Says you kicked him into a garbage can."

Pernie shrugged. "I only tripped him. They were trying to take me to a *seen-o* to get Sophia's chips."

"*Ca*-sino," he corrected. "And either way, that was well done. You should always stand up for yourself."

Pernie nodded and smiled back at him. "That's what Kettle and Master Altin and even Master Tytamon always say. Djoveeve and Seawind showed me how."

He laughed, a few notes anyway, wry and with a tinge of admiration beneath. "Yes, that they did."

"And you are going to encourage this behavior?" Sophia said. "She was nearly abducted by a gang of thugs, and you think that is a laughing matter?"

"But she *wasn't* abducted by a gang of thugs. She knocked one half out, and the rest ran away." He turned his gaze back to Pernie. "But you do need to stay away from down there, okay? At least by yourself. Your mothe—Sophia is right that it is too dangerous. You were lucky the cops came along."

Pernie made a face at that and wrinkled up her nose. She didn't know what that word, "cops," meant. Don saw it.

"Cops are the guys that brought you here. Reno PD."

She shrugged. That was good to know. She planned on avoiding cops from now on.

Sophia looked sideways at her husband before regarding Pernie once more. "So, the lesson here is that we won't be running off downtown again, right?"

"But I didn't get to the broken buildings where the dead Hostiles are."

A pained expression, the flicker of a flinch, crossed Sophia's face, but her voice remained calm. "There are no dead Hostiles down there. Only drugged-out dirtbags and transients. There are bad people on our world, Pernie. Please, promise me you won't try that again."

Pernie shrugged again.

"I need you to promise," Sophia insisted.

Pernie didn't want to promise. She looked back to the table and fussed with it again. She wondered if a plastic bone would be stronger than a regular one. Some plastics were strong but also flexible. She'd read that much. She might be able to jump very far if she had plastic bones. She decided she'd ask Jeremy if that was possible. If it was, maybe she could get her bones changed. They did lots of things like that on Earth.

"You see?" Sophia was saying to Don. "She just tunes me out. Angela never tuned me out. How am I supposed to talk to her?"

"I'd start by giving up trying to find comparisons," Don said.

That made Sophia scowl, and for the first time she actually looked mad. Pernie was glad she was mad. She would rather have her mad than talking to her in that stupid quiet way. The quiet way made Pernie feel stupid somehow. Pernie thought Sophia might be more mad at Don, though.

Sophia got up, and for a moment Pernie thought the woman was going to put her hands on her hips. Pernie thought it might be funny to see her mad like Kettle finally. But she didn't. Instead, Sophia glared down at Pernie, took another one of those closed-eye breaths, and said, "Go to your room. You are grounded and will not leave this house alone again until I say so. And you can forget about walking back from the bus stop on your own as well."

Pernie would have laughed at that as well, but she didn't. She knew how to be patient when she needed to. She shrugged yet again.

Sophia turned narrow eyes on Don, then spun and left the room.

Pernie looked to Don, who shrugged like she had. "Well," he said, "you better get in there so we don't both end up in the doghouse."

Confusion contorted Pernie's features. The Hayworths didn't even have a dog.

Chapter 24

Pernie lay on her bed, staring at the ceiling. She'd tried to watch some net shows on the monitor up there, but they were boring. She was too busy thinking about real things. Things that happened outside. She'd wanted to see a dead Hostile was all. Sophia was making a sea out of a flooded cellar, as Kettle used to say. Pernie still wanted to see a dead Hostile. And she didn't like being "grounded."

Sometimes the NTA fighter pilots got grounded. Pernie had watched a net documentary about them. If they did bad things or made mistakes, they got grounded and couldn't fly. Gryphon riders in Her Majesty's armies got grounded too. They didn't call it that, but it was the same thing. Pernie was glad she was grounded like a fighter pilot. Someday she would learn how to fly, though. Faster than sound. That would be fun. She could shout "hello" into the wind and then fly in her fighter to the other end of Earth, stop her plane, and get out in time to hear herself. She could have a whole conversation that way.

Jeremy told her she could even go faster than light if she flew in a spaceship. Then she could hear herself and see herself too. That would be fun.

What wasn't fun was sitting in here watching the world

on ceiling video. That was boring. And it was still early. It wasn't even nine o'clock.

She got up and went to the window across the room. There was electricity running through it. That's why the alarms went off. She'd looked it up on the net and knew that it was true. But Pernie also knew how electricity worked now. She just had to jump the window connection so as not to break the closed loop. Either that, or she had to shut it down at the power source.

She looked around behind the desk and the dresser for some kind of access. She thought there would be a panel of some kind that she could pull off somewhere like there were in the cars she'd crawled inside. But there wasn't.

She thought about the printers she'd seen pouring out all the new houses along the street her bus drove on. All that stuff was printed right into the walls.

She stood up on her bed and looked along the edge of the ceiling. Sure enough, there was a narrow seam, sealed with something soft. She could just reach it if she stood on her tippy toes.

She pushed a fingernail into it. It gave way a little bit, like the bark of the sacred trees in the cove. Like rubber and some plastics here on Earth. She needed something to cut it with.

She looked through her drawers, Angela Hayworth's drawers, but there wasn't anything she could use.

She went out of her room, intent on sneaking into the kitchen for a laser knife. Sophia was coming down the hall and spotted her. The woman started to say something, but Pernie pointed to the bathroom door nearby and went in.

She hated being under guard.

She rummaged through the drawers and found a small pair of scissors in one drawer and in another a small box that read *Light of Luxury—Laser Depilatory Kit.* The front of the box showed a lady wrapped in a towel, sitting on the side of a bathtub, rubbing something oblong down her leg just below the knee. The lady looked very happy doing it and had a great big smile on her face.

Pernie opened it and found an oblong object just like the one on the cover of the box. She turned it over. There were three dark lines, barely two millimeters wide, running opposite the object's length. That was it. There was a button on the side. Of course Pernie pushed it.

All three lines lit up, bright blue, glaringly bright. Pernie reflexively jerked it away so it wouldn't hit her in the eyes. Jeremy had warned her about laser light. She wasn't sure the object was really emitting lasers, since the lady on the box was smiling and all, but that's what it said, so it must be.

She wondered if she could use it to cut through the soft stuff on her wall.

She took the object and the scissors and hid them under her blouse, tucked into the waistband of her skirt. She took the precaution of flushing the toilet before she exited and went back to her room. Sure enough, Sophia Hayworth was standing there waiting when she came out, and watched her until her door was closed.

Pernie dragged the dresser to the window, first tipping each end up and tucking a blanket under it to reduce friction and noise and also to make the work easier. She jumped up onto it and looked at the joint along the ceiling and the wall. She pulled out the scissors, opened them, and, using one sharp edge, cut through the seam.

The soft material sealing the seam where the wall covering and the windowsill met gave way easily enough, and in short order, Pernie had cut a line the length of the window plus a foot and a half on either side. She carved out as much of the soft stuff as she could along a three-inch stretch of the cut, making a gap into which she could get her fingers, albeit little more than her fingernails. She pulled down on it, bending her knees and giving a few trial yanks as she tried to peel the wall covering away from the wall beneath. She knew there was concrete behind it if she could just get the outer layer off.

The material buckled a little, bending and warping as she tugged on it. That proved that it was as thin as she suspected, but it wasn't as flimsy as she'd hoped. It didn't peel away at all, which meant she'd have to cut into it as well. That was going to be harder than cutting the soft sealer in the seam.

She tried with the scissors, even though she knew it likely wouldn't work. She dragged the tip of the scissor blade in a long line, several times in rapid succession, each stroke on top of the path of the last, all halfway down the length of the windowsill. No luck, barely a scratch.

She set the scissors down and retrieved the Light of Luxury. She placed it against the paneling, laying it so that its length was parallel to the ceiling. She pushed the button. Filaments of blue light, thread-thin, radiated a short way out from the edges of the device, marking where the three bars of laser light were. Or at least that's what Pernie hoped was happening.

She didn't know how long she ought to wait, but since the lady on the box was shooting herself in the leg and not screaming, Pernie left it there for quite a while. After a period of time had passed to challenge patience, she pulled it away, hoping to see the panel burned right through.

There were three faint brown marks. They were more like smoke stains than incisions cut with a laser knife.

"Hmmph," Pernie grunted.

She jumped down from her perch and took the scissors and the Light of Luxury to her bed. She'd seen Jeremy take enough stuff apart in the lab to know how it went, so she used the scissors to pry the top and the bottom of the Light of Luxury apart. Soon she was looking at its insides. She didn't know what much of that was.

But she was getting pretty good about using the global net.

By midnight, she had swapped out the power source for the one in her tablet and routed all of it through one of the three lenses on the Light of Luxury. The new contraption was rather a mess of wires, and it all hung apart, but Pernie didn't care. Her first trial with it melted a two-inch gash into the plastic surface of her desk. Victory!

Cutting the paneling away from the window was the work of less than a half hour, and when she finally pulled the veneer back, all the pipes and conduit were exposed exactly as she had known they would be. It didn't take her long to figure out which wires went to the window alarm after that, and jumping the connection was the work of only a minute and a half.

Moments after, Pernie was headed back downtown. She was going to see a dead Hostile today, and no attempts by Sophia Hayworth to be her "guardian" were going to keep her from it. No way.

Chapter 25

"They're still alive," Tytamon called to Roberto as the ship's captain came down the *Glistening Lady*'s ramp. "I know that much for certain." The ancient magician's relief was evident as he reported the findings of his divination spell. "I can hardly tell you more than that, but it's something. I saw them both in a fog of yellow. They stared back at me, unblinking, motionless, but I sensed no fear. I tried to discern the nature of the fog. I thought it might have something to do with the Liquefying Stone. I cast another version of the divination spell with the stone as the center of the inquiry, but that didn't seem to resonate, so perhaps not. I want to say the fog is heat. It feels like heat, as if the color of the heat or the fog is hot and yellow, or something of that sort. I know little, but I am encouraged. So much so, I've invited Doctor Leopold to come for dinner tomorrow night that he might help me try again. These damned divination spells are fraught with vagaries in the worst ways, but the man is brilliant. I cannot do it alone. The gods throw our wisdom and our ignorance back at us together, all in a knot. But I think between the doctor and me, we can figure it out. Or perhaps at least get you something you can use."

Roberto nodded. "Well, I know you said the more you know the better, and I might have some information that can help. But you have to keep it quiet for now." He looked around, out of reflex more than need. There were no spies at Calico Castle, nor any this close to the walls. Prosperion's only Eight had seen to that after the orc invasion, and he'd added more since his return. He was adding even more beyond that, as it seemed the more frequently he visited Crown City, the more Tytamon sensed the tensions growing in the Palace. The Queen was in nearly constant absence, and the TGS councilmen were becoming increasingly arrogant.

"Then come inside, young man." Normally the nearly eight-hundred-year-old sorcerer would have repeated his standing offer that the crew of the *Glistening Lady* should avail themselves of Calico Castle's kitchens and other amenities, but such was his apparent worry that he skipped all such courtesies.

He led Roberto and Deeqa up the winding stairs to his study in the castle's tall centermost tower, and soon the three of them were shut inside with the door locked tight. "I don't trust anyone anymore," he said. "You aren't wrong to fear for it. There are more counter spells and magic blocks upon the Palace now than there ever were, more than any time in history. And here we are at peace, with no real enemies in sight."

"Well, I guess we're going to find out about that soon enough," Roberto said. "Because here's what I just heard. Lord Vorvington thinks the Queen has raided Blue Fire for Liquefying Stones. If he's right, then we could be seeing Hostiles swooping in any day now. Blue Fire knows where both Earth and Prosperion are. And we don't have her heart chamber wired up to blow like we do Yellow Fire's. And worse, even if we did, how jacked up would it be for us to blow her away just because she's trying to fight the Queen and her raiding parties off?"

Tytamon started to say something, a little black hole opening within the gray bramble of his beard, but he stopped. The hole lingered a moment, then closed. His eyebrows, like drapes to match the bearded carpet below, lowered as he thought behind closed windows for a time. Finally he did speak again. "No," he said. "I think not."

Roberto and Deeqa both regarded him, sure that more would come. It did not.

The ancient wizard stared into the distance for a moment after, but pressed on. "Whatever the truth of it is, what I need first is to discover what we can do about my apprentice and his new bride. Does the yellow color or heat mean anything to you?"

"Not a damn thing," Roberto said.

"Yellows and reds are the colors of warmth in a heat scan," Deeqa said. "It's how they show up on our sensors when we look for heat sources, be they geological or life-forms. Although it's relative by degree and scale."

Tytamon's cracked lips pushed through the tangle of gray hair, and he let out a hum. "Perhaps that is it. Although I'm not sure why a divining spell I cast would incorporate such a thing."

"Have you been to Little Earth and looked at the feed General Pewter has from our satellite? He's got the codes for the entanglement array below. Has he shown you the ships down there? We've got a camera on the surface, too." Deeqa looked to Roberto, who nodded, agreeing it was a good idea. "You can't see much through the storm, but it's got to be better than nothing."

"I may have seen it on the monitor when last I was there," Tytamon said, "but I'm not sure I knew what it meant."

"Would it be helpful to go look now?" Roberto said. "I can take you over there, or, you know, we can just teleport." He wiggled his fingers in the air.

"Well, I have a system for reading your messages here now," Tytamon said. "Out by the platform we're working on for your ship."

"Is that what was in that little shack we saw when we came in? I was wondering what that was. Why do you need computers here other than what's in the basement of Altin's tower ... when he gets back? Won't your magic screw it all up most of the time, all your traps and whatever you got going on?"

"It will," Tytamon said, "which is why we put it so far from the walls. Angela says it works fine out there most of the time."

"Angela?" both Roberto and Deeqa asked.

"Yes, Angela Hayworth. I am her sponsor here for a student exchange. You may not have heard, but they've arranged for students to—"

Roberto waved him off. "Yeah, yeah, we heard. But how'd you end up with one of them?"

"It's complicated. But you were with me the day Her Majesty's man brought it up to the emissary from the elves. Pernie was there. Miss Hayworth is part of the exchange, and, as the elves aren't on the charter, they needed a guardian to sponsor her. There were some ... special circumstances involved, and, well, rather than bore you with a lot of Prosperion history and the interweaving of treaties across time, I thought it best to take it on. Angela is actually a delightful girl. If you come for dinner tomorrow, you can meet her, as she'll be back from school. But for now, yes, I would like to go look and see if we can see the yellow heat you are talking about. I'm sure she won't mind the invasion of her private space in this circumstance."

Roberto was looking at Deeqa to see if she recognized the name, but Deeqa had nothing like recognition on her face. Then the name rang familiar in his own memory. "Is she the same Angela Hayworth that was Orli's lawyer back on

Earth, back when the NTA railroaded her and ran her ass straight to the execution chamber?"

"Yes, actually, she is." Tytamon looked grim. "That is precisely why she is here. She owes four years' service to the NTA, and they won't let her out of the agreement. This was as close as she could get to 'escape,' as she puts it. She is preparing herself for a diplomatic post—but just between you and me: she is resigning her commission the moment her contract is up. I think she actually hates the NTA more than Orli does, if that's at all possible. But she is very young, and very idealistic, so I suppose it's not a surprise." He studied Roberto long enough to see if his question had been satisfied, which it had. "So, let us go look to her computer for that heat reading you mentioned."

"You're not going to get it on hers. Or mine on the *Lady*. It's locked. Fleet property. The entanglement trigger in the belly of Yellow Fire is theirs. They don't want anyone tampering with it, which makes perfect sense. If that's the only way to blow up an enemy like Red Fire—at least like he was before he died—well, I wouldn't grant public access either."

Tytamon hummed. "Then yes, let's go see what General Pewter can show us."

A few moments later found them standing outside the walled compound known as Little Earth. It was forty acres square, a few miles outside of Crown City, and served at the fleet's lone outpost on the Prosperion world. Orli's father, General Pewter, was trusted by the Queen, and so it had gone to him to command the post.

The general rose and came out from behind the desk to greet Roberto, the handshake turning to a hug. He greeted Tytamon warmly and gave Deeqa an up-and-down look that prompted him to smile. He knew a smuggler when he saw one. But she came in good company, so he shook her hand and welcomed her.

"General," said Roberto. "We need a look at those alien ships. I'd say more, but God knows which one of the flies on the roof up there is working for some faction or another on Kurr." He looked up to the ceiling to prove that it was true. It was. There were several flies buzzing about here and there, flown in through the open window, along with a moth in one corner and a crane fly hanging lazily from the thatch.

The general nodded and retook his seat behind the desk. Roberto watched him as he worked the controls on his console. He couldn't help remembering having stood before this desk on numerous occasions in the past, the worst of them being the time he and Orli had been commanded to leave the planet for good by then-Captain Asad. That's when Orli was first stationed on the base on Tinpoa, a moon around the gas giant Naotatica several planets farther out from Prosperion around the sun. So much had changed in such a short amount of time. And yet it seemed like trouble never stopped. What was wrong with people, with the universe, anyway? Was there ever going to just be peace and happiness, ever? If not for everyone, at least for someone? Anywhere?

"Here it is," the general said. He turned from his desk monitor to the large one mounted on the wall behind his desk. "That's the view from orbit."

It wasn't much to look at. It was a smear of colors, lots of yellows and oranges, a few places where the yellow crept toward green.

"I'll zoom in closer to the top of the clouds so you can see them," he said. "One sec." A moment later the shifting patterns of yellow and orange on one area of the screen began expanding. Soon four lines became visible, deep red, their arrangement symmetrical, like four red spokes radiating out from a hub of yellow and orange.

"Well, Tytamon," Roberto said, "that look like anything

you saw in your fortune-telling spell?"

Tytamon shook his head. "No. Sadly it does not."

"Well, it was worth a shot."

"Is that as close as you can get?" Tytamon asked. "Can you not see them directly, like this ...?" He muttered a few words, and there appeared in the air above the general's desk a perfect likeness of the four alien ships, a section of the mountains visible behind them, and even the movement of the violent wind blowing sand around them and churning the clouds.

"A little," said the general. He tapped his console and brought up the feed from Roberto's camera, attached to the relay he'd set up on the surface. They could see dim, shadowy silhouettes in the distance, barely visible through the haze of so much blowing sand. "That's as close as we can get under the clouds. This is better than most days, although every once in a while, it's not so bad. I can't get you anything else down there without another probe. And the fleet won't clear one for me, for fear of agitating the enemy."

"So they *are* an enemy?" Tytamon said. "It's been determined, then?"

"They captured my daughter, so, yes, they are."

"But has the NTA officially pronounced a state of war?"

"No." The general did not look happy about it. He looked back at the illusion Tytamon had cast above his desk. "Can you move that around? Is that live?"

"If you mean, is it linked to a scrying spell, no, it is not. It is simply from memory of my last seeing spell. And I still can't get inside the ship. The seeing spell simply stops working at the hull. I am certain that is why I can't learn anything directly. It is as if I am chasing shadows of memories and time. It's the strangest thing. But as I told our young captain here, I have invited Doctor Leopold to dinner tonight. If the two of us can't solve it, well, then they are in serious trouble indeed."

"What about that crazy cat lady Altin talked about?" Roberto asked. "The Z-ranked nut bag out in the woods. She helped him before."

"Ocelot, yes. I started there," Tytamon said. "She is the one who told me they would be lost in time. If I did not know she was so gifted in the school, I'd have to say it was that bit of information that is muddling the rest of the magic up. So, hopefully the doctor will help me break through. Perhaps these images here will help as well, somehow, even if I don't understand how just now. And your news from earlier, Captain. All of it adds to the divining. And we must hope more than just confoundingly so."

The general looked like he was going to ask about what news Tytamon was referring to, but the old wizard pointed to the flies buzzing around the room. The general rolled his eyes, but let the question pass unasked.

"Come to dinner tomorrow, General. This sort of information tastes better with elven wine."

Chapter 26

Orli drifted in the wind, gripping her Higgs prism, gasping in the heat of the rising steam. She knew she was being cooked alive. She thought about trying to get into the spacesuit she'd caught in the wind as she fell, but it was so torn apart, it would only serve as a heat trap. What she needed to do was get out of the damn steam cloud.

She tried angling herself to ride the wind up, working back the way she'd just so precipitously fallen. She immediately collided with an alien soaring past, the massive creature emerging from the dim mistiness like some phantasmal behemoth made real from a misty nightmare.

The alien billow mashed around her, carrying her along with it and striking her hard enough to make stars swim in her vision, all the worse for the pain of what was now likely two broken ribs. She tried to catch her breath as she lay pinned against it by its momentum. The indentation her body pressed into the relatively soft tissue offered her a measure of reprieve from the heat, not much, but some, in the manner, perhaps, of being removed from a bed of coals and simply hung over the flames.

She let herself be carried along and pulled the spacesuit to her. She took the utility belt off it and wound that around her waist. She extracted a combination tool from one of the pouches and opened up the knife blade. She quickly set to work cutting the helmet seal and its metal ring away from the suit itself.

When it was done, she folded the knife and put it away, then tied the sleeves and legs together respectively. Even with the huge rent down the open front, she could still maybe use the spacesuit as a sail. If so, she could get herself someplace safe, collect her wits and her bearings, and then have a look around. If she could get back to Altin, she could cut him out of the jelly and they could get the hell out of this hellhole.

Once she had a makeshift billow of her own, she started crawling up the rounded expanse of the alien upon which she'd been caught. She wondered if it could feel her like she might have felt a mosquito or a flea. Taking the example from that, she made sure she did nothing that might constitute a bite. Maybe she really could get away.

She got to the top edge of the creature's natural parachute and found that she could walk if she set the Higgs prism appropriately. It was remarkably calm traveling with the wind as she was. The air no longer roared, even if the churning roil below was still monstrously loud. She got to her feet and set the Higgs prism just high enough that she could get traction to run. The flesh of the creature's billow was soft, like running on a feather bed.

But run she did, and she leaped off to the side when she'd built up enough speed, turning the dial back to zero gravity as she flew free. Soon she was drifting along next to it. It was moving past her gradually, its billow more efficient in the wind than her body was.

She immediately realized she was going to drift past one of its big damned eyes, so she set right to work getting her spacesuit sail experiments under way.

She had to wrestle with it for a time trying to make it

work, but eventually she found that by hooking her feet through the loops created by the tied sleeves and tied legs, she could spread her legs far enough apart to catch the wind in the scoop of the spacesuit. It wasn't elegant, but it was effective, and with a little practice using her flattened hands as rudders and ailerons to help guide her, she was making gradual upward progress.

She didn't know exactly what level she and Altin had been on, but she suspected that in terms of fore and aft, the alien that she'd just been stuck to had to have taken her at least two or three miles the wrong way. The one before that, the alien whose tentacles she'd bounced around in, well, where that had taken her, she had no idea.

All she could do was try to catch the opposite wind current in the level above and blow back the other way. Hopefully she could find the updraft that had, without a doubt, saved her life, and, maybe, use it to find Altin and save his.

She sailed her way up to the nearest grate, squeezing her ankles together to reduce the pull of the wind. She wasn't just going to shoot up through it and get blasted back the other way. With the Higgs prism working as it was, she'd end up getting bounced along the surface of the damn thing back the other way and break all the rest of her ribs. And whatever else too.

She managed to slow enough and to slip up into a gap in the grate. She stopped herself, absorbing her momentum with her legs, then pulled herself through the squared opening. She peered up over the edge and searched for aliens anywhere around. She didn't know why she bothered, since her previous captors hadn't been too concerned with her, but she looked anyway.

Three aliens were strung out into the wind, downwind from her. They were bound to the grate by four tentacles apiece, wrapped tightly around a beam like tethered kites, and they bobbed gently as their long bodies stretched up into the dimness and steam. The wide mushroom shapes of their billows were shadowy in the distance, but the lights flickering along their bodies shaped them well enough, particularly the nearer parts of them. Each had anchored itself with the lowest portion of its body, the slender end where the puckered orifice was, angled downward and situated close to the grate. Only five or six yards of stretched tentacles kept them from touching their rumps on the grate, and they looked like three long, billow-topped reeds bending in an alien breeze.

The three of them were flashing colors back and forth, obviously communicating to one another as they lay in the wind like that, while a fourth creature, much smaller than they were, scuttled along the grate using three short tentacles attached to its leading end to pull itself along. This fourth alien was long in its own right, perhaps fifty yards or so, with skin that was milky and whitish, and which had red veins visible beneath. At the tail end of its body—which was something like a cross between a prawn and a wasp— grew a long hook, which it poked down through one of the gaps in the grate. It was thusly that it secured itself to a beam. After doing so, it fanned out a section of its abdomen, spreading the length of its body like the skirts of a crawling snail, and swung upward at a roughly forty-five-degree angle in the wind, bobbing gently in the air currents in much the same way that its much larger counterparts did.

It was a few yards closer to Orli than the larger aliens were, and as it rose and fell gently on the blowing air, it pointed itself at the nearest of them. On its head, or just above it—it was hard to say what was what with the creature—there was a puckering sphincter sort of apparatus, right above its three short tentacles. It looked rather like pursed lips about to whistle, and she decided that end must be its face.

A droplet—or at least it seemed as one compared to the size of the thing—of brown fluid formed at this puckering cervical orifice. The larger alien nearest the little one was apparently aware of this operation under way, and it curved its lower end toward the growing droplet and puckered its own orifice—the same sort of opening from which ochre jelly had been spat at Altin when he'd cast the fireball in his attempt to rescue her. That seemed like a million years ago, though she thought it couldn't have been more than some span of minutes at best. Less than an hour certainly.

The hook-tailed alien let the droplet go, and the wind caught it and blew it right into the orifice of the larger alien. The bigger one sucked it up, and for a moment neither it nor its two large counterparts flashed any lights at all. Then its whole body began to light up again, just that alien that had imbibed the droplet. What began as a dull, mucous gray turned blue, then darker blue, then a deep purple that began to darken nearly to black. The alien became so dark it almost disappeared into the darkness around and beyond it. Its whole body went rigid, and most of its tentacles stiffened straight as morphine needles for a time. It actually lost its grip on the grate with all but two of its anchoring limbs, and the other two aliens had to catch it so that it wasn't blown off by the wind.

These other two flashed blue and green and yellow in alternating patterns. Despite the dire nature of her predicament, Orli couldn't help thinking they were beautiful. If she hadn't been in fear for Altin's life and her own, she might have watched for as long as the strange ritual went on.

As the rigid and purpled alien returned slowly to the normal mucous-colored state, the smaller alien with the hook angled its flowing body skirts and guided the bulk of its body back down upon the grate. It crawled toward the next alien in the line. The big three began flashing colors of every variety in what seemed an excitement of color. Orli used their distraction to duck down and pull herself along the bottom of the grate, getting herself underneath and then downwind of them by several yards. She had to get beyond them so that when she pushed herself up into the wind, she didn't just blow right into them.

When she was far enough, she drew herself back level with the top of the grate and peered back again. The three aliens were tilting up into the darkness angling high above. The little alien was angled into the wind again too, just releasing another droplet of the brownish liquid. The droplet floated up, struck the larger alien's orifice just a bit off center, and went in, sending just the barest splash into the wind.

Orli felt it more than she saw it as it blew right into her face. She realized it immediately, and with horror prepared for some kind of agony.

Instead she lost her hold on the grate and fell back into the wind, her whole body wracked with ecstasy. She bounced along the grate like a leaf on the wind, helpless in orgasmic contortions.

Before she could recover herself, she'd blown all the way past the end of the platform, several miles of it, and another mile out over a dark abyss that separated that platform from another just like it far in the distance. Her whole body quivered, and her muscles ached. She could hardly move. It was only by dumb luck that her spacesuit sail hadn't blown off her left leg, as the right one had come free of the loops she had tied.

As she regained herself, still blowing farther across the abyss formed between what she thought of as stacks of platforms that ran through the ship, she wondered if she would hit an updraft like she had earlier. The thought came to her lazily, almost dreamily, as the effects of the brown droplet wore off reluctantly.

And it was through that lazy sort of fog that she realized where she was and what was happening to her, and to Altin. That realization and the resulting fear for how far she'd been blown, even greater distances from Altin perhaps than before, jolted her to motion again, allowing her to shake off the last of the numbing afterglow.

"Good God," she gasped. Her whole body still tingled, but she shuddered anyway. "Okay, that was freaking gross." She shuddered again. "Sort of." She would definitely make a point of avoiding the little ones. That kind of pleasure she didn't ever need again.

She hooked her free foot back through the spacesuit and started angling upward again. Soon enough, she sailed her way to the stack of grates across the abyss. She'd lost a lot of distance and a lot of time. She still wondered if maybe this abyss had another updraft. It seemed likely, and if so, it would sure save time having to, in effect, tack her way upward back and forth in the alternating layers of crosswinds. She had a lot of altitude to gain to get back to where Altin was. That was the only thing she knew for sure. Her fall had been long, and that distance had to be undone.

She pulled herself along the edge of the grate platform, checking to see if there were any aliens on it nearby. There weren't.

She hauled herself along for what felt like it had to be at least a mile, gauging the distance by the nearing presence of a large oval of pale orange light. Still no updrafts. She probably had to be farther out over the abyss to find one.

As she neared the pale orange light, she realized that she just wasn't going to catch a break on the updraft thing, so she began pulling herself up onto the platform, getting ready to jump into the wind. She did that right as an alien came blowing straight toward her at speed.

Its billow was open and full, but it was high above her, and she was terrified that it had seen her head and shoulders coming up over the edge of the platform. She ducked down and held her breath, staring up along the edge of the grate, waiting for one of those goddamn tentacles to snatch her up and ... well, maybe just throw her away again. Who knew? But she didn't want to find out.

She waited. Knowing it would show up any second now.

It did. But it showed up over the orange oval of light. It flew right over the light, and then its billow seemed to empty some, deflating by perhaps half. Right after, it began climbing down, stretching tentacles to the platform beneath, and descending without any trouble from wind.

Orli realized immediately what she was looking at: a chimney of calm air. Not the same as an updraft, but perhaps just as workable.

She looked down and realized there were orange lights just like it above and below as far as she could see. She saw others in a neat vertical line across the abyss, back the way she had come, paralleling those on this side.

Of course they had a way to change directions more easily that what she was trying to do.

She waited to make sure that it was gone, watching it climb down four layers before continuing on in the direction it had been going when she'd first spotted it. She grinned. Finally a bit of damn luck.

She pulled herself along the edge of the grate and got herself even with the orange light. Sure enough, the wind died down quite a lot. It still blew, but it blew in gentle whirls and gusts, and not enough to change her direction much. With a glance up and down to see if anyone—anything—was coming, she gave a great pull with her arms and set herself gliding up the nearly dead-air column, at least heading in the direction from which she had come: up. Maybe she would find Altin soon, now.

Maybe now it wouldn't be long before they could get the hell out of here.

Chapter 27

Roberto set the *Glistening Lady* down on a rocky flat a mile from the road and a half mile from the cliff that overlooked Murdoc Bay. A careful sensor sweep showed there was no one nearby, and for at least the hundredth time since beginning his Goblin Tea enterprise, he was grateful for the discovery that illusion magic did not fool light. It fooled minds, but not optics and computers, and somehow computers filtered out the effect for human brains and eyes. There was no one out there.

They shut the engines down. All the lights had been turned off since they crossed the Gallspire Mountains. Roberto leaned back and watched out the ship's forward window, dimming the monitor below it so the light wouldn't spoil his ability to see. The darkness was nearly complete. The moon, pink Luria, was in its red phase, a gentle curve that turned deep red during this time of the month, beautiful but providing little light.

"I can't believe you told Master Tea no on that extra half ton," Deeqa said, shaking her head as she looked at the parchment manifest. She set it down on the control panel before her and looked at him. "That was free money. If you are so worried about your conscience, you could have split the profit with the Queen. That's all she cares about anyway, is it not? Raking in coin?"

"Look, I got everyone pissed off at me right now, and the last thing I need is to introduce a new idea into that woman's paranoid head. I start out with 'Hey, so your tea master is offering side deals to me, so I'm splitting it with you,' and what ends up happening is I get the tea man screwed and her wondering what other sneaky shit I'm doing that I'm *not* telling her about. It just makes me look guilty. And as far as keeping it for myself, I don't need that kind of karma. I'm trying not to piss off God right now, because I need God on my side for Orli and Altin's sake."

"I think your God would not hold your behavior against others."

"Wouldn't be the first time, and I'm just not taking any chances. I don't mind end-running the rules for lots of things, but this thing, our Goblin Tea setup, well, we can't screw with that. That has to be by the letter, or the whole thing comes crumbling down. There's already little enough I can do for my friends right now. I'll do even less if I am banned from Prosperion and put on permanent cock-block status by the TGS. Hell, talking to Vorvington right now is probably going to screw me anyway."

"He is a regular adviser to the Queen, and a relative of Her Majesty's, is he not? I do not think that is going to draw heat. Why should it?"

"Look where we are," he said, pointing out the window. "If this don't scream some kind of guilty, nothing does."

"There they are," Tracy announced from her post at the helm. "Just appeared."

Roberto squinted into the darkness in time to see a torch bloom to orange a hundred yards distant. He turned up his monitor and saw the spike on the magic detection graph. "Not bad," he said with a glance at the device as he got up. "Picked up a teleport at a hundred yards. You see, I told you it was worth eighty-five grand for that upgraded module."

Deeqa nodded. "I admit, I thought they were lying when you bought that."

"Well, on the subject of liars, come on, let's go talk to one."

They got up, and Tracy shifted into the pilot's seat.

The Earl of Vorvington waited in the darkness, his round face and long jowls painted golden in the torchlight, the wattles of his neck casting shadows like black vines rooted beneath his collar somewhere. The wind stirred the torchlight and the weeds around his feet. Four figures waited in the darkness behind him, barely visible beyond the glare.

"It's a cold night on the bluffs," the earl said. "The sea breeze still has its teeth this time of year."

"We talking weather here or looking at your star maps?" Roberto said. Deeqa stepped out of the torchlight, clicking off her flashlight as she went.

"Now, now," Vorvington said as she disappeared. "We've no need of all that. We're all friends here. With common cause."

"Then let's get to it," Roberto said. "Show me what you've got."

Vorvington produced a square of folded parchment from his cloak, which he unfolded and handed over to the Spaniard. It was large, and the wind buffeted it so much that Roberto had to kneel and set it on the ground. He looked at it for half a second, looked up, looked back, and clicked up his flashlight to a brighter setting. Then he laughed. "Are you kidding me? It's six dots. You can't be serious. How in the hell am I supposed to tell you anything about this?"

It was true. The parchment had six dots. Five in a little cluster near the bottom left corner of the parchment and one at the top right, almost off the edge of it. Roberto wouldn't have even noticed that last one if he hadn't looked a second time.

"My understanding is that those five at the bottom are the suns of Prosperion, Earth, Blue Fire, Yellow Fire, and Andalia," Vorvington said. "That other is the location we are interested in."

Roberto looked back at the map, then back at Vorvington.

"I thought you said you were trying to figure out if Her Majesty was mining Liquefying Stone on Blue Fire."

"We are. Or, I should say, we were. I did mention on our last meeting that I had some additional divining to do."

"Yeah, you did say that, all right." Roberto shook his head. He knew he'd been played that day. Now it was more a matter of trying to figure out why. And what the real game was. So for now, he had to keep playing along.

He looked down at the map again. "Well, if this thing is supposed to be anything remotely close to scale, that star up there is seriously far away. Yellow Fire is a thousand light-years from Earth, and it's hardly showing any farther away from Earth on this than Prosperion, which is essentially right around the corner by comparison. So we're talking tens of thousands, even a hundred thousand. Hell, it could be another galaxy. Even if we draw the line between these dots with a laser, the width of the damn beam just on the dot is going to be a massive area, a couple hundred light-years at least. Do you have any idea how big that is?"

"No, Captain. I admit to complete ignorance. That is why we came to you."

"Well, you got what you paid for, because I can't tell you shit from this." He got up and made to hand the parchment back.

"Wait. I said we'd bring an illusionist." He turned back and motioned with the torch. At first no one moved, but then one of the dark silhouettes, the one with the wide-brimmed hat, shoved the figure in the center into motion. A woman in her middle years staggered forward. Bits of straw stuck out of her dark hair, glinting golden in the torchlight. Roberto raised his flashlight and shone it on her, clicking the beam's brightness down a notch. She looked like she'd just come from rolling in the dirt. Vorvington reached back and drew her forward by her upper arm. "Go on, then, show him what you got from the rest of them."

She trembled as she cast the spell, and Roberto was pretty sure it was not due to the chill blowing in on the sea breeze. But soon after she began chanting, an enormous globe shaped itself in the air about a foot off the top of the wind-bent grass. It was vast, twenty-five feet in diameter. It held no images other than the fact its shape was visible by the presence of an uncountable number of tiny lights. They were obviously stars.

"You see there, Captain, an illusion that our diviners, working in concert with our illusionist here, were able to construct. It was no small feat, mind you, and as you suggested, we did elicit some help from students at the university. But it was mainly technical. Now is the moment of truth. Can you put the two together? It is my understanding that this is the sort of magic that the Redquill girl and the Sunderhusk boy provided to aid Sir Altin and Lady Meade in finding the red world."

Roberto stared up at the glittering ball of stars. It was beautiful to look into. But he wasn't sure, even with a holographic simulation of sorts, how he would be able to find which star was the one they were looking for. The parchment star map was a joke.

Apparently they saw the look on his face, because the man with the wide-brimmed hat stepped forward, though he was careful to keep his face in the shadows of that broad brim. He tapped Vorvington in the back with something. The portly nobleman turned and took it. He turned back to Roberto and proffered it to him straightaway. "Ah yes, and of course Lady Pewter used one of these to ... to somehow combine them, the map and the illusion."

Roberto took it. It was a computer tablet, the standard sort of thing one would expect on Earth, other than the fact it was wrapped in a fancy alligator case. There was something familiar about it, but he couldn't fathom why. It was certainly not what he expected to get from a Prosperion. Roberto tilted his head sideways and tried to get a better look at the man in the hat, but Vorvington was fat and the man was completely shrouded in shadow. Roberto was curious enough to raise his light and shine it on the man anyway. All he saw was the hat, its brim warping this way and that in the wind but otherwise mashed down securely upon the man's head.

Roberto harrumphed, but let it go. He wasn't too sure how much use the tablet would be, but he'd come this far, so there was no use not giving it a try.

He opened it up and turned it on. He flipped through screens until he found the star charts application. He crouched and set it in the grass long enough to lay the parchment map out on the ground next to it. He took up some rocks and laid them on the map, then used the tablet, scanning the drawing into its memory. A few taps and slides later, he ran the star dots against patterns on file. It came up with four hundred twenty three thousand nine hundred and eight possible matches. He actually laughed again. "Well, that's not going to get anywhere."

"Yes, Captain. I believe you need this too." He pointed with the torch to the star globe illusion. "You!" Vorvington snapped at the woman. "Show him with the sounds. Make them chime like the Sunderhusk map. Like you did this morning."

Roberto frowned, but hid it by glancing back at the map on the ground. This morning? He looked up at the woman. Her teeth chattered, this time for the cold, no doubt, as she was only wearing a thin shift that barely came to her knees.

Her arms were bare and so were her feet.

"Why don't you get her a blanket or something?" Roberto said.

"Captain, we don't have time."

Roberto stood and tapped his com badge. "Betty-Lynn, can you bring out a thermal?"

"She's already on the way, Captain," came Tracy's reply.

"Vorvington, I have to tell you, I'm not impressed with the way you treat your people."

"I'm not here to impress you, Captain. I'm here to get our friends back from the aliens."

"Right," Roberto said. He didn't buy that for a second. He looked down at the parchment star map in the grass again, moving the sun shape of his flashlight's narrow beam to the far corner where the single dot was. "I'm going to be honest, Lord Vorvington, that don't look like it's going to be much help to Orli and Altin."

"The diviners assure me it is exceedingly relevant."

"Yeah, I'm sure they do. They do that this morning, or after we talked?"

Vorvington lifted his nose and rolled his eyes skyward, above responding to such a thing.

The stocky-framed Betty-Lynn approached, a laser rifle crooked casually over the elbow of one arm and two thermal blankets folded over the other. She proffered the thermals to Roberto. He took them and thanked her, but did not ask her to go back to the ship.

Roberto set the tablet down and unfolded one of the blankets, his flashlight beam cutting wildly through the night as he worked. He went to the illusionist and wrapped it around her. "Here you go," he said. "I'm sorry we dragged you out here for this. You can keep this when we are done. These are great blankets. Think of it as a souvenir from planet Earth."

She looked up at him, gratefully, but she didn't smile.

There was something in her eyes that he couldn't pin down exactly, and he didn't like it at all. He looked past her to the three figures behind Vorvington. He shone his flashlight back at them. One was a large man, broad shouldered and muscular. He was young, but his face was tan and had the look of someone who spends most of his time in the sun and wind. Next to him was a slender man in gray robes. He was pale and looked uncomfortable. The third figure was, as before, shrouded in blackness, cloak and hat. Roberto flicked the light back and forth between them and held the other blanket up. "Any of you need this?"

"I'll take it," the big man said, a big grin on his face. "It'll sell for a heap bein' as it's from Earth and all."

The black hat moved side to side as the man beneath it shook his head, but he didn't say anything. Roberto handed the blanket over and then went back to the star maps. He debated quitting, but he had a feeling that might be a bad idea. And if there was even a chance this could still help Orli and Altin, he supposed there wasn't much to lose if it was not. A few more minutes of his time. No sense causing an incident.

He looked to the illusionist. "Are you okay to try?" he said. She shook her head, as if saying no, but she closed her eyes and started chanting again anyway. There followed a succession of chimes, six of them, five higher notes and one an octave lower. With each note, a star in the glowing sphere flared briefly, though Roberto missed the first three, not realizing what was happening.

"There, you see," Vorvington said, pointing to the star globe. The highest note is Prosperion, the next is Earth, the one below that Andalia, then Blue Fire, then Yellow Fire. The last and lowest is the world we need to find. That is where the secret lies."

"What secret?"

"The one that might free our friends."

238

"I notice you have already shifted to *might*." Roberto didn't know why he was even bothering to point this stuff out anymore. So he didn't wait for a reply. He picked up the tablet and went closer to the globe. "Can you ping them again? Slower so I can see them."

"Do it," Vorvington ordered the woman unnecessarily.

Again came the chimes. This time Roberto saw each star as it pulsed, once for each note in turn. There were five together on the opposite side of the star globe from where he stood, and the last one pulsed right in front of him, nearly on the surface of the globe. He had the illusionist repeat the tones several more times as he walked around the star map hanging there, the only thing unaffected by the wind.

"I'm still not sure how this is going to help me," he said.

"Well, I surely have no idea," said Vorvington.

He circled twice more, then raised the tablet and circled it again. "I can't pick it up on this thing. This is less help than the paper one. These illusions aren't real."

Deeqa came out of the darkness to stand beside him, looking into the star globe. She stepped into it, put her hand in the cluster where the five suns with the five known habitable worlds were. She went to the new one near Roberto. "Let me see the tablet," she said.

Roberto handed it to her. She quickly found his original star map scan. She squeezed it together on way, stretched it another. She went into the code and changed the scale. When she hit the reconfigure, it came up with a new list. She handed it back to Roberto. His four hundred twenty three thousand nine hundred and eight had been reduced to nine.

Deeqa cocked an eyebrow, but said nothing. He saw what she had done. He looked up at Vorvington, who was standing on his tiptoes, trying to look over the top of the tablet, even though he was ten feet away. Roberto was tempted to key in the code to the ship's computer and flick the record to his own system, but he didn't know what these guys were capable of in terms of recovering that access later. Who knew who else they knew from Earth, and those goddamn diviners were freaky in the extreme. He committed the system names to memory instead, then handed the tablet back to Vorvington. "There you go," he said. "Best I can do."

Vorvington's grin was hideous, a globular movement of his face and neck, flesh shifting like gelatin being squeezed. "This will do fine, Captain. I'm sure it will do fine. The beauty of divination is that it works with what you know. If I can give them nine stars to choose from, they can surely rule out eight of them. The gods favor those who get themselves to where the gifts are given out."

"So should I stay up late waiting for my copy of whatever results the gods are giving out?" Roberto asked.

"Don't lose any sleep at all, good Captain. You have my word that as soon as I know how to get poor Sir Altin and Lady Meade home safely, you will be the first one I notify."

"Yeah, that's what I thought." He glanced to Deeqa and shook his head. "Come on, let's go." They started to walk away, but he stopped and turned back. "Hey, you, illusionist lady. Are you okay? Do you want a ride somewhere before we go?"

The four figures vanished before he got the last word out.

Chapter 28

Pernie trotted along the sidewalk at a steady clip. She wished she had Knot with her. Running on her own feet seemed very slow compared to being on his back. In the time it took her to run past the bus stop and reach the park on her own, with Knot she could already have been downtown looking at Hostile husks in the rubble of the broken buildings. She sighed, but she kept on running anyway.

She ran around the park and down the street she'd taken after school, the one that had brought her to the tall buildings. As she made her way steadily down it, imagining how big some of the Hostile corpses might be, a vehicle rolled up beside her in the dark. It was one of the older kind with wheels that touched the ground, not one of the gravity kind like Pernie was going to get someday. Its headlights were bright, and they lit up the street for a long way ahead. A cat's eyes glowed green under a parked car, bright like a basilisk's eyes will when it is about to turn someone into stone. Pernie heard that gorgons didn't do that when they turned people into stone. She didn't think the cat was going to turn anything to stone, but she thought it looked very impressive in the dark.

The vehicle didn't drive past her like the scant few that she'd seen earlier in her journey had. The lights turned off as it neared, and then it was rolling along beside her, keeping pace. She could hear bits of gravel popping under its black wheels. She glanced over to see who was inside. She recognized the man she'd seen in the park yesterday.

"Hi," he called out through the open passenger side window. He scooted across the seat and leaned through the opening, leaving the vehicle to drive itself. "Where are you going this late at night?"

"None of your business, that's where," Pernie said. She'd heard someone say that at school and liked the way it sounded when it came out. She ran a little faster.

The man said something, and his vehicle sped up. She looked back at him. The vehicle looked very old. It was very plain, like a box, dirty and with plastic and metal visible in places where paint should have been.

The van caught up to her easily enough and drew closer to the sidewalk next to her as she ran toward the corner. "You need a lift?" he asked.

Pernie frowned. Why would she need him to lift anything? She wasn't even carrying anything. She thought he was probably very stupid. She'd met stupid adults before on Prosperion too. Kettle said that the gods kept all the peoples' brains in baskets and handed them out to babies when they were born. She said some babies got the brains that were on the bottom of the basket, and they were kind of smooshed. She said Pernie was supposed to be nice to those people, though, because nobody got to pick their own brain, even the smooshy ones.

"No," she said. "I'm not carrying anything."

The man laughed. "You're funny," he said.

That made her frown some more. She wasn't trying to be funny. There wasn't anything funny about not carrying anything. She thought she'd been nice enough, though, so she didn't feel bad about cutting through some trees and across someone's yard to avoid him now. Sophia Hayworth said it was rude to go in people's yards, but Pernie thought that peoples' yards were dumb. They grew grass but then cut it too short for any animals to eat. They paid for water to water it, and complained about the cost. They also complained about the shortage of water that made it cost a lot, which they'd known about before they planted the grass they knew would need water. People from Earth didn't make sense a lot of the time. So Pernie ran across the short grass and hopped the fence, then ran through another yard, and turned down the street that would take her directly to downtown Reno.

The dirty white box vehicle rolled up beside her a little farther down the street.

"Hey," the man said. "I'm just trying to be nice."

"Me too," said Pernie. She wished he would just go away.

"So where are you going? I really don't mind giving you a ride."

She looked back at him. "You'll just take me back home and tell me I'm too small to be out at night. That's what you all do."

"Not me," he said. "You look like a big girl. Old enough to be out if you want to."

"I am," she said. She could see the rows of green and yellow and red lights now, down the slight incline, all straightening up and marking where the streets crisscrossed the downtown. It was still pretty far away. And the big buildings were even farther than that.

She looked up at the moon. Earth only had one moon, like Prosperion. She'd learned in school that some planets had lots. Even hundreds and hundreds of them. It didn't matter that Earth only had one, though. Pernie still hadn't figured out how to tell when morning would come with it. If Sophia Hayworth stopped trying to be her guardian all the time, she might get out more and find out. She didn't know precisely how long she'd been working on deactivating the window alarm, though. It might be closer to morning than she thought.

"Come on," urged the man. "It doesn't matter how far. Wherever you want, I'll take you there. We can even get pizza on the way. Or ice cream. Whatever you want."

"I don't know what that is," Pernie said, "but I want to go downtown. Where the buildings are broken from the Hostiles. Will you take me there?"

"Sure," he said.

Pernie slowed to a walk. "Do you know where the dead ones are?"

He frowned for the barest moment. Pernie saw it in the glow of the streetlight a few yards up ahead. She started to run again, but then he said, "Oh, yeah. Sure I do. Whole piles of them."

"You do?"

"Yes. I just hadn't been over to look at them in a while. Not since, you know, they all died and all." He stopped his vehicle and pushed open the door. He slid over to the far side of the seat. "Hop in. I know the perfect place."

Pernie grinned. She'd just known she was going to see a Hostile tonight. She was very glad she hadn't given up on trying to cut through the paneling on the wall.

She climbed into the vehicle and waited for the door to close.

"You have to pull that thing shut," he said. "My poor van is shot to hell. Motor's been dead on that side for ten years."

"Who shot it?" Pernie asked. "Was it the Hostiles?" She felt stupid the moment she asked it. The Hostile war hadn't been over for even two years yet, so it couldn't have been ten.

"I'm Marty, but everyone calls me Zest," he said. "What's your name?"

He didn't sound like he thought she was stupid like a lot of other grown-ups did. That was good. She pulled the door closed as she said, "I'm Pernie. What does Zest stand for?"

"I don't know," he said. He tapped in a destination on the van's console.

"Sophia won't let me learn to drive," Pernie said. "She says I can't have my own car until I am sixteen."

"Yeah, that's not very fair," he said as the van lurched into motion. Soon they were moving right along.

Pernie looked out the window as they drove. She liked having the wind blowing her hair again. The windows on the bus only came down halfway, and it never went fast enough to make much wind. It made her think of Knot again.

The man wasn't very talkative, so Pernie contented herself with watching the buildings going by. Soon the tall buildings were climbing toward the stars, or at least what few stars there were. Pernie thought that Earth didn't have half as many as Prosperion did. Maybe less than half. Sophia said it was light pollution, but Pernie wasn't sure that made any sense.

They wound their way through a few blocks of downtown, and Pernie found herself growing more and more eager to see a dead Hostile.

"So how big is the biggest one?" she asked.

"Biggest what?" he said.

"Hostile. How big is the biggest Hostile corpse? Or are they just shells, and the Hostiles are dead inside?"

"Oh, uh ...." He glanced into the monitor that showed the street behind him, then looked out the windows on either side. She thought he looked very nervous doing it. "Very big. Bigger than the van." She thought he sounded nervous, too. It was kind of silly for a grown man to be afraid of a dead Hostile, but Pernie was polite enough not to say anything.

She wanted to tell him that Master Altin killed Hostiles all by himself, and that she had magic and would protect them, too, if she had to. But she knew that she actually couldn't because of the promise she'd made to Tytamon and Djoveeve. "No casting magic, no matter what," Djoveeve had said. "You promised. And you know what a promise is from the Sava'an'Lansom."

Pernie did. The Sava'an'Lansom couldn't tell a lie. Djoveeve said that the protector of the High Seat had to be absolutely trustworthy, or the whole world would fall apart. She said that trust was the glue of civilization. Pernie didn't know about all that, though, and she'd said as much. That's when Djoveeve got her good.

"You said you want to marry your Master Altin one day," Djoveeve had said. "Marriage is a promise, don't you know?"

Pernie hadn't ever thought of it like that before.

"It is," the ancient old assassin had pressed. "It is a promise to be faithful until your dying day. A promise is not something to enter into lightly, child. And it's all the more important for you. When you become Sava'an'Lansom, your promises must be stronger than your steel. When you promise to protect, when you promise to kill, there must never be a doubt in anyone's mind. Ever. That is how the Keeper of the High Seat on String, and the Royal Assassin in your lands of Kurr, help hold the peace. It is their promise of death that makes the knot of peace between us, the humans and the elves. You, little Sava, must never make promises lightly. One day, your promise might hold together everything."

So Pernie had promised not to use her magic. Which was fine. Especially here on Earth. Nobody else had magic anyway. Including a dead Hostile.

They turned up another street and were now driving toward the mountains. Pernie saw that they were leaving the tall buildings behind.

"Hey," she said. "The Hostiles are back there where the broken buildings are."

"I know a better place," he said. "A great big one that crashed into the trees."

He didn't look scared anymore, and Pernie thought he might be running away. She didn't want to call him a coward, though, because that would not be polite. His brain did come from the bottom of the basket, after all.

"Well, you said you would take me to the broken buildings," she said. "And that's where I want to go. So take me back like you said you would."

"We're going to see the big one way up in the trees."

Pernie frowned at him. He looked back at her only briefly, flashed a flat smile, and looked back out again.

"Speed seven," he said. Pernie knew he was talking to the car.

"Well, I don't want to see the big one," she said. "So if you are afraid to go to where there are lots of smaller ones, then you can just let me go myself. Take me back."

"Just wait," he said. "You'll like this one."

"Take me back," she said again. She was getting mad.

"No, be patient. I told you there is a big one up here." He was staring straight out the windshield now. "Window up—passenger front," he said. Pernie's elbow had been resting on the window frame, and the glass suddenly rising startled her.

"Hey," she said. "Put that down. And take me back right now."

"No." He spun on her. "Listen, brat, you're going to see the one up here in the trees. You're going to like it, and that's how it is. So shut up before I make you shut up." He turned back and leaned over the backseat. He pulled out a roll of something silvery. He unwound a length of it, which looked like parchment made of very thin steel. "Give me your hands," he said.

"No. Let me out."

He snatched her by the wrist and tried to wrap her arm up in the crinkling metal parchment that he held.

She kicked him in the face, twice rapid-fire, then a third time in the throat. He made a gasping sound, and his head rebounded off the window on his side of the van. She lunged for him and grabbed him by the back of the neck. He was mostly limp anyway, so she was able to bounce his forehead off the dash three times right in a row. He slumped against it and didn't move.

Pernie stared at him and shook her head. He wasn't only stupid, he was mean, and maybe a little crazy too. Kettle had told her once that sometimes grown-ups lose control of their minds. Then they get sent to places like Goffa House in Hast. That's where they sent the sight magicians and diviners who forgot themselves.

She pushed him up against the door and looked at the destination panel. It was smeared with blood. She picked up the wad of silvery parchment metal from the seat and wiped it away as best she could. If they weren't almost to the giant Hostile, she was going to jump out and head back down the hill.

She looked out the window and realized that they were up in the mountains now. There weren't as many trees as she had thought there would be, but in patches there were. She supposed the forest would be higher up. But she didn't want to stay in the van for very long.

She could teleport out if she wanted to. But she didn't want to break her promise not to. She tried to open the door, but it was locked. She couldn't find anything to open it with. There was a little empty hole on the side near the window where the lock on Sophia Hayworth's car was.

She looked back at the destination monitor. The green bar was just past three-quarters of the way. She supposed she could wait that long. And maybe there was a big Hostile.

If not, well, maybe there were other things. She had wanted to explore the forest up here anyway.

She just wasn't too sure she was going to be able to find her way home before sunrise.

Chapter 29

Pernie did not make it home before sunrise. At least, she did not make it home on her own. In fact, she barely got to explore the forest at all. She'd only been out of Zest's van for maybe twenty minutes at most when the first aircraft arrived.

She was just on her way up a tall pine when over the treetops came a light that seemed bright as a sun. It was even brighter than the light the Reno PD man had shone on her only a few short hours before. She was getting very tired of people shining bright lights on her and ruining her exploration time. She hadn't gotten to see a Hostile yet, and now here was another light trying to do it again.

She'd jumped down from the tree and run out of the light, dodging side to side behind trees as the infernal light chased her through the forest. She was doing a fair job of it until a second aircraft came. It didn't have its light on until after Pernie heard the hiss, two of them, *ffft*, *ffft*, right in a row. She'd managed about another step and a half, and then everything got blurry and she fell down. When she woke up, she was back with the stupid Reno PD again.

Two days later, she was finally back at school. She only got to go back to school because Don had had a big loud fight with Sophia Hayworth about it. He kept telling her that Pernie was perfectly safe and just had to learn how to be on Earth some more, just like he and Sophia had to learn how to be Pernie's guardians. Pernie had laughed at that from her place in her room, where she was "grounded" again.

Sophia Hayworth was really mad at Don, though, and she shouted at him and told him, "I can't live like this." She said that Pernie had been in the clutches of a "pet on file," or something very similar, but Pernie didn't know what that was. She figured it must be pretty bad or Sophia wouldn't be so mad, but Pernie had been very careful as she'd gone through the woods. The scariest thing she'd seen was an owl, and she was sure it was nobody's pet. Still, Sophia was super mad, and it was actually a little bit like Kettle that time. But only a little. Mostly Sophia just sounded mad. She told Don Hayworth that she thought they should send Pernie back.

That was the first time Pernie was afraid.

She didn't want to go back. If they sent her away, she couldn't learn all the Earth things that made Master Altin love Orli Pewter so much. Going back to Prosperion now would ruin everything.

For a moment Pernie nearly panicked. What could she possibly do? She thought she might go out and beg Sophia not to send her away. She could apologize and promise not to go outside ever again. She could get a net visor and just play video games all night until bedtime like the other kids did. Or just read books and study on the net like their daughter Angela supposedly always did. Pernie could do all of that. She didn't want to go home. Not yet.

But then she remembered what Sophia had told her the day before, about how there were treaties and things Pernie didn't understand. Promises that the Queen had made with the leader of the NTA. Pernie was part of a contract between them somehow. Plus she knew there was some kind of a promise between the War Queen and the elves. That was part of Pernie being Sava'an'Lansom. That was why Djoveeve had made such a big commotion about Pernie and her promises.

So maybe Sophia Hayworth couldn't send Pernie home.

Still, Pernie's heart was actually beating very hard when Don Hayworth finally came into her room.

He sat down on the bed beside her and let out a long sigh. He looked at her a few times, then looked back toward the floor. Pernie was sure he was going to tell her she had to go back to Prosperion. Then Master Altin would never love her. She'd be stupid just like the man in the van with his soft basket brains. Everyone would be mad at her. Everyone. Two whole planets full of humans and all the elves as well.

"Well, kid," Don Hayworth said finally. Pernie grimaced and waited for it. "What are we going to do with you?"

Pernie didn't answer. She didn't know what to say. She didn't think begging him would work anyway. Sophia Hayworth would make him do what she wanted him to do. Pernie had been here long enough to know that.

"Why did you go out again?" he asked.

That was good. That was better than coming right out and saying she was going to go back.

"I wanted to see a Hostile," Pernie said. She figured honesty was best right now.

He nodded. "The same as last time."

Pernie nodded too.

"There really aren't any Hostiles over there, you know," he told her. "We're not hiding them from you." He reached across her for her tablet on the bedside table. It all fell apart. He held what remained of it in his hands, and looked at her. His eyebrows made the question as he tipped it toward her some.

"I had to take the power out of it," she confessed. "The

Light of Luxury wasn't strong enough." She pointed to where her homemade laser cutter was.

He got up and went to where it lay on the dresser near the window. He set the remains of the tablet down and picked the modified cutter up instead. He turned it over a few times. The new power source dangled loosely from the wires, too big to fit inside the case. He looked at the huge section of missing paneling on the wall, then down at the blankets under the dresser, where she'd dragged it across the room. He looked back to her, then to the box with the picture of the lady running the Light of Luxury down her leg, her big smile still just as happy as it ever was. He started to laugh.

"What?" Pernie said. She hoped he wasn't laughing because she was so stupid she thought she would get to stay. She looked at the wall and realized how much damage she had done. Earth people spent all their time worrying about how many credits everything cost. She thought fixing all of this might cost a lot of them. "I have credits, you know," she said. "I'll pay to fix the wall." He frowned at her. "And the Light of Luxury. I'll buy a new one. I didn't mean to ruin it."

He laughed again, even harder than before. That made Pernie frown. He saw it, and stopped. He came back over and sat down next to her again.

"Don't worry about the wall, kiddo," he said. "It's not the wall."

Pernie was still frowning at him, but she thought that maybe he was going to say something nice.

"Look. We don't need you ... carving up the house," he said. "But that's not it at all. Hell, if I'm being honest, I'm impressed. You're one smart little cookie, I'm not going to lie."

Pernie's frown shifted to the other side of her forehead, a sort of lateral wave of confusion washing from eye to eye.

"Pernie, what you did today is dangerous. And I know

Sophia already told you that. But you have to understand something, here. You can't just go wandering off yet. Not all alone."

"I wandered off all the time at home. And I did on String too. I'm not a baby, you know."

He laughed again, though it was short this time. "Yes, by God, I know that's right. Hell, I'm more a baby than you are in that way. But, Pernie, listen to me. Earth is a different world. It's a lot different. I don't know anything about String or Kurr beyond the few hundred pages that I've read. But it's not the same. You have to be patient. You have to give yourself some time to understand how all this works. It's hasn't even been three whole weeks. You can't just run off like that. Please."

Pernie pursed her lips and moved them from side to side. She wondered if he was going to make her promise to stay inside. Grown-ups always wanted promises. She wasn't sure she wanted to go that far. She had enough promises to deal with so far. But she didn't want to go home either.

"Look, it's pretty obvious you're not the kind of kid who takes well to being told what to do. If we're being straight with one another, I'm not sure we could keep you here even if we tried." He looked up at the wall and the window and shook his head. "But I like having you here. You're a great kid, and I think one day you're going to have the whole world—hell, the whole universe—by the throat, just like you did that creeper that took you. I just know you will. But not if you do something reckless first, before you have a chance to see it all through, to, you know, learn what you need to know." He looked frustrated, made a face not so unlike the one Pernie wore. "Does any of that make sense?"

She thought that maybe it did. At least he didn't try to tell her what to do. Or make her promise anything. At least not yet.

She nodded but didn't say anything.

"Good," he said. He stood and faced her. "Now, since you are so damned smart, I tell you what I'm going to do."

She looked up at him, one eye narrowing. Here came the promise he was going to try to make her make.

"Since you are the one that wrecked my house," he said, "you can be the one to put it back the way it was."

She blinked at that. She hadn't seen that coming.

"That's right. You broke it, you fix it. And you aren't going to break more stuff like that over there to do it, either." He pointed to the Light of Luxury and shook his head. "Do you even know what that is?" he asked. Laughter began playing at the corners of his eyes again.

"No," she said.

The laughter came in full again. But it was a kind laugh, so she didn't mind.

"Well, this weekend, I'm going to rent the tools and get you what you need. Then you, Miss Grayborn, are going to *make* something instead of breaking it. You hear? That's what matters in the end. Anyone can break things. The world needs more makers, you know? The whole galaxy does."

There was a gentleness in his eyes that made her think he really wasn't going to make her promise anything. And he certainly hadn't told her she had to leave. Maybe if she fixed the house, they'd let her stay. She wasn't too sure about that, though. She had no idea how to put all that stuff back. He was right about that. It was definitely going to be a lot harder trying to fix the damage she had done. But she would. Somehow. She wasn't going to let him down. If he could convince Sophia to let her stay, then he was her best ally on Earth. He and Jeremy. And Jeremy was a maker. Maybe he would know what to do.

Chapter 30

The marchioness paced back and forth, waiting. She glared at Vorvington from time to time at one end of her course, and on the other end she would stop and look to the two diviners working with Conduit Wanderfrond, then back to Black Sander, who sat still as a statue in a chair near the window. He'd been sitting there, motionless, for nine hours, ever since the divination began. He could tell it irked her that he hadn't moved, as if his lack of movement was an indictment of her inability to be as emotionless as he. She scourged him with a look worse than the one Vorvington got, then peered through the curtains to the position of the sun. It was long past midday now.

She spun back and repeated the path across the room twice more. At the end of the second pass, she stopped and hissed at Vorvington, "What's taking them so long?"

The earl shrugged, his round shoulders pinching a slab of his throat forward, making it look like a frog's. Then he raised his forefinger to his lips. She speared him with the ice lances of her stare for it, but she spun back and resumed pacing again.

Finally, a half hour later, the chanting from the diviners stopped, the abrupt silence like deafness had fallen upon the room. All three of those not involved in the casting looked to the conduit expectantly. "Well?" demanded the marchioness.

"It is true, My Lady," the conduit said. He let go a long breath, and licked his lips before going on, a gray-tipped motion across his mouth like a lizard peeking out. A gray tongue was a familiar feature of those who used sanza-sap regularly. "The War Queen is once again at war. There can be no doubt."

He stood and stretched, placing his hands upon the small of his back as he did so. He had been sitting for a very long time. He took up two pieces of parchment, the topmost being one upon which Black Sander had written down the names of the nine star systems that the captain of the *Glistening Lady* had provided for them. It had been a central component of the spell. He carried it to the marchioness and handed it to her, pointing with the long fingernail on his pinky. "It is this one, My Lady, the third one on the list."

She looked down at the paper and read the name aloud. "Cas 98213." She frowned at it, then addressed the conduit again. "Does that mean anything? Is it enough? Can you tell who she is fighting with? Is she there for the yellow stones?"

"It does mean something, My Lady. And I can say for certain that her desire for the yellow stone is what led her there. I cannot say who she is at war with, but the cast left us without the least suggestion that it was the Hostile world called Blue Fire."

"Then who or what is it? Did you see? Are they the aliens that have landed on the red world?"

"I got the sense of giants, My Lady. Many of them. They fight with weapons as long as trees. And I did see your ring of fortresses, just as depicted in the drawings Lord Vorvington procured. That I saw as clear as you please." He presented her with the second piece of parchment, the one that Vorvington had taken from Aderbury's seemingly abandoned home. "This, I assure you, is part of it. There is no doubt. This fortification is on a world near that star." He licked his lips again, the gray lizard of his tongue dragging itself drily from one corner of his mouth to the other. Its retreat left flecks of white spittle in its absence like bits of discarded skin.

"So whose fortress is it? Does it belong to the giants? We do not have time for all this eccentric conduit nonsense on top of the cryptic diviner rubbish. Just speak, man."

"It is our fortress, My Lady. It belongs to Prosperion. The War Queen has built it on that other world."

"For what? By the gods, who are the giants? Was it they that sent the ships to the red world?"

"My Lady, I am trying. But I cannot tell you who Her Majesty is at war with. I know only what I have told you. She is at war with aliens on another world. If it is the world from which those aliens on the red world come, I have no sense of it. But I have no sense of them at all, so the absence of it neither confirms nor eliminates anything."

"Well, I already knew all of that," the marchioness said through clenched teeth. "Beyond the giants, anyway. And of course you can't tell me anything." She turned back to the window, her body rigid as a spear. "Diviners. Useless."

"You didn't know which star it was," he said.

"You said yourself the star name means nothing to you."

He shrugged, but she did not see it. She shook her head at the sun, then turned to Vorvington. "Does it mean anything to you?"

Vorvington arced his gaze to Black Sander, deflecting the question.

"It means nothing to me," Black Sander said. "But it will to our friends on Earth."

That seemed to warp the spear in her spine some. "Then you must go to them at once and find out what it means.

259

Return with what you learn, and we'll try the spell again. We must discover where that woman is."

"Yes, My Lady. When I go, I'll be taking the O-class illusionist and a satyr that an associate of mine found. Together, they will purchase another batch of laser rifles and a few cases of plasma grenades. It will be a profitable trip."

"Rifles!" she spat. "Plasma grenades? Were you even listening?"

Black Sander tilted his head to one side and manufactured a patient look, masking his surprise. "My Lady?" He let his voice fade away, shaping the question.

"The man said they were giants. Giants! Fighting with weapons the length of trees. And you want to bring me rifles and plasma grenades?"

"They served the Earth forces well against the demons, My Lady. The demons, too, were large and armored things."

"The Earth forces had the entire Palace full of magicians helping them, and all the mages on *Citadel*."

"As will we, if your intent is to go help Her Majesty extract herself from the war she has gotten us into."

"My intent is none of your concern." She turned away from them, toward the mirror in the carved bone frame. She gazed into it at the image of Sir Altin Meade and his new bride. They seemed to be staring back at her, their vacant, unblinking eyes watching sightlessly through the amber they were in.

Black Sander and all the rest waited in silence for whatever came next.

"I want the golems," she said at length. "I want the armor that is a fighting machine. That's what the Earth forces had. More than mages, that was what gave them victory."

"The mechs, My Lady?" Black Sander flashed a look to Vorvington, who made a face that said the earl was as surprised as Black Sander was.

"Yes, if that is what they are called. I'll have no more of these small arms. I might as well be paying you to bring me crossbows with flame-enchanted bolts."

"Oh, now please," said the earl. "Don't you think that might be a bit in excess? We have no one to operate those contraptions. They need riders! Which means you are suggesting we start bringing in Earth men as well. Mercenaries, no less. All those wandering minds for Her Majesty's diviners to find. All those drunken idiots. You can't possibly have thought this through."

"You forget yourself, Vorvington. Remember your place." That seemed to wound him more than a flame-enchanted crossbow bolt would have.

"My Lady," Black Sander suggested, his voice low and lubricated. "His Lordship is correct in that. I do not think bringing Earth men here is a good idea just yet. The sort of men and women who are trained in the use of those armor machines are not the type who will take to slavery, nor are they likely to be easily contained. And even if they are, at some point you'll have to let them *in*to those machines. Which means, as Lord Vorvington suggests, to employ them and their mechs to our advantage, they must be free—free enough upon our world to tip your hand before the time has come. Unless you intend to pay for them and leave them on Earth. And if so, I must remind you how limited our teleporting capabilities are just now."

She turned from the mirror, straight and calm, her mouth a fault line of thin, cracked lips. He saw in her eyes a look of power, a sense of it, a variety that comes with storied blood and the kinship of kings. "You will get them, and you will do it now. You will bring them here. If you cannot do it, I will find someone who can. If your friends on Earth cannot handle the request, then you will find new friends. Do I make myself clear?"

"Have you any idea of the cost of such things, My Lady?"

"I have more gold than that royal warmonger does. A whole mountain's worth. And it's been waiting for just this moment. So be silent and do as you are told." She turned back to the mirror, and because in it could only be seen the faces of Sir Altin and Lady Meade, no one in the room saw her smile.

Chapter 31

Orli couldn't be sure how many levels she had plunged after the aliens had tossed her away. She thought it had to have been at least ten, but perhaps closer to fifteen. The problem with hurtling through a dark spaceship at meteoric speeds while being blasted with scalding steam and trying not to hit protein beams thicker than oak trees was that, in doing so, she lost her ability to count how many oak trees she hadn't hit. Somehow, avoiding becoming a red stain on a numberless alien deck took precedence over tallying grates on her way into the boiling nightmare at the bottom of the ship. So, it was only with her best guess that she reached a level she thought might be fifteen levels above where she'd first discovered the column of dead air. She decided this was the one she would use to send herself into the wind again.

One major advantage of this level over the ones she'd just come up through was that she was well above where she'd encountered the aliens with the orgasmic mist—or whatever the hell that stuff the little alien spat was. That little accident had nearly gotten her completely lost, if not worse, and if there were any forces of mercy in the universe, she would not encounter that stuff again. What she needed to encounter was Altin. But damn, the ship was big.

She pulled herself along the edge of the grate, out of the dead-air column, and back into the wind. It pulled at her with increasing strength as she went along. The Higgs prism set at zero gravity made movement easy, so long as she maintained her grip.

Sure that there were no aliens swooping toward her—as sure as she could be, given how fast they came and how suddenly they appeared out of the darkness and steam clouds gasping all around—she adjusted her makeshift spacesuit sail around her ankles and hoisted her feet up into the air.

The wind caught it and puffed it full, and whoosh, she was on her way. She angled her arms out behind her and tilted the flats of her hands, gently guiding her flight as she soared out over the vast divide that separated the layers of grates across the abyss. It was only a matter of a few minutes before she crossed the dark expanse and was once again flying over a grate. She set herself to searching for Altin as soon as she was above it, flying high and glancing ahead warily, leery of being blown into some massive hunk of alien machinery. If she hit one of those constructs at sixty or so miles per hour, she'd still end up being little more than a steamy red smear somewhere.

She must have flown for five minutes before she came to the end of that grate. The dark sprawl of another black span yawned in front of her. If her guess was right, that was the one she'd ultimately ended up falling into after being tossed away by the alien.

Thinking of it made her glance behind, wary of aliens overtaking her. All was clear as far as she could see—which wasn't saying much.

She shifted her feet and hands, directing her flight diagonally across the wind. She had to get back as close as possible to where she thought she'd been when last she'd seen Altin, trying to reorient herself after the lateral shift she'd made when she'd pulled herself toward the orange light.

Soon she was over it and flying across another grate. She looked for anything familiar, hoping she'd gotten a good enough look at the machine upon which she and Altin had been placed, as well as at those others that she'd seen on the level below. So far there'd been nothing familiar: nothing similar to the big tanks resting in the woven tubes like nests, nothing with a big platform of bright light beneath a pronged protein microscope. In a way, that might be cause for optimism. If those machines were unique, then when she did come across them, she would know she'd at least returned to the scene of the crime, so to speak.

She angled back and forth as best she could, her eyes darting back and forth and her heart pounding. Twice she nearly collided with giant piping that ran up through the grates, seeming to lunge at her out of the darkness before plunging into darkness again on the level above or below or both. As she flew and searched, she tried not to worry, to panic, to fear for what might be happening to Altin right now. What might have already happened. She told herself it was as possible that he had escaped, or been discarded too. He might be drifting about looking for her this very moment. She could even hope that he had somehow managed to get home.

The updraft hit her without warning. She was closing in on the edge of the grate, a little over four hundred yards away, and then, wham, like a volcanic blast of steam, she was blown upward. It hit her so hard it snapped her head back and sent jolts of pain through her ribs. For a moment her vision swam for the brutality of it, but she blinked her way to clarity as she gritted her teeth and waited out the pain.

She was rocketing into the darkness like an insect pinned

to an invisible windshield. Up and up she went, so suddenly that she lost count of how many decks the updraft carried her past. Orange lights at the edge of them flickered by one after another in a vertical line. She was dimly aware of the fact that she ought to have noticed herself approaching that line.

It also occurred to her that she ought to look up.

She did so with exactly enough time to utter, "Shit," before she hit the upper reaches of the ship. A bright violet oval ringed another type of grate, the cross members narrower and closer together. She struck the intersection of two of these at speed. Not so fast as free fall, nor so fast as the crosswinds between levels, but hard enough to knock her out.

When she came to, moments later—minutes? hours?—she was lying against the vent pinned to it right where she had struck.

She lolled her head from side to side, assessing her situation. She was on a vent, pressed firmly there by the updraft, which now seemed from the sound of it to be more like an in-draft, drawn in by whatever it was that was making a tremendous roar. Though her whole body ached from the impact, it quickly became apparent that if she'd not hit the grid and instead gone through, she might be hamburger right now.

"Shit, shit, shit," she said, trying to get her bearings. She had no idea what level Altin might be on now.

She forced herself to calm and looked around. The violet light glowed brightly all round the vent. Off to her right was another oblong ring, shaped just like the violet one, but this one dull and gray. It too encircled a sprawling vent.

Making sure to keep herself pressed against the narrow crossbeams of the one she was on, she rolled onto her stomach and crawled toward the edge. She realized as she did that she'd lost her spacesuit sail. Not much she could do about it now.

She made it to the edge. The violet light came from a raised ring of protein, looking rather like the humped bead of a giant weld. It was rough to the touch, slightly different from the rest of the hull. Definitely not like any light source she'd ever seen. She crawled over it, clinging to the ceiling like a fly. Immediately on the other side of it, the airflow that had held her to the surface was gone. Once again she was drifting in zero gravity.

A much gentler wind blew lengthwise along the hull, so gentle she was barely moved by it at all. She bounced lightly against the hull like a helium balloon along a ceiling after the birthday party has gone. She got herself closer to the other vent, which was encircled by the light ring that didn't glow. There came from that vent the same roar of machinery blowing air. When she was near enough to reach her hand over the edge of the lightless light mound, her suspicions were confirmed. "The down elevator," she muttered to herself.

If she pulled herself into it, she wondered if she could get out again at the time and place she wanted to. It was either get in there and try it, or try to descend on her own, using her Higgs prism ... while dealing with the alternating crosswind. Without the help of her spacesuit sail.

She swore and pushed herself into the downdraft.

She plunged downward at a steady clip, braced for a wave of terror that never came. Being prepared for it made a huge difference, and she wasn't in free fall. She counted down five levels ahead of her, a guess at how far she'd come, and angled out of the air column.

The wind blowing over the deck snatched her immediately, and she fought to straighten out. She'd just gotten level with the deck when the gray smear of an alien soared right over her.

The air swirled beneath the edge of its billow as it blew

past, and it spun her wildly. The lazy waves that ran the lengths of its tentacles caught her twice as it continued by, the second knocking her almost to the grate. She saw the gridwork coming up at her and managed to get her foot down in time to absorb the impact some. A glancing blow, the pain in her ribs made her head spin, and the wind caught her and blew her along the grate, tumbling along it like a bit of trash down an alien road.

Her vision cleared in time for her to spot a huge triangle of light looming out of the darkness at her. It came from the top of a massive machine at which she was being blown. Fifty yards away tops, and she was going to hit it dead center and at high speed.

She angled upward, reached with her leg for another push off the grate. She gained altitude, but not enough. She was still going to hit it. Even if she cleared the edge, she'd likely hit pipes rising from the top of it.

She looked down. No chance she could cut an angle fast enough to get through one of the gaps.

She glanced down at the beam she was hurtling just above, her flight carrying her along its length, barely a foot above it. She'd only just managed to stop herself from glancing off it as she was blown along, the rough protein already having scratched her up all over. But she knew what she had to do.

Twisting to center herself around, feet first again, she reached down and rolled the Higgs prism to one Earth gravity. She dropped right out of the wind, onto the grate, and skidded to a halt like one of those old-time baseball players sliding into a base.

The surface was rough, and the abrasion that it made down the length of her hip and leg burned like fire. It stung so bad she had to wait for a wave of nausea to pass. When it did, she looked up. She was four yards short of the machine. Close, but far enough.

Glancing back to her leg, she saw blood welling up like tiny rubies all up and down her leg. As they grew larger, they would run together, then simply run. She shook her head. That was going to be a mess. But there was nothing she could do. She had nothing. Spacesuit utility belts didn't include medical kits.

Looking around, she concluded that this definitely wasn't the deck she and Altin had been on. But there was something familiar about the machine. It had a triangular bit of prismatic light on it near the upper edge. It was huge, perhaps thirty yards on a side. The colors in it whirled together in seemingly no pattern at all, but they were all there, the full spectrum of the rainbow along with many patches of lightless gray mixed in. She wondered if this was the same machine she'd seen while looking down through the grate shortly after getting out of the yellow gel herself. She hadn't noticed the pipes, or shafts, or whatever they were, rising out of it before, but she also hadn't seen a bright triangle like that anywhere else on the ship as she'd been flying around. It seemed like a long shot, but she had to hope it might be the same one. If it was, then she was close.

She made her way to it. She had the advantage of the wind blowing her against it on that side, so a minor adjustment to the Higgs prism made scaling it easy and quick. Soon she was at the top.

A bank of lights and a large oval patch showed her where the device's controls were. Only a few of the lights were illuminated, and the oval thing, which she thought might be a viewing screen, was as blank as the rest of it was. Only the texture of it was different, smooth and slightly soft to the touch.

Careful not to touch anything that looked like it might activate something, she climbed through the massive control panel and made her way up to one of the thick columns that rose from it like smokestacks. It was extremely hot, and it rattled. She could feel that rattle through it, like something gurgling inside, boiling or bubbling. She thought maybe it was a steam stack.

She looked around for something to wrap her hands in, something insulating, anything at all. There was nothing. No cloth. No paper. No duct tape. Nothing like rubber or foam or even a damn tree leaf. She looked up at the grate above.

There were aliens moving about up there.

What if that really was the level she'd been on, the level where Altin was? Could she have that kind of luck?

She grunted and set the Higgs prism to a tenth of Earth gravity. She just had to get up there. She told herself that the steam stack wasn't so hot that she couldn't touch it a couple of times on the way.

She gritted her teeth and wiped her hands down the front of her thighs. They were slick with sweat and steam. She was soaked through and through.

The wind cooled it enough that she hoped the moisture would work.

She jumped upward, and half climbed, half ran up the column, trying to launch herself upward with the least contact possible, but needing enough contact to stave off being carried away by the wind.

It burned. But it worked. She was up in under two minutes, and her hands and feet merely throbbed.

She pushed herself off the stack and grabbed the beam downwind of where the steam stack went through. She panted and winced at how bad her hands hurt. She wasn't sure how much more of this place her body was going to take. Her ribs threatened to black her out when she hit the edge of the beam, even though she'd timed the movement pretty well, and her right thigh along the side felt like there was acid burning the entire length.

She had to wait until enough things stopped throbbing

and burning and aching to see clearly. She looked around, hoping that somehow she'd actually find herself where she thought she ought to be.

There was a blocky machine perhaps six hundred yards upwind of her that had three hoses coming out of the side. That was just like what she'd seen before.

There were aliens beyond it; she could see the top half of them glowing in the steamy dimness. She couldn't tell if they were the same aliens or different ones. They all looked the same.

She crawled up onto the beam, her ribs screaming at her to stop. She set the Higgs prism to a click above Earth normal and turned into the wind.

When she got to the machine with the three hoses on her side, she glanced to her right and saw rows of nesting melon-shaped tanks. Hope flared even brighter.

She worked her way to the edge of the machine and peered around it toward the aliens. Sure enough, there was the work table with the brightly lit examination deck.

One alien was just leaving, pulling itself against the wind. It dimmed with distance, maybe three-quarters of a mile or so. Then it apparently found the upwind edge of the grate. She could only barely make it out in the darkness as it climbed up and slipped away. The other was still working at something on the controls of the machine.

Orli hoped it was Altin being examined like she had been. Maybe she could get up on the table unseen and ... what? Use her utility knife to cut out the creature's eye? The little flea could finally bite. But maybe that would buy her some time for ... something.

She didn't even know if Altin was up there.

She pushed her way through the wind, fighting toward the examination table. It was hard to believe she was actually moving back toward that thing. She knew it would be easier to climb it if she went around to the far side and got some help from the wind again. So she did. With the Higgs prism adjusted down, she let the wind hold her to the surface as she made her way up.

Her hands didn't hurt as bad as she feared they would. Maybe there really was a chance.

She glanced over her shoulder to make sure the other alien wasn't coming back. It wasn't. She saw it pull itself up a level and get blown away. She thought she might have seen it suddenly shoot upward after, but she couldn't be sure. Too much steam, too much dimness, and it was barely a phantom smear of gray from that far away.

At least it was gone. She turned back and finished climbing. She peered over the edge of the machine.

There was Altin. Right where he had been when last she saw him, trapped in the ochre goo.

His back was to her, and it was all she could do not to run to him and shout through the jelly that she was okay. That she was going to get them out of there right away.

Somehow.

Instead she crept along the edge of the machine until she could take advantage of shadows cast by the alien working the controls.

She crawled up on top of the machine and snuck up behind Altin's gelatinous enclosure. The alien was still working on the controls beneath the eye-shaped viewing screen above.

Orli got out her utility tool with its little folding knife. She didn't know what the hell she was going to do with it. Something. Maybe the jelly could be cut through or scraped away.

She got to the lump of jelly. She touched it with her hand. It was hot—big surprise—but not so hot she couldn't leave her hand there.

And there he was. So helpless. Unmoving. From the back she couldn't even tell if he was alive.

She wanted to see him, to look into his eyes.

That would be stupid. The alien would see her. If it bothered to look.

She took the knife and attempted a cut, knowing full well it wasn't going to work.

She carved away a slice. The stuff was tougher than it seemed, like a chunk of semisoft plastic. But it could be done.

She set herself to carving.

The damn knife was small, and it wasn't shaped well for gripping, at least not for work like this. But she cut anyway. Her scalded hands shook as she worked. She looked around the jelly blob and up to the alien.

She could see Altin in the eye-shaped monitor the alien itself glanced into from time to time. She saw herself in the image on it, just the shadowy shape of her head along the edge of the encapsulating gel. She ducked back. Damn, she'd looked enormous on that alien monitor.

Scrape, scrape, scrape. She hollowed out a bowl-shaped indent that was almost a foot around, maybe six inches deep. She had another two feet to go to get to him. It was going to take her at least an hour to cut him out.

She wondered if she had that much time.

As she worked, the ring clip on the knife rattled against the handle. She tried to pin it to the body of the knife with her palm, but it gouged into her hand, making the work a misery. She had to hope the sound was lost in the wind.

Two feet wide, maybe eight inches until she got to him. She hoped he could feel her coming for him.

Or maybe not. Maybe he would feel something terrible eating its way into his back?

She scraped and carved some more. Twenty minutes. Still the alien worked. It was looking at pictures of a human brain. Orli recognized the mythothalamus on the model depicted on the screen. It was Altin's brain. She'd seen it often enough on the *Aspect*'s computer, modeled by Doctor Singh.

She carved some more. She had to switch to her left hand. Her right hand was a bloody mess. So was her thigh. Most of the cuts on her leg had stopped bleeding, but every time she shifted her weight, crouching as she was, she broke the fresh scabs open here and there, and the blood ran freely again.

She hoped nothing could smell it on the wind. That would be bad. But then again, she'd been working for a half hour at least, and the alien hadn't looked for her even once, despite its being downwind. Maybe they couldn't smell. She didn't think she had that much luck.

She dug some more. Two and a half feet long, two feet wide. Barely a quarter inch and she would be able to touch the back of his spacesuit.

She pressed into the jelly with her hand. It was soft enough she thought he might be able to feel it now, if he hadn't felt it before. She wanted him to know she was coming. She wanted to feel him herself.

She dug some more.

The shadows she was crouched in grew darker. She looked up. The machine was off. The alien turned around.

Why? Had it heard the goddamn clip rattle?

The alien snaked down a tentacle for Altin, winding it around his jelly cage in the same moment it sent more tentacles forward to grab the grate. It sent others to grab the grate above. The long reach of those tentacles went taut, and the alien began moving into the wind, just as the other one had done. Altin was snatched up and hauled right over Orli's head.

The alien hauled itself against the rush of air to the edge of the grate. Orli tried to follow, but only as far as the edge of the machine. She was helpless to give chase. It moved away so quickly, like some mangled spider climbing up parallel webs. When it got to the edge, it hauled itself up to the level above. Orli watched in horror as it blew its billow out then, up into the wind. The arc of that strange parachuting appendage inflated in an instant and carried the alien away. And Altin.

Orli screamed and reached for her Higgs prism, intent on jumping into the wind anyway, but she stopped. That would only make it worse. If that was possible. How could it be worse than him being totally lost? She watched the alien dim to nothingness, heading toward ... somewhere Orli couldn't possibly hope to know.

She screamed Altin's name. Calling to him. Reaching for him with her bloody hands. Then she collapsed to her knees and wept.

Chapter 32

"Well, did it work?" Jeremy asked when Pernie got off the bus. "Did you get the seam in that wall paneling to blend all the way up like I said?"

"Yes," she said. "It worked just like you said. And it did smell really terrible. That might be the worst smell ever."

"Yeah, that resin is nasty stuff, and the catalyst is even worse. Put the two of them together and it's like burning barf."

Pernie laughed at that as they walked together toward the front steps of the school. She saw that the boy she'd beaten at the video game was standing at the top of the stairs with his friend Ritchie. They were watching her as she came up.

"Hi," said the tall boy, smiling.

"Hi," said Pernie as she walked past.

"Hey, wait up," he said, falling in beside her.

Jeremy glared across her to the boy who had joined them. "She doesn't want to play games, Kyle. She's got better things to do."

"Look whose nuts have dropped," the boy named Kyle said to his friend Ritchie. He turned back to Pernie. "Hey, so maybe at lunch you want to come hang out with us? I want a rematch. You owe me one."

Pernie tilted her head and turned to look at him, frowning. "No, I don't."

It was his turn to frown. "No, I mean, well, yeah, you don't owe me one. But, I mean, you could give me one anyway. It would be fun. Or I think it would be fun." His cheeks started turning very red. "Anyway, we hang out at the picnic table by the swings." He practically ran away.

Pernie watched him and thought he was kind of weird. Ritchie paused before going after him, long enough to get close to her ear. "He thinks you are pretty," he said. "He wanted me to tell you he likes you." Then he melted into the herd of kids staring down into their tablets or up into their visors as they shuffled along.

Pernie looked to Jeremy, who was staring straight ahead. "Those boys are weird," she said.

"What did Ritchie say?"

"He said his friend thinks I'm pretty and he likes me."

"So do you like him?"

"I think he's weird. I can't say if I like him or not, though. I don't really know him very well."

"Are you going to play with him at lunch?"

Pernie could tell Jeremy hoped that she would not. That seemed weird too. But she didn't want to play video games with Kyle and Ritchie anyway. "No," she said. "We should work on your robotic arm."

Jeremy smiled then, looking more than just a little relieved.

After they'd eaten, Pernie and Jeremy worked on his robot. Jeremy had completely rebuilt the wrist unit over the weekend and was ready to get it reattached. "So was Sophia still super mad today?" he asked as he slipped the new parts in. "Did she say if you were going to have to go home or not?"

"I can stay," Pernie said. "But she made me promise not to sneak out at night anymore and that I wouldn't try to go downtown alone." Thinking of that made her shake her head. "They both say there aren't any Hostile bodies in the wreckage downtown either. They say the NTA cleaned them all up. Do you think that's really true?"

Jeremy frowned as he worked, thinking on it. Finally he shook his head. "No," he said, "I doubt they got it all. There's probably no big pieces left, at least not where you can get to them without backhoes and cranes, but there's probably smaller parts. You know, the little bits of shell or the glowy stuff that came out of them when they died. I'll bet we could find that kind of stuff if we tried."

"We? You mean you would come with me?"

"Sure. We could be like paleontologists digging for dinosaur bones."

"I don't know what that is," she said.

"Well, it doesn't matter. But yes, we could go look sometime."

"When?"

"I don't know. When do you want to go? How are you going to get out?"

"Well, I don't know. Sophia had some man come and put in a prock-see-me alarm. She said I can't leave the house now without it seeing me and going off."

"*Proximity* alarm," he corrected her. "It's tuned to your chip."

"What chip?"

"The chip in your arm. Everyone has a chip. I'm sure they made you get one too. It's how they know who you are if you are dead and all chopped up. Or burned up real bad and stuff. It's also how they find you if you are a criminal."

"Well, I'm not a criminal," she said. "I don't think I have one. They never gave me anything."

"Did they give you any shots before you came? You know, with the long needles?"

"Yes. They said it was so I wouldn't get Earth disease."

"Well, then you got chipped." He put down his tools and

reached across the table, tapping her on the forearm right above her wrist. "Did you get a shot right there?"

She nodded.

"Then that's your chip. That's where they put them. That way when you reach for the screen on kiosks or public consoles, they can track where you are without even having to activate the city scans. Those they're supposed to have a warrant for, but Gabby says they scan for people all the time anyway. The NTA doesn't care too much about warrants and stuff."

Pernie didn't know anything about warrants or scans. But she didn't like having something in her arm. "So now I can't go anywhere without Sophia seeing me?" she asked.

"Oh, no, she wouldn't have access to that. She'll just know if your chip gets out of range of the monitor in your house. She'll get notified."

"How do I get it out?"

"You can't get it out without cutting it out, and it's in deep. But you can just cover it with tinfoil. It's the oldest trick in the book. Technically it's illegal to knowingly blind your chip, but it's not like anyone is watching if you do. Not unless you are a known criminal."

Pernie harrumphed. People who used their magic wrong could blind their mythothalamus, the organ of magic. Then they could never cast spells again. She thought it was interesting that someone could do the same to technology. "What is tinfoil?"

"It's like paper made out of metal. Shiny paper. There's some in the second drawer over there by the other workbench."

Pernie got up and went to it. She opened the drawer and right away found a long roll of shiny, thin "tinfoil." It looked just like the stuff the *pet-on-file* had tried to wrap around her arms that night in the van. She wondered if that was what he was trying to do, to blind her chip. The Reno PD people had certainly said that he was a criminal, so it seemed fitting that he would try to blind chips to hide from them.

Pernie closed the drawer and went back to Jeremy. She would cut hers out instead. She didn't want to be a criminal.

"I think we should go look for Hostile guts after school," she said.

"But how? You have to go home on the bus."

"I don't have to. I can walk home from downtown. I know the way now. We can just leave from here."

"The bus driver will know if you don't get on. He'll call Sophia. They'll come look for you right away."

Pernie shrugged. "Can you go or not?"

"Gabby won't mind. I just have to tell him is all. But you're still going to get caught."

"Nope," she said, taking up a laser cutter from his tool kit. "I won't." She cut right into her arm, right where she remembered the needle went. She opened it up wider than she needed to, and gave herself room to fish around with her fingers. It took a few seconds for the blood to flow.

"Whoa," muttered Jeremy. He leaned forward and stared into the hole. "Is that your bone?"

"Yes," she said. Her grimace was partly from pain, but mostly for concentrating on feeling around for the chip. "How big is it? I can't feel anything, and I don't really know what I'm looking for."

"Pretty small," he said. "But I've never actually seen one, so I don't know either."

She felt something then, right against the bone. Something hard. She tried to pinch it, but the blood was running freely now and her fingers were slick. She had to keep pinching at it, trying to grasp it. "It's stuck on there," she said, grimacing in frustration now.

"Doesn't that hurt?" Jeremy said, looking up at her, then down at the blood that was beginning to pool on the tabletop.

"Not really," she said. "Maybe a little, but I've had worse.

I had a sargosagantis horn right through my guts. It was as big around as your whole leg, bigger even. Getting stabbed through the guts hurts really bad." She used her fingernail to scratch at the thing. She was squishing more and more blood out over her arm, which ran over her wrist and off the back of her hand, droplets spotting the metal tabletop like rain, which in turn began to pool together as she worked.

"Wow, that's a lot of blood," Jeremy said. "I've never seen that much before."

Pernie glanced briefly to the puddle forming there. She shrugged. "It's not that much." She pointed toward a pair of slender, needle-nosed pliers near the robot arm. "Can I have that?"

He handed it to her reverently. She took it and pushed the nose in, smearing the handles with blood. She rubbed the tip of it across the chip stuck to her bone. She could feel the bump as the tool slid over it. But it wouldn't scrape off.

"Can you hit it?" Pernie asked. "Tap the back of the pliers. Just a little bit. I don't have enough hands."

His eyes widened, as if she'd just asked him to shoot her in the face.

"Hurry," she said. "The bell is going to ring."

Hands trembling, he looked about for something to use. There was a wrench closest to him, so he took that from the toolbox. "You're serious?"

"Yes. Just do it. Not too hard, though. I don't want to break it."

He leaned over her and placed the wrench across the grip ends of the pliers. He gave a gentle tap.

"Harder," she said. "Just a little bit more than that." He struck again.

She felt the chip break free. She set the pliers aside and fished around in the cut some more. She found the chip right away and pulled it out, holding it up to the light. It looked like a little black ant.

"That's it?" she said.

Jeremy was staring at all the blood. Pernie saw him and looked at the table. It was something of a mess.

Pernie went to the drawer where they kept the shop towels. She wiped away most of the blood, then bound up the wound. She really wanted to use her daffodil healing spell, but Djoveeve's stupid promise made that impossible. Keeping promises made making them seem dumb. She was definitely going to be more careful about making them in the future.

Jeremy came over and grabbed a bunch of shop towels and went to work cleaning up the table. Pernie took a few more and worked on the floor. They needed to hurry before the science teacher came in from lunch. He would be mad and make Pernie go see the nurse, who would in turn call Sophia Hayworth, and Pernie would once more be in trouble, she just knew.

Soon enough, however, they had it all clean. The table, the floor and the tools. Pernie got the bleeding stopped. She swapped out the first towel for a strip of a clean one, which she wrapped tightly enough to close the wound. Djoveeve had shown her how to do it right.

She went to where she'd hung her backpack and her sweater upon entering the room. Even though the weather was pretty warm, she pulled the sweater on. The long sleeves would cover up the binding on her wound. She pulled her ponytail out from beneath the collar and gave it a flick before turning to Jeremy. She lifted her arms out to her sides. "How do I look? Can you tell?"

He shook his head, but he was looking at her in a funny way.

"What?" she said. "Do I have blood on me?"

"No."

"Then what?"

"Kyle was right. You are pretty."

Chapter 33

A ltin stared out over the edge of the examining table for a long time after the alien threw Orli away. He yelled himself hoarse. He wept himself dry. Still he stared. He didn't know what he was expecting. Some miracle. Some reappearance somehow. He waited and watched, and she was just gone.

He spent quite a while in cursing the alien, using every threat and epithet he knew in the languages of two worlds. He was helpless. All alone. Orli was lying somewhere below, dead, or if not dead, horribly broken and dying. In agony.

He realized as he thought it how many times he'd thought it before. He was trapped in a loop of stupidity, a moronic cycling repetitiousness in which he was incapable of learning a most singular and essential thing, dating all the way back to a dead mouse, so very long ago. His curiosity the death of fragile things. And here he was again, so many deaths later, once more responsible ... and this time it was Orli. Again. He'd actually thought it was a good idea to approach the ship. How could he possibly have thought that was a good idea?

Orli had tried, over and over and over, to talk him out of it. But, as always, some insipid and inescapable part of him just had to prove it could be done. Always. He just couldn't stop trying to push just a little more. One more step. One more planet. One more star.

He'd challenged the gods that day upon his tower, not so long ago, a few years really, him all alone, barely off Prosperion's moon, Luria. He challenged them, defied them, dared them to be real.

And what had they done? They gave him the gift of Orli. They gave him love. They brought love all the way across the damned galaxy. And what did he do with it? He killed it. He killed her.

He wept until his eyes were dry and then begged the gods to forgive him. He begged them not to take it out on her. Why should she suffer for his arrogance? For his stupidity? He begged and pleaded that somehow she be kept safe, that she was safe. That somehow, someway, something had happened, something she deserved.

Maybe some of the aliens were like her. Maybe these aliens here with him now—there were two of them—maybe they were like him: stupid, selfish, and cruel. Curiosity burning in their guts like poison fire. Maybe they waded into worlds like this one and cut out beating hearts and threw away the shells. Maybe these two aliens were like he was, inquisitive tools of hateful, destructive gods. But maybe, just maybe, there were aliens like Orli here too, somewhere on the ship. Maybe there were kind and gentle ones. Compassionate creatures who would find her and nurse her to health, scoop her up, and carry her back to safety as he'd seen Orli do so many times herself. Every cricket, spider, and moth ... they all were treated so gently at Orli's hand. She'd gasp this little gasp when she saw one. "Oh, look," she'd say. "There's a fuzzy spider there. Look how cute he is. Look at his eyes." She'd taken one onto her hand once, a little colorful thing, and smiled so happily as she showed it to him. "Look, he's staring right at you," she'd said of it. "He looks like a little clown."

It was a tufted little invader in Altin's eyes, more like the demons they'd fought along the Palace walls than some "cute little clown." But she'd cooed and sighed at it, told stories about how hard it must have worked to get all the way to the table in the dining hall. Even Kettle, whose heart was as big as they come, couldn't be made to feel sympathy for the thing. She'd have smashed it just as Altin would have. But not Orli. Orli took the damned thing all the way outside Calico Castle's gates, setting it free in the grass of the meadow beyond. "Go make baby spiders," she'd said to it.

Tears burned again as he thought about it. Babies. That's what she wanted. A family. A life. Not this. Not this. Never this. It had to be the hundred billionth time he'd had these exact same thoughts. Again. It was hard to imagine a universe could contain selfishness the size of his.

He wanted her to be safe somehow. But he knew it couldn't be. He'd seen her flung away. She was in the arms of Mercy now. Or perhaps some version of Mercy that looked over the very best of planet Earth. She would be fine. The gods would see to that. But him, no, him they were going to leave alive. Long enough to drag himself through the hell of a Seven's lifetime, century upon century knowing what he had done.

Better that he had been a Six. They only killed themselves.

Motion drew his attention, and he saw that one of the aliens was dragging itself away, drawing itself away from the machine and upwind. It passed over him, out of direct line of sight, but he was able to watch its departure reflected in the black glass dome of the inspection machine until he lost it in the distance.

Then there was only one alien nearby.

It was the one that had thrown Orli out over the edge of the tabletop. It was the one being in all the universe he hated most. He reached for the mana, wanting to melt the monster with fire drawn from the very center of a star. He couldn't hate hot enough to burn it as it should be burned. There was nothing that could cause it enough pain.

Movement caught his eye again. He thought perhaps the alien, as it looked into the eye-shaped viewing screen of the bulky machine and pressed its controls, had set the prong with the glass dome in motion again. But it had not. Something was moving in the reflection.

He strained to see it, but the damned machine was too far away to make out fine detail. The surface of the glass too dark and too curved for clarity.

Whatever it was, it was small, like him, and creeping up behind him. He thought for a moment it might be Orli. He prayed it was. But then it vanished in the darkness, lost behind the warped image of himself—the image of a stupid mage trapped in ochre jelly while his brand-new wife was dead or dying.

He thought absently that it might be Roberto come to get him. It had been man sized. But it was all warped and bent and shadowy in the reflection. It could have been anything. It was probably nothing. He was delirious. Racked with grief and self-loathing. He needed to get it together. He needed to think. There was still a possibility. There really might be nice aliens. Maybe he hadn't been totally wrong in that. He and Roberto both had felt that there were at least some odds that such might be true. He and Orli had worked out rather famously from opposite ends of the galaxy, after all; surely there was some evidence in that.

He had to keep trying. He had to hope. That's what Orli would do. Orli loved hope. It was her favorite star. So he would not give up.

He drew in a few deep breaths, talking himself down from the heights of anger and sorrow that had driven him to unproductive thoughts. There was always a chance. For gods' sake, Tytamon was alive after being dead for over a year. Anything was possible.

Something moved behind him again. A little black dome shape behind him in the shadows. It moved. It was obviously someone's head. But whose? If it was Roberto, then he wasn't wearing a spacesuit. At least not the helmet. But of course, Altin knew he wouldn't necessarily need one. And the steam did condense on it and make it hard to see.

He wanted it to be Orli. That almost made sense, despite what he had seen.

He spent a long time hoping for that. So long that he might have dozed off. He couldn't tell. Someone was pushing against his back. He could hear the sound of something shifting against the dorsal unit on the back of the spacesuit. He felt it again, definite pressure.

Orli, or maybe Roberto, or ... well, someone might be trying to get to him. He could hardly allow himself to hope for such a thing.

He looked up at the alien. Was the alien watching? Did it know?

It was looking at more images of Altin's brain. Altin hoped it could read his thoughts. "I will kill you when I get out," he thought as clearly as he could. He thought it in words and in images, as if he were communicating the idea to Blue Fire. He thought it and filled with a whole galaxy's worth of hate. He knew what that felt like too. He'd felt hate from Blue Fire before, and thought that an enormous, crushing sentiment. But then he'd felt hate from Red Fire, and discovered a whole new form of it, hatred of such volume that it dwarfed Blue Fire's to relative nothingness, malice on scale to fill galaxies. Altin poured all of that out at the alien as it watched the images of his brain. If the creature had felt it, it would have died.

Instead, the creature shut down the machine. A few flashes of light on its own skin, a wave running down one of the tentacles it had jammed into the machine's holes—

which Altin assumed were filled with various controls—and all the lights went off. It got a lot darker on the tabletop. Only the glow from distant lights on machines several hundred spans away, and a few others on objects up above, prevented him from being plunged into darkness.

The creature sent out a few tentacles to the grate above, and others off behind, to where, Altin couldn't know. Another tentacle came down and wrapped around the jelly blob he was in. Then he was flying, or at least that was the sense of it.

He dangled and whipped about. He thought he was going to bounce once off the tabletop, the alien carried him so casually.

He saw Orli kneeling there. Right there. Not fifteen paces from where he was. He could just barely make out her face through the filter of the ochre jelly. Her beautiful face.

She'd been the one digging him out. It *was* her. She was still alive.

She was still alive!

He shouted back to her. Shouted with every ounce of his strength. "Orli!" What else could he say? He just wanted her to stay alive. She had a fast-cast amulet, he knew. His hand tried to lift itself so he could point to his own neck, get her to use it.

Although, he realized it wouldn't work. There was no mana here. It wasn't just being channeled into a different form here. It was gone all around the damnable ship. What he found was absence. The amulet wouldn't work. The thought of it horrified him. It occurred to him she'd probably already tried.

If she had, then she was trapped down there. If they shut off the mana block somehow ... if he shut it off somehow once he finally worked out a way to get free, she'd still be trapped.

She wouldn't know. She hadn't known, most likely.

In one moment he hoped she'd think of it, in the next he hoped she would not ... that she had not.

By the gods, the universe was cruel.

But she was alive. That was all that mattered. He would get out of this damn jelly box, and he would burn the aliens to slag. Then he would get her home. He would get her home, and he would never leave Prosperion again. He would give her babies. As many babies as she wanted. They'd fill up Calico Castle with babies until they overflowed the walls and spilled out into the meadow beyond, if that's what she wanted to do, so many that even Kettle would beg for no more. Then he'd bring home puppies and kittens for them all. Maybe some of those little desert drakes whose breath was glitter dust. All of Calico Castle would sparkle with rainbow sand, and the kittens could piddle in it while the puppies barked and all those babies laughed.

Altin watched Orli fade into the distance. He laughed. "As many as you care to have," he promised. "You'll see." Then he cried.

Altin Meade had finally learned. The cycle would be broken this time ... if he was not too late.

Chapter 34

"**S**he wants what?" El Segador asked, stopping midway through his inspection of the 0-class magician Black Sander had just delivered to him. The middle-aged woman trembled in his grasp, tears running down her cheeks to be soaked up by the knotted cloth tied tightly in place as gag. "Mechs? Does she have any idea how much those things cost, even just one of them?"

Black Sander looked to Jefe, who was stooped over and staring into the crate where the satyr was. The fact that the mustached man did not look up indicated that he either hadn't heard or didn't care. Or perhaps that he was very good at making deals.

"Yes," Black Sander said. "I told her. She was adamant. We have received new intelligence, and our requirements have changed. We understand the cost may be greater than the number of magicians we can supply, or perhaps that you even require. I understand that gold is not without value on your world."

El Segador glanced back to the woman for a moment, then shoved her toward a short, stocky man holding a projectile rifle in his hands. "Take her to Gaspar," he said, "before she tries to call someone telepathically."

"She won't," Black Sander said. "She's kindly sacrificing herself for her children. She and I have an arrangement." He sent a smile toward the woman, which caused her to sob.

El Segador nodded and waited until the guard had led the woman from the room. He regarded Black Sander for a moment, drawing in a long breath that filled his chest all the way. He hummed once, audible in the expanse of that expanded cavity, and exhaled.

"I don't know that it will be possible to get them for you. Those are NTA machines. There's no black market for them because there is only one company making them. Rifles and small arms, that's one thing; the networks of suppliers for global skirmishes are wide. The NTA keep them going, even as they talk about fighting to shut them all down, because the money is good in keeping the arms trade alive, even air power to a degree. But not in mechs. No way they're going to risk anyone getting ahold of one of them. You can bomb a town into rubble from the sky, but to take it and hold it, you have to be on the ground. There is a very large difference."

"I was not under the impression that your NTA feared any entities on Earth. It was my understanding it has total dominion via the economy and very little territory to hold. Is the NTA not rather like your credits currency, all existing only in the machine?"

"Yes, but part of how that all works is that they keep people believing they are the good guys. If video gets out showing NTA mechs marching around burning down third-world slums and hosing babies with fifty-cal Gatling guns, well, it can become harder to keep people drinking the Kool-Aid."

Black Sander frowned. "I am unfamiliar with the last word, but I believe I take your point all the same. However, my employer has no interest in preventing anyone on Earth from drinking whatever the NTA chooses to serve them, and her operations have always been discreet. Not to mention, no one is taking video on our world anyway."

"Oh, don't fool yourself about that, my friend," El Segador said. He went to the crate and looked in at the satyr as Jefe was pushing the end of an electric cattle prod through one of the small air holes. Black Sander heard the arc of the spark, followed by a goatlike bleat and the crate thumping and rattling for a time. Jefe laughed and jolted the creature again. El Segador straightened and came back to stand before his Prosperion counterpart once more. "You have a strange world, Mr. Sander, but I'd be surprised if the NTA hasn't already mapped every inch of it and counted your population twice."

"I don't imagine that will please the War Queen if she ever learns of it."

"I gathered you are planning to make your employer Queen."

Black Sander watched him for a time, not surprised by the deduction he had made. He supposed at this point it was obvious. "I will not confirm it or deny it. But if it were the plan, it wouldn't happen until we got our hands on those mechs. If you are unable to deliver them, perhaps you can refer me to someone who can." He made a point of maintaining an air of absolute cordiality. He even smiled as if they were two friends chatting over tea.

El Segador's expression narrowed, and there flashed for a moment a sinister shadow in his eyes.

"I can get them for you," Jefe said from his place at the crate. He didn't look up. He was still jolting the satyr with the cattle prod.

"You are certain it is not too difficult?"

After one last shock, Jefe pulled the cruel device out and laid it atop the crate. He came to stand beside El Segador, a full Earth foot shorter than his hired man. He looked up into Black Sander's eyes, and unlike those of El Segador,

Jefe's eyes gleamed with greed. "Nothing is too difficult for the right price."

"That is as my employer sees it as well. Name your price and you shall have it."

"How much armor does she need?"

"How many of them can you supply?"

He thought about it for a moment. Then put one finger up, and left the room. Black Sander and El Segador spent a few moments in silence, neither man the sort to be uncomfortable in it.

When Jefe returned, one curled end of his mustache rode a little higher than the other. He regarded Black Sander through smiling eyes. "Forty-three," he said. "I can get you forty-three."

"Is that all?"

Jefe laughed aloud, a great, hearty laugh that filled the room, booming from him as he held onto the big silver buckle on his belt. "You see," he said to El Segador. "This is why I like him. He makes me laugh sometimes because he is a funny man." He looked to Black Sander then. "I like you, Prosperion. You remind me of me."

"Thank you," Black Sander said. "I am honored by such a compliment. Now, about that number, is that all?"

"Yes, amigo. That is all."

"Very well. How much? What do you require in exchange?"

"How much gold does your would-be Queen have to pay?" He looked around the basement, which was not large, but a good ten paces on a side at least, the ceiling a half span above Black Sander's head. "Could she fill up all of this?" He swept his hand out to shape the space. He pointed to the ceiling. "All the way?"

It was Black Sander's turn to laugh. "Done," he said.

"Not done," Jefe said.

"What else?"

"I want armor too."

"Armor?" He nearly stammered, adding, "What kind of armor? And why?"

"I want the golden armor. I have seen it in the net feeds. They say that it is magical. I want the armor of the War Queen."

"You what?" That he did stammer. The request was absurd. "I should hardly think that is possible. It *is* magical. Deadly magical. And she is the most guarded person on the planet, besides. It is rumored that she never takes it off. She certainly doesn't put it up for trade."

"You said your employer is going to take her seat. I heard you say it just now. You have hinted at it many times before. Is your fight real, Prosperion, or do you want my mechs for toys? I am not in the business of selling toys to toothless dogs. Weak dogs are undependable."

Now they were "my" mechs. Black Sander noted it before nodding his head. "Is that all?"

"No. I also want to be there when she takes it off. I want to see the look on her face when she is no longer the War Queen."

"Why in the name of Hestra would you want that? What possible reason could you have to need that sort of personal connection with her being dethroned?"

He turned and pointed to a photograph hanging on the wall. It was in black and white, like many around the villa were. In it were three men wearing ponchos and wide-brimmed hats, wider than Black Sander's by far. The entire place was decorated with similar images. They all held rifles, and one held a bottle made of glass. "It is for them," he said. "They will see me standing on the soil of another world. They will see how strong their blood has become. They will see, and they will be proud and know that their courage lives on, that it will grow out into the galaxy. That is why."

Black Sander didn't think he could make that kind of deal.

"Your eyes say you don't have the authority," Jefe said.

Black Sander winced inwardly. He hadn't made any outward signs of his thoughts. He'd been doing deals like these for more than two decades. He regarded Jefe warily.

Jefe smiled. "It is okay, amigo. I have my own kind of magic to see. Besides, I think it is time for me and your employer to meet."

"A meeting is not on the table," Black Sander said.

"But we will have one anyway."

Chapter 35

Pernie didn't want to be pretty. Not for Jeremy and not for Kyle. She made a point of telling Jeremy that as they made their way toward downtown after school. She explained that she was going to marry Master Altin one day, and that she would only be pretty for him. She was going to try to be pretty like the lady elves, but if she couldn't be that pretty, then she was going to be pretty like Deeqa Daar and the women who crewed Roberto's ship. Pernie thought she could be that pretty if she tried. But she wasn't going to try right now, because she probably was going to have to wait a hundred years. So being pretty right now didn't make any sense.

"Well, I still think you are," was all Jeremy said, which was fine. He could think what he wanted, but she told him he needed to keep his thoughts to himself unless he wanted to make her mad. Fortie Nomstacker had tried to tell her she was pretty once, and he was lucky she didn't hit him in the throat again.

They walked together quietly after that, Pernie trying not to be mad and Jeremy trying not to make her that way. Forty minutes after the last bell, they were picking their way down abandoned streets and around trashed cars, many of which were burned out or had someone sleeping in them.

"That one over there," Pernie said, pointing to a very tall building that had its whole top half caved in. It was very sharp looking at the top, almost like a spear. Just thinking that they might find a Hostile in the rubble made Pernie wish she had her elven weapon with her.

They got to the building in no time. Travel went much more quickly with Jeremy along because he used his tablet to make maps that led them right to things. Soon Pernie was tilting her head back and staring up at the broken parts of the building high above.

"There has to be some Hostile guts up there," she said.

She looked around, but all the doors and windows were boarded up. There were lots of signs saying "Keep Out" and "Danger—Condemned."

"We can't go in there," Jeremy said, seeing where she was looking. "The whole thing could fall down on us. We need to look through the rubble around the outside." He turned to go down the side street. "Come on, a wall over there on that building fell down into the street." He showed her a picture of the next block, taken from a satellite. He started to move away, but Pernie went to a board on a window and tried to pry it off with her hands.

"I need something to lift this with," she said, bringing Jeremy back. "It's stuck."

"Good. Come on, Pernie. We can't go in. It's not safe."

"Nothing is safe," Pernie said. "Just ask anyone, and that's all they will ever say." She went to the next boarded-up window and tried to pull that one off. It wouldn't budge either.

She turned about and looked through the debris lying all around. She found an old wooden broomstick and lots of bottles made of plastic and glass. She ground one end of the broomstick against the edge of a broken slab of concrete that had fallen from above, grinding it flat like one of

Jeremy's screwdrivers back in the science lab. When it was flat enough, she took it to the boarded-up window and worked the flattened end underneath the board as far as she could. She pulled against it, trying to lever the board away from the wall, but all she managed was to snap off a quarter inch of the wooden broomstick blade.

"I need something to hit it with," she said. "It needs to go deeper. Bring me that rock right there."

Jeremy saw the chunk of concrete she was pointing at and was kind enough not to tell her that it wasn't technically a rock.

"I'll hold it, and you hammer it on that end," she said.

She ground the end of her broomstick flat again as he retrieved the chunk of concrete.

"It won't work. Look." He was pointing up to where round, nearly flat bolt heads dotted the board in nine places, lined up in rows like miniature domes at the top, middle, and bottom. "They're bolted on there. You'll just break your stick again."

Pernie frowned. She really wanted to get inside. She wished she hadn't promised not to do magic. If she could just open up that board enough to look inside ....

"Come on," Jeremy said again. "Let's just go to the other building. Sophia is going to figure out you didn't take the bus home pretty soon. Don't you at least want to look for something Hostile?"

She did. She really did. She'd been trying to get down here for days and days. It would be a shame not to even look.

"Fine," she said. She followed after him, but eyeballed every covered window and every covered door, looking for just one piece of wood with a big enough gap to get her stick in. She just knew the tall, broken spear of a building held something good inside.

They traveled all the way down the side of the building

and came out on the other street. Sure enough, Jeremy had been right. The whole avenue was heaped with massive chunks of concrete where another building had collapsed on one side. Black strands of metal reached out like twisted insect limbs. The metal was rough and surely made of iron, and Jeremy told her it was called rebar. He told her how iron and concrete are both strong in their way, but that together they become something else entirely. He said someone in Earth's history named Roman used it first, and that Roman had a great empire—or at least that is what Pernie heard while digging around looking for Hostile parts. Pernie thought Roman sounded like the War Queen, so she told herself that she would mention him and his concrete to Her Majesty the next time she was in the Palace, even though that would probably be a long time away.

The two of them crawled around on the debris pile for the better part of an hour. Pernie didn't know what she was looking for, but she figured she would recognize a Hostile when she saw one. She used her broom handle to pry over some of the pieces she couldn't move by hand, feeling a little thrill of anticipation each time she sent one tumbling down the mound. She'd get down on her hands and knees and stare into the dust until it cleared. But there was never anything. Just more concrete and rebar. Sometimes she found parts of furniture or big shards of broken glass.

She stood up and stared back down the street, along the wall of the tall building with all its boards. All the buildings around it had boards on them too. It seemed like all the best parts of downtown were marked as "Danger" and "Condemned." She wondered if maybe there weren't any Hostile parts outside of them at all. According to the signs, all the danger was inside.

A series of notes played from Jeremy's backpack. He opened it and pulled out his tablet again. His grandfather, Gabby, was calling him. Pernie recognized the school custodian's voice even though she couldn't see him on the screen.

"Where you at, boy?" Gabby asked. "It's getting dark. You get that girl back home?"

"No," Jeremy said. "Not yet. But we're going soon."

"You best get on. The school gone and called me already. That Mrs. Hayworth is all in a fuss about her now, and she got the police looking for her again. She say your little girlfriend ain't showing up on the grid. You didn't wrap that girl, did you?"

"No, Grandpa. I didn't do anything. But we're on our way."

"You want I should come get you?"

He looked to Pernie, who shook her head emphatically. Sophia Hayworth had also made Pernie promise not to get into any more vehicles with any men who "hadn't come to the Hayworth home for dinner at least twice before." Jeremy shrugged and looked back into his tablet. "She says no. We're on our way home, though. We'll still be home way before dark."

"You best make sure," Gabby said, and then Jeremy turned the tablet off again.

"Come on," he said. "Let's go. If we cut through the alleys, we can be back at your house right away."

"Where do you live?" Pernie asked.

"Not far," he said. He was already walking back down the side of the building. "Come on."

She caught up to him quickly, and the two of them made good time. She saw a man rummaging through bags of trash in one alley, and she saw lots of very mangy cats. A dirty lady with only three teeth tried to touch her, begging Pernie to put some credits in her account.

"I don't even know how to do that," Pernie said as she knocked the woman's reaching hand away with a reflexive rap of the broomstick. The woman jerked her arm away and made a rasping hiss, snakelike, as she clutched her wrist.

Jeremy shied away, looking horrified, but Pernie simply walked on.

"You weren't afraid of her?" Jeremy asked once the woman was well behind them.

"No," Pernie said. "Why should I be? She's just an old lady."

"I thought you said that lady who was teaching you how to be the Sava'an'Lansom was an old lady."

"Well, that's true," Pernie said. "Djoveeve is very strong for an old lady. Plus she was trained by elves. She could kill most anyone if she wanted to."

"Could she kill you?"

Pernie had to think about that for a moment. Her first thought was that Djoveeve could not, because Pernie had already beaten her in several fights. But those were practice fights. Djoveeve had other ways of killing people. She was a trained assassin, after all. She could sneak in while Pernie was asleep and claw out her heart with jaguar claws. Or use Fayne Gossa poison on her while her immunity was still not quite complete. The more she thought about it, the more she realized that if Djoveeve wanted her dead, the old assassin could get it done.

"Yes," Pernie said at last. "A Sava'an'Lansom can kill anyone."

Jeremy looked suitably impressed.

"Hey," called a voice from behind them. "Look who it is."

Pernie and Jeremy turned back to see four of the boys from her first night in the alley downtown. Pernie recognized one of them as the oldest one, the one that had tried to grab her.

"Oh crap," Jeremy said. "Come on, run." He took off running, but stopped ten steps down the alley when he realized she wasn't following.

"Pernie," he called to her, his voice an agitated whisper. "Come on. We have to go."

"Did you come back to pay us what you owe us?" said the

oldest ruffian. "I figure you owe me double now, seeing as how you cost me a night in jail."

"I don't owe you anything," Pernie said, squaring up to him. "And you are a criminal. Those men at the Reno PD said so. Criminals belong in jail."

The young man laughed and turned to his friends. "You hear that? I am a criminal, and I belong in jail." They laughed, although the youngest one was looking up and down the street nervously. "So look here, kid. How about you just come along with us to Gorky's Casino and get us some game chips. What's your allowance, anyway? A rich brat like you must get at least a hundred a week. Maybe two hundred. I'll let you off for seventy-five, how's that?"

"I'm not giving you anything. You need to go away."

"You got a mouth on you, sister. You should watch that."

"I'm not your sister. Now go away. I have to go home, and you are going to make me late."

He glanced at his friends. The youngest was backing away, but the other two were moving to either side. "Look. Why not make this easy? It's only three blocks away. You just go in, put your hand on the plate, look into the iris scan, and tell them how many chips you want. Give them to me, then we go away. It beats getting your ass kicked, and your friend's back there too." He looked over Pernie's shoulder to where Jeremy stood. Jeremy's eyes were wide and his hands shook terribly.

"You leave him alone too," Pernie said. "I'm not giving you any chips or anything else." She raised her broomstick and held it defensively.

"Oh shit!" he said, mocking her as he pretended to shake like Jeremy. "I got a little girl with a broomstick here. She's ... she's going to give me a splinter."

The boys flanking her laughed, and one of them went beyond her and grabbed Jeremy. Jeremy tried halfheartedly to pull away, but gave up straightaway. The street tough dragged him back and thrust him to the elder of the crew, who caught him in a headlock.

"So this is how it's going to happen," the youth said. "Me and your pal here are going to Gorky's. If you want me to not beat his face in, you're going to get me some chips. I'll call it fifty, since I'm being nice. You get them, he walks away; if not ... lots of bleeding and screaming. How's that?"

Pernie's broomstick swung flat and hit him in the temple. It dazed him, and it came so fast the other two near her didn't move for the sheer surprise. She stepped back and drove the blunt end of the broomstick into the forehead of the boy who had grabbed Jeremy. He collapsed in a heap of loose-fitting clothes. The third boy pulled a length of rusted chain out of his pocket and swung it at her. She caught it with the forward half of the broomstick, and the momentum of his swing wound the chain around the broomstick twice with a *clack, clack* even as she yanked it from his hands with a jerk. That movement allowed her to bring the back end of the stick around hard against his ear. He staggered, and Pernie jumped up and kicked him in the chin. She heard his teeth cracking, and a moment after, blood poured from his mouth.

The older boy shook off the headshot he'd gotten and quickly fished something out of his pants waistband. It was a small laser gun. Pernie saw it and knew exactly what it was. She'd been looking through weapons catalogs on the net since she figured out how it worked and how to find such things. There were so many wonderful weapons out there, at least a hundred of which she wanted to own one day.

"Put that shit down, bitch," he said, gesturing to her broomstick with a movement of his chin. "I swear, I'll do this little bastard right now." He pressed the laser against Jeremy's temple.

The flattened end of Pernie's broomstick sank a full two inches into his eye socket. He screamed and fell to the ground before he'd even realized she'd thrown it. His laser and Jeremy both fell to the pavement beside him. Pernie snatched up the laser and put it in her sweater pocket. She helped Jeremy to his feet as the blinded youth grabbed his face and rolled about making a ruckus.

"He ... he could have shot me," Jeremy said, looking down at the figure thrashing on the ground.

"No, he couldn't," Pernie said.

"Yes, he could. What if you had missed? He could have shot me, and I'd be dead right now."

Pernie pulled the laser back out of her pocket. "No," she repeated, pointing to the three lights along one side, none of which were lit. "Look. The battery is dead."

Jeremy looked at the laser, his mouth slowly opening as he thought about what she'd said. He looked back at the young man lying in the street. The youth had pulled the broomstick out, and now blood was spewing everywhere. He was screaming at the top of his lungs, a high-pitched, piercing wail. Jeremy watched him for a moment, then looked back at Pernie again. "Damn," he said.

Pernie shrugged. "We should hurry. There's still plenty of daylight for me to get home."

Jeremy was nearly dumbstruck, but he stumbled along with her, alternating his unending dialogue between how he'd almost died and how Pernie was like one of those Darma Force commando guys. Pernie didn't know what "Darma Force commando guys" were, but she did know she wanted to get out of there before all that screaming got the stupid Reno PD to come get her again. She'd gone to all the trouble to cut out her chip and wrap it in tinfoil in her bag so they *couldn't* find her, and she sure didn't want to get hauled back to Sophia Hayworth by them again now. That was likely to get her sent back to Prosperion for sure.

Unfortunately, the police cruiser was waiting for her at the end of the block.

Chapter 36

By the time Roberto and his crew arrived at dinner at Calico Castle, the meal had already begun, though just barely so. Kettle caught them entering and gave Roberto a scolding look as she passed him by. "I should say ya could find the time ta show up proper fer a grand meet such as this," she said. "Kept the master, the great doctor, and the general all sittin' there o'er an hour waitin' on yer leisure." She winked after it, though, and patted him on the cheek, whispering, "I made that duck-stuffed swan what ya liked so much afore."

Roberto grinned. "Two birds are better than one," he said. "And sorry I'm late. Those guys at the TGS are assholes."

"Well, ya can watch yer mouth in mixed company in this house," she said, the long habit of admonishment readily upon her. She looked to his entourage of corseted crew and frowned. "The ladies'll not be too keen to eat with that offal comin' from yer mouth."

"Right. That was me. I apologize." He turned and winked at Deeqa as the rest of his crew was filing past, greeting Tytamon and being introduced all around. The two of them joined right after, with Roberto and Deeqa sitting across from each other. Roberto sat between the now slim Doctor

Leopold and Liu Chun, whom the doctor had brought back with him from the hospital in Leekant, finally recuperated from injuries caused by a broken coolant tank. Deeqa sat between General Pewter and Tytamon's exchange student, Angela Hayworth.

"Sorry we're late, everyone," Roberto said after giving Liu Chun a hug. He sat down and dragged the heavy chair in behind him with a grunt. "I'm telling you, the TGS has a real stick up their ass. We sat there for nine hours getting back, and our teleport for this trip was booked before we came here last time."

Kettle sent a grunt of displeasure and a sour look at him before scuttling off toward the kitchens again.

"It's only going to get worse," said General Pewter. "There's been another death on the council."

Roberto grabbed his goblet and drained it. A girl in her early teens swept out of the shadows beyond the candlelight and refilled it almost immediately. "I didn't know there'd been a first one," he admitted. He looked to the girl and thanked her. "You guys sure have better service than any restaurant back on Earth." She smiled and, seeing that half his crew had already emptied theirs as well, set herself to work.

"Interesting that you should mention it," the general said. "Councilman Stropleather choked to death on a spinach salad two weeks ago during his first visit to Earth. That raised a few eyebrows, but nobody said much. Bad luck, maybe. But now, they are locking everything down with the death of the new first councilman who replaced Stropleather, Councilman Spinnaker."

"Yes," agreed Tytamon. "The death of them both, two weeks apart, suggest not only a conspiracy, but arrogance."

"Or stupidity," suggested Roberto.

"I think not. That is a bold move, and a statement."

"Who is the next in line?" Deeqa asked. "Are they suspect

or trembling, new number one?"

"Both, I imagine," said the general. "The new guy's name is Ivan Gangue. I've never met him, but he looks like a typical bureaucrat."

"We've met him," Roberto said, pointing with his fork to Deeqa across from him. He swung the fork toward Angela Hayworth then. "He was the one who set up your coming to Prosperion, and he didn't look too happy about it when that elf dropped the bomb about Pernie going to Earth."

"He wasn't," Angela said. "And it was the big stink it raised that put it on my uncle's radar in Fort Reno. That's the only reason I got to come here. I know there was some trouble with her here—I've heard the whole story about that"—she paused and cringed as she glanced to Tytamon—"but I'm glad I got out of there. The NTA just isn't what I thought it would be. I mean, it did start out not so bad, but the longer I was there, the more it changed. Slow at first, but that was like the first bits of snow tumbling down the slope before the avalanche. Maybe I was just naïve, but now it's crazy there. Nothing they say is true, or at least not exactly."

"It's hardly better here, my dear," said Tytamon. "Which is why I've asked you all to come. There are things afoot that, as Miss Hayworth suggests, portend an avalanche. A large one. I haven't felt such tremors in over two hundred years."

Roberto snorted. "Well, I thought the whole Hostiles-and-demons-from-hell thing was kind of an avalanche-sized cluster fu—" Kettle had just come in with a tray of the very same duck-stuffed swan she'd promised him. The woman had a gift for that sort of timing, and her glare shot across the flicker of the candles like a thrown knife to cut off the epithet. "That was bad enough," he finished. "You're saying it's going to get worse?"

"The priests are saying that was how it began."

"Damn. You guys need to get some better priests. The

ones you got are major downers." Roberto looked to Kettle and shrugged.

That got a few chuckles from his crew, but Doctor Leopold was deadly serious when he spoke.

"I looked into what some of the Church gossip has been putting out. In particular, the Church of Anvilwrath, who seem determined that the time of Tidalwrath's return is imminent. The Grand Maul's last statement was over nine months ago, and no one has seen him since."

Roberto cringed, but he wasn't so bothered by it to be prevented from stabbing several slices of swan and duck together. "I thought he came back already, that Tidalwrath one. Wasn't he the one that pissed off the giant rock monster with the long arm that the orcs brought?"

Doctor Leopold shook his head. "Anvilwrath's return was prophesied. His judgment would fall upon the people. If the pleas of Feydore could sway him to spare them—us—then the sacrifice of love would be complete. The gods would once more protect Prosperion, and Tidalwrath would be allowed to return and once more rule the seas. All would be whole again. Even the priests of Mercy agreed, which is rare. They say that she will intercede when time comes to bring love back."

"Yeah, that's a hell of a story, I'll give you that," Roberto said, despite his mouth being stuffed with duck meat. "I definitely like having just one God to worry about."

"Well," said Tytamon, "however much of that is accurate divination, and how much is story to fill in the gaps, is a matter aside. The real issue is still as it has been. We must first find a way to get Altin and Orli free. We must also learn the nature of the aliens and their intentions on Yellow Fire."

"I'm not supposed to tell you this, but I'm going to," the general said. "I'm going to because I'm tired of being strapped to the deck in all of this. Command is planning to blow Yellow Fire straight to hell the moment those aliens get to the heart chamber. There's a hundred-megaton nuke sitting in one of those crates down there." He looked straight to Roberto. "That wasn't all simple mining charges you put down there, regardless of how they labeled the crates."

Roberto nodded. "I figured as much. And I knew that's what they were going to do. If that was supposed to be a secret, it's a pretty obvious one."

"Yes, but now it's not a secret you all don't have. And I'm damn sure not going to push the button."

"Who else has one to push?" Roberto held his goblet up for the serving girl, who was refilling the general's cup just then.

"Director Bahri, of course. And Admiral Putin."

"Putin? Are you serious? He's one of Asad's cronies. How could they have given access to that guy?"

"It's the fleet, Roberto. You more than anyone should know how it works."

Roberto looked to his empty goblet as he shook his head. Maybe he should just get his own pitcher if this was how the night was going to go.

"Regardless of which of them plans to push the button," Tytamon said, looking to the general, "we must get my apprentice and that sweet girl of yours before they do."

"Well, you said you can't look through the hull of that alien ship," Roberto said. "So they got a block on your magic somehow. At least defending the ship. Like maybe that anti-magic stuff you guys were casting on our nukes, right? Or some of that warding stuff like Altin put on my ship?"

Tytamon nodded as he leaned aside and allowed Kettle to change out his plate for a clean one.

"Which means I need to go," Roberto said. "Like, now. If magic isn't going to work, then we just need to handle this old-school style with an ass whipping. So I need a way to get back here after, in case Altin is jacked up somehow after

I get him out. So you have to come with me, or I need some harbor stones. Both would be better."

"I can send you there," Tytamon conceded, "but as I said, Doctor Leopold and I have work to do. Brute force is not enough. At least not until we know what we are dealing with."

"He's got a thousand mechs and a handful of fighters," Roberto said, pointing at the general. "I think you underestimate what brute force is capable of."

"Yes, but the ships are large, and we don't know what they are capable of in terms of brute force on their own." Tytamon forked meat onto his plate, though the portion suggested he hadn't much of an appetite. "And as I understand it, the fleet has no intention of sending ships. We haven't finished our little platform out there ... and the reality is that we aren't in a position to wage war out of Calico Castle just yet. The outcome of our collaboration on such an operation would be seen as an act of war by the people of three worlds at bare minimum. We need to know more."

"Man, no offense, but it seems like the older people get, the more they want to think about stuff. The clock is ticking on this shit. Yellow Fire's heart stone was only a three-week dig. Orli did the math. I'm telling you, those spaghetti-bastard aliens are right there. They have to be. We need to go. Tonight."

"Well, I can make you a harbor stone," Tytamon said. "But it will take many hours to complete. I haven't got a Liquefying Stone to speed it up, and getting one would take longer than we have, for reasons too numerous to relate. But I can have one ready by tomorrow night."

Roberto grunted and speared another slab of duck. "They might not have until tomorrow night." Kettle set a tray of some kind of root on the table, long and fat tubers with small hairs that had curled up from the heat. She cut one down the middle with a wooden knife, sending filaments of honey-colored light crackling around its surface like lightning. A heavenly sweet aroma wafted up on a cloud of steam. She set it on Roberto's plate and set to doing the same for Liu Chun.

Tytamon's expression conveyed that he clearly understood Roberto's impatience, and shared it. But it changed little. "I'm afraid the work of finding out how to get them out is more essential than getting you there and back just yet. Chariots before chargers and all that rot. The doctor and I will be all night at the divining spell first."

"Fine, then just send me and the general and as many mechs as my cargo bays can hold," Roberto said. "That is, if the general wants to come along."

"I do," he said. "I'll need some time to get the mechs and pilots together."

Roberto nodded and looked to Tytamon. "You can send me, then send the general and whoever he can round up when they are ready, and when it's done, send me the harbor stone too. And if you can't get it done before we could use it, well, we will just up and get the hell out of there the old-fashioned way, and that's how it will be. The *Lady* is fast enough."

"And if you run into a problem before you have that opportunity?" Tytamon asked.

"Sometimes you just have to improvise, Tytamon, trust your instincts. Those are my friends up there, and I don't have time for ... for the crystal ball treatment. No offense. This shit is on, you know?"

Tytamon sighed and nodded. "It is. I agree. I worry about how we will communicate. You have no mages on your ship. You must have a way to communicate telepathically at least. You have other crewmembers to think of."

"Do you have anyone you can recommend?"

"Her Majesty has tapped the entire nation, I'm afraid.

With the losses from the war, the TGS efforts, and whatever Her Majesty is up to, there's hardly a B-class illusionist to be found for the start of summer festivals."

"Then I'll get one of those homing lizards you guys use. How many have you got around here?"

Tytamon huffed at that. "None. The world teeters on the brink of something spectacular—or terrible—and an entire generation of blanks wastes the first magical access those creatures gave them in sending short notes and silly drawings back and forth. I abstain on principle."

Roberto turned to see if the doctor had a homing lizard to spare, but the old fellow was nodding right along with Tytamon. Roberto shook his head. Old people. Always crapping on change. Some things never changed.

"Fine," he said. "Where can I get one this late at night? Is there someplace close? In Leekant?"

"Murdoc Bay," Tytamon and Doctor Leopold said together. Tytamon continued, "Everything in Leekant will be closed, but down there, well, they shutter more businesses during the day."

Roberto nodded. Not his first choice, but any spaceport is better than none in a meteor storm. "Fine. I'll go after dinner. You happen to know the name of any shops?"

"I don't. Be careful if you go. It's not a safe place during the day, and the danger there multiplies the longer the sun has been gone."

"I know. I'll bring my people," Roberto said. "We've done that run before."

"After dark?"

"No."

"You'll be better off with less of you, not more. And I'd cover those Earth weapons of yours."

"I'm a big boy, Tytamon. And Deeqa grew up in a place that makes Murdoc Bay look like a pirate-themed kiddie park."

Tytamon nodded. "Very well. I'll send you along before the doctor and I start the divination. Sooner is better. We've got a lot of work to do."

"We'll take ourselves," Roberto said. He jammed the last of the duck into his mouth as he stood. He scooped up a fork load of the lightning root and stuffed that in as well, then snatched the uncut half of a loaf of Kettle's now galaxy-famous bread. "I'll go now." He didn't have to say anything and Deeqa was pushing out her chair, the rest of his crew only a few movements behind. He nearly made it to the doors, then came back and wrapped up the rest of the root on his plate in the napkin he'd dropped beside it when he got up. "Damn," he mouthed around the food he was still working on getting down. "That's freaking amazing." He grinned so wide that his stuffed cheeks nearly closed his eyes. "I love this planet. I really do. Can't wait until we can cut the crap and just get to having fun." Then he was off after the rest of them. A couple of homing lizards from Murdoc Bay and then he was going back to Yellow Fire to get Orli and Altin. Her Majesty had had her chance. Way more chance than he should have given her. Now was the time for action.

Chapter 37

Black Sander watched through the window as the poplars beyond Galbrun Hall's eastern garden wall swayed in the night breeze. The uppermost branches, black silhouettes, swept lazily across the sky, masking and unmasking the star that sailors called Hope. He watched it blinking in and out as the black clouds of the leafy poplar limbs blew over it, on and off, over and over again. There was hope, and there was not. Hope was a coin toss, about the same odds Jefe was looking at in his suit to get the royal armor from the marchioness as a prize.

Black Sander glanced to the water clock on a table in the corner and saw that they'd been waiting for almost an hour. He knew she was doing it on purpose. He looked to where Jefe sat, a pleasant smile on his face as if he were some young boy about to watch an enchanted puppet show. That was good. Black Sander didn't want to be in the room if two colossal egos were going to collide.

As if reading his thoughts, El Segador, seated next to his boss, looked to the clock as well. Black Sander could tell the Earth man didn't know how to read it. El Segador's gaze slid to Black Sander. He gave the slightest movement of one shoulder and even less movement in the tilting of his head, a question. Black Sander made no movement, nothing at all to serve as response.

When a full hour had passed and one minute more, the door opened to the marchioness' sitting room. The Earl of Vorvington stuck his fat face out and announced, "My Lady will see you now."

Jefe sprang up with youthful energy and strode right in. El Segador and Black Sander followed less eagerly.

"Buenas noches, Mi Señora. I am—" he began, addressing the marchioness with utmost courtesy.

"I know who you are," she cut him off. "Do you think I am an idiot?" She did not look at him. She stared into the mirror instead.

Black Sander cringed and started running through his mental list of contacts back on Earth. It wasn't a long list, but he'd likely have to start working it now. They were going to be back to square one.

"Do you see here?" the marchioness said, stepping back from the mirror enough to grant the others in the room a look. "The aliens are moving them now. It's most interesting."

Shockingly, she looked to Black Sander as she pointed to the mirror. He knew why she was doing it. She wanted Jefe to understand his place. She would address her own kind, those with magic in particular, first.

Black Sander went to the mirror and looked into it. The image that had been there for weeks was different now. There were long, ropy things, grayish-white strands, dangling around the Galactic Mage and his bride, and they were moving, although Black Sander could not say how. There was a bright light shining on them, and they seemed to be traveling through mist.

"It started twenty minutes ago," the marchioness said. "Those tendrils came down and pulled one of the tubes out of the amber. Then the light came on. They've been moving along like this since."

Black Sander leaned forward and looked into the faces of each, Altin, then Orli, in turn. They were still in the gelatinous ochre material, and it was hard to make out if they were moving inside of their spacesuits. "I still can't tell if they are alive."

"We may be on the brink of finding out. Perhaps they have been in cold storage all this time, little more than slabs of meat on ice."

"It would explain the mist. It's likely frost, though it looks a little heavy in this view."

She nodded, and they stood watching for a time.

"She'll be right with you," the earl muttered to Jefe and El Segador nervously. Black Sander knew how badly the nobleman wanted to get the mechs. The idea had surprised him at first, but the earl knew an advantage when he saw one. His palpable eagerness was going to up the cost.

Black Sander was himself a bit uncomfortable with standing there as long as they did. It was rude, and grossly so, and with each minute that passed, he became more aware of it. He could not look away, however, for this was the marchioness' game to play now. She'd not been happy to have her hand forced like it had been.

"What's that?" she said, more to herself than to Black Sander.

Two of the tendrils that waved around Altin and Orli in their amber cocoons swung up and out of view, and shortly after, the edge of a platform came into view. The two newlyweds were lifted up over it and placed on a wide beam. The beam was so long it disappeared into the distance with no end in sight. There were others like it nearby, some in parallel, others running crosswise at even intervals, all together like latticework, albeit a very great one. Large, shadowy things loomed in the distance, shrouded by darkness and blowing mist, frost perhaps, as the marchioness had suggested.

The two of them were placed upon the beam together, Orli slightly ahead of Altin. The tendrils released them both and then seemed to simply float away. Soon after, there was little more to see, Altin and Orli, once again, just sitting there. Black Sander almost turned away to look at Jefe and El Segador, compelled to by the audacity of their wait, but then Lady Meade blinked.

The marchioness saw it too, for she said, "Well, there we have it. She's not dead." She turned from the mirror then as if that had been the signal she was waiting for. "Now, you," she said, gazing down her nose at Jefe. "What is this about the royal armor?"

Black Sander finally turned, relieved that the wait was over and curious to see how much damage she had done. But the expression on Jefe's face was just as sanguine as it had been when he was out in the waiting room. Black Sander let out a silent breath. He had to give the man credit: he was good at what he did.

Beyond good. A half hour later, Jefe and Vorvington were laughing like old friends over a bottle of elven wine, and the Earth man was making promises to deliver, in exchange for a case of the fine libation, a case of another fine libation from his homeland called "tequila," which he promised was the very nectar of Earth. The marchioness, while hardly so convivial as those two, had actually deigned to let everyone sit down. Everyone but the "minions."

Black Sander and El Segador were dismissed like children soon after the wine was poured, with Vorvington even calling after, "Take him into the city and show him around." It was a suggestion to which Jefe had boisterously agreed, acting tipsier than he could possibly be.

Black Sander gritted his teeth, but nodded that he would comply. If his part in securing the mechs required that he play tour guide, then that was how it had to be.

"Let's get you into something less conspicuous," he said,

looking El Segador up and down. "There's no sense shouting to every blank on Prosperion that you are here."

Chapter 38

Roberto and Deeqa Daar left the *Glistening Lady* not far off the road, a quarter mile west of the Decline. They'd come in slow and set down quietly and with lights off. As soon as they were off, the ship turned on its camouflage, vanishing into the night.

As it had been last night when they'd met with Vorvington, the wind whipped around them, whipping the folds of their cloaks, garments that Kettle had forced on them after having chased them down as they left Calico Castle's front gate.

They bent into the wind and made their way onto the road, and soon after, they were winding their way down the Decline. Despite Tytamon's comment about businesses in the city shutting down during the day rather than at night, there were scant few of them lit up as they went down. There was a candle shop with lights on as they passed, but not invitingly so. Deeqa commented that it had the same name as the warehouse through which they contracted several of their Goblin Tea suppliers: Gevender's.

"Yeah, I think that sneaky little bastard Tenderthrift has his stubby fingers in everything, probably on all sides," Roberto replied. "And frankly, I'll be perfectly happy to buy homing lizards from him too if he's got a shop somewhere up ahead. At this point, I don't really care where they come from."

Two men fell in behind them as they rounded the first of the steep hairpin turns that bent the Decline back on itself as it cut its way down the cliff. Roberto and Deeqa both saw them. The tail was still with them after they passed through a better-lit stretch where four businesses in a row were open—none of which promised homing lizards inside.

As the lights were fading behind them, Roberto glanced to Deeqa, who nodded. They stopped and turned around, Roberto throwing back his hood as he spoke. "You got a half second to back off, or we're going to drop you both where you stand," he said. The barrels of both Deeqa's nine-millimeter pistols pushed pointedly in the direction of the men from beneath her cloak, revealing the source of the menace if not the nature of it. "Actually, she's going to do it," he amended. "I'm just going to laugh."

The taller of the two men glared out from beneath his own hood, but saw something in the aspect of his intended victims that turned him and his companion around. Roberto watched them go until they were beyond the light, heading back to the hairpin. He shook his head and grinned at Deeqa, who shrugged. They set off again.

They made their way down the rest of the Decline without event, and without homing lizards, and moved into the city, where the lights grew brighter and more frequent the closer they got to the harbor.

They turned down this way and that, expecting at any point to find something promising, but nothing stood out.

"How does a town support this many bars and taverns?" Deeqa marveled. "Where do this many drinkers come from?"

"The ocean," Roberto said. "They come in with the tide."

Finally a man and what looked to be his wife came along

the walk, moving quickly with their heads down. "Hey, excuse me," said Roberto, doing his best not to sound threatening given where they were and what time of night it was. "Any chance you know where a guy could pick up a homing lizard this late?"

The woman gripped the man's arm tightly, and he drew a dagger from beneath his coat, one he'd been gripping all along. "Back off, thieves. I'll cut you open, don't think I won't." Roberto could tell by the way he said it that he was as terrified as his wife. They hugged the wall of the shop front they were passing and scooted past as quickly as possible. It was a mystery what the two of them were doing out this late, but the woman's eyes were red rimmed. Roberto suspected they might be going to or coming from having had to post some ransom or pay some awful bribe.

"Maybe I won't retire here," he said, glancing to his companion. "Not much for hospitality."

A man lurched out of a bar and staggered toward them. Roberto eyed him, wondering first if he might be a threat; second, upon deciding he wasn't, wondering if he might be of some use; and third, upon his having pivoted and blown the contents of his guts against the wall, deciding to give him a considerable grant of right of way.

They asked a few others that they encountered, but everyone was either too drunk, too afraid of them, or too busy sizing them up as potential victims to be of any use. The one group of sailors who would have been useful were just ashore from Sansafrax and had no idea about homing lizard vendors at all. One of them did remark that Deeqa had pretty eyes and an even prettier mouth, which almost got him shot, which in turn would have been a shame, given that the lads were apparently the only marginally civil people in the entire city.

After making their way back and forth through town for nearly a half hour, Roberto decided they needed to just go in and ask somewhere. He looked up and surveyed the street they were on. Three taverns, an opium den, two brothels, and two businesses proclaiming themselves the finest choice for something called sanza-sap, which was something neither of them were familiar with. However, based on the comatose people lying along the walks in front of these places like stacked garbage—and knowing what he knew of Orli's plight on the slaver's ship—Roberto decided a regular old tavern would be the least likely place to piss him off.

He scanned the signs above the doors of the nearby drinking establishments. None of them had dancing illusion magic on the rooftops like the brothels did, but one of them made Roberto laugh. "Look there. The Harlot's Pocket. That's funny." He started for the stairs.

"Why is it funny?" Deeqa asked as she eyed the monster of a bouncer standing outside the door.

"It's one of those double entrées Orli is always talking about. You know, two meanings: one plain, one sexually delicious."

She looked at him, for a moment even more bewildered than before.

Roberto frowned at her. "Girl, you need a sense of humor. It's right here next to a whorehouse. Think about it. That shit is hilarious. Maybe the proprietor is a halfway decent guy."

She thought about it a moment more, then shook her head. "It is *entendre*, not *entrée*. And you are like a child."

"I know," he replied, putting on a grin. To the bouncer he said, "What's the cover, my man?" He tried to sound a little like Altin with that but failed.

The bouncer looked at him, then tilted a little to look into Deeqa's shadowed cowl. He was nearly as tall as she was. He grunted a single note under his breath, then motioned toward the door with a sideways twitch.

"Thanks a lot, old sport," Roberto said, still trying to

sound Prosperion. He winked at Deeqa, and together they went in.

The place was almost exactly what Roberto had expected it would be. Smoke clung to the ceiling in a thick cloud, the worst of which Roberto was just short enough to clear. The interior was dark and drab, and nobody seemed to have ever cared in the least about decorating. Patrons sat around tables, making noise and cursing over dice and games of cards. Others sat quietly, peering out from under hat brims and hoods, watching who came and went. Two buxom bar wenches roamed the spaces in between, one of them laughing and giggling gaily every time someone groped her, while the other poured drinks on those who treated her likewise. The doused men would laugh and order another, and Roberto figured she'd probably been playing that game for the proprietor for years.

"There," Deeqa said, nodding toward a brutish man standing behind the bar, pouring drinks for two sailors who looked as if they were about to slide off their stools and sleep beneath the bar. Roberto noticed a young man in the shadows nearby watching them, a lean fellow with a tuft of red hair that glinted dully like copper wire in the darkness.

They made their way directly to the bar, Roberto watching those who watched him and matching their stares long enough for them to recognize that he didn't care. He bellied up to the bar, with Deeqa beside him turning her back to it so she could watch out into the room.

"What can I get you?" the barkeep asked, not looking up at them.

"I need a homing lizard," Roberto said.

"What do I look like?" the man said, gazing up at that. He flipped his hands over for a moment to convey how dumb he thought Roberto's statement was. "Buy a drink or get out."

"Fine. Two of whatever isn't poisonous. Ale or wine."

"Which is it?"

"Wine. House wine is fine."

The barkeep turned and got a pitcher off the back counter, a crude clay thing and a far cry from the silver they'd been served from barely an hour past. "Show me your color, friend."

Roberto paused, the question on his face. The bartender rolled his eyes and started to turn away, but Deeqa turned long enough to place a gold coin on the bar.

"Hestra," said the man. "You're either brave or fools."

"It's all we got," Roberto said, keeping his voice as low as he could.

"Well, you'll have half these bastards following you out," the man said, taking it and pouring the drinks. "You'll have to give me a moment to get your change. I don't keep that lying around."

"Keep it," Roberto said. "Look, I need a damn homing lizard. Where can I get one, like, right now?"

"If I had one, I'd give it to ya," the man said. "But I ain't."

"So who does? Someone in here have one? Or at least somebody sell them that's open still?"

"Bleck's on Front Street sells them. So does Carper's Carrier Pigeon at the bottom of the Decline. That's it. But I doubt you'll find either open now."

"Well, crap. We walked by that carrier pigeon place, and it was definitely shut up tight. I thought this town was a round-the-clock affair."

"I can get you one," said a voice from the shadows near the wall. The young man who'd been watching the sailors drinking themselves into oblivion stepped into better light. Roberto pulled back reflexively upon seeing how pockmarked his face was. Huge scars like craters all up and down his cheeks and jawline. There were angry red lumps in other places, likely making more craters to come. Roberto almost offered to introduce the youth to Doctor Singh, but bit his tongue. "Where?" Roberto said instead. "How fast?"

"How fast do you need?"

"I need it like an hour ago."

The boy frowned. "Well, I can't do that. But I can get you into Talbin Bleck's."

"You his kid or something?"

"No."

"Then how we getting in?"

"How you think?" the boy said.

"That's okay," Roberto said. "Someone will have one around here." He was half-tempted to just shout it out, when Deeqa put her hand on his arm. She crooked an eyebrow in the direction of the boy and shrugged, barely discernibly.

"Fine," Roberto said. "Let's go."

He turned to go.

"You gonna drink those?" the youth said, pointing to the cups.

"No," said Roberto. "We're good for now."

The boy swigged down Deeqa's cup and chased it with Roberto's. Then he led them back out through the crowd.

Two men jostled them as they came through the door, and for a moment, Roberto was staring into the bright blue eyes of a man he was sure he knew. The man looked out under a cloak pulled down just as low as Deeqa's was, but Roberto saw him, and he saw the flash of recognition there. Or at least he thought he did, but the man pushed past him, driven by the hand of a man in a wide-brimmed hat and a cloak to match, both black as starless sky. Roberto thought he looked familiar too, and he turned back to look, but both of them were gone. In their place were two other men, shorter, broader at the shoulders, dirty like miners or men who work digging in the earth. Roberto blinked and shook his head. He looked up into the smoke, and groaned. Maybe he wasn't short enough to be clear of it after all, whatever it was.

Deeqa and the red-haired youth met him in the street. In the light of the illusions and lamps up and down the street— those that were lit, anyway—he could tell the boy couldn't be more than eighteen or nineteen.

"This way," said the boy. "It's only six blocks from here."

"Don't screw with us, dude," Roberto said.

"So why you want them, anyway?" said the boy. "And what's it worth to you?"

"Shouldn't you have asked that before we came out here?"

"You just paid a crown for two drinks and gave them to me. My take from a pair of homing lizards will be good." He flashed a greedy smile over his shoulder at them. "And why does an Earth ship captain need a homing lizard at all? I thought you all sent your messages through the air somehow, with some kind of machine."

Roberto exchanged glances with Deeqa before answering, measuring his reply. "Who says I'm an Earth ship captain?"

"I'm not stupid, you know. I make my living by paying attention to things."

"I guess so." They walked in silence for a time.

"So you gonna tell me?" he asked finally, as they turned another corner. "It's just up here," he added as they went along. "Third one there, on the left." He pointed to a low building, near the end of the block. The sign above it read Bleck's Bakery.

"They sell homing lizards at a bakery?" Roberto made a face at Deeqa, but she was too busy looking around.

"We've got four of them," she said. "Three between those two buildings back there, one more by the broken rail. Been on us since we left."

"Figures," Roberto said. He'd missed them completely. "I should have known you were a shithead," he said to the boy.

"Wasn't me, swear," said the kid. "I'd be dead if I was a double-crosser all this time. Look at me." He looked down at himself. "I ain't got nothing for a fight."

"Size doesn't mean much. Any monkey can learn to shoot. Or sword fight, for that matter." He looked up ahead of them along the street. He didn't see any movement up there.

"I can handle myself with a sword," the boy said. "Can't afford one, though." He moved to the walkway on their left. "Come on. We can move quick, get in through the back. They won't know which we went in."

"You want us to follow you down that dark alley, with four guys on our ass, so that we can get a homing lizard from a bakery?" he asked. "I mean, I get that you figured out we are from Earth, but you should know that it's not a whole planet full of morons. I mean, we have plenty, but, you know, not all of us."

"Up to you," said the youth. "But I give you my word. Thief's honor, I swear it."

"Why does that not mean anything to me?" But Roberto was moving along behind. "You die first, thief, just so you know."

They slipped into the narrow space between two buildings, Roberto having to squeeze through sideways, for his shoulders were too wide. He pulled his blaster out and was ready to come out firing on the other side.

The boy was waiting for them when they came through.

Roberto looked left, then right. Deeqa reached up and grabbed the roof by its overhang. She pulled herself up and vanished into the darkness.

"Down here," the boy said as they went along. "My name is Breks," he said as they crept along the wall. "But everyone calls me Squints on account of me always watching everyone. I never met nobody from Earth before. I heard there ain't no magicians nowhere at all on the whole planet. Is it true? A whole world with just us blanks?"

"Yeah, it's fantastic. Now get us in so we can get the hell

out of here before they drop the ambush on us."

"They'll wait till we come out," he said. "No lamps down the street there, and if we break into something like they probably heard we were doing, we might set off the alarms."

"What kind of alarms?"

"Shrieker ferns, mostly. Enchanted as best they can pay for, smoke and fire, maybe breaking glass and shadows moving inside. But I got you covered. I been in Bleck's before."

They stopped at the back of the building, third from the end of the back alley. Squints left Roberto by the door and crept along to a small window, peering inside through the iron grate that covered it. Roberto could barely see him, and it was all he could do to resist pulling out his flashlight. Were it not for the dim moon, a clear sky full of stars and the light of a lamp bleeding through the narrow alley out onto the opposite street, it would have been pitch black.

Squints squared to the window and took two paces back toward Roberto, which brought him just short of the door. He placed his hand on the wall and began muttering. A moment later something dull thumped down onto the floor inside.

"You're a wizard?" Roberto asked, under his breath.

"A-class transmute," he said. "Not good for much more than warping wood, but it's got its usefulness."

He started chanting again, his hand on the door. He had just looked up at Roberto again when two gunshots rang out. Footsteps sounded, lightly running across the rooftop right above them, followed by a brief silence, then the sound of someone landing on the roof next door and running again. Another shot sounded, a single sharp crack.

Roberto gripped his weapon and went to the alley, peering around the corner, ready to smoke whoever came through. Nobody was there. He was just about to head into the street, when Deeqa dropped down behind him, near the door where Squints was.

"One got away," she said. "We need to be quick."

The boy didn't even look sideways at her as he opened the door. He crept inside, holding a hand out behind him as he did, indicating that they should be silent for a time. He disappeared into the darkness. They waited, each of them watching warily into the dark on either side.

"Gorgon's gaze," came a curse from inside.

Roberto and Deeqa exchanged glances. It was clear she didn't want to wait.

Roberto leaned into the door. "Hurry up, kid. We're leaving in thirty seconds, homing lizards or not."

The boy came toward him then; he could see him silhouetted in the front window, the lamplight coming from the street shaping his hunched form and that of a small cage swinging in his hand.

"You get them?" Roberto asked.

"Not exactly," said Squints. He came out into the semi-light and held up the cage. "They're gone."

"Great. We pick the night the damn baker cooked all his damn lizards into a pie."

"He probably sent them home with him or something," the youth said. "They're pretty hot these days."

"Let's go," Deeqa hissed. She was already moving down the alley toward the far end of the street.

"Sorry, kid," Roberto said. He fished a gold coin out from beneath his cloak. "You made out like a bandit anyway. Stay safe. That asshole that got away might bring his friends."

"You got a cabin boy?"

"A what?" Roberto glanced back, but set out after Deeqa, Squints following.

"Cabin boy. Every ship has a cabin boy."

"No, they don't. And you're too old to qualify." He stopped long enough to wave him off, shooing him like a dog. "You need to go on, now. I can't be dragging you around. This shit just got real. So, go. I can't watch out for you."

"I been watching out for me down here for a long time, Captain," he said.

"Good. So good luck. And thanks for trying."

He set off after Deeqa again.

The boy was still following him.

"Dude!" Roberto said. "You're about to piss me off."

"I can get you out of town without trouble."

"You were going to get me a homing lizard too, remember?"

"I still can."

"Really? Where, at that other place? The pigeon store? I got news for you, chief, we already went by there on the way down. It's closed. And I'm sure they sent theirs home at night too."

"Why you need one, anyway? You never said why."

"That's right, I didn't. Now you need to get going. My friend up ahead there ain't nice like me, and if she decides you're just trying to lure us into the next trap, well, she's liable to do some crazy Somali pirate shit to you."

"You need a telepath, don't you?"

"Fuck off, kid. I swear."

"You'll need to talk to someone from here while you are back at Earth. I heard they aren't letting magicians go there. So you got no telepath on your ship."

"Your information is old. They sent some wizards. And I'm telling you, if I have to tie your ass up and leave you in the street, you're not going to have that gold I just gave you for very long. Just take what you got. Seriously, dude. Last time I'm asking nice."

"I can do it."

"Do what?"

"Be your telepath."

"You just said you are just an A-class guy. Even I know

that's weak as hell."

"Telepathy don't work that way. You just have to know the other guy. And, well, you know, they have to let you in."

Roberto frowned down at him, then looked back at Deeqa, who had just come back. She looked like she was actually considering what the kid said.

Roberto saw it in her eyes. "Dude, he's a thief. He even said so." He held his hands up as if to ward her off. "I'm not bringing a damn thief onto my ship. We've been trying to avoid that since we first got here, remember? No thieves. Period."

She looked at him, one eyebrow arched and her head tipping sideways. She was waiting for something, waiting for him to figure out something obvious.

"What?" he said. She cocked the other eyebrow, patiently. Then he figured it out.

It was her. *She* was on the ship. He shook his head emphatically. "No. That's different. You're different." He turned and pointed to Squints. "He's different."

"How many more bakeries do you want to break into?" she said. "Or would you rather wait until sunrise?"

"God damn it," Roberto said. He looked at the boy. "How do I know you're not just going to screw me somehow?"

Squints pulled out the coin. "You just paid me with this," he said. "I've never even held one before." He held the coin toward Roberto, giving it back. "I'll work for food and a hammock. And if I work for you right, you'll take me to Earth."

Roberto pushed his hand, and the coin, back at him. "What the hell do you want to do on Earth? By the time I am dumb enough to drag your magic ass to that planet, it's going to have to be legal to put you there. So you won't be any more a big shot there with your A-class magic than you are here."

"Yes, I will. It's a planet full of blanks. There's no way I won't be something more than I am here."

Roberto glared at him, and back to Deeqa, who gestured that he should make up his mind. "The clock is ticking," she said.

"Shit." He glared at the boy again. "Fine. But I'll throw your ass out an airlock if you screw with me, even one time, you hear?"

"I won't," he promised. "Thief's honor."

"Well, how about you honor that first by getting us out of town."

Chapter 39

"Well, Miss Grayborn, it seems that everywhere you go, you leave a trail of blood behind." That was Lieutenant Hammond of the Reno PD who said it, and Pernie was pretty tired of the way he kept walking back and forth when he talked. Sophia and Don Hayworth had been called, and they were on their way too. Pretty soon everyone was going to be lecturing her. Pernie thought maybe Sophia and Don could get in line behind the lieutenant, and they could all walk back and forth like a parade telling her how bad she was. "Do you understand that here on Earth, people don't just go around beating everyone up?"

"Everyone doesn't put a laser to Jeremy's head," Pernie said.

"You should have called for the police."

"That would take too long. And I didn't have my tablet anyway."

"Well, that was reckless, too. You should never have been downtown. Little girls, no matter where they are from, do not go downtown all alone."

Pernie rolled her eyes. Everyone on this whole stupid planet said that. They all sounded like dumb cawfrats, big poisonous parrots echoing back the same set of sounds over and over again. *Don't go downtown. Don't go downtown. Squawwwwk. Don't go downtown.* Pernie had already been downtown three times, and the only bad thing that ever happened was that the stupid Reno PD always showed up and got her in trouble every time.

A knock on the door of the small room sounded. Lieutenant Hammond called, "Yeah," and in came Sophia Hayworth and her husband, Don. Both of them looked worried, but Sophia mostly looked mad—mad in that calm way she had when she was going to talk a lot and talk like she thought Pernie was dumb.

"Mr. and Mrs. Hayworth," said the lieutenant. "Please, sit down."

They both looked from the uniformed man to Pernie sitting there. Pernie made a point of ignoring them. Mostly Sophia, though.

"I was just explaining to Miss Grayborn here," said the lieutenant, "that we can't have her running loose all over the city, leaving a wake of carnage everywhere. I've had a look at her file, and in barely three weeks, she's already managed to collect quite a history of ... wanderlust."

"She is completely unmanageable," Sophia said in the exact same moment Don Hayworth said, "She's got heart, that's for sure."

The lieutenant looked back and forth between them and harrumphed. He looked back to Pernie. "So which is it, Miss Grayborn: are you unmanageable, or do you simply have too much 'heart' for your own good?"

Pernie's heart was exactly the way it was supposed to be. Just like her brain was. The longer she stayed on this planet, the dumber they all seemed to be. Except Jeremy. And Don Hayworth. And maybe Gabby, but she didn't know him very well. Mrs. Beckman, her teacher, was nice too.

"Well, I can't do it anymore," Sophia said. "I can't. I volunteered to take her because Angela was in such a big hurry to get off world. Her people assured me she would behave, but as you can see, this child is completely out of hand. I can't control her, and she clearly can't be trusted to keep any of her own promises, much less those of her people back on Prosperion." She glanced at Pernie when she said that last, and made a face at her as she pronounced "her own promises" like somehow Pernie had broken one.

"That's a lie," Pernie spat.

Sophia let out a windy sort of breath, and looked insulted. "You little brat!" she snapped. "How dare you? What single—"

Don Hayworth cut her off. "Honey, honey," he soothed. "It's okay." Sophia glared at Pernie but allowed herself to be silenced.

"I never broke any promises," Pernie said, looking to the lieutenant. "Not one single one."

"Then why are we here?" muttered Sophia as she rolled her eyes up and stared at the ceiling. She crossed her arms over her chest and looked as if irritation might blow her to pieces from the inside.

"I didn't," said Pernie. "I only promised not to use magic, not to sneak out at night, and not to go downtown alone. I did not use magic; I did not sneak out; and Jeremy was with me today." She crossed her own arms over her own chest and gave a smug, singular nod as she glared at the lieutenant again. Then she thought about it and amended, "And the sun was perfectly in the sky."

The lieutenant looked from her to Sophia and then finally to Don. Both men sighed.

"So what now, Lieutenant?" asked Don.

"That's up to you two. If you really can't keep her, then I have to put in a call to the NTA. Her file is pretty specific with how we have to handle this, and it's some kind of file, I'll tell you. Seven layers of access in the thing, and six of them are above my pay grade."

Don looked to Pernie, and his eyes were very sad. "Pernie," he said. "Can't you please just follow the rules?"

"Forget it, Don," Sophia snapped. "I'm not going to live like this. This isn't what we agreed to."

"But honey, it's only been three weeks. She's from Prosperion, for crying out loud. She needs time."

"No, Don." That came out with ice on it. "No. You said it yourself, she's no Angela. Well, she's not. And I am too old to spend four years with ... with some kind of alien sociopath."

"Jesus, Sophia!" Don said. He turned back to the lieutenant, who seemed sad now.

Don got up and tugged Sophia up with him. She looked into his eyes and saw something there, and her expression softened. She glanced at the lieutenant, sighed, then turned and let Don lead her to the door. She paused and turned back to Pernie with tears in her eyes. "I'm sorry," she said. She was sobbing as Don led her away. He looked back through the window glass as they passed down the hall, and Pernie could tell by the way he looked at her that he was sorry too.

Pernie didn't care. Fine. She didn't need them anyway. She could stay with someone else. Maybe Jeremy's grandpa would take her. Gabby seemed very nice, and he looked out for Jeremy even though he was only one old grandpa. And he didn't try to lock Jeremy up in a jail with *prock-see-me* alarms on the windows like a criminal. She would just ask Jeremy tomorrow when she went to school.

Assuming they let her go to school. It occurred to her they might not.

The lieutenant watched the Hayworths pass beyond the window, then went to the door and closed it again. He leaned on the table with both hands. He studied her for a time, not like a bug or something, not like Master Altin and Tytamon had that day the last time Pernie had tried to kill Orli Pewter again. But he clearly didn't know what to do. Pernie had always thought that people named "Lieutenant" in the army were supposed to know what to do. But he didn't. She could see it in his eyes. Djoveeve said that when people look like that, they are vulnerable.

But Pernie didn't know what to do with his vulnerability. This wasn't the kind of combat they'd trained her for. So she just watched him and waited to see what he would do next.

"You want a tablet or net visor?" he said.

"For what?" she asked.

"To play with until the major comes."

"What major?"

"The one from Fort Reno. From the NTA."

"Fine," she said.

He brought her one. She couldn't get access to the global net, or even call out to ask Jeremy if she could stay with him and Gabby and go to school. All it had on it were games for captured kids to play. Pernie knew what it was. But she didn't care. She would wait and see.

She opened up the only game she recognized, *Blades of Death XIV: Return of the Lich.* She spent the next three hours turning all the other stupid game warriors into piles of guts with Starfaze. Starfaze with her big bosoms and her broomstick.

Chapter 40

The major came into the little room in the Reno PD headquarters and looked just like Pernie thought he would, just like all the other fleet officers she'd seen back on Prosperion. There was actually something comforting in that. He looked a little like Roberto, only taller and not quite so broad across the shoulders and back. He had dark eyes, but there wasn't anything funny glinting in them, though, not like Roberto's always had.

"Well, Miss Grayborn, it seems you've already worn out your welcome with your host family. Although, Lieutenant Hammond there has told me that you've had some bad luck in at least part of that."

Pernie thought he was going to lecture her about going downtown like everyone else did. But he did not.

"You've put us all in an awkward place," he said instead. "But I'm not sure how we are going to find a new host family for you if you are going to continue running about drawing attention to yourself."

"I didn't draw attention to myself." She didn't really know what that meant anyway, but she didn't care. She didn't do it on purpose if she had.

"Well, sweetheart, yes, you did. I've got one Martin 'Zest'

Boyle, a registered sex offender, still in a coma at Pfizer Corporate Hospital. I've also got a Calvin McLeary, Ryan Perkins, and Lashon Zaparto listed as hospitalized. The McLeary and Zaparto kids have been released, but it looks like the Perkins boy is probably going to lose his eye unless he can come up with enough money to get it regrown. That's a lot of carnage for one ten-year-old girl in under seventy-two hours. If that's not drawing attention to yourself, I don't know what is."

"They started it," Pernie said.

He actually laughed. He reminded her of Don Hayworth in that way. Which was also comforting.

"Well, that may be so, but I'm afraid that, by our agreement with your government back on Prosperion, if you can't be ... kept in check, we are authorized to send you home."

"I'm not going home," she said. "I need to learn how to do all your sciences. Plus I am going to learn to fly the planes that go as fast as sound. And a starship."

"Well, that's just it, Miss Grayborn. That's what we all want for you as well. But you can't run around ramming broomsticks into people's faces and putting them in comas."

"I already told you: they started it."

"Yes, that's what you said. But they wouldn't have started it if you were in your house where you were supposed to be."

"They have alarms on my house and I can't leave, like I am in jail."

"But you aren't in jail."

"People in jail can't leave when they want to."

"That is true, but—"

"Well, they won't let me leave when I want to. The man who brought me here the first time told me that criminals are supposed to be in jail. But I am the one who has to stay inside, and all the criminals are outside."

"Miss Grayborn," he said. "It doesn't work that way. I can

see how you—"

She cut him off again, because she didn't want to listen to any more grown-up lies. "No," she shouted at him. "Everyone wants me inside. But they don't keep the criminals away." She pointed at the lieutenant accusingly. "That's why all the criminals are outside. You should make him go get the bad men and leave me alone."

She felt tears burning in her eyes, though. They were going to send her back home. They were. She just knew it. They were grown-ups, and grown-ups always did whatever they wanted to, even when they were wrong. And so she'd go back to Prosperion and she wouldn't know anything. She'd know how electricity worked and how to fix a wall. And that was all. Nothing else. Master Altin would think she was stupid, and he'd just be married to Orli Pewter forever, and Pernie wouldn't even be Sava'an'Lansom, because she didn't do like Djoveeve and Seawind said. She hadn't even been here for three weeks, and they were sending her back. She even kept all her promises.

She put her head down in her arms upon the desk. She didn't want the Earth men to see her cry and know that she was weak like a little girl. She tried not to cry, but it all just kept coming out.

The man from Fort Reno tried to touch her shoulder, but she turned on him and growled and made her most terrible face. He recoiled from her as if she were a viper. She was glad to see it in his eyes. He was afraid of her.

She set her head back in her arms and stared at the darkness inside. Enough light came through that she could see a pool of tears and spit on the table. After a time she wished she hadn't cried like that.

She blinked her eyes dry and tried not to make too much noise sniffling up all the snot that was running in her nose. She wiped her face on the shoulder of her blouse as best she could, then finally looked up again.

"I'm not going home," she said.

"Well, we'll see about that," he said. "But for now, you're going to have to come with me." He glanced up, and nodded out the window at someone standing outside the room. The door opened, and in came another man in an NTA uniform much like his. The new officer handed the major a square, flat box made of metal, dully reflective in the bright lights of the small room, then moved around to stand behind Pernie.

The major opened it, and Pernie saw a large metal object, round like a collar or a tiara, though held closed with a small, locking clasp. At even intervals around it were small metal boxes, hardly bigger than one joint of her finger, three of them in all. Each had two lights on it, one a dull green and the other flashing yellow.

"I'm going to need you to wear this," the major said. "Just for now."

"What is it?" Pernie asked. She glanced over her shoulder at the man behind her, then back at the object. She didn't know why, but she hated it on instinct.

"It's just to help us ... keep you from doing anything we'll all regret."

Pernie glanced to the cut she had made on her arm, where the police medic had stitched it up with tiny black things he'd called staples. He'd told her they would dissolve and the "new skin" he'd painted on her would help it all regrow. He'd put another chip in her arm too. Pernie thought the metal ring in the box was going to be worse than the chip.

"I don't want to wear it," she said.

"It's just for now. Until we can, well, until we know what to do."

"I won't wear it," she said.

"But you don't even know what it is. You might like it."

"If I was going to like it, you would have said what it is."

He turned to the police lieutenant, who nodded and

raised his eyebrows in a way that seemed to say, "You see?"

"Well, you have to wear it. That's just how it goes."

"I won't." She pushed out her lips and crossed her arms again. She was watching him, though. She'd been in enough fights in her life to recognize how those things go.

"Vincent," said the major, meant for the uniformed man behind her.

The man in uniform behind Pernie stepped up and grabbed her arms, pinning them to her sides. Pernie started to jump up from the chair, intent on flipping backward, over his head, but in the same motion as he was snatching her arms, he shoved her chair forward and pinned her to the table's edge. He was extremely fast, like he was a trained fighter too.

The major took the collar out of the box and unlocked it with the pass of a plastic key. "It doesn't hurt," he said, "as long as you do as you are told. So please, let's just all stay calm. It's just a precaution. That is all."

Pernie thrashed in the man called Vincent's grip. He was very strong, and the edge of the table was jammed up under her ribs. She flung her head back, trying to head butt him, but she only thudded against his chest, which was muscular and strong.

The collar opened up like a set of jaws. The lights were all blinking red now. The major stooped and approached her, reaching it for her throat. The throat was the most vulnerable part, Djoveeve had said. Never let them at your throat.

She tried to kick the table over, but it was attached to the floor. Her knee clanked against the metal painfully. She thrashed even more violently in Vincent's grip. He was too strong.

"Come on, Miss Grayborn, please." The collar was only inches away.

She wanted to do magic. She wanted to teleport.

The tip of the collar latch brushed against her neck. She batted his arm away with the side of her face.

"Miss Grayborn, stop it now." That was absolute command.

Pernie batted it away again. She smashed it hard with the side of her head, and when he tried to shove it back, she bit him as hard as she could. He shouted, and when he tried to jerk his wrist out of her mouth, his skin tore. She shook her head like a dog as he tried to pull away, biting harder. His blood tasted much different than Seawind's had when Pernie bit the elf. The major's blood tasted like Earth.

"Lieutenant," ordered the major, finally pulling his arm free, "for Chrissakes, come help. Hold her head."

The lieutenant moved to comply.

Pernie thrashed. She really wanted to teleport away. She hated her stupid promise.

The lieutenant grabbed her head, crowding Vincent behind her to get position. He mashed his hands against her forehead, covering one eye, and squeezed her skull front and back.

"Watch her teeth," the major said. He came at her with the collar again. She felt its leading edges scrape against her throat.

She should teleport.

"Move your hand, I can't get it locked," he said.

The metal was cold as it slid around her neck.

"Hurry up, before she casts something. Move your damn thumb."

Promises were stupid.

The collar clicked shut as Pernie finished the second word of the spell. She felt something bite her on the neck, electricity perhaps, but when she reached for the collar, it wasn't there. She turned and looked at the three men through the window. They were still in the room. She wasn't.

She ran down the hallway in the direction she'd seen Don

and Sophia Hayworth go. She remembered the way the police people had brought her in. She didn't want to go that way. She ran left and right, running through corridors. All the doors had little windows in them, so even the locked ones were easy to get through.

She teleported past one lock after another.

She ran past a wall of monitors and saw herself on them. The Reno PD people had cameras everywhere.

She ran through another series of corridors. There had to be a door that would take her outside. She found a door that was opening all by itself. A man was coming down another hall. He shouted at her.

She jumped through the opening door but found herself boxed in. It was a very tiny room. The doors were closing behind her. She turned to leave, but more men were running down the hallway where she had come.

The doors closed on them. She looked for a lock to keep them out. They were heavy-looking metal doors; perhaps they would buy her time to think.

There were so many buttons. All of them numbered. None looked like locks.

She pushed them all.

The little room started to move, upward, by the feel of it. She wondered where it was taking her. The men were taking her somewhere.

The doors opened again right away, and she was in another set of corridors. She looked out, and there were people passing by, but not the men chasing her. These people weren't looking at her at all. She ducked back. The doors were closing again.

The little room went up again. The next floor was the same as the floor before. People were out there in corridors. She ducked back again. Three more floors went by before she found a corridor where there wasn't anyone right outside. She ran down the nearest hallway, then left and right and left again. Still there were no doors leading outside. She kept running.

Finally she saw a big window that looked out into darkness at the end of a hallway. She ran to it. The night sky beckoned from between buildings that were tall like the ones downtown. There was no way to open the window. Just glass in a wall. Thick glass.

She was at least a hundred spans off the ground.

Shouting came from behind her. The lieutenant and the two NTA officers were running after her. Someone came through a door at the opposite end of the hallway, and there were footsteps coming from another corridor halfway in between.

Pernie looked out the window again. She spoke the words of her teleport spell and broke her promise again. She appeared outside the window. She looked back in time to see the major's mouth shape the word "no" as she began to fall.

She fell toward the street, faster and faster all the way down. Just before she hit, she cast the teleport again, reappearing on the sidewalk on the opposite side of a police car. She ran around the corner, once more heading for the broken buildings in the distant part of downtown. She couldn't go back to Sophia Hayworth's house, that was sure. At least downtown she sort of knew.

She ran in a series of sprints and teleports. She'd already ruined her promise now, anyway. She had to get far away. Quickly. She had to get the chip out of her arm again.

In only a few short minutes, she found a vacant lot, where a smaller building had been demolished and left to the weeds. There were amber streetlights all around. Light glinted off broken glass. Sirens wailed in the distance now.

She snatched up the neck of a brown bottle and went right to work on her arm again. She cut through the "staples" and back to the bone. It hurt a lot more with a piece of glass than it had with Jeremy's laser knife, but she didn't care.

She cut in with one long, neat slice and stuffed her finger in, searching for the bump that marked the ant-sized chip was there. She found it right away. She slid the jagged point of the bottle up against it, and with a sideways swing of her arm, she struck the mouth of the bottle against a streetlight pole. The chip gave way from the bone.

Tossing the bottle aside, she fished out the chip again. She dropped it and mashed it flat with a chunk of concrete.

The sound of sirens surrounded her, echoing between the buildings from all directions. She couldn't tell where they were really coming from. Or else they were coming from everywhere.

She picked up the broken bottleneck again. It was a decent knife for now. There was blood all around her feet, running down her forearm and dripping off her elbow. She glanced up and down the street. No time to heal it now. She ran toward the one place remotely familiar to her down here, the big, broken building that looked like a spear. She teleported in fifty-span leaps as she ran, blinking in and out of the pools of amber light cast by the streetlamps, in and out of the darkness. Light and dark. Light and dark.

The siren sounds got fainter as she fled. She paused long enough to sing the daffodil healing song. Her arm closed up by the second time she sang it through. The wound was still angry and red, but it wasn't bleeding anymore.

By the time she got to the big spear-shaped building, she'd sung even the red away.

Chapter 41

The fatigue and frustration bent Orli for a time, but they did not break her. When the sobs had passed a few minutes later, she lifted her head and glared up through the grate of the deck above her. The alien had taken Altin away, it was true. But it was also true that she had found him once despite thinking him lost to her. She would do it again.

She wiped her hands as best she could on her underwear, then examined the damage to them. It wasn't too bad. They hurt, and they were going to be a mess tomorrow, if she lived that long, but today, she could still make them work.

She set the Higgs prism to zero and jumped once more into the wind. She'd had enough practice that angling herself up to the next level was easy enough. She crawled through the grating, checked for oncoming billowed-alien traffic, then thrust herself into the wind that had taken Altin and his captor away.

Without her spacesuit as a sail, she couldn't direct her flight as effectively as before, but she made her way along at a good clip and managed not to hit any more goddamn alien machines. One of the billowed creatures flew by to her left, overtaking her and passing her by at a seemingly leisurely pace, but it paid no heed to her. She angled herself just a little higher up, closer to the deck above her, just in case. She didn't want to be seen, and she certainly didn't want to be mashed into the pillowy lampshades of their parachute sails if another one or two came by—not too close, though, for this was tricky business. If she skimmed along the bottom of the next level too finely, a wayward wind gust might push her up into a gap, and, well, she thought she might be running out of ribs to break.

The wind carried her over what seemed like endless fields of alien machinery, the patchwork squares of the grating like vast pastureland, the quilted fields of an alien landscape seen from high above as if viewed from a spaceship high in the atmosphere.

Eventually she flew across one of the wide, empty spaces, then over the grate on the far side of it. She had to veer left to dodge a huge steam stack that rose from another bulky machine, and then for a full five minutes she flew over nothing but bulbous brown tanks like those she'd seen nesting in the strange brown piping.

Eventually the stretch of tanks and the platform itself came to an end, and once more she was flying over an abyss. She looked up and saw a violet ring, oval shaped, high above, but on the same line as her flight path. She knew immediately it had to represent another upward column of air. She shifted the direction of her flight so that she would fly by it rather than into it, not wanting to be driven back up to the uppermost reaches of the ship.

As she neared the next stack of levels, she saw the telltale orange lights in the distance, marking where the dead-air column must be. Either she was back where she had been before, or more likely, the aliens definitely lined those lights up with consistency. Predictability was one thing Orli desperately needed in this place.

But there was still no sign of Altin.

She flew over the next level, another long platform, an

endless-seeming grate stretching for mile after mile. It was astonishing how massive the ship was. As she neared the end of this one, she found herself flying between what looked like a forest of steam stacks on either side. There were hundreds of them, all climbing through the grate from down below, and through the one below that as far as she could see. They rose up through the grate above her, and above that one as well. Beyond that they were lost in the dark. The puffs of steam that she flew through grew more frequent.

Shortly after encountering the dense assemblage of steam stacks, she shot out over another wide black abyss. Again she found the violet ring above her, though not in a line with her course, and shortly after, the orange lights, one above the next, marking the edge of yet another level.

She flew over platform after platform, in what seemed an endless stretch, the vastness of the ship becoming increasingly staggering, experienced in slow, desperate reality. Each was in some ways different from the previous, but all were essentially the same to her untrained eye. The only thing she recognized for certain was that there was no sign of Altin anywhere.

She flew over another large cluster of machines, where six aliens were at work on something. She hoped it might be Altin at the same time she feared it would be. They clustered around one another in a huddle, looking to her like a ring of mucous gray dumbbells, their long bodies and uneven bulbs bent toward each other as they blinked down at something unseen between them. Orli stared down through the wisps of steam, into the shadowy place between them, hoping that the flashes of color one or another of them emitted would illuminate her missing husband there.

Just as she was nearly too far to see, she saw a flash of something long and metallic. Not Altin, at least. At least she hoped it wasn't him, stuffed into some new kind of alien thing. But she was already flying out over the edge of the grate again.

This could go on forever, damn it.

Three more sections of platform came and went, and then, finally, there was something different and new, something very loud ahead. There were no lights beyond the abyss over which she flew, and what little ambient light there was, coming from behind, kept lighting up puffs of steam around her rather than revealing anything.

As she began to curse the steam for its puffy obstruction, a blast of it hit her full force. In the blinking and sputtering that followed, something smashed her left hand so hard that she felt the bones breaking. The sound changed in that same instant, growing louder, and whatever hit her had her spinning around. She struck something hard with her back and then her head. She bounced and slid along, tumbling down some kind of tunnel. A giant duct, like the one she'd discovered within the violet ring. Except this time she'd blown right through the vent into the ductwork itself.

She skidded and bounced along the rough surface, collecting abrasions like mad. The wind was lessened some as the turn of the duct slowed both it and her. She tried to brace herself between the edges as she might have trying to climb a chimney, but the duct was too wide to reach across—not to mention her hand was throbbing worse than her leg and about as bad as her ribs.

She reached for the Higgs prism as she was drawn deeper into the shaft, bouncing along the upward curve, carried by the wind. Dim light now came from above her, along with a frightening increase in the volume of the machinery sounds. Whatever it was, it was getting closer. Much closer.

"Shit," she muttered just as she blew up and around what was essentially a long horseshoe curve. She fumbled for the Higgs prism frantically. She tried at first with both hands, and the pain in her left nearly blinded her. With her right, she dialed up gravity hard and slammed herself to a stop, pinning herself to the bottom with a full four Gs.

She lay panting, her whole body aching everywhere. She stared up at the rough ceiling of the duct and waited for her heart to slow. She was fit, and it did so right away. She let go a steadying breath, then turned down the Higgs prism to one and a half. She lifted her left hand and examined it in the dim light. It looked terrible. Three fingers broken for sure, and at least a few carpals opposite her thumb. Mangled, basically. Blood ran freely into her left eye from a cut on her head. Her elbows and knees were waterfalls, the blood and sweat mixed to rivers. She laid her head back down and sighed. "Don't I look lovely for my honeymoon?" She almost laughed.

A painkiller or ten would have been nice, but she had none, so there wasn't much to be done about it but grit her teeth and go on. Even after resting for a time, breathing still made her ribs ache. And she really did need to find Altin.

Looking in the direction of the airflow, she saw that, forty feet from where she was, the duct came to another vent, which opened out into the ship proper again. Between her and the dim lights of the distant stack of decks beyond was a series of valves, enormous and long, opening and closing sequentially, each slamming in turn with thunderous regularity. There were at least six of them, giant things that squeezed laterally like a digestive act, forcing air through them and out into the ship.

Somehow she had to get out of there and back to looking for Altin.

With an effort that was so fraught with agony from what felt like literally every source possible in her body, she rolled over onto her hands and knees. Her left hand, braced on the heel of her palm, shook as if with palsy. It throbbed. She had to wait for dizziness to pass. She stood and leaned into the air flowing by. There wasn't any way she was going to try navigating her way through the mashing brutality of those valves, so she had to go back out the way she'd come in.

She bent into the wind and marched back through the duct, having to jump down into the horseshoe curve with some added gravity to overcome the wind. That did little for her battered body, but soon enough, she was around the bend and back on a level surface. Shortly after, she was back at the intake vent she'd blown through, and upon which she'd mangled her hand. She peered at it and shook her head. She was damn lucky it was just her hand.

After being in total blackness coming round the bend in the duct, the ambient light coming through the vent seemed brighter than it had been. It reflected wetly off the slickness of the steam that coated everything, though she thought perhaps a bit of that sheen was her blood.

She climbed through the vent, bracing herself against the wind, and looked out over the abyss toward the layers of grates far beyond. Glancing up, she gauged it had to be nearly a mile to the upper hull. The bottom was so far away she couldn't see it at all. Seven or eight miles at least. Maybe more. She shook her head. He could be anywhere.

Something scuffed and scuttled to her left. It startled her, and she ducked back through the vent. It passed along the edge of the vent and then moved down below, its course marked by the huffing sound it made, like something trying to intentionally hyperventilate. She risked looking out after it.

It was one of the little aliens, the ones with the three-tentacled faces and the hooks on their behinds, like the one that spat the ecstasy-inducing bubble that nearly got her killed. She shuddered.

It crawled along the bulkhead, oblivious to her. She wondered where it was going. More huffing sounds had her glancing up again. Two more were coming down.

She ducked back inside. What if they caught her? What if she was lunch? The big ones had ignored her, but these little freaks might not. They could blast her with their orgasmic sauce, and she'd be done for. Not one damn thing she could do.

They didn't. They moved along just as the first one had. She looked out once they were beneath her and watched them go.

She thought about following them. Maybe they were going somewhere useful. But doing so would be as random an action as not following them.

Think, Pewter!

She caught herself. Smiled a forlorn little smile as she shook her head. *Think, Meade!* Lady Meade. "Get it together, Lady Meade." Saying it made the smile a little wider.

She needed to gather the facts that she had. Which weren't many. The air streams blew through vents. That much was obvious. There were lights marking air columns for up, down. The aliens spoke with lights on their bodies, or at least she was fairly sure that was what they were doing. They used machines, maybe—probably—built them, which meant they were smart. The fact that they had lights to mark things meant they needed some kind of guidance to get around the big ship, much like human ships had signage, too—meaning the creatures weren't perfect, and, therefore, not infallible. It also meant there might be a master schematic of the ship. That's what humans did as well, and, all in all, this ship wasn't so much different than a human one: decks, atmosphere, and machines.

She also knew from extreme personal experience that they threw things away. And not just her. They'd thrown out her spacesuit and helmet. They'd done likewise with Altin's helmet. Although, as she thought about it, he'd gotten that back. She'd seen it fall, and yet, when she was trying to cut him out of the jelly blob, he'd been wearing it.

Something or someone had gotten it back for him. Or gotten another one.

Maybe they didn't throw things away. That made her glance back up again. Nothing was coming.

The fact that they had retrieved or recreated Altin's helmet suggested they understood how it worked or at very least why he had it. The fact that they threw it away to begin with suggested either that they hadn't understood that at first or that it was broken and they had to make another one. Or else that they might even have had an extra one.

It occurred to her that they might have encountered humans before. It was certainly possible. The humans of Earth had discovered there were humans on the planet Andalia, and after that, they discovered more humans on Prosperion. That made it very likely that there were more humans other places too. Blue Fire had said that humans were like dandelions, and the seeds of humanity—and maybe the seeds of Hostiles, for that matter—blew across the stars. So if that was true, then humans might be everywhere. And Hostiles. Maybe these alien assholes too.

Whatever they were, they were damn sure more advanced than humans were. That rift they'd opened up, that was something else. The ships might be largely similar for all their differences, but the humanity she was familiar with wasn't anywhere near opening up rifts in space. Hell, her people had barely mastered the gravitational wave. Without Altin and the Prosperions, Earth ships would still be crawling around at cosmic glacier speeds.

So these aliens had probably already been all over the galaxy. Maybe all over the universe. Humans were probably old news, and the aliens might have a whole ship full of human technology, much of it likely far more advanced than anything she or Altin had. But if that was the case, why had they been so interested in examining Orli and

Altin? Why the table and all the weird microscope machines?

Then it hit her. They'd had Altin's brain imaged up on the monitor. *His*, not hers. She'd been the one they threw away. They weren't interested in examining her at all. Not anymore. But him they kept. Maybe humans were old news. But perhaps *magic* humans were not.

The humans on Andalia hadn't had magic. Just like the people of Earth, the Andalians had relied entirely on technology.

Orli wondered if these aliens relied solely on technology, too, though she thought they likely did not. How else could they have so easily shut Altin down? That didn't bode well for the chance of escape. If they wielded magic, she and Altin were in trouble. And it was certainly possible that they did. The Hostiles used magic, so the precedent for magic use was well established in the universe. Perhaps it was just not common in humans.

Which meant they might view Altin as an oddity. That would explain why he was the one they were going to keep. Perhaps they planned on putting him in some specimen jar like a rare butterfly or some grotesquely diseased organ. Orli they didn't need. She was just a dumb old primate, a cosmic cockroach to be tossed down into the boiling bottom of the ship.

She couldn't prove it, but that seemed plausible. And it was all she had to go on. She'd seen the image on the monitor. So, if she was a cockroach, and Altin was a collector's edition human, then where would they take him? Where was the teaching lab? Or the museum?

She looked out over the abyss and shook her head. She still didn't know. Her theory didn't mean jack.

So where would a cockroach go?

She looked up, then down. The little aliens—if fifty-yard-long creatures could be called "little"—had gone down. A cockroach would go down and get under things. A cockroach would be down where the garbage was. Maybe she could find something down there that would help. Some evidence of Altin they'd cast off, or maybe some rocking hard-core weapon from some other alien species they'd collected. Something with which she could blow a hole through the ship or take some hostages and demand Altin back.

That was her best strategy, bad as it was, because it was her only strategy. It wasn't much, but it was something. So, with a sigh, and a wince as her ribs protested it, she set the Higgs prism to half Earth's gravity and dove out into the wind, a cockroach headed for the sewers and hoping for some luck.

Chapter 42

The *Glistening Lady* appeared in orbit above the huge red world. Battery power came up right away, and the crew set itself to the familiar routine of a five-hour post-teleport restart. Roberto did his part on the bridge while Tytamon and Squints, the newest member of the crew, watched.

"So you are sure you will be all right without me?" Tytamon asked once the initial flurry of activity had passed.

"You have your own work to do," Roberto replied as he reinitialized the navigation computer. "Get that divining thing cast, and then get to Little Earth and send the general and however many mechs he can get for us into the cargo bay I showed you."

"You are rather defenseless out here just yet," Tytamon observed, glancing about the bridge and taking in the blank screens and flashing warning lights all around him. "A measure of prudence while I wait, perhaps."

"It's only five hours. Maybe less if we don't jack around. Besides, you said you can talk to this kid telepathically. As long as you are sure his little A-class pea brain can shoot that far—you know, and so you don't close the mind gate or whatever you guys do—then go do what you need to do with Doctor Leopold."

"Yes, I will be available to the boy," Tytamon assured him. "And to put your mind at ease, we'll confirm it the moment I get back." He turned to Squints and nodded, which the youth returned in kind, though his was openmouthed and wide-eyed. The pedigree of his circle of friends had just gotten a serious upgrade. Soon after, Tytamon began chanting the words that would take him home.

The dim lights dimmed further in the moment Tytamon disappeared, then brightened again following the sucking sound of the great magician's absence snapping in the air.

Squints looked around himself then, as if finally realizing where he was. He crept across the deck to the forward window and stared out into the stars and down at the big red planet beyond. "Wow," he said. "So we really are all the way up in the night sky."

"We're a hell of a lot farther than that," Roberto said as he shifted to the copilot's chair and started up the sensors and weapons system reboots. "That ain't Prosperion down there."

"So who lives down there, then?" he asked. "Are there more people like us?"

"No." Roberto's answers were necessarily short as he worked through the access codes. He glanced once over his shoulder to see if the kid was trying to see them as he typed, but recognized immediately that the young Prosperion didn't even know there was such a thing. He didn't think it would take the thief long to figure it out, though—being as his "gift," after all, was "noticing things."

"So whose ship is that?" the boy asked as Roberto worked. Roberto didn't hear him until he asked again.

"Do we know those people? Or are they pirates?"

"Who?" Roberto asked, annoyed, and having to retype the code to access the satellite orbiting the red world of Yellow Fire.

"Those guys."

Roberto let out an irritated sigh and turned to tell him to shut up until the restart was finished, but he saw that Squints was pointing outside, toward the wormhole.

He looked up and out. An alien ship had just come through the rift. It was moving away, its invisibility function inactive and therefore perfectly, worrisomely visible. Worse, right behind it, he could see a shift in the flickering pinkish fringe of the rift, indicating that another ship, this one invisible still, was slipping into local space. Roberto watched as the invisible smear blurred the pink line and the stars beyond it; then it too was free of the tear and, for a moment, seemingly gone. Like the first, it became visible shortly after. A third ship was coming through right behind.

"Damn it!" Roberto cursed. He tapped his com badge. "Speed it up. We got company. Three more alien vessels just came through."

"We're going as fast as we can, Captain," came Deeqa's response.

"Just letting you know," Roberto said. "Get me power to hide us at least."

"On it." That was Liu Chun. Roberto was glad to have her back aboard. He just hoped it wasn't simply in time to get her mashed by the next set of ships passing by.

A fourth ship slipped out of the opening and, shortly after, joined its three companions in visibility. Roberto watched, his hands numbly moving across the controls, but there wasn't much he could do without power. If the aliens came at them, it was over. He was about to tell Squints to get Tytamon back when the ships began to move away.

Unlike the original alien ships to come through, which made their way straight down to the planet, these new arrivals began to glow, and after a few moments of it, a blinding white glare appeared near the split tail section at the back of each of them. There was a slight blur that followed, and then the four of them shot out of sight, too fast to be seen.

"Whoa," said Squints, the sound pouring out as if his tongue had melted. "Did you see that?"

"Yeah," said Roberto. "I did."

The lad looked at him then, his attention drawn by the foreboding tone in Roberto's voice. "So who are they? Pirates? Something else? Like invaders or something? Why won't you tell me?"

"Because I don't know, man."

"Where are they going?"

"Look, you want to help?" Roberto paused long enough to look at him. His expression was dire serious. The boy nodded. "Then shut up. When Tytamon contacts you, you tell him to get word to General Pewter at Little Earth. Tell him there might be aliens on the way to Prosperion. Or Earth. Can you do that?"

"I can." He actually had sense enough to look scared.

Chapter 43

Pernie ran around the outside of the spear-shaped building, looking for a door or window she could get in. They were all boarded up, all the way around, and she couldn't find a single crack or knothole to look through.

Ten spans up she saw a ledge wide enough to stand on. There were windows above it all along the wall. Most of them were broken. She wasted no time and teleported to the ledge near one of them. She looked inside. The dull glow of the streetlights cut an angle across the darkness. Broken glass and a few rocks and bottles lay inside.

She used her own bottle to break out the jagged teeth of glass along the windowsill and stepped inside. Turning back, she peered out toward the street. She saw one of the black-and-white Reno police cars floating by on its antigravity, barely a span above the ground. There were others higher up in the air, police aircraft like the one that had captured her in the woods three nights ago after she'd escaped from the *pet-on-file*'s van. They were everywhere.

She'd been reading about the flying machines, and she knew that they could see heat through walls, so she quickly made her way deeper into the building so that her heat wouldn't give her away. She didn't know how much heat they could see, or through how many walls, but she had to try.

She made her way to what she hoped was the very center of the place. She wished she'd read more than she had. There was just so much to learn. So many weapons, so many fighters and spaceships. So much technology. It was going to take a long time to know more than Orli Pewter did.

She wondered if that was possible. Orli Pewter was older than Pernie by more than ten whole years. That was more than Pernie's whole lifetime again. How could she ever hope to catch up? It would never be possible. She would always be over a decade behind.

Although, she had learned about percentages, and it was true that while twenty was twice as much as ten, ninety was only ten percent less than a hundred. Maybe she could catch mostly up in time because of math. And if Orli Pewter wasn't working as hard as Pernie would, then maybe Pernie could know more by then that way too.

That calmed her some, and she tried to relax. She used the breathing techniques Djoveeve taught her, breathing that wouldn't give your location away. Breathing to help your strength and agility. Elves don't make mistakes in battle because they don't get scared. They don't get excited and do dumb things. Humans have to protect against being scared and dumb. That was the price of instinct. That's what Djoveeve said.

So Pernie calmed herself. She had time. She just needed to think. She had to figure out what to do next.

When she woke up, there were voices coming down the hall. She cast her invisibility illusion, masking sound and smell as well. Nobody had ever taught her how to hide her heat before. She knew even as she cast it that they would see her that way.

As if to confirm it, one voice called out, "In there."

Pernie wished she had sight magic. She wanted to teleport

out, but what if one of them was where she wanted to go? Altin had almost teleported into her once. Her hand throbbed simply from the memory, a pulse of phantom pain where his robes had become part of her flesh.

She didn't want to hurt the Reno PD men or the men from the NTA. She knew they were not criminals, or at least she didn't think they were. But she thought she might have to hurt them if they tried to get her again. She wasn't going to let them put that collar with the biting electricity on her again. She wasn't going to let them send her home. Not until they taught her how to fly. Not until she knew everything about technology and guns.

Two men burst through the door. They held weapons that Pernie could not see because the lights they carried were too bright.

"Got her," one of the men called out.

Pernie heard the *ffft, ffft* of the weapon firing as she began the teleporting spell. She felt the bite of the projectiles like bee stings, one in her shoulder, another in her cheek.

Her magic finished as the second one struck, and she appeared in the hallway outside the room, right behind the men. She got a half step before her vision went blurry and she collapsed to the floor, felled again by the same Earth trick that got her the last time. It occurred to her, in the moments before darkness took her, that she would have to develop some kind of immunity to their knockout serum in the same way she'd developed one for small doses of Fayne Gossa. Apparently the resistance to "all poisons" supposedly imparted to her through that exposure on String did not include the poisons they brewed here on Earth.

Chapter 44

The Marchioness of South Mark stood as she had been since the man called Jefe and the rest of them had left. Jefe was going to bring her a "mech" and a driver for it. He said he had men, ex-NTA forces no less, who would operate them for him ... for her. For a price. They both knew he held all the cards on that front. But she had magicians, and so she'd had to up the game. Her contribution to his enterprise would have to be more subtle: diviners and seers to help him do his dirty work. And he would need it. Even with her magicians working to hide his plans and his activities well after his campaign began, his efforts would be, ultimately, obvious. Her people would take pains to hide his intent and his activities on Earth for as long as it was possible to do so, from prying magicians working for the TGS and perhaps even the NTA, but that would only work for so long. Ultimately, NTA machinery would see, someone would see, and, after, well, Jefe would have to look to his own interests in his pursuit of his coveted "Texas."

And while the marchioness was looking quite well to her interests on Prosperion, what interested her most in the absence of the Earth men and her minions was what she saw in her enchanted mirror. For the last two hours she'd been standing stock still before it, staring. It was mesmerizing.

Lady Meade and the Galactic Mage had somehow gotten themselves into the hands—or tentacles—of some variety of alien animals. The Galactic Mage was nowhere to be found in the view—he hadn't been for an hour or so since Jefe and company had departed—but Lady Meade, upon whom the mirror's enchantment was locked, had been slapped about on some luminous plateau, half-naked, where she was prodded with some kind of three-pronged conical device for a time. Not long after that began, she was picked up and simply discarded, thrown off into the darkness, where she flew to gods knew where.

The marchioness had watched it happening and watched for nearly five full minutes as the newly made lady of Calico Castle plummeted through latticework grating of some alien variety and eventually lost herself in clouds of fog, or mist, or steam, upon catching hold of the torn remnants of some alien clothing.

There had followed quite a bit of drifting about, and some collisions with large gray things, which the marchioness thought might be the massive alien creatures, though the limited view she could manage with the mirror had frustrated that, forcing her to call for Kalafrand.

For the next hour or so, she and the seer had watched as Lady Meade was blown about, exploring the alien spaceship. It was quite clear that was what she was doing, sailing in a way, and it was nearly impossible for the wizened Lady of South Mark to tear herself away when came a tap upon her door. But tear herself away she did, for that tap was one that announced events for which she had a great need to attend.

The thief, Black Sander, waited beyond the door with the Earl of Vorvington. The earl's round face was florid, and his chest heaved with eager breath. She could see in his gleaming eyes that her mechanized armor piece had arrived.

"It's here," he said unnecessarily. "Come, you must see. It

is truly spectacular."

She allowed herself to be led down the stairs and out of her own house. Vorvington grabbed a hooded lantern as they went out, and Black Sander extracted a bit of wax from somewhere inside his cloak and summoned a luminous illusion to guide them through the darkness.

She glanced up and saw that Luria had slunk off behind the horizon already. Sunrise was still another four or five hours off. That was good. The Queen's seers wouldn't be watching now.

They made their way down a paved path, around the fountains, and over the massive fishponds on a series of arched stone footbridges. They rounded the hedge maze and eventually came to the smokehouse, a long, flat-roofed structure of unpainted wood.

"I apologize, My Lady, but this is the most convenient place," said the earl. "I thought it prudent."

She waved the apology off. "Go on, go on." It was not without some effort that she hid her own excitement. She hadn't been this close to finally doing it for forty years. Forty years of waiting. Two hundred years of it. But finally, it was right there in her grasp. The smoke was clearing and reality was taking solid shape.

And solid it was. They went into the smokehouse, and there it stood in all its magnificence: an enormous, gleaming mech. The machine armor of the Earth Marines. It stood half again as tall as she was, and across its shoulders, it was nearly as wide. It had great arms, jointed like a human's, but broad and spectacularly made of metal that shone like steel. Beneath and between the plates of its heavy armament ran tubes and silvery rods of metal. There came a dull hum from it that rumbled even in the ground.

She let her gaze wander up its length, from its titanic feet to its windowed canopy. She peered through the glass and saw a man inside. He stared back at her, his features expressionless. She noted that he wore a mustache that curled in the same way that Jefe's did, a pair of black hooks pulled out to either side.

Jefe stepped out from behind the mech and came to stand before her. With a flourish, he swept his arm out and presented the machine.

"This, My Lady, is as I promised you. You can see that it is working fine. Ignacio will show you, if you do not mind."

Carefully restraining any sign of enthusiasm, the marchioness nodded. "Carry on."

Jefe lifted his arm and spoke into a bracelet on his wrist. "Go on, Ignacio. Show her."

The hum of the mech grew louder, and something of a whining sound ensued. It spun at the waist, halfway around, and lifted one of its arms. A cylindrical appendage, wide like a keg but made of separate black metal tubes, was directed at a side of mastodon that was drying near the back of the smokehouse. The corner of the marchioness' mouth twitched up with a smile she could not entirely contain.

Fire erupted from the end of the Gatling gun accompanied by a loud, cracking sort of whine. A red spray of meat flew across the space and spewed all over the smokehouse wall beyond where the side of mastodon hung. Perhaps a second and a half went by before the lower half of the mastodon fell to the floor, the upper portion swinging lazily on its squeaky hook. Smoke rose from both halves, and little flames flickered for a moment before they went out.

"That is the gat, My Lady," pronounced Jefe.

The mech's giant feet stomped a few steps around, turning so that its whole body faced the mastodon meat. A narrow nozzle emerged from the lower portion of its torso, and suddenly a tongue of flame like dragon's fire engulfed the meat lying on the ground. It blew past the meat even, and against the smokehouse wall.

The meat and the wall were aflame.

Right after, a spew of white issued forth. The flames were extinguished entirely.

"I apologize for the damage," Jefe said, though he didn't sound sorry at all. "All part of the demonstration."

"Carry on," was all she said again.

"Go on, Ignacio," Jefe said.

Ignacio marched the mech to the farthest end of the smokehouse, some thirty spans away. Then the mech jumped right out through the roof, boards and bits of roof tile falling in after. It was gone from sight for a seven count before it came back down again, landing so hard several pieces of meat fell as the rail to which their hooks were mounted broke loose from the beams.

There followed a blasting out of the far wall with an incendiary device of some sort, after which they all followed the mech out back and watched a brilliant series of maneuvers that ultimately ended in the complete destruction of the smokehouse, a small smithy, and three five-hundred-year-old oak trees.

The marchioness could not have been happier, and she watched for over the course of an hour as the mech stomped about destroying outbuildings and remote garden structures. Finally, when the demonstration was complete, the mech came back and stood before them again. It hissed and ticked with a distinct *ting, ting, ting* as various hot metals cooled. Ignacio's smile inside was not quite so big as Jefe's, but it was big enough.

"Is my Prosperion friend pleased?" Jefe asked.

The marchioness drew herself straight and tried to look just a little bored. "It will suffice. Tell your man his performance was acceptable. I will take the forty-three at the agreed-upon price."

Jefe laughed. "Of course."

"See that it is done," she snapped at Black Sander. "I want them all within the week."

377

He inclined his head, losing his devil's eyes beneath the wide brim of his hat.

She glared at Vorvington then. "You. Inside."

Vorvington looked startled, then afraid. He followed her inside, panting in her wake. She grinned wickedly as she led him on.

When they were back in her chamber, she locked the door. She glowered at him, which made him wince and fall back like a beaten cur. Her eyes narrowed, and he slunk down even more. Then she made him pleasure her for the remainder of the night, lying on the couch with her father's famous sayings beneath her and looking past her lover as he huffed and labored and sweated, looking beyond him into the bone-framed mirror where the Galactic Mage's new bride crawled around the alien ship doing the most extraordinary things.

It was almost sunrise when the magic mirror went blank.

Chapter 45

Orli was familiar enough with the wind shifts now to make falling through the opposing layers efficient if not quite simple. It might almost have been fun were she not in agony in her ribs, her hand, and her leg—and were it not for the fact that Altin was lost and, for all she knew, dead and stuffed in a jar or hanging on a wall like some trophy fish. But other than the agony and dread, it might have been enjoyable. She thought Roberto would probably have been having fun anyway.

She guessed her fall to be on the order of six or seven minutes, plenty of time to think, but thoughts of Roberto and even Altin vanished as the bottom finally came into view. The steam was thicker, and the wet clouds that had been simply hot and wet became miserable again. It was almost impossible to breathe by the time she was four levels from the thickest of it—the same layer of blinding fog in which she'd been lost after getting her free fall under control the first time. And as if breathing in steam as if it were liquefied air wasn't painful enough, the temperature was nearing the point of scalding.

She feathered the Higgs prism back, slowing her fall. From beneath the steam came a rumble, a roiling, popping

379

rumble that sounded every bit like water boiling. Massive quantities of it, a river's worth or a lake.

She couldn't go down into that. Even cockroaches couldn't handle that, no matter how determined they might be.

She looked to the bulkhead, where the hook-tailed aliens crawled along with their three-limbed mustache faces. She wondered if they could swim in whatever that was down there. All she could see was hazy gray, but onward she fell, angling back and forth across the wind with each successive level.

The heat grew.

She blew back toward the bulkhead, realizing as she did that she was, at some point, going to have to figure out how to stop without hitting the damn thing so hard she'd break the rest of her ribs and who knew what else.

As she got closer, she saw more of the hook-tailed aliens, "hooks," as she thought of them. They looked like ants in a line. Most of them moved angularly, heading down into the dimness or coming up from below.

She paralleled a line of them moving downward toward the starboard hull, or at least what she thought of as the starboard hull. God knew how far off her bearings were at this point. After what seemed an eternity, she found it, a great dark expanse rising up out of the steam as if it were the end of some fog-filled universe. Soon she was sliding along the rough surface of it, braking her momentum with her left elbow and leg—agonizingly—and working the Higgs prism to lower herself down.

Finally she found the bottom, and, to her great relief, it was solid, at least along the hull. That was the only bit of relief, however, for it was so hot and the steam lay upon it so heavily that she started to panic. She crouched, prepared to leap back up, and fumbled frantically for the Higgs prism dial. The device had gotten so hot she could hardly handle it, and her hands trembled terribly. The broken one was useless.

She realized she was losing it, and closed her eyes, calming herself. Making herself breathe in long, hot breaths of all-but-liquid air. Agony, but not instant death.

She could still see, at least a little bit. The steam whirled around, thicker and thinner in wisps and whorls.

The sound of the boiling was incredible, like an avalanche rumbling from everywhere in the mist, under her feet and thrumming beneath her hand upon the hull, like a million unseen hammers were beating upon the bottom of the ship, up and down all its length. The noise filled the space all around her, although perhaps more so from off to her right.

A few more moments spent calming herself and she realized she could endure it for a bit longer, long enough to look for something that might help. Maybe she wouldn't have to go back up just yet. Maybe there really would be a weapon she could find.

She knew that was a ridiculous hope, but that was what she was running on at this point. A wave of heat washed over her that nearly set her to panicking again. She looked to the flesh on her forearm, the soft, paler skin on the underside. It wasn't blistering, but it was turning blotchy and pink.

Get moving, damn it.

She started along the hull, heading in the direction where she'd seen the hooks angling toward.

Something whooshed past her head. She felt the brush of it against her hair, and couldn't tell if it was something physical or just a gust of wind.

A huffing sound accompanied it as it rustled past. She ducked reflexively and crouched down. She couldn't see more than a few feet in any direction through all the steam. More huffing was coming from above and behind her. She waited, staring into the mistiness. She was fairly sure she was being slowly cooked as she waited.

Something dark whooshed by, something curved. A hook. She just saw the shadowy arc of it coming at her and jerked her head aside. The alien huffed and hustled past. She shuddered. At the speed it was traveling, that hook could have taken her head off, or sunk right into the back of her head and hauled her off like a pig carcass in a slaughterhouse.

She shuddered a second time, then listened for more aliens coming. Silence. She had to keep moving; she didn't have time to linger down here, or she'd be a cooked pig anyway. A cooked little human cockroach.

She headed in the direction of the bulkhead, the direction the hook that had almost hit her had just gone. She wove back and forth away from the wall a little, looking at the ground for something that might help. She didn't know what. Anything. Altin's helmet. His backpack unit. An alien ion rifle with a full stock of plasma grenades. Anything.

No such luck.

She came to the bulkhead and found nothing at all. Although she could hear the sounds of the hook aliens running around in the steam above. From the noise of them, and the way the sound shifted sometimes, a bit of an echo, she thought they might be running into some kind of corridor. Some of them sounded hollow, and she could make out little grunts as well.

She crept along the base of the bulkhead, moving toward the boiling sound. She crouched as low as she could, but the heat grew too intense. There was some shielding effect as long as she stayed low, so she knew she was nearing some kind of edge—she was on a ledge perhaps. She wasn't about to discover where that edge was on accident, however, so she backed off. One thing was not hard to locate, however, for the roaring of a wind vent came from just above, loud enough to be distinct from the massive, rolling boil.

She backed away and listened to the sounds above her,

parsing the noise of the hooks moving in and out of something from the rest. She looked at her forearms again. They were turning pinker, like a bad sunburn on the way. She had to get out of this.

She set the Higgs prism and jumped up along the wall. She hoped she didn't fly right up into the path of one of the damn hooks. Might as well jump into freighter traffic. She didn't.

She drifted up out of the thickest steam and found that her suspicions had been correct. There was a hole in the bulkhead: a big one, twenty yards across, roughly circular, as if it had been burrowed by the hooks themselves.

Hooks were coming in and out of it in a steady flow. The ant analogy worked almost perfectly. Some of them were angling up along the hull, heading back down the length of the ship. Others peeled off and angled up and across the bulkhead.

They ran along the vents and gripped the cross members as they went across, preventing themselves from being blown off the wall. The wind blew the length of their bodies out like shrimp-shaped flags, but their mustache tentacles held them tight and they traveled right along anyway. They'd get to the narrow horizontal bands of unvented protein that separated the levels and scurry along flat again, making the transitions from calm to windblown easily and without ever losing speed.

The vents ran the length of the bulkhead as far as she could see. Each layer of the ship was defined by this incredible wind factory. Impressive, but impossible to appreciate given the nature of her current agonies.

She turned back and regarded the opening in the bulkhead. If she went in, she could probably keep herself above the backs of the hooks traveling in and out of the corridor, like a cockroach crawling on the ceiling.

She got herself to the opening, drifting over the top of it.

She reached down to feel for any wind. There was none. So her plan might work.

Except she didn't know what her plan was now.

What was her plan?

Hell if she had a clue.

She waited to see if any of the aliens coming and going paid any attention to her.

They did not.

She wondered if they could even see her. It was possible that the big aliens with the billows were too big to notice a puny human, but it seemed like these smaller creatures ought to.

Or else they really didn't care. Maybe cockroaches didn't bother them.

Maybe there were poisoned traps somewhere. Or an exterminator.

Ugh. She could be running right into one.

She shrugged. She had to do something, so she was committed now.

She lowered herself down into the corridor. No more than eight or nine yards separated her from the back of an alien running in, but as long as she moved carefully, she could pull herself along the top and stay above the scuttling traffic of them all.

She peered down into the darkness. There were no lights ahead, no round rings of violet or ovals of orange light. The hooks themselves, they glowed a little, though. The farther into the tunnel they got, the more they did, a pale gray light that formed a line in the distance. From the way the light of their wide bodies turned to a thread in the darkness, the tunnel was very long.

She looked back into the long stretch of the ship behind her, at the stacks of grates climbing up out of the steam and out of sight. One guess was as good as another.

She pulled herself along the ceiling, heading deeper into

the tunnel. The going was slow, and she had to do it with only one hand. It was very dark. The aliens didn't throw off much light. She was tempted to pull the small flashlight out of her utility belt, but decided against it. If the damn things communicated with light—at least the big ones did, she didn't know about the hooks—she didn't want to turn it on and announce that she was here. They were doing a fine job ignoring her still, and she didn't want to ruin it.

She pulled herself along. She must have done so for a half hour or more. Finally she came to an intersection. Hooks were crossing ... on the ceiling.

Of course they were, the bastards.

She made her way carefully to the intersection and looked left and right. The aliens stayed on the ceiling as they traveled down that one. That wasn't so troubling. And there was something glowing in the distance to the left.

She inched across the ceiling and waited for three aliens to scuttle past. She pushed in after them and rotated the dial on her Higgs prism. Soon she was standing on the floor.

It is hard to appreciate simple things like walking and gravity until one has done without them for a very long time. Improvised travel along ceilings and through wind-blasted deck levels gave her a new respect for simply being on her own two feet.

She looked back and saw another hook coming her way. Her first instinct was to run, but instead she crouched down and let it run past. It never slowed at all. Not even the twitch of a tentacle or the dip of its hook as it ran past. She might as well have been invisible.

She tried to jog along in its wake, but the jolt of each step was too much for her ribs, sucking the wind right out of her lungs. She wouldn't be any use to Altin lying there unconscious for an hour. So she had to walk.

She went toward the distant glow, ducking each time an alien scooted past even though she didn't quite need to.

The light grew steadily brighter as she went along. She thought she must have walked well over an hour that way, until eventually she discovered that it came from a corridor branching to her right. She peered down that one and saw that it ran another several hundred yards ahead. Something was very bright beyond.

She crept toward it.

A massive chamber opened out above her. It reached well up into the distance, several miles at least, and in its center, filling almost the entire space as far as Orli could see, was what appeared to be a giant bubble. It was filled with a clear fluid, like water, as clear as any she'd ever seen. She couldn't be certain it was water, but there was no odor in the vast chamber, so she thought it likely that it was. That and the fact that there were plants growing inside, long, sinuous vines reaching upward like a kelp bed, though these were brighter shades of green, and some were red or orange or black. They grew in wide clumps, and were illuminated by the brilliance of the blue light that filled the chamber and the giant ... well, tank, for that's what the bubble seemed to her. In fact, the longer she looked into it, the more it reminded her of the giant fish tank her mother had kept back on Earth when Orli was a child. Except this one had to be ten miles wide and at least three or four high, and of course all the water was boiling.

She glanced around the outside of the tank, suddenly aware of how long she'd been looking into it. Nothing was coming at her. There didn't appear to be anything inside looking at her either, though from her current location, she couldn't see much for all the long ropes of green and orange and black.

A narrow space ran around the edge of the tank on either side, no more than ten yards separating the massive liquid-filled vessel from the chamber wall. She touched the side of the tank as she peered around its edge, tentatively testing its temperature with the palm of her hand. There was very little heat coming off. It was softer than she'd expected it to be as well, like it was made from a membrane, something grown, and perhaps even alive.

She moved around the tank a little ways, trying to see deeper into it through the forest of long, ropy plants, waggling their way upward and out of sight. She got to a wide gap between a clump of them and discovered that, more astounding than the giant tank, or even plants that could grow in boiling water, there was a monster floating in the middle of it all.

Filling perhaps a quarter of the tank's total volume was a great spotted blob, its flesh awash in black and gray and yellow. It looked like a dirty oil cloud churning beneath the sea. The colors of its skin moved around as if independent, the shapes of each cellular, like hundred-foot-wide microbes crawling around on it. They flattened or grew oblong as they squeezed around on it, pinching together into figure eights sometimes or stretching out into long, gooey-seeming strands. They'd shift from black to yellow to gray, none of them staying the same for long. Every so often one of them would flicker with light, then several nearby would follow suit, and then a prismatic blast would follow for a time, beaming out of the tank against the chamber wall, painting it in rainbow colors and patches of gray. Orli thought the patches of gray might actually be colors she just couldn't see.

Whatever they were, they had to mean something, though she had no way to know what. It didn't look like anything. It wasn't shaping images like the aliens that had examined her and Altin had done.

The wall upon which the colors were projected, the wall around the tank itself, was soft and white. And for the first time since coming onto the ship, she realized it wasn't rough in the way of the hard protein from which everything else seemed to have been made. This was rough in a different way, like sandpaper or, given the pale white color, maybe more like the belly of a shark.

The thing in the tank, the creature, shone its prismatic display on the pale wall for a time, and then the pattern went away. Then the creature was simply black and gray and rather golden for a time. It had a luster to it, as if it were polished and very smooth. She thought it was beautiful, though for some reason it terrified her too.

She watched it and finally noticed that inside the giant boiling fish tank there were hook aliens as well. Several of them crawled around along the bottom, apparently gobbling up small blackish objects that had fallen down there. She thought they might be excrement.

They opened up their little puckered protrusions and, with their tentacles, handed the round globules into themselves. Lots of them were doing it.

Others were crawling around on the flesh of the undulating mass, the big thing inside. Seeing them crawling around on it, looking like larvae or little bits of wriggling rice, gave her a sense of scale for the monstrous thing. She set her Higgs prism to zero and pushed off from the ground, wanting to get a better look at the colossal thing.

When she was nearly a mile off the ground, she was high enough to see that the little ones were blowing bubbles of something syrupy and brown. She had a feeling she knew what that was. Others were blowing bubbles of pink or gray. She wondered what those did, but she was pretty sure she didn't really want to find out, at least not firsthand. The bubbles clung to the giant alien's skin, placed there upon it like stitched-on beads. Orli had no idea what was going on.

From this height, however, Orli got a better idea of the sheer enormity of the alien within. Suddenly the long, tentacled aliens with their billows and bulbous cores seemed like nothing, bare wisps of stringy servitude. Drones, entirely insignificant. That thing in there was at least three miles across at its thickest parts, though it was hard to say for sure. Its soggy form kept changing, stretching and globing about, making it impossible to estimate.

She pulled herself up the surface of the tank, making great time at zero gravity using her hand and both feet. As she did, she angled herself around it as well. When she got perhaps a quarter of the way around the tank and just past the halfway point, around the widest of its bubbled bulge, she saw that the big alien had a tuft of tentacles growing out of its top, almost like a patch of hair. It reminded her of the writhing threadlike roots on a garlic bulb, the alien one monstrous bulb of shifting color, turned bottom up and reaching out of the water with all those filaments. There were thousands of them. She knew they were not threadlike, though. She was sure the tentacles were no less thick than those of the long, billowy aliens, but by comparison to its sheer mass, they seemed delicate fibers—at least from this distance.

Whatever their size, they waved up into the heights above the creature, out of the boiling water, where they vanished into steam coming off the surface. The steam concentrated itself at the top of the chamber, thick like smoke, and shaped into a whirling disc like a massive hurricane cloud viewed from space. She had no idea what the creature was doing with all those arms reaching into it, for its purpose within the steam cloud was entirely obscure.

She also couldn't say how any of this was going to help her find Altin.

She continued to pull her way around the tank. It was widest at the midway point, so she was able to adjust gravity a little and make even better speed with some help from it sloping upward now.

She pushed herself along with her feet, just enough gravity to give her contact, but not enough to slow her down. Her runner's legs gave her speed, and eventually she rounded far enough to count herself on the back half of the tank.

She watched more of the oil-cloud alien's light shows on the wall for a time, wondering if she might maybe translate it somehow. She'd learned the common tongue of Kurr easily enough. Maybe she could figure this language out.

That's when an image of the *Glistening Lady* appeared.

It came from the big garlic-glob alien in the fishbowl, a projection that was obviously Roberto's ship, for it could be no other, the slender, silvery ship clear as it could be backed by a field of star-speckled black.

Orli wondered why it was beaming that. Roberto's ship was on Prosperion, wasn't it? Was that, like, a recording? Or was Roberto out there somewhere? Perhaps he really had gotten away.

And come back.

Hopefully that wasn't an image of the ship they'd captured.

She pulled her way closer to the prismatic light show playing on the sharkskin wall. She wanted to call out. To wave.

The lights went out.

She could still see the ship.

She panicked. Was that a damn window, or just an image left there now? The alien hadn't done that with its other projections.

She ran along the curve of the tank toward the image. She ratcheted down gravity and launched herself up at the wall, rolling the Higgs prism back again to brake her speed, and then set it to zero when she got there.

It was a window. A huge one, deep. She was looking through a half-mile-thick pane of window glass, or something just like it. But that was the *Glistening Lady*. There could be no doubt. She waved. She did shout this time. "Roberto! God damn it, get us out!" She pounded on the glass. It felt rough like the protein of the hull and grates. She pounded anyway.

She turned back, faced the big alien with its onion hairs all rising up into the steam.

"Let us go, God damn it. We haven't done anything to you."

She saw as she looked back across that there was another image on the far wall. It was so far away she could hardly make it out, even though it was probably a mile wide. It looked like Yellow Fire. The red world. The planet viewed from orbit.

"No," she said, realizing what was happening. "No!"

The *Glistening Lady* moved out of view, laterally, as with the motion of this ship, not Roberto's. Orli screamed Roberto's name. The window went away. She was staring at the white wall again.

A blinding flash of light shot out from the alien in the tank, rolling over her. She had to turn away. It passed over her and played on the wall a few hundred meters left of where she was. It sparkled and glowed, and then there was the rift in space, visible through it, a great black rent with a pale pink flicker at the edges like fire. The stars around the rift were like the flesh of space, making the tear itself seem a bleeding gash.

It was growing bigger. Or for a moment, at least, she thought it was growing. Then she realized what was really happening. The ship—with her in it—was moving toward it.

It was huge, widening as they drew nearer and nearer, yawning darkness. The fiery pink flickers of its rim disappeared beyond the edge of her window's view. Total blackness.

Then the alien ship was through.

Chapter 46

Sensors came online shortly before navigation did, weapons right after. They were just over the four-hour mark on the restart and making great progress. The specter of the four alien ships Roberto and Squints had seen coming through the wormhole had given the crew a forty-five-minute bump in efficiency that none of the crew would have thought possible prior. And that accomplishment might have been met with appreciation by the *Glistening Lady*'s captain had it not been for the fact that the first thing he saw when the sensors came up was a ship lifting off the surface of the planet. From its position in the formation around the dig site, he knew instantly that it was the same ship Orli and Altin had been taken into.

The great craft rose steadily up from the rocky red soil. Roberto could barely see it through the camera relay on the surface, due to a particularly nasty storm blowing down below, but between its shadowy shape rising above the rest, and the confirmation via other wavelengths, there was no doubt: it was leaving. The only question was, was it *leaving* leaving or coming the *Glistening Lady*'s way?

"Deeqa, get up here," he called. "We may need to kick some ass in a minute." He turned to Squints. "Strap yourself into that seat back there, junior. Do it now."

The redheaded youth did immediately as he was told.

Roberto's ship only carried four nukes, but he armed them all. The ion cannon and both lasers were charging by the time Deeqa slid into the copilot's seat. She only needed a minute to assess what was happening. "Well, this will be fun. You sure it saw us?"

"Planet rotated us into range just before I got camo up. Be surprised if it didn't."

"It's going to read our heat signature anyway."

"I know. But you never know."

The alien vessel took its time about breaching the clouds, and in the twenty minutes it did so, the *Glistening Lady* had prepared itself should the vessel decide to attack.

The alien ship took a position just above the upper atmosphere and stayed there, its orbit in perfect synchronicity with the planet itself.

"What the hell are they waiting for?" Roberto asked.

Deeqa swung her chair around, stretched her long body to the navigations computer, and tapped something into that console. She retracted herself and tapped in more commands. "Not picking up any scans on us," she said. "Not saying I could if they didn't want me to, but not seeing anything coming this way. Maybe they still don't see us, just like last time."

"Yeah, they didn't seem to pay any attention to us down there on the planet either ... until they did. Then Altin and Orli were gone. I never should have talked them into it."

"The last time you told this story, Sir Altin was eager to go as well."

"He was. I'm just whining. I hate not knowing what they are up to."

Tracy came briskly in and took up her place at navigation. "Sorry, I'm late," she said, and quickly set herself to assessing the situation, as Deeqa had.

"So are we going to fight them?" Squints asked.

Tracy turned back and looked as if she'd forgotten they'd gotten a new crewman. She looked back to Roberto after, though. It was a fair question.

"Not if they don't screw with us," he said.

"What if they take off like those other ones did?" the young Prosperion asked. "We gonna chase them down?"

"If we have to."

Tracy grimaced, but Squints looked eager for the fight. "I need one of those light-beam rifles you guys carry," he said. "And a sword. I'll fight. Wouldn't be my first."

"I'll holler if it comes to that," Roberto said. "Now be quiet. We need to think. Tracy, what's the depth on the dig now?"

"Eighteen point six miles. The heart chamber is breached."

"Shit. I knew it. They probably pulled him out of there. God damn it. What if he's dead?"

"It just opened," Deeqa said, pulling up the readings. "It's still hot around the edges where the diggers were going at it. They'd have to have worked pretty fast to get him out, and even more so to harvest all the Liquefying Stone."

"Are we going to go save him?" Squints asked. "Whoever he is."

"Shut up, kid."

"If we're going to save him, we need to go now," Deeqa said. "You know Putin is sitting there right now ready to push his button, even if the general and the director aren't."

Roberto couldn't help being glad that at least the ship Altin and Orli were on was off the surface now. He felt guilty for it, for, in a way, not caring about Yellow Fire like that, but, well, Yellow Fire—Blue Fire, for that matter—was an intangible. A bunch of glowing rocks that Altin and Orli said was alive and in love. Roberto loved love, but, he loved his human friends more. And he loved his crew. He wasn't going to risk them for some damn Hostile world. He'd feel guilty about it forever, of that he was sure, just as he would never forget how it felt to blast the doomed spaceship *Liberty* into oblivion. But he wasn't going to go down there for Yellow Fire. He couldn't. Not with the other ship in sight. What if they did try to get away, shoot off after the other four or, God help them, even back through the goddamn rift?

"Tracy, see if you can detect the gravity wake on those four that left. Deeqa, you're watching that one for the same, right?"

"I am."

"You guys with me if we have to chase that fucker into that wormhole?"

Deeqa turned to him, her expression stoic and, by her tone, the question not rhetorical. "Are you being serious?"

"As a heart attack. Orli and Altin are on that thing."

"How do you know they weren't moved?"

"I don't. But that's where they went, that ship. Why would they move them?" He watched her study his face. He shrugged. "I'm going. Period. The rest is up to you."

She shook her head, but then showed her teeth with her smile. "You're a crazy goddamn Spaniard," she said. "I'll go."

"Good. I need a crazy goddamn Somali for some shit like this." He turned to Tracy. "You going to have a problem with that order if it comes?"

Tracy shrugged. "I've never been through one."

Roberto grinned. He opened up the all-ships com. "Attention, everyone. I need a little gut check here, just in case we have to jump through that wormhole in a minute or two. I know you guys signed up for commercial enterprise, so, if you aren't up for it, I need to know now. I'll arrange for anyone who can't muster for it to go home. But I need to know *right* now. I can't have anyone hesitating if it happens, and we're about out of time. Speak up now."

No one answered.

Roberto tapped the console where the com pickup was. "Hello? Is this on? I need to know. I need to hear *in* or *out*."

To the last of them, they were all in.

"You're all nuts," he said. "But I love you. If we don't all die, everyone just made a million-credits bonus when we get back."

"Hey, what about me?" Squints said. "Do I get that?"

Roberto looked over his shoulder as Deeqa began to laugh.

"Do you even know what it is, boy?" Roberto asked.

"No," said Squints. "But I want it."

Roberto laughed. "Fine, you too."

Squints grinned broadly, clearly having no idea exactly what a credit was, but clever enough to know he was going to be pleased with a million of them, whatever they were.

"Let's hope it doesn't come to that," Deeqa said.

"It might come to something worse," Roberto said. "They're moving now."

"Heading toward us at eighty thousand miles per hour."

"Bastard better not hit us again," Roberto said. "Or shoot our ass."

"I hope those new tank braces hold," was Tracy's comment.

Roberto groaned.

The alien ship stopped abruptly in its course. Directly over the *Glistening Lady*.

"Now we're being scanned," Tracy reported. "And who knows what else."

"What's that mean?" Squints asked, sounding perfectly at ease now.

Nobody answered him.

"Man, I'm not going to have time to do shit if they fire on us," Roberto said.

"Your call," Deeqa said. "You armed the nukes. Say the

word."

"I can't open it up. Altin and Orli are on there."

"As far as we know."

There was an edge in her tone that irked Roberto some, and he turned a terse look on her. "That's right. As far as we know."

Deeqa nodded, although so slightly it was nearly imperceptible.

The ship was in motion again. It snapped off its scanning beam and cruised right over them. Right over them and into the wormhole.

"Fuck."

"Yep, fuck," Deeqa agreed.

"Tracy, send word to the general we're going after his girl without him. Squints, tell Tytamon we're going through as well. Tell them to catch up as soon as they can."

"Through what?"

"The goddamn hole in space."

The Prosperion smiled as he did as he was told. Then the *Glistening Lady* gave chase.

Chapter 47

Pernie woke up lying on a cot in a small room. It was all very white inside. The light came from a strange ceiling that glowed all over so that she couldn't tell where the source was really coming from. It was an ugly kind of white. Lifeless and unnatural. She hated it immediately.

She sat up and put her feet on the floor. It was cool and hard, but not cold and coarse like the flagstones of Calico Castle were. Not alive. She looked around and realized that there was something around her neck. She felt for it and confirmed what she already knew: a metal collar, narrow with three finger-sized boxes and one locking clasp. She didn't have to see the lights to know they were there too.

She looked for a mirror anyway, but there was none. Only one small window in the door across from her. She got up and went to it. She could see out into the hall. It was lifeless and white out there too. She craned her neck left and right, looking down the hall in both directions. There was no one there.

She tried the handle, but, of course, it was locked. Pernie was in jail like a criminal again.

She spoke the words to the teleport that would take her outside, but before she could get the second syllable out, the muscles in her neck and face seized up with terrible cramps, violent spasms that yanked her jaw back and jerked the corners of her mouth into a contorted, trembling grimace.

It lasted a pair of seconds at most, but it dazed her as if it had gone on for half an hour. It took her some time to blink through the haze. Casting magic had never done that before.

She tried again immediately, trying to speak the magic even faster. The same thing again. A terrible jolt, electrical, shocking her right out of her spell, pain from the collar on her neck twisting her muscles up in an awful way. It was as if the collar was watching her in the mana in the same way Djoveeve and Seawind had taught her to do: watching for the first signs of movement in the mana stream, and then, if you were quick enough, you could counter your opponent's spell, kick them or stick them with your spear and knock them right off the magic they were trying to cast. Sometimes that alone could be the end to them.

But that was impossible. All the people on Earth were blanks. They could not see mana at all. Even stupid Orli Pewter had said so. She said nobody on Earth had ever heard of mana before. Roberto said it too. He said that people on Earth thought magic was all made-up stories and that even he hadn't believed until Master Altin almost turned him into a toad. He said then he would have believed.

So how could they be watching the mana with the collar on her neck? Why would they all have lied? Of course Orli Pewter would lie, but not Roberto. He was nice for real.

But he was Orli Pewter's friend. That's why.

Pernie growled as she touched the collar. Master Altin didn't even know how much danger he was in. They were all liars, and he was surrounded by them. She wondered if maybe they wanted to take all his gold that he got from Master Tytamon. What if that's what this was all about? It was all for money. That was all anyone talked about on this world. They talked about it all the time. Sophia Hayworth and Don Hayworth and even Jeremy. The criminal in the alley wanted to take her to the casino for game chips. They all cared about money all the time.

That's what Roberto had been talking about with the Queen!

Suddenly Pernie understood it all. All of it. It was all about money and credits and gold. And poor Master Altin thought Orli Pewter loved him.

Realizing it filled her with such rage as she'd never known. Not even when she'd killed the sargosagantis king had she been so furious. She glared out the window and cast the teleport spell again, speaking the first word as if it were a curse and trying to hold on to the mana no matter what.

The electricity struck her and felt as if it were strangling her. Even the python that had grabbed her in the tree on String and choked her in its coils, squeezing her to silence and darkness, had not hurt so bad.

She clawed at the contraption, gasping and trying to choke out the next word. The contractions of her face and neck squeezed tears from her eyes as she tried to force that second sound. Her whole face was in rebellion, the muscles in her neck betraying her. She fought with all her might to finish the spell, but her jaws were locked tight and her whole body began to shake. Still she forced herself to channel the mana, to try to get it out. Just the second word. She pushed, and the air rasped and gurgled in her throat. She saw spots in her vision, and when she woke up she was lying in a pool of her own saliva, much like the one on the table back at the precinct.

She hadn't even known she'd passed out.

She got up and glared out the window. She beat on the door and screamed. Then she tried the spell again. She seethed and growled and grunted, and her neck squeezed and cramped and twisted up into knots. Her jaws locked up so tight it made the veins in her temples throb. The electricity burned hot against her skin.

When she woke up again, the major was sitting in a chair that someone had brought in. The door was open, and there were two men outside. Visible on either side of the doorway, Pernie could see the butts of their rifles and part of one uniformed arm and shoulder for each of them, enough to know she was under guard. Exactly like a criminal.

"Miss Grayborn," said the major. "I hope that we can dispense with any more attempts at magic now. If you hadn't figured it out yet, that necklace you wear prevents you from doing so. Please spare us both the trouble and keep your magic in your head."

Pernie's little blonde brows dropped low over her eyes, like crouching predators. She watched him and made no attempt to conceal the hate.

He lifted a small black object, flattish and roughly oval shaped. He held it casually between his fingers, with his thumb resting on a silver button at the object's center. "I can activate the necklace even if you don't try magic, so if you decide to ... get out of hand, I'll have to shock you until you will behave. And, I want to tell you, Miss Grayborn, I don't want to shock you at all. In fact, I want to help you."

Pernie didn't believe it for one second. She knew that he was the real criminal in the room.

"Miss Grayborn, we are down to two options at this point. We can send you home, or we can continue to provide you with an education here on Earth as accorded by our agreement with the TGS and Her Majesty of Kurr. It is my desire to—"

"Let me go," she said. "And take this off me." She pulled on the collar but knew better than to try casting a spell. She didn't think she could beat the major and the men with guns. The men who had shot her in the broken building downtown had gotten her incredibly quickly. Their guns didn't have to channel mana at all. They could cast faster than elves, and there was no mana to watch to see it shaping up. And even if they didn't shoot her with bullets, she had no resistance to their tranquilizer darts.

"It is my desire," the major went on, "to give you exactly what you have expressed interest in before. You want to train as a pilot, and you want to learn the tricks and secrets of our military. Our weapons, that sort of thing."

"I don't care about your military. I want this collar off me."

He ignored her protests and pressed on. "We know you are interested in these things because we have your net logs. We know exactly where you have been going and what you are looking at while you are there. We also have several recordings of you and your friend Jeremy discussing your plans at school. I have to tell you, Miss Grayborn, you are a very intriguing girl. Far more so than anyone expected when they granted you your status in the student exchange."

She frowned. How could they know that?

He saw it in her eyes, and smiled. "Miss Grayborn, you don't think that the NTA would allow a teleporter loose on Earth, or any magician, for that matter, without observing everything they do, do you? Watching you was part of the contract. It's just that nobody expected, well ... you."

"Master Grimswoller taught us at magic school you aren't supposed to watch anyone when they don't know. He said it's bad and against seers' laws, and Her Majesty will cut out your heart when she finds out. That's the penalty." She realized they probably weren't using seers, but she did know about the "saddle lights" in the sky. She hadn't read about them, but she'd heard enough to know that they were probably like gryphon riders made out of technology. She knew about drones and cameras and video. They must have stupid cameras even in the school. Why hadn't Jeremy told her?

"Her Majesty's people signed the documents. It's all by

treaty and contracts with the TGS. But look, I don't want to bore you with all that. I'm trying to tell you that you have an opportunity. We want to—"

"I don't care what you want. The Queen might let you spy on me, but Master Altin won't. Not when he finds out. Or Seawind. Seawind will come and slice you up into meat, and Knot will eat your eyeballs."

He smiled and sat back, shaking his head. "That won't happen either." He looked down into the tablet in his lap, scrolled through a few pages. He looked up. "Seawind is your elf friend. So, no, he won't be coming at all. We have no agreement with them, and the new councilman from the TGS assures us that no elves will be processed through any TGS depots. So, there will be no pieces of me anywhere. And as for your friend Mr. Meade, well, I'm afraid he's gone."

Pernie started to say something, but stopped. What was that supposed to mean?

He saw her pause, and sighed, the smile on his face turning into a patient thing. "That's right, Miss Grayborn. Mr. Meade is gone. Permanently, by all best estimates. It happened yesterday."

"You're lying," she said, even though she didn't know what he was lying about exactly.

"Mr. Meade and his wife vanished into a wormhole that appeared above a planet in the Cep 128a1 system, along with the captain and crew of a spaceship registered to one Captain Roberto Levi, whom, according to your file, you also know."

Pernie wanted to call him a liar again, but she didn't know what most of it meant anyway.

"A wormhole," he repeated, sensing her ignorance. "It's a hole in space. A rift. Some say it's a rip in the fabric of space-time. Others say it opens onto another dimension. Some say it opens to nowhere at all, although that seems unlikely, given that data uploaded to the NTA from Captain Levi's ship show alien spaceships coming through."

"Then he'll come back, and then you will see."

"That is possible. But may be unlikely. If it is a space-time rift, he may not come back for a thousand years. Maybe ten thousand. Hell, he might have already come back ten thousand years ago."

Pernie's whole expression was one of absolute bewilderment. The man was talking nonsense.

At least, she thought he surely must be.

She wanted to talk to Jeremy very badly. He would tell her if this NTA man was a lying criminal or not.

But what if he wasn't?

"Look," said the major then. He flipped his tablet around. "Here is the video from the satellite above the red planet where it happened. If you look up here in the left-hand corner, you can just see the *Glistening Lady* going through. And if you look at the date here, at the bottom, you'll see that it was, in fact, yesterday." He paused and looked at her.

She glowered at him again. He had to be lying. Master Altin wouldn't go through a wormhole and come out ten thousand years ago. Why would he? That would make him ...

That meant, if it was true ... if it really had been ten thousand years ago ....

She wouldn't even think it. Ever. It was just a worm's hole. Master Altin had tamed a dragon. He could easily tame a worm. Or just kill it if he wanted to.

She glared back at the major, her hatred so hot it melted his smile away.

"Hey, I didn't do it," he said. "I understand your anger, but it wasn't me. It wasn't the NTA." He turned the tablet around and replayed the video. "Look. They went in all on their own. All of them. And that's what I'm trying to tell you. You glare at me like all of this is my fault, like it's the

NTA's fault somehow. But it's not. And I'm trying to help you, if you will listen and hear what I have to say."

One of Pernie's brows stayed low, still crouched there warily, but the other let go a little bit, leaving only some of that rage upon her face.

"I can give you what you want, Miss Grayborn. You're a very special little girl. I can make you a pilot. I can arrange to have you taught how to use our weaponry, our systems, our technology. Whatever you want to learn—within reason, I'll admit; they aren't going to give you top NTA secrets ... at least not right away. But I can teach you what you want to know. All those things you wanted to have and see: the guns, the planes, the starships ... the Hostile bodies. All of it. In time. But you have to work with me."

"But what about Master Altin? We have to get him back before ten thousand years." She really didn't want to have to wait ten thousand years if she didn't have to. A hundred had already seemed very long. And if he went into the past, somehow, well, how could she wait for that?

"Well, that I can't help you with. The NTA isn't going to throw any ships into that rift. Not until we get some data back from the probes, which, if you and I are going to be friends, I'll tell you a secret about."

Pernie didn't think she was ever going to be his friend, but she was smart enough to say, "Okay."

"They've already sent eleven of them through. Top-end equipment, every one. And yet, we haven't gotten back one lick of data yet. Eleven probes, not one single byte back."

Pernie pressed in her lips, thinking about that, about the missing data. She knew what *data* meant, but who cared if the worm bit the probes? Why would it even want to, given that they were surely made of metal and didn't taste good? But there was something obvious he was missing. "Did you look in the history?"

He leaned back, a mildly amused, partially curious

expression on his face. "What history?"

"At Carson-Millerton Junior Military Academy. They keep it there. They were always making us learn history about the past. I thought it was boring and I didn't pay attention. But if you look, won't there be data from ten thousand years ago? What if Master Altin came back and needed help? Did you look to see?"

He tilted his head a little, regarding her seriously, then after a moment of that, he began to laugh. He laughed so long Pernie started to get mad again. She watched his throat as he did, saw how exposed it was, and thought how easy it would be to jump over there and punch his windpipe in.

But she didn't.

What if he really would teach her the things he promised her? What if he taught her how to fly a starship? Then she could go into the worm's hole and get Master Altin out. She could pay attention to the boring history and learn if Altin came home ten thousand years ago, and she could go back and get him because she would know where he was. All she had to do was learn.

She gritted her teeth, almost like the collar made her do. The amount of time she was going to have to wait was getting very long. And she had a lot to learn.

"You're a clever girl, Miss Grayborn. I hope we can get past our misunderstanding earlier. I don't like that collar any more than you do. I know you don't believe me, but it's true. I hate to have to clip your wings, but you did promise, and your sponsors, Mr. Tytamon, Mr. Seawind, and Ms. Djoveeve, all signed that you would not do magic while you were here. And there were conditions attached for if, well, if you did."

He nodded and glanced at her neck, indicating that the collar was one of the "conditions." A snarl shaped itself on her mouth, but she didn't give it sound.

"I know you are angry right now. And you have every

right to be. But if you can come to grips with it, then I give you my promise that I will do as I have said. You'll be a pilot by the time you are twenty. Perhaps even sooner if you work as hard as you have been at Carson-Millerton. Like I said, we've been watching. You're something else." He stood and looked down at her. "So what do you say?" He put out his hand for her to shake.

Pernie glared at it. If she had a knife, she would have stabbed him through it, right between the knuckles at the back of his hand and out through his palm.

He pushed it a little closer. "Come on. You're going to have to trust someone at some point. And we have the resources you need."

She felt like she was walking into a trap. But she had broken her promise. And now Master Altin needed her even more. She had no choice.

Still glowering, she took the major's big hand in her little one and gave it a single shake. "Fine," she said. "But I want to start learning today."

Chapter 48

Dark stone formations thrust up from soupy green fluid, rocky columns built by some natural force and forced out of the quagmire from somewhere deep below. The fluid, once water perhaps, was thick, and it moved like rendered fat, lapping in slow, shallow waves against the base of the stone formations. The columns rose some twenty spans out of the swampy ooze, nine in all, eight of them loosely arranged in a natural kind of symmetry around a slightly larger central one. All of these were surrounded in turn by short black trees, half-starved by the look of them, with twisted limbs and gray leaves like tarnished silver, which glinted in the light of a pea-green sun as it burrowed through hazy gray clouds above.

Dark shapes darted in and out of the clouds, creatures with two pairs of wings, one in front of the other like dragonflies. They flapped and circled over the formation of stones in the way that vultures do, and they seemed to be waiting for the spoils of the fight taking place below, the resolution of a mighty siege.

Black Sander shifted his weight from his left foot to his right as he maintained the illusion spell through which the images were being channeled, watching what unfolded right along with all the rest. Conduit Wanderfrond held the spell together, taking the spell from Black Sander just as he took the seer's feed. The diviners who had found the distant world, Cas 98213a4 the ungainly name given it by the star charts from Earth, had already done their work, and the place was found. The old priest, the Grand Maul of Anvilwrath, sat in a chair atop a small wheeled platform, feeding mana into the concert cast. His eyes were closed, and the loose folds of map-lined flesh dangling from his neck quivered slightly as he worked. Black Sander could feel the smug satisfaction coming from the man, as evident in the cloudy essence of the concert as it had been in his yellow-toothed smile before the casting began. The Grand Maul. The marchioness had found herself some powerful allies.

Kalafrand's powerful Z-class seeing spell loaded more imagery into the conduit's memory. As the seer watched the scene upon the distant world with his far sight, he bundled up memories that he fed to Black Sander telepathically, fed to them all, really, but to Black Sander for his exquisite gifts as a W-ranked illusionist. It was Black Sander's job to replicate the sequences of events for the small crowd of observers in the marchioness' private sitting room.

Between just the three of them, the U-ranked old priest diviner—a Five, no less—Kalafrand, and Black Sander, they had a monstrously powerful bit of work under way; they would have made a more than adequate concert to complete almost any task upon the world of Prosperion, at least in normal times. But these were anything but normal. With the inclusion of the two teleporters, the captive T, Paeter, and the marchioness' man from the TGA, Ivan Gangue, who was an O, and with the introduction of six other diviner priests that Black Sander didn't know, the concert had finally found the place where the War Queen made her war. And her war was well under way. And so it was that they, and through them the marchioness, observed.

Atop each of the outer eight columns in the swamp, the War Queen had built small stone fortresses. The stone was dark like the formations themselves, and the blocks rough cut, as if by transmuters and stonemasons in a hurry to get it done. Each of these was joined to a larger fortress, a blocky, three-story structure on the centermost column. They were connected by a series of bridges, which arced high above the soupy currents flowing and sloshing underneath, the high bridges like arcing spokes leading to a stalwart central hub.

They didn't have to watch long to understand why the War Queen had chosen such a place, for there were giants sloshing through the muck beneath the high fortresses, their huge feet stomping and splashing as they thrust upward with long spears like men with sharp sticks trying to poke garbage out of the sky. They were enormous and unfamiliar to all who observed, unlike any giant on Prosperion—at present or out of recorded history—just as the diviners had predicted they would be.

The giants were roughly human-shaped, bipedal but with four arms, and eight fingers to a hand. Their heads could be, in part, called humanlike as well, with two eyes and one mouth, but there were no noses to be found. And these heads sank down between the giants' shoulders as if pressed down by the enormity of their own weight, with faces that looked out from the center of broad chests, their mouths apparently chanting rhythmic war cries in a pulsing, steady way that made it appear as if their jawbones might grow right out from their beating hearts—although there was no way to say if the creatures had hearts at all. Beyond those marginally humanlike attributes, for the rest of them, these creatures could only be described as alien. They were massive, ten spans tall, and they seemed as if they were made from the same stone that fortresses sat on, though it appeared scaly in places, and striped here and there by something loose and fibrous like shredded rope or even tree bark. Whatever they were made of, it was hard, and when the arrows and spears of the Queen's men fighting in the towers came down at them, those projectiles bounced off and left no evidence of having caused injury at all.

Spells and visible magic appeared to fare much the same, and the humans, the Queen's personal soldiery, were on the defensive. Fireballs rained down amongst shards of ice half as long as the giants were. But these all seemed to do little or nothing to the monstrous things, all of it, arrows and magic alike, crashing and flashing against invisible shields that protected the misshapen monstrosities from harm.

The Queen's army, on the other hand, had no shields to save them. And the giants would thrust up with their long spears and spit a soldier through the face the moment he or she looked down to throw or cast. With phenomenal speed and accuracy, this giant or that one might spike a Prosperion fighter on its spear like a fisherman, and just as casually flick with its great wrists and send the caught warrior flying out into the swamp as if throwing back a fish too small to bother cleaning, cooking, and eating. The flailing human would fly off, then splash into the thick soup, where the vomitous liquid would roil and bubble and froth around the body until it was gone, leaving only wisps of black smoke rising from the scene. Black Sander couldn't know what the soup was, or what was in it, but he was grateful that there were no sounds associated with the divining spell the marchioness' caster was sharing with him now. Even he did not delight in that much agony.

The flying creatures swooped down after a body vanished into the goop, and they hovered with their leathery dragonfly wings over the smoke that rose, breathing it in. Their long, toothy beaks opened, and Black Sander was sure the sound must have been awful to hear as well.

He watched two of these creatures suck up a patch of smoke, then fly away again, rising up to join the circling of their fellows. He allowed himself to watch them as they flocked together above the swamp. That's when he noticed *Citadel*. The flock of flying creatures gave it away, the swarm of them wheeling like a dark cloud around some unseen object in the sky, shaping the perfect sphere of its invisibility as they bounced, rebounded, and ultimately avoided it, a bubble of vacant sky in the dark cloud of their circling mass.

Citadel hovered over the ring of fortresses, and yet it wasn't doing anything.

The conduit saw it as well, and he took Kalafrand's magic and pushed it up to where *Citadel* was. Black Sander knew he would not be able to push a seeing spell through the space fortress' magical defenses, though. That was the most impenetrable possession of the War Queen. The attempt was a waste of time, though he could not say it now. He half expected to hear the marchioness shout the conduit down for not going inside anyway.

But the seeing spell pushed right through the birds and right through *Citadel* and plunged into the darkness of the stone.

The vision slid through its many floors after, light, dark, light, dark, up they went. Wanderfrond guided the concert's vision right through to the core of the place, right to where he knew the mighty concert hall was. The heart of the War Queen's own giant, it too encased in stone.

The room burst into view, and Black Sander faithfully rendered it for the marchioness, the rings of plush red stools around a plush red-and-gold ottoman. The concert hall seating spread all around the outer edge, stadium style, wedges of seats filled with robed wizards from every guild. There were supposed to be eight hundred of them in there, and rumored to have the yellow Liquefying Stone, every one of them, if the Queen could force herself to give them out again.

At least, there were *supposed* to be eight hundred. That's what Black Sander had heard. But there were not. Not exactly, anyway.

At least half of them were dead. Perhaps more than half. Blood ran down the stairs between the sections of the concert hall, dark red smears on the Queen's bright crimson. Black Sander rendered it all exactly as Kalafrand's spell revealed, the conduit handling it well, for all his sanza-sap haze.

The War Queen and a handful of soldiers were beating back the last of what appeared to be an invasion force. There were perhaps eight of them left. The invaders looked human.

The conduit squeezed Kalafrand some more and chased the retreating scene through the massive bronze doors, out into an area filled with Prosperion plants. It was bright and lit up like a Crown City park in the middle of the day—all illusions, of course—and the battle crashed through the illusions, revealing the untruth of them all. One by one as they watched, the illusions failed, and soon they were simply watching the Queen and her entourage slaughtering what was left of the enemy.

Four men, and they were men, human in every way and in leather breastplates, hard leather, and draped with bronze chains. The leather was dark, dyed the color of wine, and the men wore helmets that looked as if they were made from some kind of animal shell. They fought with hooked swords and pole arms, bardiches made from something blue like glass.

But they didn't fight long, and finally the last of them were gone.

The War Queen stood panting over the bodies. Black Sander watched as she spat on one of them.

She turned and reentered the concert hall, having to step

over the dead as if wading through the swamp below *Citadel*.

Black Sander guessed there were at least as many dead invaders as there were dead wizards. Many of the invaders held wands rather than weapons in their dead hands. The holes in the walls, and the gaps in the red coating of the ceiling with its strange, twisting golden tentacles, all suggested a long magical fight had taken place.

The Queen's assassin, the elf called Shadesbreath, appeared beside her.

"There!" shouted the marchioness.

The conduit stopped chanting, locking the perspective of the seeing spell in place. The Queen and the elf moved through the injured, picking up the dead invaders' wands.

"That's him. *Now.* Now is the time." She turned to Jefe, who was watching with eyes wide. He'd obviously never seen a concert before. "Now! Do it now, the stunning device. Quickly."

Jefe turned to El Segador, who pulled two objects from a pocket of his jacket. One was a stun grenade. The other a flash. He went to the conduit and held them out for him to see. "Tell me when."

"Now," hissed the marchioness. "For gods' sake, do it now."

The conduit nodded. "Now is when."

Black Sander watched expectantly. This was the whole plan, the core of its success. Neutralize Her Majesty's two deadly pets, and she had nothing left: with the Galactic Mage gone well over two weeks now—eaten up by a hole in space, the reports on both worlds had said—he would not appear, and the elf was standing there in plain view. This was the time.

El Segador handed the conduit the grenades. Wanderfrond took one in each hand, as he'd been told to do before the spell began. He held them up, gripping the triggers, and let El Segador pull the pins. "Be ready, Gangue; be ready, both of you."

He picked up the cast where he'd anchored it, staring up into Black Sander's illusion just before he began. He smirked at the image of the War Queen and her assassin, and then he was lost in the magic again.

The chants from the two teleporters grew louder, and in a moment after, there came two hissing sounds, *ssst, ssst,* and the grenades disappeared.

They reappeared a moment later, a half span in the air before the Queen and the elf. Both flashed before they'd even had time to drop to the bodies lying on the ground.

Both the War Queen and the elf staggered backward. Both tripped over bodies and fell down.

"Now!" shrieked the marchioness. "Send them now!"

Suddenly the draw on Black Sander's mana was immense. It was beyond immense. The drugged-out conduit seemed to have lost his mind. He sucked mana out of the sky in impossible ways, yanking through Black Sander's mythothalamus so brutally it burned. He could feel the conduit doing the same to others as well, riding hardest on the Z-ranked Kalafrand. Kalafrand screamed. The teleporters were chanting like maniacs.

Black Sander saw the marchioness' small clean room in his mind, in the concert mind, a teleportation chamber outside on the grounds. He saw it, and saw it disappear from beside the great house. It appeared in the spell, barely, the seer only just holding on to the view.

But there it was, the marchioness' teleportation chamber, sitting crooked atop the bodies nearest the central crimson stool. On *Citadel.*

Four mechs erupted through the clean room wall. So carefully built into it as they had been, now they burst forth from it in a spray of bullets. In seconds, half of the remaining wizards in the room were gone.

Two men climbed out of the wrecked stone box after the

mechs. Black Sander recognized one to be his big brute henchman Twane. Twane held a truncheon nearly as big as a mammoth leg. With one stroke, he dropped the elf to unconsciousness even as the Royal Assassin was clambering to his feet.

"Hurry, you fool," Black Sander heard the marchioness say breathlessly.

Twane bound the elf up quickly.

The conduit was casting more teleports; another clean room flashed through Black Sander's mind, the concept of it more than a vision, larger perhaps, or perhaps just a crate of wood. It all went so fast, he could hardly hold on to ideas. Again he felt as if he were going to have his brain ripped out. He couldn't understand how the conduit was casting in such a way. The mana wasn't working properly. It was as if ... as if it had turned to water somehow.

Then he realized that the conduit must have Liquefying Stone. Suddenly he understood. The marchioness had one. She'd had it all along. Or perhaps she'd gotten it from the ancient priest. But she had one.

Black Sander knew enough of its power to hope that idiot addict didn't get them all killed. He considered letting go of the spell. But he was second in the cast. If he did so, the release would whip back through the chain and kill all the rest.

Still, it was better than dying himself.

But the next part of the spell was cast. He still had his life and his magic intact. For now.

The other man that had emerged with Twane was Black Sander's right-hand man, Belor. Belor looked pale and doughy compared to all the rest. It was obvious the screaming, silent in the seeing spell but apparent in all the O-shaped mouths of the wounded wizards who had survived, unnerved him. It must have been a tremendous cacophony. It embarrassed Black Sander to see how timidly Belor picked his way over the bodies in the concert hall. He held a sack limply in hands that trembled. Perhaps they should have let El Segador go instead, as the man had asked.

But Belor did as he was supposed to, if too slowly for Black Sander or the marchioness, and he gingerly pulled the sack over the elf's head and handed Twane a length of cord. The burly young sailor, long used to working with rope and tying knots, made quick and secure work of it from there. And just like that, the elf was rendered harmless, a simple anti-magic spell and a plain old burlap sack, the former the invention of the Queen's own favorite enchanter, Peppercorn.

"Take us up top. Quickly. I need to see." That, of course, from the marchioness.

The conduit had to fuss with poor, addled Kalafrand, for the seer was terrified. But eventually he managed to get the spell under way, and the vision fed to Black Sander, at first, and once again, lots of flashing light and dark as the sight slid through the floors of *Citadel* up to the battlement. By the time the sight magic emerged, the scene was much the same as it had been in the concert hall, bodies strewn all over the redoubt decks. The tightly packed combat towers were littered with dead wizards and dead invaders from … well, from the alien world they were on, apparently, dead human aliens—again. The remaining Prosperion wizards—having repelled the invaders as had the Queen and those in the concert hall below—had not been so lucky against the unexpected attack of the marchioness. They were already being herded together by ten more mechs, sent in one of the large shipping containers used for freight on Earth. It sat crookedly, bridging the space of two redoubts and looking just as alien as any of the bodies lying there.

The *Citadel* commander, Aderbury in his brown robes, stood among them, looking angry and holding a cloth to an enormous bleeding cut at the back of his head.

The marchioness' men, Jefe's men, had done their job.

"All right," commanded the marchioness. "It's time to do the rest. Send our friends to *Citadel* so that Master Jefe can claim his armor from the Queen. And Councilman Gangue, get your people at that Amphitrite TGS depot near Earth to send the rest of my mechs to the Palace. Vorvington is waiting for us by the entrance he's built for us in the wall. The time has come to take Kurr back from the ruinous reign of the War Queen."

THE END

For more information about the author, his
other novels and his works in progress, please visit
DaultonBooks.com.

If you would like to be notified when
new releases are made available, sign up for the
Daulton Books newsletter.